SEEDS OF THE GRAY

DAVID WENDT

Copyright © 2020 David Wendt
All rights reserved
First Edition

PAGE PUBLISHING, INC.
Conneaut Lake, PA

First originally published by Page Publishing 2020

ISBN 978-1-6624-0015-5 (pbk)
ISBN 978-1-6624-0016-2 (digital)

Printed in the United States of America

For Jake, Rachel and Jessica, my source of all Joy!

CHAPTER 1

Aaron snapped awake to the sound of that old, shitty fuckin' alarm clock screaming bloody murder, with a high-pitched blast of designed intensity. Instinctively, Aaron's left hand came flopping down on the foul device like a fat, limp dick. The vicious noise came to a grinding halt. The thoughtless action was seamless, and over the years a level of precision had been obtained, and the brain-drilling sound had ended mid shriek. Unfortunately, a steady hum remained in Aaron's rum-soaked melon.

The first few moments of waking from an all-night bender are much like jump-starting a car battery! One's life begins slowly, easing its way back into the dehydrated and not quite functional body. A battered human form that was beaten and abused by its master's hand begins the journey back from the abyss. Then there is the pain—nasty, mean, teeth-grinding agony. It starts behind the eyes and, in slow deliberate waves, pulses through the body, only to break back to its point of origin, right in the middle of the skull. There is no atheism in these dire moments; suffering always gets you closer to God.

It is in these waking seconds the body only wants peace, and the mind automatically seeks out divine intervention. Aaron thought about the concept of hitting the snooze button, but the thought of moving from this bed was frightening and unadvisable; sleep needed to be extended at all costs.

A baby like whimper emerged from under the blue flannel blanket.

"Holy shit," gasped from his dry, barren mouth.

Aaron's first attempt to lift his head from the pillow landed somewhere between comical and excruciating.

He thought to himself, *Isn't it amazing how a night of fun and frolic had turned so ugly with just a few hours of sleep?*

The voices in Aaron's head ran like a river of random gibberish mixed with prayers to stop the pain. The party was officially over; the only thing left to do was to deny everything. For all those questionable events that couldn't be shrugged off, many apologies would be forthcoming. If that didn't work, his standard speech about mixing Captain Morgan and Coke with oxycodone would have to calm the critics.

Aaron scanned the room with his bright red eyes.

"This is not my beautiful house," he said out loud just to hear his own words ease from his dry foul mouth.

He lifted his hurting frame, fully realizing that he was in Gina's apartment. Small bytes of memory were seeping to the surface. He recalled leaving McSorley's alehouse with a little assistance from a bouncer named Burger Bill. Bill was quite upset with Aaron after he was found in the back of the house, urinating under the painted lady picture.

Aaron recalled yelling, "The Bambino would be proud of me!"

The thought of going uptown at that time was not even an option.

Then he remembered having Gina's key. He tried to give it back to her before joining the team at MIT. He knew that there would be little time for the type of relationship she deserved.

Gina slid the key back into his pocket and told him, "Nice try, asshole, but you're my bitch. Get used to the idea."

He had no problem living with the shame and guilt of it all. She was in London for the past few weeks, so it wouldn't be an issue if he crashed there.

Slowly, Aaron let his feet swing off the bed; blood was moving too fast into his pitiful noggin, and he felt drugged.

"Oh, my dear God, if you let me survive this, I promise never to drink another fucking thing. God have mercy on my wretched soul," he said with a pathetic wail.

He was saying this out loud, too, simply to feel his mouth work. There is a moment when all drunks wake from the horrific fog, where an actual physical inventory takes place. Aaron wiggled his toes, and then counted his fingers. His tongue ran across his top teeth then the bottom, making sure that none of the choppers were missing. Fully satisfied that there was no permanent damage, he then initiated a random scan for blood. He noted a small laceration on the left wrist with only minimal leakage of his own personal stock of red high test. He thought, *Not even Band-Aid worthy.*

Aaron started thinking about why he initiated this all-night soiree. The fact was that Aaron Goldstein from Valley Stream, Long Island, had made the breakthrough of a lifetime, and it would change all life on planet Earth, forever.

Slowly, it all started dribbling in, ten years of his life eating and sleeping in that shitty lab, smelling his own ass. The endless battery of tests, mixed with all those failures. The worst of it was the self-doubt year after year, the beatings he gave himself.

Then it worked.

My God, it really worked! Essentially, it was accidental; the process design had been reversed by a faulty computer input, but the result was undeniable. Aaron had been working on a synthetic fat burner for the last ten years. There had been some limited success, but nothing that would break wind in any of the hundreds of labs throughout the country. That was all bullshit at this point; he was now the Grand Wazoo, the alpha of the fat breakers. The crap on the market today would be obsolete within six months. He had no fear about any FDA holdup; after all, it was the fucking high priest who was funding his research.

Not to mention that this could be the primary weapon on the American obesity outrage! For just a brief moment, Aaron considered the countless benefits that people would derive from his discovery.

He had really done it; the formula was spinning in his head along with way too much alcohol. As soon as Aaron's eyes started to focus, he scrambled back to bed.

Oh, that is so not going to work. Aaron sat back on the bed; just closing his eyes for a few minutes was so damn helpful. His phone started buzzing across the nightstand, and he reached out to grab it, failing several times. Finally, he was able to wrap his fingers around the fuckin' thing.

"Hello." But he was too late.

As Aaron looked at the phone, he was stunned to see twenty-three missed calls. *What the fuck!*

As he reviewed the numbers, he saw that most of the calls were from Sidney, and some others he didn't recognize. He scrolled down to the last number and hit "Send." Moments later, Sidney's voice came over the phone.

"Where the fuck are you? Do you have any idea what is going on at this place?"

"Sidney, please stop yelling at me. The terror in your voice is cutting through my brain like a Marine's Ka-Bar," Aaron snapped.

"Aaron, please stop talking and listen to me. Ditusa learned about the breakthrough last night. He is fully freaked that you can't be found. He thinks you're selling out or going rough to a competitor!"

"Sidney, can you tell me how in hell does Howard know about my formula?"

"Well, the way I hear it, some drunken asshole called him last night screaming, 'I fuckin' did it.' I hear you also threatened to bone his wife and the English sheepdog named Alfie!" Sidney responded.

Aaron sighed, slightly recalling verbal threats against that poor dog's anal cavity.

"I am jumping on the subway right now, twenty minutes. Tell Howard," Aaron said.

"Dude, there's something else you need to know. Gerard Ditusa himself has descended from above, and he looks pissed," Sidney said with obvious tension.

"What!" Aaron responded with alarm.

"The weird thing is he is flanked by two suits that smell like government, and these guys have been all over your office like Russian housekeepers."

"Oh, that motherfucker!" Aaron screamed into the phone.

"They can do whatever they want. The formula is in my head. I will be there in twenty minutes!" Aaron screamed.

Jerry Ditusa was the Trump of the pharmaceutical world, except he was self-made. Daddy didn't hand him the keys to the kingdom.

If he was in London last night, and now tearing my office apart, he was on a mission. They had truly now entered the "holy shit" phase; Aaron really needed to pull it together. Water intake was an empirical necessity and critical to his survival.

He was a scientist, and he understood that last night's alcohol was still pilfering valuable fluids and amino acids from within his agonizing skull.

He slid from the big, puffy bed, realizing he was wearing one of Gina's Victoria's Secret outfits. The silk felt really good on his skin, and his dick was really enjoying the sensation as his big one eye stared right at him.

He didn't bother to change; water was his primary mission. The refrigerator was one of those stainless steel monsters with two equally large doors. He thought to himself, *That bitch weighs all of a hundred pounds. She really needs this much fuckin' fridge space?* Of course, Gina needed to keep up with the Joneses; he had spent countless hours trying to educate her on this pointless endeavor, but it fell upon deaf ears. She would nod her head in agreement, but broken self-esteem can't be fixed with even the sincerest dialogue.

Aaron eased the door open like a safe cracker praying for an ample water supply.

"Champagne, vodka, and two big bottles of Fuji, yeah, baby, relief is on the way!" Aaron yelled.

He grabbed the large cool bottle like a junkie after a dope drought. The cap flew off the top with one fast, effortless move. There was no real swallowing involved; his head tilted back, and the contents of the container were poured down his throat. Some gagging was involved initially, but the body so needed the fluids, and necessity far outweighed the brief discomfort. The mind was starting to motor up, and focus was returning; he was beginning to organize.

Clothes, money, keys, and out the door, in that order. Keeping everything simple was extremely important; deep thought could be problematic.

Aaron was on the move now; there was no time for a shower, and food would never stay down. The thought of projectile vomiting was not very appealing. Gina most likely had a clean shirt somewhere. He lived here for nine months; there had to be few leftover garments.

Bingo! The blue shirt he knew she stole from him last year; this will do nicely. The hangover was still kicking the shit out of him, but the rage he was feeling was sending plenty of adrenaline through the pipes. Why the fuck was there government running through his paperwork? This made absolutely no sense; Ditusa hated any outside influence, especially the government, and he had enough money and power to keep their asses out of the sandbox. This shit just didn't make any sense. *We were working on fat busters, not anything these fuck heads could use. What in the world was going on?* he thought.

I left for nine hours, and cats and dogs are living together in sheer pandemonium.

Aaron rolled out of the elevator, moving quickly for the door. He was pretty incognito in his blue shirt, Mets cap, and sunglasses. Aaron always liked the Mets, and that wasn't an easy thing in Yankee town, but you know the old saying, "Fuck the Yankees!"

Tito Pagan had been the doorman at Gina's building for the past six years; he knew everything about everybody. He took one look at Aaron and started laughing and shaking his head.

"Hey, cabron, nice to see that your ass is still alive. You know, it took three of us to get that drunken ass upstairs last night," Tito said, still laughing.

"Tito, I am crazy late. I owe you big time," Aaron managed.

"Oh, don't worry, you blew all three of us. We're even," Tito joked.

"I thought I tasted refried beans when I woke up," Aaron shot back.

Aaron would usually laugh his balls off when Tito cracked on him, but not today; he needed to be on a subway heading midtown, pronto. Aaron was flying down Thirty-Third Street double time; the fresh air felt extra good in his lungs. The thought of fresh air in New York was a foreign concept to most, but nothing could be further from the truth. The smells of coffee and that early morning bread baking were as close to heaven on earth as one thought possible. Aaron loved this city; as he looked around, people were on the move, and it seemed that everyone was on a cell phone. He laughed to himself.

How could so many people live in one area and be so disconnected from one another? Aaron wasn't too sure why these thoughts were circling through his head, but he knew today was a new day. The impact that his breakthrough will make over the next few years is really unfathomable on so many levels. Total joy was rolling in and out of his head, only interrupted by the thoughts of what was going on at his lab.

Government dickheads in my fucking office, he puzzled with that concept again and again. *What the hell is their angle, and why would they even be slightly interested in a fat-extracting agent?*

As Aaron entered the park entrance, he started to contemplate the basis of the process itself. There was such simplicity to the mathematics surrounding the formula; he couldn't understand how so many before him failed to align the proper formulation. These thoughts raced around his alcohol-soaked melon at the speed of light. He was so dammed confused about Sidney's call; it just didn't line up. *Why the fuck is this allowed to happen in my office, and why is Ditusa letting it?*

CHAPTER 2

Upper East Side, New York

Jimmy Cosgrove snapped out of bed at seven twenty-three, more than a half hour earlier than his alarm clock was set for. That was something that just didn't happen in his world.
"What the hell!" he said out loud.

If Jim had one outstanding and endearing quality, it was consistency. This was extremely odd and a little disturbing for him, but he didn't let his mind dwell on it. He started suiting up for the morning run, or what he liked to call the AM constitutional. Everything he did in the morning was of a methodical nature—first, sweatpants, T-shirt, then sneakers, and finally his iPod.

Jim was a huge Pink Floyd fan; he always had some old classics geared up for his morning run. Side A of *Atom Heart Mother* was on the menu this morning. He had tried running with several different bands, but nothing really gets deeper than the Floyd! And he loved to go deep while he was out on his run. That blast of endorphins made all things worthwhile.

He had recently gotten his ten-year chip from the rooms, and his health was improving. It had been a long, hard road out of hell; however, there was never a shortage of inner strength with Mr. Cosgrove.

Jimmy let himself out the back door. This was always part of his pattern—gear up and slowly sneak out the back door. The key was to avoid waking up Katie at all cost.

SEEDS OF THE GRAY

He had been married to her for only a few years now; his first marriage had failed painfully. However, three outstanding children had risen from the ashes of that marriage, gifts paid in full. For this he would always be somewhat grateful, but he has finally found true happiness with Katie, his angel and partner.

His life had been a strange and beautiful journey with peaks and valleys that most people couldn't possibly fathom. He had spent ten years with the police department, until common sense got the better of him. He was now with the NYFD, and life was finally starting to fall into place.

A slight smile ran across his face as he stepped out onto Ninth Avenue. He always started his run with a few-minute stretches to avoid injury, but not this morning. Jimmy had an overwhelming sense of purpose this day, not fully understanding what that was all about. The air was crisp this morning; Central Park was full of runners as was the case this time of year.

As Jimmy turned into the path by the lake, he began noticing that he was off his regular morning course and that was so unlike him. His thinking started to drift, the pace of the run was increasing, and his body was adjusting without any difficulty. Something wasn't right, and that was the last thought Jimmy had before his brain went on autopilot. Jimmy hit the downtown traffic area without slowing down; however, seconds before he reached the street, the lights changed, allowing him safe passage. The same thing happened for the next few blocks, until he reached the subway entrance. He took the steps two at a time, bypassing the big board of scheduled train timings; he clearly knew his intended destination.

He approached the gate leading to the downtown subway; standing on the left side of the iron swing gate were two men. The first man, Officer Frank Niavez of the NYPD, and the second man was Private Michel Maloney. It was not uncommon to see military in the subway system since 9/11; it was all too familiar now.

Officer Frank saw the man in his jogging gear approach; when the man came within three feet, the two men started feeling a building pressure in their upper sinus area. This was nothing that would be considered painful, but enough to wince slightly.

They both knew it was important for the jogging man to pass without incident, and so he did. Jimmy walked through the gate, not even glancing at the two authority figures on his left; he proceeded to the escalator. As he rolled slowly down to the platform, his brain scanned the 224 people currently on the platform. Initially, he was able to systematically eliminate the 72 females, 14 Afro-Americans, and 6 children, but before he could complete this process, he identified his target.

Aaron Goldstein was standing 21 meters away; he was wearing a blue shirt and a New York Mets baseball cap. The ground started to shake, and the noise from the incoming train was intensifying as Jimmy took each step toward his designed target.

The C train express rolled into the downtown station with no intention to stop; the noise from the horn was deafening. It was so strange how New Yorkers became practically oblivious to loud sounds that surrounded them.

Aaron stepped back over the yellow line as the oncoming train approached from uptown. He knew it was silly, but he always had a deep fear of being sucked into the train's back draft. He looked over to his right and saw a young Asian girl was standing there looking at him. She was smiling a little after witnessing him take that step back. Aaron smiled back at the young girl and couldn't help but notice how beautiful her skin looked next to her dark hair.

This was Aaron's final thought as he felt the sharp shove to the upper center of his back.

He knew his body was being projected toward the oncoming train. Disbelief and horror filled his eyes. Aaron instinctively turned to look behind him, only to see the man in a jogging outfit with a flat affect turning to walk away.

The train hit Aaron at sixty-five miles an hour; the effect was similar to Nolan Ryan throwing a tomato at a brick wall. Aaron's body exploded, spraying blood and bone over everyone in a forty-foot radius. The blistering screams of horror filled the platform after a brief pause; these were slightly drowned out by the grinding of the C train braking system.

The young girl who seconds ago was smiling at Aaron was now frozen, covered from head to toe with blood. As she worked the spit out of her mouth she realized it was Aaron's blood, and a fairly large piece of skin was working around her teeth. She attempted a scream that just would not come. Hysteria was running rampant through the terminal; people were vomiting and desperately attempting to move away aimlessly in all directions. Some simply passed out, unable to deal with the gruesome reality.

Yet, there were still others who couldn't get enough of the carnage and were twisting their necks in almost impossible configuration to see the ugly. That is the duality of who we are as a people; we bathe in the ying and yang of good and evil on a daily basis. It's just how we are wired.

Jimmy kept up a reasonable pace as he exited the station without a single drop of blood on him. When he hit Eleventh Street, he retraced his previous course to return to his apartment. As before when he approached the intersections on both Park and Broadway, the traffic lights turned in his favor almost with perfect rhythm. When he entered a more residential area, he started to slow down, until he came to a full stop. Jimmy was unsure how he had reached this part of town; side A of his album had completed, and dead air filled his ears.

Jimmy glanced at his watch; he was confused, but not overly concerned since this has happened to him while running in the past. He fiddled with the button of the iPod, resetting it to the "On" position, and proceeded back to the apartment for a shower, and hopefully a blowjob.

As he ran his hands through his hair, he picked out a small piece of bone fragment; he quickly discarded it and resumed his run back to his apartment to start a new day. Absolutely no recollection of the events that took place just seconds ago.

James' thinking pattern began to clarify, and he thought of plans he had made for the day.

DAVID WENDT

On the corner of Fifth Avenue clicking away on his Minolta 950 sat an aging Asian man inside a green sedan. As Jimmy jogged down toward the lake, the man spoke into his handheld transmitter in the Chinese Mandarin dialogue of his home, "Cosgrove subject M671, seventeen minutes outside parameters now reentering the park. Will adjust surveillance feedback. Out."

CHAPTER 3

Lt. Robert MacDonald was an eighteen-year veteran of the New York Police Department. He stood close to six foot one, with a slim frame and a well-muscled upper back. He was a hard worker both on the job and off, often thought of as a bit of a roughneck. Mac didn't frequent the gym but was always able to remain in good shape, despite the smokes and booze. His stock answer concerning his physical condition was that his father lived well into his eighties.

The man hated every day after seventy. I am hoping the smoke and the drink will pull off ten years and let me die with some dignity, he thought to himself.

He got the call twenty minutes after the incident. Several people had to be taken to the hospital immediately, mostly shock. He would need to catch up with them later. He hated these cases; the manpower and paperwork weren't worth it. Lieutenant Bob paced back and forth on the platform at the downtown station, placing yellow cards every few feet.

The uniforms knew Detective MacDonald. His nickname was the Mac; he was a good cop and well respected. He had made his way up the ranks from the streets, spending nine years in Brooklyn narcotics. The uniforms knew he was the real deal, not one of these college-made dicks that slide into plain clothes right out of school. The word on the block was Mac was a hard-ass if you weren't doing the job; one didn't want to slack on his watch.

Everyone worked to stay out of his way; keeping the endless flow of commuters off the platform was no easy task. New Yorkers hated being redirected, even by the police. One smashed-up bone bag in a city of nine million didn't seem that critical in the grand scheme of things. The city was funny that way; as he looked around at the crowd, he could read the agitation on their faces. Nobody gave a shit about this dumb dead fuck, and the Mac got that. He knew the unwritten rule in this town; deep, deep down in the belly of this fuckin' city was an angry brat that wanted more toys. Bob thought to himself, *Do your job and do it fast. Don't hold up the show.*

The blood pattern was consistent with a direct impact at four to six inches above the platform; Lieutenant Bob was leaning toward suicide. He had seen too many of these tragedies, and he knew these direct hits were well-timed. Someone who was pushed usually was hit at a much lower trajectory. The thinking was really pretty basic, no rocket science going on here. There have been many people who have been pushed or jumped into oncoming trains over the past years.

In the early eighties, thousands of people were released from several psychiatric facilities throughout the state of New York. This was no mystery; they were considered low-level psych cases, and the state really didn't want to fit their bill any longer, so they had to go somewhere. Some actually transitioned well into society; most didn't. If you had spent any time in this city, you knew they were always around, talking with themselves, begging, and afraid. We walk past it every day, not giving it a second thought. New Yorkers were fully immune to the zombies and noggin defectives who walked the streets. Bob had a soft spot for the crazies in this town since they really didn't go looking for trouble. Unfortunately, they spent a good deal of time swimming in it. On way too many occasions, they would bring Bob here to scrape up the pieces, attempting to make sense out of the madness.

He looked around for a uniformed officer named Steve; he was first on the scene.

"Steve!" he called.

A young black officer walked over, purposely keeping his eyes fixed on Bob's face, wishing not to acknowledge the body parts lying about his feet.

"Yes, sir, Lieutenant?"

"I need statements from everyone you came in contact with the moment you hit the platform! I am also going to need someone to follow up with MTA! There are three separate cameras that may have captured something."

Officer Steve followed writing the directions down, eyes still averting from the bloodbath that surrounded him.

"What am I working with so far?"

Officer Steve fumbled through his pad quickly. Finding what he needed, Steve turned to address Bob, "The dearly departed is Dr. Aaron Goldstein. He's a scientist from MIT. He is unmarried and lives out on the island. He has an apartment uptown. The weird shit is that I have been hearing that name all night long."

"What do you mean?" Mac asked confused.

"At two AM an all-points went out on this guy. Everyone and his mother have been looking for him," the officer shot back.

"Who sent up the flag?" Mac added, puzzled.

"This is where it gets fuckin' wacky. From what I am hearing, there are five separate agencies trying to tap that dead broken ass, or what's left of it," the young officer added.

"Who?" Mac probed.

"The FBI, DOD, and even the Department of Health. There are a few others that I don't even know what they do," said the young officer as he listed the top few.

"Are you fucking kidding me?" Mac snarled.

"I shit you not, boss. As we speak, there are three white shirts and a Fed at the top of the platform," the officer tried to emphasize the craziness.

"Steve, listen to me real good. I need you to move out double time, get me that film. I don't need any of these limp dicks working their own investigation!" Mac snapped and pointed to the ceiling cameras.

Steve started to move out when Bob reached out and grabbed his arm.

"Wait! Why hasn't the Fed come down here?"

Steve smiled as he turned back to Mac. "She told me that she didn't want to get her new shoes full of red vino. Apparently they're Italian."

Bob smiled at the thought of the big bad FBI agent being blood shy.

He stepped back from the platform, taking in a deep breath. "Shit," he said.

As he rescanned the area, his brain started to process the puzzle. The likelihood that this was a standard suicide was starting to look unrealistic. Now, if that was the case, then this was one extremely well-timed assassination. Why would anyone want to kill a geek that bad?

There was nothing left to do down here. forensics was doing their thing; Steve was after the tape. As he made his way up the stairs, he began to think about the victim. If he was pushed, did he understand what was going on? Did he have a chance to scream, or was he in a state of disbelief?

Bob neared the top of the stairs; the brass was everywhere. He could feel their cold eyes being fixed on him; clicking and flashing broke his thought pattern. This was new, he said to himself. It never ceased to amaze Bob how fast a news story moved through this town. The first feeling that shot through Bob was fear; the press could really put a choke hold on one's ball bag. Mac quickly took the helm and puffed up his chest; he put on his best John Wayne and walked through the fire.

"Are there any suspects, Detective?" asked a young reporter.

"Sure, you and everyone else in this fine city, Sara!" Mac snapped.

"Detective, can we rule out suicide?" asked the blonde woman thrusting a microphone way too close to Bob's face.

"Sara, if you're ready to confess to the murder today, we will be good to go!" Mac shot back, fully aware of how to deal with the media from years of practice.

"Detective, is there anything you are able to tell us at this point of your investigation?"

Mac knew how this game worked; if he walked away leaving these scavengers to their own devices, the bullshit would be so deep by morning, he would need a ladder to pop his head out. His best course of action was to put these assholes to work for him.

Mac drew a breath and turned sharply to address the band of reporters, "Now listen, what we have is a horrible tragedy. A young man is dead, and we are still processing the evidence. His family has not been notified, so please show some discretion! We are hoping to find someone who saw something down there." He paused for moment, scanning the pack. He contemplated giving them the "right thing" speech, then he realized this was a gang of New York press. He shook his head and walked toward the door, and the press followed for a few more feet; then realizing that the interview was over, they broke pursuit.

Mac hit the fresh air outside the terminal; he squinted his eyes from the sun's glare. Looking at his watch, he was stunned to see that he had been down that hole for four hours. His nose picked up several amazing smells. The first was the doughnut shop across the street; it was a Krispy Kreme. If God came down from heaven tomorrow, his first stop would most definitely be the double K.

The thought of some coffee and Boston creams was making his mouth water. Mac rubbed at his belly and started to play head games with himself. He was in his forties now; he was in good shape, but he wanted to stay that way. The trick to staying in good shape in your forties is half sacrifice and half starvation. Across the street was a little Thai takeout place; he knew that he should be making that move for the good of the waistline.

At that very moment, all good thoughts ran screaming from his mind; the smell of pizza hit him like a sledgehammer. Ray's Pizza wasn't the best in this city, but it never let you down, big fat slices with lots of cheese and grease that pooled on top of that Grande Cheese! The trick was to fold the pizza and let the oil drain off.

Mac was moving double time across the avenue, holding up his arm, gesturing the oncoming cars to slow down.

This was a game New Yorkers played with one another; most of the time, it would just piss off drivers to pick up speed. The pizza joint was almost empty; he had beaten the after-work crowd, and this was good.

"Let me get a slice of that fresh pie coming out, and two Sicilians." Mac pointed to the slices he wanted.

The young kid behind the counter pulled the earpiece from his iPod and said, "You staying or going?" in a perfect Brooklyn accent.

Before Mac could answer, a woman walked up from behind, handed the kid a twenty, and said, "We're going to stay."

The blonde turned to Mac and said, "Hi! My name is Agent Magen Cummings."

Mac fumbled around for something intelligent to say. She was incredibly beautiful, and he was more than slightly out of practice.

The best he could do was "Thanks for lunch. Now who the hell are you?"

The moment it came out, he wanted to take it back. It was hard for him sometimes to stop being the cop. *My God*, he thought to himself, *she really is a beautiful woman*. She made him slightly uncomfortable, but he liked it.

Magen smiled as she flipped open her identification. "I am with the Federal Bureau of Investigation. I need just a few minutes."

This time it was his turn to smile as he looked down at her expensive Italian shoes. He closed her ID and handed it back to her.

"It is really nice to meet you, Agent Cummings. How is it you think I can help you?" Mac smiled and gave his best cute look.

Mac was not unfamiliar with the Feds involving themselves in his investigations; their presence has been strong in this city since 9/11. He had handled countless agency identifications over the years, and the one that she just handed him could have been made last night. He could actually smell the ink drying. *This case is starting to get interesting,* he thought.

A scientist getting himself lambasted by the C train, press gang tackling him at the starting gate, and now the blonde Jennifer Love Hewitt handing him a dummy badge.

"I am not looking to stick my nose into your business, Detective MacDonald. I was only hoping to review the platform film with you."

"Oh! Is that all, but you don't want to stick that pretty nose in my investigation?"

She lowered her eyes from his, briefly puffing out her bottom lip. "Detective, it's really not like that!"

Mac flashed a phony smile, thinking to himself, *Wow! Did this agent just pout at me?*

This was getting weirder by the moment.

"Listen, Ms. Cummings, call me at my office after six, and I will get you down to review the film."

Magen stood up from the table, a glib smile dancing across her face. She shot her hand out in front of herself like a politician. "I can't thank you enough, Officer MacDonald, I will call you later."

She turned on her heels and walked out the door like she could have been on a midtown runway. Mac looked around the room then stealthily shot his eyes at her firm, tight ass. This was one of those things men couldn't really help; if a nice ass was walking out the door, it was practically impossible not to shoot at least a quick glance. The rest of the pizza joint had also caught Magen's act as she rolled out of the building.

The Italians appreciated a nice ass the most, and when she was gone from sight, the crew behind the counter turned to Mac with a look of newfound respect; no words were exchanged but an understanding among the swinging dick club had been reached. Mac sat at the table finishing the rest of his pizza, thinking about the events of the day. There was a feeling moving through him that started to worry him. This thing wasn't adding up! A bubble of fear rose up from the pit of his stomach, wreaking havoc with the tomato sauce. He knew deep down that he was slightly irregular and he better document well. This was not your routine case that he was going to deal with overnight, file a report, and move on. Mac was going to need some help; the beautiful thing was that he knew where to get it.

Mac was through with the last piece of pizza crust in his mouth; he loved the taste of New York pizza crust. He had lived for several years outside Baltimore while getting his degree in criminal justice at Maryland University; they were real big on crab cakes down there, best in the world! Unfortunately, their concept of good pizza was a shit wheel with a burned condom chaser. There really was no substitute for Manhattan pizza. Sometimes he would get a small saucer of garlic and olive oil and use the crust to soak it up. It was one of those things you took for granted but really missed it when it was gone. Man! He found that more and more he was not indulging in the dago dip, as he called it.

Lately, everything has been about watching one's weight. He couldn't stand that he really loved to eat. Unfortunately, the weight packed on so fuckin' fast, he couldn't keep up. Mac finished chewing and walked back on the avenue. It was getting darker, and the streets were filling up with the going-home shift. He pulled out his phone and flipped it open; hitting a series of numbers, he held it up to his face.

After about a half dozen rings, a hard, scratchy voice answered the phone, "What the hell do you want?"

"Paul, it's Mac. I need to come over!"

"That's cool, kid, the door is open. I need some Camels, and my beer supply is low and no damn filters." With that, Paul was gone.

The phone went dead, Mac looked down at the cell, and he shook his head and walked down to the deli.

Paul Major was the poster boy for old-school New York City cop, from the womb, squeezed out of his mother in the back of a black-and-white. He liked to tell everyone that his first human contact was an Irish sergeant who wrapped him in his winter blues. Although this could never be proven, it was apparent that Pauli was born to do the job. Retired for the past six years, he had been spending most of his time swallowing painkillers, smoking grass, and drinking way too much.

Paul was a good cop, but not a great cop by any stretch of the imagination. Mac would run things by his old friend every now and then; not so much because he felt he was some great criminologist, it just helps to sound things out sometimes, and Paul had the feel for this town. He felt comfortable with his friend, and he knew that anything he would say would never leave the room; Paul could hold his mustard. That may not sound like much in the grand scheme of things, but it was really important to Mac.

Lately, he found that most men were worse than women when it came to holding their tongue. He couldn't put his finger on any one thing, but there had been a lot of changes since he joined the force. He could remember the cops that hit the streets when he first got started; every one of them tough, hard, and mean. Today, the force looked like rejects from computer camp, and everyone had phones in their ear.

The crazy thing was that it wasn't only the job; it was everywhere. We are a softer society! We amuse ourselves to death, eat everything that's not nailed down, and we come up with ideas to minimize our work every chance we get. He called it the metrosexual pussification of the modern man!

Mac pulled the Crown Victoria in front of the ugliest house in Bayside, Queens. He grabbed a bag out of the front seat of the car and walked up to Paul's shithole. As Mac approached the door, he could hear music coming from the open window. He could immediately recognize the voice of Jim Morrison and the Doors. Mac couldn't help but smile. Mac loved the Doors, and the song he was hearing was "When the Music's Over," one of his favorites. Off the left side of his eye, Mac caught movement that could only be human. In one swift motion, he broke his progression and shifted the bag in his hand, freeing his gun hand. He shifted his head toward the tall bushes at the corner of the property. An easing feeling soon relaxed his guard as he saw the stern-faced old woman materialize from behind the bush.

She acted slightly offended at being caught red-handed, snooping; she gave him a disapproving look and walked toward her *metic-*

ulous home. *Apparently not a music fan*, Mac thought as he headed back on track to the front door. The neighbors never fucked with Paul regarding his music or the presentation of his home. Once, they attempted to form a committee in hopes of discussing front-yard cleanup. The next day all of their cars were impounded.

CHAPTER 4

The door to Paul's house was never locked; he tried to talk to him about negative patterns and leaving himself exposed, but Paul would only laugh at him, call him a pussy, and lean in to his face and try to stick his tongue in his mouth.

Mac turned the handle and walked into the house. The smell of stale beer and cigarettes hit him like a bitch slap, and there were plenty of other nasty smells in there as well. The music was practically deafening as he moved closer to the living room. Paul stood in the middle of the floor; a faded blue robe draped around him like a potato sack.

He turned to see Mac standing there; he gave a slight smile and then yelled, "The scream of the butterfly!" which was a feeble attempt at the Morrison classical lyrics.

Paul was singing into his .357 Magnum, and the head of his penis was winking at him from underneath a filthy robe. There was something almost haunting about a man nearing sixty years of age acting like a frat drunk. Mac stood there looking at the scene before his eyes, trying desperately not to laugh.

Paul paused for a few seconds then reluctantly opened the cabinet to the stereo and turned down the music enough to talk.

From somewhere outside, they could hear the sounds of cheers and clapping. There was a woman's voice yelling, "Thank you!"

Paul looked at him with anger in his eyes, then turned and ran to the window where he stuck his head and screamed, "Ingrates!"

He closed the window and ran his fingers through his hair, as if he was working to compose himself.

"So, how are you, Mac?" Paul offered.

Mac lifted the six-pack of Schmidt's toward Paul. "Things could always be better."

Paul grabbed the beer and the small bottle of Jameson like it was gold, his face showing elated happiness.

"Kid, you should be a fuckin' captain by now. You're an obvious genius, with excellent taste in the finer things," he said as he crept off like Gollum off to the cold fridge, clutching his fresh stash.

Mac kicked some papers off the sofa, checked the area closely for bugs, then finally settled down. He realized that this was the first time since 6:00 a.m. that he had stopped moving. He rubbed his eyes and let his body relax into the sofa. The madness of the day flashed in his head. Mac wanted to run a few things past Paul, but he was having trouble finding a starting point.

Paul had come back into the room, sat down in front of Mac with a fresh drink in his hand. "You look like shit, boy," Paul offered between hard slugs of his drink.

Mac became really serious then began speaking slowly, "How many bodies have you pulled off the tracks in your day?"

CHAPTER 5

A puzzled look grew quickly across Paul's face. "Damn, kid, I don't know, more than I want to remember. Sometimes I still see their twisted, broken faces gazing at me," Paul stated with fresh pain on his face.

"In all that time, did the FBI or the Department of Defense ever show up at your crime scene?"

Paul smiled and added, "You got yourself a hot one. I was wondering why you popped your pecker in here today."

Mac tried to smile along with his friend, but he was finding the situation unnerving.

"This is much more than a hot one. This one could be out of my league," Mac said, lowering his head.

"Bullshit, boy! You don't have any idea what level your league is. I can tell by the look on your face that whatever is going on has spooked you pretty good."

"So much of this damn thing just isn't adding up," Mac offered.

"Mac, you are killing me with all this suspense! Please, start from the beginning, and stick to clear details."

Paul took another slug of the whisky and pulled deep on the uncircumcised cigarette.

Mac started to unravel the story, from the moment he stepped onto that platform a little past eight this morning. He tried to stay as close to the facts as he could remember them. Paul sat back, taking in the full story, not saying a word. As Mac finished the breakdown of the day's events, he realized that he had not heard from Steve regarding the platform video. Paul took a long pull on his smoke, and then gulped hard on his drink. He smiled at Mac and got up from his chair and headed to the fridge. Mac pulled out his cell phone and called the desk commander at the station.

"Officer Miller!"

"Miller, this is Lieutenant MacDonald. I am looking for Steve Anderson."

"Hold on, Lieutenant, I saw him two minutes ago."

As Mac sat on the phone, Paul came back into the room and sat back down on his chair.

Steve came back on the phone. "Chief! I have been looking for you. I have your film."

"Listen, Steve, I am on my way. I need you to head to the lab and find Bill Lange wherever he is, and don't let him leave."

Mac hung up the phone.

"Paul, listen, I have some film to look at."

"Yeah! Keep me posted! Hey, what was the name of that Fed with the nice rack?"

"Cummings, Magen Cummings," Mac said.

"I will make some calls, see what I can see. You just stay in the mix!" Paul stated.

"Thanks, I'll take anything you can get your semen-soaked hands on!" Mac joked, and let himself out.

A few feet outside the house, Mac could hear the music start to blast. He stopped for a moment, not even turning back; he got into his car and gunned it down the full length of the block.

CHAPTER 6

Bill Lange sat in the lab with the look of total disgust on his face. He was clutching Knicks tickets in his white-knuckle hand and sweating bullets from sheer anger. Three plainclothes officers were standing between him and the door. There were no words spoken between them. Bill Lange sat in his overcoat staring past his three captors, occasionally adjusting his glasses. The door crashed open, and Mac came in with two cups of coffee in his hand, and a sharply dressed female who seemed overly excited.

"Thanks for coming down, Bill. Would you care for some coffee?"

Bill Lange stood up with a face full of shock and anger. "No, I don't want fuckin' coffee. I want to know why I'm not at the ball game."

"Listen, I'm really sorry," Mac voiced.

"Sorry about what, me missing the game or you having me kidnapped by these fuckin' goons?"

"Bill, I really need you now."

Mac stepped closer to Bill, holding out the second cup of coffee. "Please."

Bill started to calm down; dropping the tickets into the trash, he turned to Mac.

"So, what is it that is so damn important?" Bill said as he visibly calmed down, realizing this was something big.

"Thanks," offered Mac.

One of the large plainclothes officers who was close to the door walked over to the table and emptied a large bag of tapes.

"As you are most likely aware, Bill, we have a high-profile case unfolding in this city." Bill looked at the faces seated around the table.

"Is this about the pureed scientist?" Bill asked.

"Yes, sir! I am not sure at this point what we are dealing with. Suicide versus foul play. Steve has scooped up all the available tapes from the scene, and you are the best film man I know. So, let's get this bitch going!" Mac's face was all business at this time as he pointed his finger at the film board.

Bill picked up the closest tape, gave it a once-over, and plugged it in.

CHAPTER 7

Mac slowly picked up his coffee and walked to the back table where Magen was sitting. She was entering a series of numbers into a miniature keypad, and coordinating this with a secondary device. Mac quickly identified the device as a satellite uplink.

"So, when did the FBI start getting into global surveillance?"

Magen gave a slick smile and continued her assembly. As Magen moved to plug in the final USB cord, Mac grabbed her arm.

"I don't like surprises, Magen! Before you plug that in, I need to know who is going to be on the other end of that uplink."

Magen studied Mac's face, and paused for a moment.

Mac was wondering what she was thinking; he was half expecting a line of federal bullshit. Magen placed the camera unit on the table, and with her right hand, she grabbed at Mac's grip that was holding her arm. With a sly smile, Magen dug her long thumbnail into the fleshy meat between Mac's index finger and thumb. Mac was familiar with the aikido-style defense methods. He had spent over fifteen years studying several versions of martial arts. The strange thing was that even though his hand was in severe pain, he felt himself getting highly aroused.

Mac blissfully smiled and gave an apologizing glance. They both released their grips, and took the chairs surrounding Bill. Mac was happy to sit down before anyone realized his new development. Magen continued with the uplink setup; she turned to see Mac struggling with himself and was confused at first, then it dawned on her. She thought to herself, *I still have it.*

Magen finalized the frequency and then plugged her cell phone into the device; she spoke briefly into the phone and set it on the table. Magen took the chair next to Mac. She slowly turned to look at him with a smile, leaned over, and, in a purposefully husky voice, said, "I don't like to be grabbed, but apparently you do."

Mac said nothing, only smiled, and kept his head forward. Bill Lange yanked the first tape out of the soundboard, turned to the back table. "This is shit. The camera has been pointing at a brick wall for just about forever."

He placed the second tape into the device and began to spin it to the desired time frame. The film started to slow down, the focus was off, and the picture was dark and grainy. Bill quickly made some adjustments by turning a few knobs. The time highlighted on the screen was moments prior to the death.

As the camera swept back and forth through the crowd, Bill turned out the lights in the room to emphasize the quality of the film. Mac utilized the opportunity to peek down at Magen's perfectly long legs. As he shifted his head back to the screen, he jumped to his feet and yelled, "Stop!"

The lights went back on in the room, and everyone moved closer to the screen.

"Mets cap!" Mac called out.

Bill slowly turned the tape back, stopping frequently to allow the film to adjust. The team focused intensely on the screen. The problem was that this was a sweeping camera, moving the full length of that platform.

Bill caught eye of him first. "Hello, Dr. Goldstein, let's find out what the hell happened to you."

The moment they locked on to Aaron, the camera began its sweeping pattern back down to the other end of the platform. There was a collective sigh throughout the room. Bill sped the camera, being extremely careful not to overshoot the mark or to damage the film, and slowed down as the camera swept back to the area that they identified as the crime scene. The Mets cap came back on the screen; Aaron Goldstein was stepping backward and smiling at a young Asian *woman* who was next to him on the platform.

Magen's excitement wavered for a moment as she realized that the man on the platform was a person, and not just an assignment. This thought was broken by two events; the first was the sound of the C train, and the second was Bill Lange's voice stating, "I don't think this guy is thinking about suicide."

He looked straight into Mac's face and asked, "What do you think?"

Mac said nothing, but his facial features were indicating that he fully agreed with Bill's assessment. The camera started to sweep out of the area, clearly frustrating everyone at the table.

Bill said, "Shit! I don't think we're going to catch this by the next go-around."

The level of intensity in the room was intoxicating. Magen looked down at her hands; they were drenched and shaking. She quickly dried them off in her dress, gripping the fabric white-knuckle, and took a deep breath.

There was no attempt on Bill Lange's part to speed up the machine; the team sat pensively as the camera slowly stopped at the far end of the track. The light from the train was visible, and the C train's horn reverberated throughout the room like dynamite blasts.

Mac timed out the camera sweep in his head. "This is going to be close," he said out loud. The camera finished its pass and landed square on the back of Aaron Goldstein. At that very moment, there was a distinctive jerking motion at the base of Aaron Goldstein's neck, as if he was being pushed from behind, but there was clearly nobody there.

The next thing the team witnessed was Aaron Goldstein exploding against the C train. There was a feeling of puzzlement and disgust throughout the room. Something had happened on that platform; it was caught on film, yet still unclear. Bill Lange sat perplexed for a few seconds and then snapped up out of his haze.

His hands jumped to the dials on the board, stopping the film progress.

"Hold on there. I think this needs a second look!" Bill slowly moved the dial back over the event. Even in reverse, the gruesome scene was difficult to watch.

"There's no suspect that I see, Bill. He jumped at the train!"

"No, look here." Bill pointed to a shadow that came in direct line with the sweeping camera.

If it weren't reviewed in slow motion, it would have been easily missed.

"Watch his back."

As the tape sped up slowly, it was clear that the shadow came in contact with Aaron's back.

"Now watch his head."

Mac watched as the shadow came into contact with the victim; his head jerked straight up and flew forward.

"Now watch this part," Bill stressed.

Slowly the film moved to the point of impact. Bill froze the film to the exact moment of the murder; there, on the screen, was a wide-eyed Aaron Goldstein in the throes of pure horror.

"This is the face of a murder victim," Bill said.

The image on the screen was twisting his body around to look behind at something.

"I understand what you're saying, Bill! Unfortunately, I can't send an all-points on the shadow. Give me some time with the tape, Bill," said Mac as he stood to his feet, stretching out his stiff muscles and easing some of the tension that had built up over the past hour.

He placed his hand on Bill's shoulder and said, "Thank you for everything, and I am sorry for kidnapping you!"

Bill's right eyebrow rose up as he watched Mac walk away.

"That's okay. The Knicks suck this year. The nuns from St. Francis could give them game."

Mac smiled as he fished his cell phone from his coat pocket; he hit a speed dial number and put the phone to his ear.

"Steve, I need to get back down in that tunnel. It really is starting to look like this was no accident."

Mac listened for a few more seconds then hung up the phone. He looked over at Magen who was dismantling her satellite uplink; she looked unhappy. Mac stepped closer to the back desk, rubbing his wounded hand.

"Agent Cummings, you seem disappointed," Mac said, looking into her soft blue eyes.

Magen stopped what she was doing and turned from the table to see that Mac was closer to her than she initially thought. Mac saw the surprise in her eyes and instinctively stepped back. "I was hoping for some resolution," Magen said openly.

Mac's eyes opened widely as if he was stunned by this response.

"Resolution to what exactly were you expecting to see on that tape?"

Magen became guarded and turned back to the dismantling of the uplink.

"I was hoping to catch a killer!" she said firmly.

Mac reflected for a moment, looking at the back of Magen's head; he then walked around the table and sat directly in front of her.

"I have been a cop for a long time, Agent Cummings. As you can well imagine, being in this business for as long as I have, one gets a feeling about truth and the lack of that truth. Now, I don't think you are lying to me, but you are sure not giving me the full story," Mac stated in full cop form.

Magen considered a feeble protest and then thought better of it. She moved her suitcase to the floor and sat down next to Mac.

"There have been other scientists who have turned up either dead or missing, and it is not locally isolated," she said with uncomfortable resignation.

Mac could feel the hair on the back of his neck stand up; there was also a strange sense of relief. This was not totally his problem anymore!

"Magen, how many scientists are we talking about?"

The beautiful agent from the Federal Bureau of Investigation waved her hair away from her eyes. She moved in slowly to limit her volume to a whisper. "That is a difficult question. Do you mean this year or since 1972?" Magen stated in an almost matter-of-fact tone.

Mac couldn't comprehend the response to his question. At first, he thought maybe she misunderstood what he was saying. Then the scope of her answer hit him square in the face like a shotgun blast.

"Does the FBI believe that there is a serial killer in my town who has been active for the past four decades?"

"To be perfectly honest with you, the bureau has no position on this case. We simply have confirmed several patterns of interest."

"You know for a moment you sounded like Scully from *The X-Files*," Mac jested as his nervousness grew.

"Officer MacDonald, it has been nice meeting you! I will be catching a flight to Virginia in a few hours," Magen said with some regret.

Mac held up his hand in an effort to halt the conversation. "Stop right there! I know you're not going to drop this bomb on me and then go running back to your office," Mac stated, practically blocking the door.

"That is something that's totally out of my hands. My orders were to review the data and report my findings at 0600 hours in Langley."

Mac didn't really want to engage in a battle he knew he couldn't win. He understood orders all too well. He also knew this soldier wasn't going to disregard her orders.

He had figured her for military the first moment they met. Asses don't get that hard polishing a seat. Mac knew the best way to play this one out is to continue a soft approach. "Well, this sucks. Can I at least give you a ride to the airport?"

"That will not be necessary. I have a car waiting downstairs!" Magen said sheepishly as she turned to the door.

"Agent Cummings, I need to know one thing before you leave. Just how many patterns of interest has the bureau identified?"

Magen visibly stiffened, although she must have anticipated the question because she jumped right into bullshit need-to-know commentary.

In the middle of Magen's prepared avoidance speech, Bill Lange stood up from the video board and yelled out at the top of his lungs, "What the fuck!" he shouted.

The room went totally silent as everyone turned to see what was going on with Bill.

Bill stood in front of the machine in what could best be described as absolute shock. He kept looking at the screen and then at Mac.

"Bill, what is it?" Mac asked gently.

"I don't know," he mumbled as he slunk back down in his chair. "I was reviewing the tape at different speeds when I decreased the speed to minus times sixty, and this is what I found in that shadow."

Bill Lange rolled the tape back prior to the impact, and then he calculated his device and slowly moved his hands away. "Now watch!"

Slowly a figure started to materialize directly behind Aaron Goldstein. Bill waited to the last possible moment then hit the freeze button. "There, do you see it! Do you all see it?"

There on the screen, clearly defined, was the Chuck Jones cartoon version of the Road Runner. Its face was smiling directly into the camera, and its big yellow foot was strategically placed on the middle of Aaron Goldstein's back. Everyone in the room was familiar with the Looney Tunes cartoons; there was no mistaking what was there on the screen. Mac turned to see the reaction from the beautiful agent to what she saw on the screen. Unfortunately, she was halfway out the door talking into a cell phone. Mac squinted at the screen one more time and then lowered himself close to Bill's ear. As he touched Bill's shoulder, he jumped, as if afraid.

"Easy, Bill, I need you to focus for a moment," Mac said, but his deep breathing and body language told a different story.

"Focus on what?" Bill Lange said with the look of sheer confusion.

"How could someone manage to get that image into the tape in such short notice?" Mac asked, trying to make sense of all this.

Bill looked at Mac with a look of sheer puzzlement and then broke into uncontrollable laughter.

"Are you kidding me? That is just a total impossibility. You don't get it," Bill said, still slightly amused by the whole thing.

Mac considered Bill's response for several seconds, and then turned back to the screen.

"There has to be a way," he offered.

Bill put both of his hands together at the fingertips, and in a calm, low tone, he turned to Mac.

"Do you remember why you kidnapped me from the ball game at the Garden tonight? I know why, because I know my shit when it comes to film. That's why I am not upset. Now, Mac, I am telling you, for someone to actually pull that off, they would need technology far beyond what I know to be available. And if there really is someone capable of doing that, then the question would be why?"

"It's a message! He is telling us that he's smart!" Mac stated.

"That's one hell of a message, but it's not a he. It must be more than one, possibly a network," Bill stated firmly.

Mac moved to protest Bill's position, "You can't be sure of that, Bill!"

"Mac, I know you're fishing for possibilities, but the facts still remain. It is a physical impossibility for one person to manufacture this in the time frame specified. You're not convinced. Okay, let me explain. First, there are no splices in the tape. That means if there was some form of signal manipulation, it must have been at the primary site. Now, to my knowledge, there is nothing available to interrupt a video signal and inlay an overlapping signal." Bill continued to educate the room, "So, on the outside chance that there is some radical new technology that is leaps and bounds beyond anything in production, you still need someone to operate the device."

There was a moment of silence in the room as Mac searched the faces of the two other detectives to see if they were able to follow the logic. They looked at each other and then at Mac with confused reactions.

"Bill, I need to be honest, I'm not following you!" Mac added mildly.

"The fact still remains that if someone is utilizing this state-of-the-art magical device, you still need someone else to push the victim," Bill added.

"Shit," said Mac.

Now realizing that the simple logic was unavoidable, this was not the action of one delusional mind; the reality now setting in was even more frightening, the possibility of group conspiracy.

CHAPTER 8

As Mac thought about the developing information, he began to feel out of his element. His line of thinking kept pointing to government involvement.

"Where the fuck is that FBI agent?" he said out loud, the vein over his temple pulsing.

Mac stuck his head out the door and peered down both hallways; there was no sign of Magen. The more he thought about this situation, the easier it was to tie the government into this. He contemplated the events for a while, recalling how good Magen looked when he turned to see her in Ray's Pizza. Mac walked slowly to Bill's table, deep in thought regarding the chain of events. He leaned close to Bill Lange, not wishing to be overheard by the other detectives.

"Bill, I need to ask something. Knowing what you know, would you say that it may not be totally inappropriate to consider that we may be dealing with some form of internal government scenario?" Mac probed.

"I don't know, Mac, but it truly makes more sense than the possibility of an individual conspirator," Bill said, shaking his head as he watched the Road Runner's tongue waving at him.

Magen Cummings's hands where shaking as she fumbled with her cell phone. She walked out the front door of the station slightly frustrated because her phone couldn't hold a signal while in the building. There was no problem on the fourth floor, but as soon as she got into the elevator, the signal was lost. As she dialed the number for her superiors, she realized that it would be impossible to hear them with all the noise from the avenue. Magen caught sight of her driver halfway up the block and began to wave him down. He pulled the car into traffic and began to make a sweeping U-turn. Without saying a word to the man behind the wheel, Magen jumped into the back seat of the dark blue Crown Victoria.

She put the phone to her ear and waited until the voice came on the other end. "I have a level-three breach in New York. Code name request secure line for data retrieval." There was a long pause as Magen slid her laptop from the floor of the car. "I have a video anomaly in the death of subject Goldstein, Aaron, NYC, downloading now."

There were a few moments of silence as Magen waited for the processing of her data.

"Received," said a deep voice on the phone.

Magen began to disconnect her laptop; she reached for her earpiece and began to discuss her extraction from New York. "I can be at LaGuardia Airport in twenty minutes," she added.

"That is a negative on extraction. We require additional information, and you are the closest to the data source," the voice continued.

Magen had anticipated this position from her superiors.

"That will not be advisable. My current status here is under deep scrutiny. I believe the law enforcement primary is considering me a suspect!"

There was some muffled discussion on the phone as if someone was holding his hand over the phone.

"The primary needs to be taken to a level-three clearance. We are sending prior files to your lap. They will be encrypted. Pass codes will be on your cell within the hour," the handler added.

Magen knew that protest would be futile, so she simply packed up her gear and opened the car door. There was purpose in her step as she walked back toward the station. She was not oblivious to the instant attraction between the lieutenant and herself. It had been some time since her last interest in anyone. She had been extremely career minded the past few years; the bureau had kept her really busy with the abnormal aspects of this case. Magen welcomed the work or maybe the distraction that accompanied that work. Short of fourteen months ago, she was wrestling with the concept of love and marriage with the most beautiful Special Forces sergeant she had ever seen. Afghanistan had ended that dream for her and left her with a sense of emptiness that was always right there under the surface.

The pain from that loss was the worst time in her life. It started with a phone call just before lunch on a dreary Friday. It was Randy's sister crying, "He's gone, Magen! He's gone."

The first three days were spent in a dreamlike world, phasing back and forth between denial and the reality that her life was dead. When the numbness finally ended, it was easy to invest herself totally into the job. It was the obvious answer to her problem—keep working; stop thinking. She locked up a serial-killer case in Miami in six months that could have dragged on for years.

She knew that it was mostly luck; the asshole's ego tripped him up. Fortunately, it was enough to get her noticed by someone deep within the company who pulled a lot of weight. Almost overnight, her whole world changed; for all intents and purposes, she was no longer an agent for the Federal Bureau of Investigation. She really wasn't sure what was going on around her. This was a forty-year-old case that held the highest internal priority and absolutely no budget restrictions. The military plays some role in this case; that she knew for sure. Air Force jets are always on standby at the drop of a hat. No questions were ever asked. This assignment felt like standing in plain sight but being absolutely invisible. The extent of who she had become really became clear to her when she ran into a friend of hers from the academy one morning coming out of Starbucks in Maryland, the look of total shock as her mouth hit the floor.

"Magen, is that really you?" Sara Amos said.

Magen smiled, recognizing her friend. "Sara, how are you?"

"Are you kidding I'm fine, but we heard that you didn't make it back from Iraq!"

"What?" said Magen.

Sara suddenly started to look uncomfortable. "We sent cards and flowers."

Magen started to get a little spooked. "That's crazy!"

"Magen, I have to run," Sara said sheepishly, and then she was gone.

The rest of the day was a blur; what was going on? She remembered asking her immediate supervisor about the morning interaction. It wasn't so much his response but the look on his face that told her it wasn't some mistake.

There was no doubt in her mind that she was in deep, and the things that she had seen over the past few months working this case had confused her. The insanity of the information that she had been feeding back to her section chief was never questioned. Maybe that was the single most bizarre fact that concerned her the most. Mission after mission, they would send her all over the planet to investigate horrific murders, missing persons, unidentifiable situations. Initially, the insanity of these cases didn't have any real impact on her. Unfortunately, that was starting to change; she could feel herself becoming unglued.

Maybe, she was starting to feel the loss of Randy; she had been avoiding the grieving process for some time. Magen was smart, and she knew that eventually she would have to slow down and deal with this. Unfortunately, she knew that this wasn't the time.

It was at that minute when Magen saw the lieutenant coming through the revolving doors at One Police Plaza. He was breathing hard, and his face showed distress. The sun was bright, and Mac's blue eyes adjusted slowly to the light. He held his hand over the brim of his eyebrows and scanned the street. His eyes came to rest on her thin blonde frame slowly making her way toward him. Magen thought to herself, *It's time to make an ally.*

CHAPTER 9

Mac looked at the beautiful woman walking toward him. At first, he was contemplating calling after her, started to put on his angry face, then he stopped. Something had changed in her mannerism; her step was off as if she was giving up. A chill was running down his spine; Mac knew answers were coming, and deep down he wasn't sure he was ready to hear them.

Magen walked up the three steps at One Penn Plaza, placing herself at eye level to the lieutenant.

"We need to talk! Buy me some ice cream!" she stated.

"How about frozen yogurt?" Mac added sheepishly.

"That would be perfect!" Magen said with wink.

They popped into a small candy store about half a block up Broadway.

The girl behind the counter recognized Mac immediately; she smiled and started walking back to the frozen yogurt section. They started talking in Spanish. Apparently, the girl was slightly agitated about Mac bringing another woman into her store. Magen acted like she didn't understand and accepted the mango-flavored yogurt with a big smile. The girl gave Mac an evil glare until he hit the door, and then she blew him a sexy kiss. They strolled down the busy street as if they were the only two people in New York.

Magen started to talk about her life from her early college days and her decision to join the FBI. Mac kept his mouth shut, taking all the information in and wondering why the stage was being set. She went on talking about her tour in Iraq and the love she lost. There were several pauses during the story as if Magen didn't know how to have a long discussion. Mac began to realize that this woman had been living in a bubble for some time. This situation was getting stranger by the minute; he knew it was important for her to tell the story in her own words.

However, the clock was ticking, and there was still a murder that needed to be solved.

Magen could feel his impatience, and moved her timeline up to fourteen months ago. She came off the Miami case with a boatload of steam, and everything changed.

"They had a chopper waiting for me at Langley. Before I knew it, I was landing at Andrews Air Force Base. From there I was escorted to a black-ops jet, blindfolded, and taken to the desert."

"Was it military?" Mac asked.

"To be honest with you, I am not sure who was running the show, but they weren't all American. There were a lot of medical personnel. They ran six hours of tests on me, from MRIs to blood tests. After that, there was a three-day debriefing. This is a case that has been floating back and forth from agency to agency for the past four decades. The initial pickup began in the early part of 1963, after a double homicide at Procter & Gamble."

"The assholes that make my sensitive-skin shaving cream?" Mac added.

Magen smiled. "They are much more than that. They cover the market in consumer goods. One of their departments was the creator of Crisco oil. A group of scientists were working a healthier HDL cholesterol alternative, when all hell broke loose. Initially it was thought that two of the leading researchers killed each for other bragging rights. After revisiting the case nine years later, we escalated the case to homicide of a suspicious nature. Mac, the term 'suspicious nature' is going to take on a whole new meaning as the information is disseminated," Magen added with great emphasis.

"I take it that the FBI is positive that this was the first identified case from this killer or killers?" Mac asked.

"I have been authorized to upgrade your clearance to my own. I am waiting for a file download that will bring you up to speed on the past forty years."

"Forty years of this vicious insanity and not one arrest!" Mac openly stated, not trying to be critical of past detective work, but more or less struggling with the elusive ability of his adversary.

Mac slowed his pace as he neared the small park by the corner. The day's events were beginning to take their toll, and he could feel the anxiety creeping in. He was no stranger to stress and anxiety. The first two years after his bump to detective, the stress and daily madness had him in weekly therapy. His shrink had him on a brief run of Zoloft to take the edge off. Unfortunately, the meds did a job on his libido, and a limp wang was totally unacceptable.

He thought of a statement his therapist used to slam him with whenever he got too deep into the job, "Mac! The world is a cruel and ugly place, and some days it has absolutely no desire to be saved. So, you do your job, then go the fuck home."

Mac looked over at Magen and wondered if she ever left the job at the office and went home. His guess was that little Ms. Cummings was all job, and the more he learned about her and this case, the more he realized that she was so far over her head. The trick is to find the player on the other side of that phone she keeps updating.

Then Mac began to consider the possibility that Magen might not be the only field agent tracking this case. Clarity is a strange animal, but you know it when you feel it. Bells were going off in his head just thinking about the complexity of the layers that could be involved. And there was no way in hell that Agent Cummings was even the primary field contact on this monster.

"Tell me about your Langley contact!" Mac probed.

"What do you mean?" Magen looked puzzled.

"I want to meet him, talk about this case. There is only so much one can learn from reading files!" Mac said in a low, even tone. His cell rang, and he moved a few feet away.

"Officer MacDonald, talk!" he said low into the phone.

"Hey, kid, I got something. Did you know that your little princess is a phony? The real Magen Cummings died in battle!" Paul Major informed.

CHAPTER 10

"That is interesting. Keep digging, see what else you can find," Mac requested.

"Will do, Mac. Watch your six!" Paul stated with true concern.

"Even that would be impossible. I don't know who my contact is. I have never laid eyes on him, and I am pretty sure that this is by design," Magen said.

Magen was not convinced he was being honest.

"Nothing is impossible! There is a murderer loose in my city, and if your boss thinks he's going to show me some files and use me like he's using you, then he is just as crazy as this fuckin' case," Mac added, continuing in the same low, even tone.

Magen seemed slightly puzzled by the lieutenant's response. She wasn't hurt or angered. This was the first time since the onset of her involvement in this case that Magen actually spoke to another human being about this mess. There was a feeling of relief that she couldn't deny. However, she didn't have time for cop tactics; what she needed was an ally, and time was of importance. Magen reached into her coat, pulled out her phone, hit the number one, and handed it out to Mac. "Here you go, Chief, make it happen," Magen added in the same low, even tone.

Mac fumbled with the phone, not really expecting the immediate response that he just received. He put the Blackberry to his ear; it was ringing. He watched as the blonde agent started walking away. His eyes trailed down over her extremely fit ass, down her long legs.

A male voice came on over the phone. "How can I help you, Lieutenant?"

Attempting to hide his astonishment and play it cool, Mac mumbled, "Well! I am hoping we can help each other. But it would really help me if I knew your name!"

"My name is Dr. Timothy Gregory. I am the field supervisor for the Federal Bureau of Investigation, Washington division. I am also on the board of directors for external activities at the National Security Agency. It may also interest you to know that in a prior life, I was a gastrointestinal surgeon on staff at Jane Haskins. Now, tell me one thing, Lieutenant, if you will?" Gregory spoke.

"What would that be?" Mac asked.

"Is there anything that I have told you about myself that can help you in the least?" the agent stated.

"Sometimes it's not what you hear, but how you hear it!" Mac said evenly.

"I see. Will that be all then?"

"Not even close! We need to meet, and we need to do this soon," he stated forcefully.

"Is that so? Well, again, what would be the benefit of this parley?" the voice on the phone offered.

"Dr. Tim, this is nonnegotiable," Mac stated.

"Well, then I suppose there is no way around this situation. Are you familiar with the name Sydney Gotlieb?"

"No!" said Mac.

"Well, the recently departed Aaron Goldstein had a partner. You might know this if you weren't waltzing down Broadway with one very attractive FBI agent. Anywho! Dr. Sydney Gotlieb, a former Harvard professor, has been working hand in hand with our dead scientist for the past five years. He is scheduled to lecture on childhood obesity at ten AM tomorrow at the Schwartz Lecture Hall over at the NYU campus. I will see you there. Are you all right with these arrangements?"

"How will I recognize you?" Mac asked.

"I will introduce myself as soon as you arrive, no cloak and dagger required."

The phone went dead; Mac clicked the off button on the Blackberry and managed a forced laugh. The whole thing was just a bit too easy.

Magen had put herself out of phone range purposely. Now seeing him click off the Blackberry, she started walking back toward him.

"I hope that was helpful for you!" Magen said flatly.

"We will see! The both of us have a playdate with Dr. Tim tomorrow at the NYU campus," Mac added, handing Magen back her phone.

"How's that?" Magen stated with obvious surprise.

"We have a meeting tomorrow with your boss, Dr. Tim. He is going to meet us at the NYU lecture hall. He tells me that the recently departed Aaron Goldstein apparently had a partner that will be giving a lecture on little fat children at ten AM. He will be looking for us."

Before Magen could open her mouth, Mac asked, "Do you like Korean food?"

CHAPTER 11

Lynbrook, Long Island, New York

Mathias MaTaigh struggled with his weight since early childhood. Heavy drinking, drug abuse, poor eating, and poor sleeping habits resulted in a physical tragedy of epic proportion. However, always the optimist, Mathias threw his right leg over the back of his big black Weber Grill to stretch out his hamstrings.

"Four…five…six…Oh yeah!" Mathias grunted through his warm-up exercise.

He had made the mistake several months ago of not stretching his limbs prior to jogging, only to come limping home with a painful pulled hamstring. Now his routine consisted of a twenty-minute warm-up in his backyard, then slightly break a mild sweat. He was now ready to proceed out toward Merrick Road and catch his pace. This was a path he had taken many mornings; the town of Lynbrook, Long Island, was mostly quiet at 6:00 a.m. Mathias could hear some trucks out on Sunrise Highway, but not too many. Merrick Road was much slower, and he wouldn't have to watch over his shoulder at every corner. The first twenty strides found Mathias at the corner of his block.

Just another three hundred feet to Merrick Road, he thought to himself.

He was starting to feel comfortable with his process, and he looked forward to it. There was always a sense of peace that filled his core for the first few seconds. Traffic was tricky at the end of the block some mornings, so one needed to be cautious.

That wasn't the case today!

Over to his left was Fireman's Field, and this morning he had company. Fireman's Field was a large wooded area between the two highways. They called it Fireman's Field because the local volunteer firefighters used it for drilling practice. There was an area set aside for children, with swings and monkey bars covering the area. As Mathias passed it, he quickly caught the sight of two children standing by one of the older swing sets.

Seeing children in the park was not always something that would concern Mathias. However, it was 6:30 a.m., and these kids couldn't be more than six years of age.

No one would ever mistake Matt for some bleeding heart, but it was pretty early. His first thought was, *Not my fuckin' kids!*

And off he went without looking back. Besides, these two didn't look right; their clothing was wrong, and they were way too pale.

Matt thought to himself, *They're giving off that* Children of the Corn *vibe*. Even at six thirty in the morning, Merrick Road was busy. Cars were buzzing up and down the two-lane block. This early in the morning, the green lights last a little longer, and that opens up the speed demons racing to the Belt Parkway into Brooklyn.

Matt had made the first quarter-mile mark on his run, and he was breathing heavy, his lungs screaming from years of abuse. If he had spent less time packing his nose with the local version of stomped-on cocaine last night, he might have enough energy to complete his routine. He was considering alternating a few shortcuts that would ease his morning run by a few streets.

He knew that he could make the distance; unfortunately, his inner thighs were chafing from his balls sweating, and the discomfort was unbearable. He picked at his tighty-whities for the next few blocks and then started to slow his pace. Matt slowly made his way back to his home. He was still breathing hard and hacking up some yellowish-brown lung butter when he turned the corner of his block.

As he lumbered down the block, he was anticipating a plate of pancakes and some additional coffee.

He started to hear faint weeping coming from the Firemen's Field playground.

Initially, he couldn't see anyone, but as he moved to the other side of a large flowering bush, Matt could make out the little girl that he saw earlier. She was alone and crying. Before he would even consider talking to the child, Matt searched the area for the other child, and was hopeful that a possible parent could be in the area.

Where was the other one? he thought to himself.

Matt painfully approached the little girl, noticing immediately just how pale this child was. Her thin hands were covering the better part of her pale face, and she was weeping sheepishly into them.

"Hey, little girl, where is your mommy and daddy? Are you okay?" he said in his best gentle and caring voice.

He crouched down to be face-to-face with the little girl. "What are you doing out here, and where was the other child that was playing with you before?" he added softly.

The child lifted her cold, dark eyes and looked straight into Matt's face. She slowly began to spread out a smile that was freakishly wide across her pale face, displaying a row of sharp teeth set in jet-black gums. The smell was beyond anything he had come across in his life.

Traces of vomit raced up his throat.

If I had to place it, he thought, *rotting meat in the sun would be close.*

Matt began to feel afraid and tried in vain to back away. Something was wrong; there was a thundering alarm now going off in his head. The child still looked at Matt; the smile began to distort into more of a sharklike presentation.

CHAPTER 12

The noise off to the left was strange, but not immediately perceived as a threat.

It came from tree level, and it could have been a squirrel or some other animal. That was the last slice of denial that Matt could afford himself.

The small male child had jumped from an eighteen-foot vantage point; he then bounced off a telephone pole and was now digging his razor-like mash of teeth deep into the floating rib of an extremely terrified and speechless overweight man.

Matt instinctively began to swing at the source of his pain, aimlessly kicking and screaming, making several attempts to remove the child from his rib cage.

The child was dug in on Matt like a ravenous tick.

There came a strange burning feeling as fluid rushed in from the child's mouth, directly into the wound on Matt's abdomen. The fluid that Matt felt invading his body was a complex breakdown of vasodilators, along with a host of blood-clotting agents that assisted the humanoid parasite with easy feeding.

Unfortunately for Matt, there were no paralytics to ease the pain from the savage beings that were now beginning to devour him. The violent nature of these young animallike creatures was worked in an absolute frenzy. The pain had reached levels that were indefinable, and darkness was close now.

Matt spent his last moment of life pleading with the young girl for some form of mercy.

Mercy was a foreign notion in the small park that morning; it was simply breakfast time.

The girl was initiating a visible transformation as she slowly reached for Matt's face. The next few moments were horrific as these two young children metamorphosed into ravenous, nightmarish animals that dragged the carcass of the portly man deep into the woods with little effort. His last thought was *This can't be really happening!*

CHAPTER 13

Soho, New York

Korean food stands apart from the plethora of Asian-style presentations you may find in New York City at fifteen minutes after 1:00 a.m. on a Monday night or Tuesday morning, depending upon your own personal perspective. After years of living in the city of life and death, one gets a feel for the food. Sometimes the thought of some good kimchi can rival that of the best heroin in town. When that illness creeps up on you, it's time to hit the Bann down in Soho.

The restaurant has been closed to the public for the past hour. However, a gold shield opens many doors in the dark hours of Sin City. Rob made a quick call on the way, and when he got to the back door, he didn't even knock. The door eased open with a scary movie creak, and out popped the biggest oriental woman that Magen had ever seen. Her presence was profound and remarkable, a living Buddha in female form. Everyone who knew her well addressed her as Mike; her real name was Mi Kiwi Chun. All of Chinatown knew her as Tiny Mi!

"Hey, Mike, how's it hanging?" Mac said with a smile.

"Good morning, Bobby boy," said the large woman.

"This is Magen Cummings. She thinks she's working for the FBI," Mac added with a touch of sarcasm.

"How very interesting, pretty lady. I myself worked with them once many ticks of the clock ago!" the large lady offered.

"Just once?" Magen added.

"One dance with Mike is all most can handle," the large woman added in a deep bellowing laugh.

"Magen, be careful. She has a thing for hot blondes, and once you go Tiny Mi, there's no turning back."

This brought a great explosion of laughter from the woman. As they marched down the long thin hall, Rob heard the woman say, "Your table is ready. You will find some adequate sake already poured at the table. Sam is still in the kitchen. He is preparing deung sim gui for you, Robert. For the tight ass, he has made a gentle saeu twigim."

"You have outdone yourself. Please allow me the honor of repaying this kindness," Mac requested.

"Yes, of course, Lieutenant." She slowly lumbered into the darkness of the kitchen followed by more laughter.

"Interesting friends you keep, Lieutenant," Magen added through squinting eyes.

"I keep nothing of the people in my life!" Mac firmly stated.

Mac led Magen to a lovely small table by the kitchen door. Out of habit they both made the initial move for the chair that would have faced the front window. Mac realized what he was doing and motioned for Magen to take the seat.

"Thank you!" Magen said, fully realizing the situation.

"What kinds of food do you usually eat?" Mac asked.

Magen gave some thought to the question, and then with a painful grimace, she said, "I am kind of complicated. I spent a good part of my life as a vegetarian. It's only in the past few years that I broke down and started eating meat."

"Well, you say that as if you have crossed over to the dark side!" Mac joked.

"In so many ways, that's how I feel, and in some ways, I know it must sound odd. But being a vegetarian has been part of my identity for so many years. Everything I did, everyone I knew was reflective of the vegetarian lifestyle, and to be fully honest, we frowned upon meat eaters."

"So, it's much more of a transition than I realized," Mac added.

Magen studied Mac's face, wondering if he was patronizing her. She often found it difficult to discuss her eating preference with the meat-eating majority. Often, people would look to engage her in a debate platform, regardless of what side of the issue she was discussing. Magen began her journey as a nonmeat eater during her first semester at Ohio State University. Initially, growing up in the country, she only understood the relationship of food as a whole and how it connected the community. It was her first roommate who started her wheels rolling. Her name was Dina, and she was the child of southern Californian hippies. Magen had come into the room on the second day of the semester eating a cheeseburger from a local grill, and Dina absolutely lost it. That was her introduction to a brave new world. Magen, who was young and willing to please, apologized for the next two weeks. Before Magen knew it, she was the poster child for happy rabbits everywhere.

Nine years without meat of any form, and a happy and healthy nine years to boot. Unfortunately, all that came crashing down last winter while she was chasing down yet another wacky lead on this all-too-crazy case. She was outside a hospital in Savannah, Georgia. When she looked up, she saw a well-known eatery called the Bayou Café. As she was running toward the front door, she spent a few moments convincing herself that she wasn't going to eat anything with meat in it. Of course, the moment the food hit her nose, she was lost and hopeless. The worst thing a hungry vegetarian should ever do is walk into a Cajun café with a fresh pot of Gumbo on the boil. The guilt behind her relapse was both painful and liberating. Initially, she was concerned with the prospect of weight gain and limiting her morning jogging routine. The strange thing was that after six months from falling from the granola wagon, just the opposite was true. Magen was in the best shape of her life, and her running had more purpose. She felt physically awesome, and the way guys were checking her out made it all worthwhile. Mentally, she could do better if this case would go away. It has been the source of agonizing pain, which has really taken its toll. There was something turning with this damn thing; she could feel it.

Not only the increase in activity that has been so evident, but also, there has been a shift. The force that has been so elusive for so long was starting to change the game. Magen was exceptionally intuitive and highly connected to the feelings surrounding this case. She knew there was a storm on the way!

"Did I say something that offended you?" Mac added.

"No! Of course not!" Magen looked at him, puzzled.

"It's just that you zoned out on me. What's on your mind?"

"I am so sorry! It's not you. The truth is this case has been working on me for some time. I need you to know that I am really glad that you are on board."

"Wow! That must have been hard for you to say!" Mac joked.

"You have no idea!" Magen said painfully.

They both grinned at each other, equally feeling a sense of playfulness that both had not felt for some time. There was a brief moment of silence that felt slightly uncomfortable, and then it was gone. The conversation ran the gambit of topics from military service to lost love, and as it went on, it became easier. The connection between them was growing; they had walked similar paths to get to this table tonight, and they were both finding their center.

"More sake," Mac added with an evil smile.

"Why are you trying to get me smashed?" Magen asked without skipping a beat.

"I don't think it was my prime objective when we came in. However, I am really enjoying myself," Mac added, half laughing.

"I bet you are a pervert!" Magen said with a slight slurring in her words.

"I know this is where I should start to profess my innocence, but I am guessing you know far too much about me for that to work." Mac laughed.

"You are so right!" Magen laughed aloud.

"What is it that the bureau's saying about me these days?" Mac asked.

Magen moved closer across the table as if to discuss some deep, dark secret that must be kept in the strictest of confidence. "To tell you the truth, Mac, there is not much you're flagging for with the Virginia farm boys. However, you have a friend named Paul Major that you are really close to. Believe me when I tell you that guy hits on everyone's radar."

"Pauli! That's crazy! He's an old man."

"Yeah! So was Caesar! I know this is a really good friend of yours, and I'm sorry for laughing about this. However, we are under the impression that he may be solely responsible for over three murders from within the New York Police Department. Internal affairs identified your crazy Irish boyfriend as the trigger guy for a then secret society of the NYPD. The FBI had taken him in for questioning on several occasions during the early nineties for that string of Russian mafia murders."

"This is all extremely fascinating! And nothing that I haven't heard before. The big question for me has always been why?"

"Why? I thought that would be blatantly obvious. Money!"

"Well, I left Pauli Trump a few hours ago, and I didn't even want to sit down in his house, too afraid a cockroach might chew my ass off," Mac added sarcastically.

"I know on the service it doesn't add up, but there were witnesses who placed him with weapons, cash payouts, and body parts for identification."

"Where are these witnesses again?" Mac added.

"Two of them are dead. One was snatched right out of a safe house in Jersey," Magen offered bluntly.

"Well, I think we could go back and forth with this all night long." Mac added in a slow even tone, "I need you to understand one thing, Magen, that really is important to me."

"What's that, Mac?" Magen added, slightly taken back.

"It's important to me that you know that at no time did Paul confide in me any involvement with illegal activity," Mac said as he gazed into her eyes.

"The documentation reports no connection or prior knowledge that you had any involvement with any of that madness. Mac, the word on you is that you're a straight shooter!" Magen added with a smile, and he was really happy about that.

"Well, thank God for that! I would hate to think you didn't trust me," Mac said in his most sarcastic tone.

"Aren't we sensitive tonight?" Magen said, smiling.

"Not even a little. My dark side refuses the admittance of any sensitive feelings," Mac said, pretending to have little emotion at all.

"I knew you had a dark side," Magen added in a playful manner.

"What about your dark side? Do we ever get a chance to meet?" Mac added confidently.

"I must admit it has been a while since that side of me has seen the light of day. I am not going to sit here and lie to you or act uninterested. I find you extremely cute. If I was thinking with my head at this point, I would best be served by running from this place like I was on fire."

Mac quickly cut her off by leaning in and kissing her hard on the lips. Agent Cummings put up no resistance and let the wave of pleasure surge through her body. Her puffy bottom lip now lost in his mouth, feeling the gentle tension that was controlling her completely. She lifted her hand in a stopping motion, not really wishing for the moment to end but slightly frightened to fully surrender herself to a man she met at a pizza joint earlier in the day.

"Wait! Please, I need to breathe," Magen exclaimed in a panting motion.

"You taste so damn good, and I have been fighting myself on that since we sat down!" Mac stated as he caught his breath.

"I see you're going to be trouble, aren't you?" Magen said as she reached for her chest, lightly brushing her small finger across her hard nipples.

The big woman slowly walked up to the table with some takeout lobster, dumplings, and warm sake in a container. "You come back and see Mike!" she said with sincere warmth and was gone as fast as she had come.

"I guess we should go then!" Magen stated.

"I believe you're right!" Mac stood and offered his hand, and Magen accepted.

CHAPTER 14

Laurel, Maryland

The light brown building outside of Laurel, Maryland, could have been any office building in the country. The grounds were manicured to perfection in the classic Maryland style. The sunrays bounced off the spotless glass, creating the illusion that the building was slow dancing against the green background. There were several compounds of this style building in the area, and they were quite unpretentious. However, what made this dwelling different was the absence of any definable name. The only method used to identify this building was the large numbers at the front of the drive, 11100.

This was the only way the rest of the world knew that they were standing in front of the Apple Physics Laboratory (APL) of Jane Haskins Hospital. The birth of APL hatched out of the heated anxieties of World War II. During that time, the Nazi war machine was evil personified on our fragile little planet. It soon became apparent as the war progressed that the Germans were far more advanced in the realm of scientific theory. Weapons, missiles, and medical and scientific theory were being seized from the moment the Allies hit Normandy beach. Attempting to understand the information and the technology that were returning from Europe took the best minds America had on hand. The most unfortunate truth regarding war is that from the beginning of time, man had made his greatest technological advancements as a direct result of violent engagement. Some may argue that war brings out the best in us! World War II was the prime example; captured German V-2 rockets changed the world as we know it. Prior to 1946, the American scientific community really didn't have a firm grasp on high-altitude weaponry. Less than two decades later, we had progressed to the point where we were successfully able to land Neil Armstrong on the moon. The sad reality here is without the horror of that vicious war, we most likely would never have made the great leap in 1969.

Most people today feel they have an adequate education regarding the Holocaust. The truth is the majority of the world identifies the Holocaust with the frail, starving bodies shuffling toward the American soldiers wrapped in dingy, soiled blankets. Most stop investigating the realities of those six years, understanding it only as an extremely horrific event that took place in the past. The frightening truth is even worse than most could imagine—six years of laboratory freedom on human subjects. All this without any monitoring from outside agencies, and absolutely no regard for the subjects involved. This was probably the evilest time in the human experience, yet the medical breakthroughs were countless. The possibility may also exist that the birth of stem cell research and cord blood studies came directly out of these atrocities. The greatest breakthroughs in psychiatry can also be linked to survivors of that war. There was no shortage of human wreckage at the end of World War II. Unfortunately, the shrinks wasted no time finding new ways to bill for all the new weirdness.

The work performed by Dr. Josef Mengele at Auschwitz is well-known throughout the world as the pinnacle of the very worst that we are capable of doing to one another. The connection between Apple Physics Laboratory and the government was not intentional; it resulted from necessity. There really wasn't a long list of potential organizations with the ability to decipher the data that was returning from Europe in the late 1940s.

CHAPTER 15

> When the lawyer opens its mouth, I was swift to shade my ears from the affront. Hence, I never had to survive cancer!
>
> —Cain

"There is something remarkably calming about feeding ducks," William Dean said out loud.

"I don't take to feeding those flying shit houses, but they do eat well with an orange glaze," said Robert Kingston.

"I keep forgetting that you are a culinary master, capable of turning almost anything into a palatable delicacy," Dean said with a smile.

"Well, thank you, Sir William!" Kingston added as he sat down, placing his briefcase on his lap.

As William Dean gazed along the pond at Apple Physics, he thought of all the covert operations that were hatched right on this spot. All the players who sat right here and made such a phenomenal difference in this country. He wondered how America would feel if they knew that their lives hung in the balance of old men feeding ducks in rural Maryland.

"What brings you down here, Bobby boy?" William added in a friendly manner.

"We have several issues that you need to be aware of that are stemming out of New York, initiated at seven AM yesterday morning."

William gave thought to Kingston's statement regarding issues. *Somewhere along the line, we stopped saying problems.*

July 7, 1947, was a problem; November 22, 1963, was a problem; but 9/11, well, that's a serious issue. I guess it became apparent that we were a world full of problems, and it didn't make sense to keep reminding ourselves of that fact.

"Show me what you have," William stated with a much more serious tone.

"Take a look at these photos. This is James Cosgrove, a retired fireman, three children, and a wife. He jogged into Penn Station yesterday, and before he left the building, this was all there was left of one Aaron Goldstein," Kingston added as he handed William additional photos.

"Goldstein! Why am I not surprised? Do you remember the time we put in trying to recruit this guy? Brilliant scientist but a bit of an ass, as I recall," William added with a mocked sadness.

"I remember all the smart ones," Kingston said with a hint of sadness.

William nodded in agreement, and he felt the pain of so many lost to this madness. "What do we know about this Cosgrove?" William whispered to his friend.

"Intel has him being hardwired by an NYFD-approved dentist, sometime back in 1998. We got a hold of an MRI three years back. At that time, we identified two implants under the back molars. There was also some stage-three hair wiring throughout the frontal cortex. This is the standard seeding process, nothing different that we can identify." Kingston added, "He's working his second marriage. The first was a disaster that ended in the late nineties. He has a distinguished history with the NYPD, and halfway through his twenties, he flipped over to the fire department. Three years ago, he retired and has been off the grid, until yesterday morning." Kingston looked at his friend for acknowledgment.

"It really is amazing that they are capable of doing this. How do you suppose they are able to stay on top of all these low-frequency implants?"

"Do you really want to know?" Kingston asked.

William turned to Kingston with a stunned look on his face. "Yes, I do. At least, I think I do!" answered William with some hesitation.

"There is only one sure way that these individuals could be tracked effectively, and that is by the utilization of orbiting satellites," Kingston added firmly.

"That does make sense, Bill, a little bit of a scary thought though," William said, shaking his head.

"The real scary piece of this puzzle is that the only viable technology capable of handling that level of programming is made right here on this campus," Robert said in a low sad tone.

"What about the Chinese?" William added hopefully.

"Sorry! That's not going to work. The Chinese are following this Cosgrove guy. That's how we stumbled upon him!" Robert added with conviction.

"So that's it. The bad guy is us!" William chuckled a little, but his gut wrenched at the news.

"Well, it may not be us, but it's someone you are sharing the executive toilet with," Kingston added with a sarcastic tone.

"That's just great!" William added, shaking his head.

"Let's be honest, I have been thinking along these lines for some time, Bill, and I know that you are much smarter than me. Why is it that we are only having this conversation at this point of the game?"

"I haven't ruled out anything or anyone from the very beginning, even you, Bobby," William said.

"I can live with that. Still, I feel that we have been wasting some critical time in this denial state. We should have things in place by now to weed out this tumor," Kingston pleaded.

William sat in meditative silence, contemplating the statements that his old friend was unloading on him. *This has been one crazy ride*, he thought to himself. William could remember his first day walking through the doors of APL one week after he graduated from Loyola. It was hard for him in the beginning. Back then, mostly everyone that was being hired was a Haskins graduate. Even with an IQ of 189, they still fought his application. There were a few Jewish kids from the area that made the cut, not that they had any real talent. It was more like Daddy was shoveling big piles of cash at the hospital. They didn't last long at APL; they were mostly kicked into managerial positions within the hospital arena, or one of the many Hopkins interests throughout the world. It wasn't about money when you got right to the bottom of things; it was all about full and undeniable control of APL. He had lived through many changes within this compound.

Lately he had been consumed by the time and sacrifices he had made over the years. Vietnam was a strange time that he remembered all too well; he didn't think the facility was going to survive that time period. The Cold War was strongly divisional on the campus, and ripples of that time are still present today. Kennedy changed so many things in this country in just a short period of time. There was a real clarity of purpose coming out World War II that lasted for almost two full decades. William remembered those days as if they were unfolding before his eyes. It was the Hopkins crew that emerged in control after that extremely difficult time.

He contemplated the information that his friend gave him today; familiar thoughts of a past time circled around his head. If something illegal was going down within the walls of APL, the Hopkins crew would need to have their hands on it, or at the very least know what was going on.

"There is something else we need to talk about," Kingston added with a hint of disdain.

He handed William a newspaper; it was worn down like it may have been old. However, as he looked closer, he realized it was yesterday's paper; Kingston must have spent some time reading it and then rereading the article in question. It was a paper known as *News Day*, a local Long Island paper. William was not really familiar with the publication.

MAN MAULED AND KILLED BY WILD PACK OF DOGS

The story went on to describe the horrific findings of a young family who brought their children out to the local park one morning, only to find the half-eaten remains of an overweight jogger.

"My God!" William exclaimed.

"Please read on! This only gets stranger," voiced Robert.

The story continued on with vague details surrounding the incident that for some odd reason no one in the area had heard a thing. There were noted dog tracks throughout the area. According to the local authorities, the algid pack of wild dogs worked its way down through the county by utilizing the nearby train tracks.

Then, as this jogger turned the corner, he was ambushed by several large dogs. Dental records made it imperative for proper identification; there were also several limbs and appendages missing from the scene.

While on the scene at Lynbrook, they did have the opportunity to speak briefly with William McLachlan, the local forensic expert over from the Fifth Precinct in Franklin Square station. Officer McLachlan was asked for his assessment regarding the breed of these rough canines. The officer stopped cold in his tracks, turned to the reporter, and, without blinking an eye, said, "I am leaning hard toward a smaller version of a velociraptor or possibly something from the great white family."

That was the end of the interview; Officer McLachlan was quickly ushered to a section thirty yards away where several body parts were located.

Several months back, there were three separate sightings nine miles to the west in an area of Hook Creek. There were no attacks reported at that time. Local animal management authorities validated this information and added that two of the lead alpha dogs were put down and the pack dispersed.

The article went on to discuss the philosophy of pack behavior and what we as concerned citizens could do if we are ever confronted by this type of horrific encounter. For the most part, the article laid out an extremely vicious attack. William began to wonder what was so important regarding this event that had his friend so worked up. He racked his brain attempting to put the puzzle together. Unfortunately, nothing was coming.

He gazed up at his friend almost slightly ashamed. "What are you showing me, Robert?"

"Do you remember the day we first met?" Kingston added with a mild tone.

William pretended to contemplate the question; he recalled the day quite clearly. William often found himself doing this; he was always aware of his genius status and his mind's ability to retain limitless information. He never wanted to come across as a smarty-pants. He started this behavior as a child, an act of self-preservation. It was very difficult dealing with other children who worked so hard on things that came so easy to him.

He lived a good part of his life pretending to be slightly not who he really was, just to fit in a little easier.

"It was in New York, wasn't it?"

"That's right," Kingston said. "You hired me to find one of your runaway scientists back in June of '04. The guy's name was Mazza, Robert Mazza," Kingston stated, watching his friend. "I spent six months chasing this asshole over three different countries. The closest I ever came to catching him was three blocks from this park. His grandmother has a house right there, and I know he was in and out of the house several times during the hunt. His grandmother is long gone, but the house stays in the family. Some attorney handles all the affairs for the estate. I got into the basement back in '04 with the help of the local police. The place is set up like a laboratory, and some real high-tech computers. I knew this guy was there on more than one occasion, but he was sharp and avoided me with some level of skill. I spent a lot of time tracking this guy. I went through file after file. This guy was certifiable, and if he hadn't taken off from APL, they would have locked his crazy ass up. I think of him as the modern-age Dr. Moreau or even the good Dr. Frankenstein. Two years prior to the good doctor going AWOL from Apple Physics, he was in line for the Nobel Prize in medicine. Apparently, he has made several major breakthroughs in behavioral genetics.

"This guy's primary objective is to alter the human being from what we are to something much more radical," Robert added with the reflection of anger in his voice.

"I remember this guy all too well," William responded. "I once pried his hands from the neck of Oliver Martin. He could possibly be the most unstable individual that I had ever had the sorry pleasure of dealing with."

"What was his connection with the hospital?" Kingston asked.

"There was absolutely no connection at all with Hopkins!" William instinctively responded.

Kingston cocked his eyebrow up and tilted his head to the left. He was amazed how someone so high in the political arena could lie so poorly.

William stood up from the bench looking out over the APL complex; he recalled the first and last time he ever met Dr. Robert Mazza. It was a budget meeting regarding interdepartmental projects between APL and the hospital. Mazza, who was working on some deep covert project between Haskins and NASA, already had a bit of a reputation as a nut ball. He came charging into the meeting yelling at Oliver Martin, making accusations that he was a traitor. He claimed that he was not living up to his end of some prior arrangement that they had going on. Later, William learned that Martin was overseeing several opiate research studies between the main hospital and one of the smaller satellite hospitals in Baltimore. Mazza had made arrangements with Martin to have two dozen new applications from the opiate study report to his lab at APL for intensive behavioral therapy. William received intelligence later that Hopkins had been involved with opiate research, specifically with young black males without significant family structures. This is an extremely sensitive subject around the Haskins boardroom. It's very much like the pink elephant in the room. One of the largest prestigious hospitals in the world existing right smack in the middle of the drug-infested ghetto. Hopkins stands alone in the research arena, and that is not by accident.

In the late eighties, one Frank Nieves, a CIA operative, sent a report to both the *New York Times* and the *Washington Post* claiming that he had brokered several large heroin purchases from the Chinese government for Haskins Hospital. Apparently, there was a smack drought after three monumental drug busts during the summer of 1986. The hospital research was being threatened by the lack of product; this was not an acceptable scenario for operations at the hospital. Of course, the information never made the papers. To smear the reputation of Jane Haskins would have a negative spin on APL, and even NASA for that matter. How would that help the humankind? Sometimes it's hard to find the truth in the mountain of lies. The meeting ended with Mazza jumping over the table and taking hold of Martin's neck. That was the last day the good Dr. Mazza was seen; after that, he went underground.

William hired Robert to track him down, but secretly he knew that he wouldn't be found. William exhaled and turned from the pond. Kingston was staring at him, with the look of long-term disappointment.

"There is something that you're not telling me, and that bothers me!" Kingston said with his eyes burning into his lifelong friend.

"I came across an invoice about six months ago for lab supplies. It was about twenty thousand, so I didn't give it much thought, but it was being shipped to a storage locker in Rockville Center, about three miles away from this!" William said as he held up the newspaper.

"Damn, you are just full of good news!" Kingston stated as he rose from the bench.

"There is more you need to hear, Robert. Please sit," William asked of his friend.

"I don't like the sound of that. What's up?" Robert asked as he sat back down.

"Do you know the term 'water mine'?" William asked with sadness in his voice.

"Sure, it was an underground missile silo in upstate New York, Tarrytown, I think. Closed down at least fifteen years ago," Robert said, slightly confused.

"The Anderson satellite picked up a monster of a heat signature from that area last night!" William stated.

"What does that mean? Who is it?" Robert looked puzzled.

"I need you back in New York. That's where this thing is coming apart. Take two teams. Find the detectives connected to the subway case. Maybe you can be helpful without tipping your hat. Stay out of Long Island. I really don't need to know the whereabouts of the good doctor," William added firmly.

"These are intense times. I have known you for the past forty years, and together we have seen some of the most unimaginable events unfold in front of us," William added. "Trust has become the most important issue on the table. We have many differences in the way we see things. However, I have learned to trust you, and I need you now more than ever," William said with solid passion in his voice.

"You're a good man, Bill. I never thought anything else. You can trust me to the end. I hope you know that. However, I must admit, my primary motivation for unquestionable loyalty to you is really quite simple."

"What would that be?" William asked.

"I can't help but notice that those people who on occasion cross you or get in your way don't really last too long!" Robert added with a smirk.

As William walked away, he smiled slightly, thinking of what his friend had said. The truth of the matter was that many have been lost during the last few years, both friend and foe. The information that he retrieved today explained a few things that were not fully clear yesterday. Reality was starting to settle in, and it was building up acid in the pit of his stomach.

There was no way around it; he knew the bad guys! The thought of this truly filled him with dread. For years, he had been attempting to sell his theory to his superiors that his house was compromised. That in his heart of hearts he believed an army of serial killers were undermining scientific advancements throughout the world. All that time he was selling that theory to those directly responsible.

Why am I still alive? he thought.

He stopped dead in his tracks, looking around the campus as the truth crystallized itself.

Why not keep him around; it was brilliant. They were always watching him.

He thought for a moment, *Could they be watching me now? Am I bugged?*

They have had years to work him out. He could have several microphones on him or near him at all times.

They have the intelligence of legions of the brightest geeks on the planet. He reached in his pocket and pulled out his Blackberry.

As he raised his thumb to speed-dial Kingston and warn him of his revelation, he froze. Then he stopped himself, thinking that his phone would definitely be their first access to any outside conversation.

William spent a long time in this game, and he always knew that the risk level was high. However, the fear that was gripping him at that moment was deeper than anything he had ever experienced. His thought process was racing around his skull like Dale Earnhardt Jr. hitting the high wall. For a moment, he gave thought of walking straight past the entrance door and out to his car.

Unfortunately, his keys were in the office.

He was going back in there and walk to the office among the purist form of evil on Earth. William recalled some dialogue from one of his favorite books, *Dune*, by Frank Herbert.

He repeated "Fear is the mind killer" several times as he walked to the elevator.

It was a mantra that gave him strength in those times when comfort was fleeting. William walked out of the elevator and scanned the area quickly, trying to find eyes that were focusing on him.

Nothing.

Everyone was appropriate and doing what they normally do. As he finished that thought, he looked up to see Mark Weinstein barreling down the hall, looking right at him with a highly aggressive face. William reached behind his back, fumbling on the desk of Matt Colman, one of the recently hired analysts. He laid his hand on an ivory-handled letter opener and quickly moved it up his sleeve. Mark was seven feet away when William positioned himself in a Kempo-style horse stance and waited for the attack.

CHAPTER 16

Mark now shook his head, his face full of anger and rage, turned right at William, and said, "Can you believe this shit?" Mark said out loud. "The Terps drop one in the last second to Morgan fuckin' State. Can you believe it?"

People in the area were laughing out loud.

Mark went on about it. "This is like losing to the maid and the yard workers," he added as he stomped away.

When Mark was ten feet away, William allowed himself a much-needed breath. He took a few more seconds to get it together before he started to walk back to his office.

This is insane, he thought to himself.

He was off-center and not thinking clearly. He really had to get far from this building and contact Kingston and everyone else he could trust.

The Hopkins crew at APL was deeply involved in the systematic assassinations of at least seventy-five scientists, he knew this now. He had to say this over in his head multiple times just to let the absurdity of the whole thing sink in.

Why is this happening? What is the goal of all this slaughter? he thought to himself.

The more he thought about this situation, the crazier it sounded. Was he losing it? Thoughts flew through his head now without any real design or purpose. He had played golf with these people; they had been to his home. He felt like his whole world was being turned upside down. William came through his office door, half expecting visitors to be waiting. It was totally empty as it should be at this time of the day. He stood in the middle of the office for what felt like several minutes. Years of training taught him methods to dismiss stress in these situations. Unfortunately, that training took place forty years ago, and too much had been lost over the years. William spent twenty-four hours out each day being in full control of his environment. That had been stripped from him in the course of one morning's conversation. William started from the beginning with a mental list of what he needed to do. Number one was to get out of this building without making anyone aware. APL appeared on the outside as a laid-back building without high-level security. The fact of the matter was that this building was more secure than the White House. From the moment you hit the parking lot, your body is being scanned not only from several different cameras, but also infrareds and chemical scans are also utilized.

As you walk through the front door, temperatures and pulse rates are being monitored from highly sensitive access points in the doorframe. There is a host of detection devices that can pick up anything from uranium, anthrax, and syntax.

So, for now, the primary question was just how he was going to get through all that without showing up on somebody's radar.

Think! You helped design this monster, William's voice echoed in his head.

Just then, William watched a delivery guy from Pizza Hut walk right out the door without any attention. William picked up the phone, listened as it rang three times. Then a young female voice came on the phone, "Seasons Pizza, how I can help you?" the young woman said.

"Yes, this is William Dean over at APL. Can I place an order for delivery, please?"

"Absolutely, Mr. Dean, what can we get for you today?" said an enthusiastic voice.

"I need a large pizza, half sausage and meatball, Greek salad, and two large Cokes please," William added politely.

"We'll get that right out to you, sir. Are you still in administration suite 310?" asked the young woman.

"That would be me!" William added.

"Twenty minutes and $15.08, will that work for you, sir?"

"See you then!" added William.

William knew he had approximately twenty minutes to formulate and execute a fairly complex plan. He took several deep breaths and repeated his mantra, "Fear is the mind killer," one last time, then walked out of his office.

He needed supplies, so the first stop would need to be in the operation room on the lower level. As he moved in that direction, he considered the personnel that would need to be in place to pull off something like this. People in power were running this show; there was really no way around that fact. Initially, he tried to convince himself that maybe it was a rough bunch that had penetrated APL and were utilizing the technology for their own goals. However, the deeper he thought this through, the reality pointed to the highest level of clearance. That would mean that this was going straight to the top.

The question was just how high?

He didn't have the time or resources to work that through at this point. He approached the supply room, or what he referred to as the gizmo room. He knocked twice and waited for a response; nothing came back in return.

William opened the door slowly and walked in. To the right, there was a small desk that belonged to the clerk, Cornell Pierce. The man had worked at the lab for a long time. However, he was one of those rare individuals who lit up a room and could make even some of the coldest fish laugh. APL had no shortage of boring people; that was one of the downsides of working with the terminally intelligent. Cornell stood out like a sore thumb as he moved through the place. He ran the football pool and organized dinners and trips to the booby bar. Extremely well-liked by all and in a place like this, that was an accomplishment.

There were keys hanging on the side of the desk labeled "Security." William knew that he could get everything he needed in the steel cabinet in the back. He reached out, grabbed the keys, and moved toward the cabinet. He smiled as he realized the cabinet was already open. He thought to himself that this was way too easy. William removed two dull gray Glocks and ammunition, lowered a microphone detector into a brown bag, and headed out. He placed the keys back on the hook and grabbed for the door. Before he could open the door, he was face-to-face with Cornell Pierce.

"Holy shit," Cornell said mostly out loud.

"Good morning, Cornell, isn't it?"

"Yes, it is," Cornell mumbled. He was trying to come to grips with the idea that his boss's boss's boss was standing in his office alone.

"Is there anything I can do for you, sir?" Cornell managed.

William suppressed his immediate alarm and laid out an easy smile.

"I am slightly embarrassed, but it has been a long time since I have been down here," he added with a mild hesitation.

Cornell, who was still relatively thrown to find the regional ops chief standing in his office, was able to repeat his initial question, "What can I do for you, sir?"

"Oh, nothing, really, I'm in the wrong part of town. Would you believe that once upon a time HR records were kept right in this room?" He recounted with a smile.

William looked up slightly to the tall, thin Cornell. He guessed the man ran about six foot one and his weight was in the two-hundred-pound zone. He knew that he had some talent in that area. Before his wife passed away, they would sit around the hospital and play the "size up" game; she wasn't too bad herself.

"We have never been properly introduced. My name is William Dean. I am in the operation end of the business," William said, trying not to present all too important.

Cornell wasn't buying it. "Operations, I see! I suppose that those operations are doing well considering all the large photos of you throughout the building," Cornell added with a rolled eye.

Both men managed a smile and a bit of a laugh at William's expense.

"Cornell, I have heard that you are very funny. You are very well-liked in this community, but I'm sure you are aware of that," William said.

"I really don't know how to respond to that. I am very happy here and get along with most. Maybe I have some struggles with the new Haskins upper-elitist pack, but I just avoid them," Cornell said, joking but not really.

"Yes! Between you and me, they don't set well in my world either. Keep doing what you do so well," William added.

Cornell was absolutely blown away that William Dean even knew his name, let alone the work that he was doing. He looked at the aging man in front of him and started to wonder what was going on. "Is this some kind of joke. Am I being punked? Are there cameras set up in here?" Cornell asked seriously, searching the room for cameras.

"No tricks up my sleeve, my good man. You are doing well. I have to get going now, but we will talk soon."

William shook Cornell's hand and then was out the door before anything else was said. Cornell stood in the middle of his office and wondered if that whole thing really happened. He picked up the phone and dialed his wife Shania. He had to talk to someone, and he didn't think anyone in the house would believe him. As he completed the dialing sequence, he noticed the gun cabinet was slightly ajar.

William made it back to the office and wasted no time scanning for bugs and micro transmitters. It didn't take too long; they were all over the office.

He also found several on his person, his watch, the phone, and some form of threadlike bug that was woven into his shirt collar.

He quickly removed everything he found then scanned his body one last time, finding a faint signal coming from his lower jaw.

Oh God, my teeth! he thought.

The realization that he was tagged by his dentist upset him more than anything else. Nine months ago, he had a root canal done by a young stand-in dentist that he hadn't used before. He came highly recommended by his primary guy. He remembered that he had to go back several times because the pain wouldn't go away.

William thought to himself, *For a smart guy, he could be quite the asshole.*

He knew there was only one way to deal with this; it would have to come out.

First, he needed to get out of this building. He downloaded a number of maps for Maryland and New York. His best shot was to head north, find Kingston, and isolate people that were loyal to him, not necessarily APL.

The CIA operative who wrote the article about Hopkins was retired and living out in the Hamptons somewhere.

The door at APL opened, and in came one of the delivery guys from Seasons with a white bag in his left hand. William moved quickly to intercept the guy before the front door guard got a good look at him.

"Seasons, I think that's for me!" William said.

"I'm looking for a Mr. William Dean," the young driver said.

"That's me. Come on in and let me pay you!" William offered with mild indifference.

The young man in an aging red North Face coat walked two steps in front of William. He carried in his hands a small pizza box directly in front of his body. Wrapped around his right thumb was a white plastic bag containing the rest of his food. Tucked in his left hand was the young man's vehicle key. Up until that moment, William was only considering utilizing his own car in his escape; however, he was a man who always maximized his options for any given scenario. As the two approached the large office at the end of the hall, the young man stood aside.

This allowed William to get the door and ease the young man into his office.

"Thank you for taking the food down the hall. My old bones thank you profusely!" William offered the table to the young man to put the lunch down.

"Thanks, what was your name again?" William added.

"Roy!"

"That's right, Roy. By the way, have you ever had heart problems? Is the ticker okay, Roy?" William added.

"Fine, I guess," Roy said, confused about the question.

"Perfect, then what is it that you are driving these days?" William said easily.

"I rock a '70 Chevy big block out there, and it kicks ass!" the youngster said with pride.

On that mark, William stuck a fifty-thousand-volt Taser directly to the nape of the young man's neck. Roy shut off like a kitchen light and fell back into the oversize office chair with what appeared to be a happy smile draped across his face. William, working quickly, removed the young man's coat and pants. He reached into his pocket, pulled out wads of cotton, and laid it out on the desk. William moved to the front of his desk and removed a pair of pliers from the top compartment.

Then, placing himself in front of the mirror, he reached into his mouth and gripped the teeth that he suspected were planted with the tracking devices. William looked directly into the mirror, and with trembling resolve within his heart, he gripped his left hand and ground down with the pliers, as tears came flooding from his eye sockets.

CHAPTER 17

William yanked the large hot molar from the back of his mouth.

"Shit!" William allowed himself and then packed his mouth with the available cotton. He was dizzy and fully nauseous; it wasn't so much pain of the extraction but the feeling of a full violation.

The long tungsten wire was the last piece to leave his body.

Disgusting, he thought to himself.

William dressed quickly and viewed the contents of Roy's pockets; cash and keys were all that would be necessary. He placed the hood over his head then put both weapons in his waistband and zipped up as he was off.

William fumbled with his cash as he rolled out toward the door. The guard at the far end desk briefly looked up and quickly nodded before returning to the monitor in front of him. William was out the door walking slowly to the parking lot. In his hands were young Roy's keys; he tapped the keyless entry only twice, and the response directed him to a 1970 Chevy SS in gray primer.

William was initially alarmed by the sight of the vehicle in front of him; then a slight evil smile came over his face, and then he broke into action. Adrenaline was running through William's body as he fired up this American muscle relic.

"Stick shift, holy crap," William said out load as he recalled the last time he worked a stick many years ago. As he put the beast into reverse, the passenger door opened, and there stood Cornell Pierce.

"Mr. Dean, is this some type of test?" Cornell added with obvious nervousness in his voice. "I know every item in this shop, and when two Glocks go missing, I know they had to go somewhere, and you were the only person with access today. Are we on camera? Is this about my merit increase?"

William was stunned and not ready to deal with a storeroom clerk who was on the ball. He raised the weapon from his waist and pointed it directly at Cornell's face.

"Please get in the car right now. I really don't wish to end your life here in this parking lot!" William shouted.

There was only honesty in his voice, and Cornell responded accordingly.

William replaced the Glock in his waistline and, without a word, grabbed a pair of dark Oakley glasses from the dash.

Cornell studied the company chief, fully confused at the turn of events. With both eyes on his new passenger, William threw the beast into low gear and lit up the wheels. The Chevy jumped out of the parking lot before they could exhale. William's eyes danced from the road to the rearview mirror and back to his guest.

"Boy, did you just hump the bunk," William added, nodding his head.

What the hell have I gotten myself into? Cornell thought.

CHAPTER 18

Brooklyn, New York

Mac straddled Magen's lower back; he was rolling a cherry up and down her small spine. Mac pulled her blonde hair apart and kissed the side of her face. She smiled and slightly parted her legs, letting Mac know that if he wanted her again, that would be fine. Mac received the massage and slowly turned Magen on her back. She ran her nails along the full length of his hard, vulnerable ass.

"*Yow*, that's the spot," he added playfully as he arched his head back. She loved the power that she had over him in these fleeting moments. With his large left knee, he parted her legs and then reached down to feel her vagina. Magen was beyond wet, and she loved it; her breathing was erratic. Mac grabbed his cock at the base of his balls and started rubbing the doorway to her wet pussy.

Magen was sweaty and hungry to have Mac deep inside her. Mac was fully aware that he was making her absolutely insane. He really was getting into the way her body was responding. He drilled the large head of his penis into her pussy, only giving her the initial thrust, and then he pulled back.

"Please stop, you are not being fair!" Magen managed with desperation in her voice.

"Oh, really, I didn't realize that you needed all of it now!" Mac jested.

The sexy, raspy voice in her ear was making the situation too hard to deal with. He was back in her now, and somehow, he had reached his hand down to her clitoris, twisting it lightly; she could feel it growing in his warm fingers. In one fluid motion, he had grabbed her by the back of the hair and positioned her against the pillows, then he fully entered her. It was beautiful and everything that she could imagine. It had been way too long to go without the physical connection that she enjoyed way too much. The tears that rolled down her face weren't only for the pure joy she was feeling but also for the release of all that time of compounded pain that she volunteered to carry around with her since the death of her love.

She was sensing a wave working up from somewhere deep, and she needed his immediate attention.

"Stay with me, Mac, I need you!"

Mac reached under her back, ran his hands up her spine, unintentionally following the same waves. He reached her long silky blonde hair; he took a large handful to his face. Her scent was intoxicating. She was close, and he knew it; as he tightened the grip on her hair, he flipped her over and positioned her on top. She loved the change; it was always best for her to climax on top. *How did he know that?* He really joined with her during their lovemaking, and she kept thinking maybe there was hope. Mac arched his back and grinded his cock as deep as he could go.

"Oh my God, Mac!" Magen called out. Mac stayed with her; their breathing was right on target. His hands slid down to her tight and perfect ass. He pumped that same ass up and down until she reached that point of no return.

"Stop," she was crying, and it was repeated until she passed out.

CHAPTER 19

Interstate 95, New Jersey

The sound of the big-block Chevy engine was unmistakable, like a large signature on the Declaration of Independence. Flying up 95 in this monster was the furthest thing in his mind, Dean would consider inconspicuous. William considered several decisions he had made since his epiphany back in front of the pond at APL. He glanced over to his left where Cornell was cramped against the passenger side door, wide-eyed and confused. This situation was beyond repair; he was running blind from the most sophisticated machine on the planet. On top of everything else, he is officially a kidnapper. If he wasn't mistaken, that was, in fact, a felony. He started to laugh out loud considering the outrageous thoughts that ran around his head. The idea of any of this actually seeing a courtroom was absurd. Dark forces were busy mobilizing darker forces with the prime objective being the ending of his life.

He recalled a book he read some time back from a woman named Kubler Ross, *On Death and Dying*. It discussed the stages that we go through as we accept our pending doom. This was why he was laughing at ninety miles an hour as he wheeled down Route 97. The sign up ahead indicated that he was getting closer to the Baltimore beltway.

He turned to his passenger who was breathing erratically. "Cornell, you need to calm yourself," William said in a raised, pointed voice.

"Calm myself? That is practically funny considering I am barreling down the highway with a man who has been talking to himself for the past twenty miles. Mr. Dean, I have been a big fan of yours since my start at APL. I always thought you set yourself apart from that tyrannical group from Hopkins. Most people at APL feel the same way. So, I am a bit thrown aback by the fact that you have snatched me up in this old beast heading toward Baltimore, and, sir, why are you spitting blood clots out your window?"

William thought for a while and then realized that he needed to come clean with the new guest.

"Cornell, I needed to pull one of my molars out of the back of my mouth," William said with transparent honesty.

Cornell was scared and found himself being extra careful with his choice of words. "Nothing to worry about, Mr. Dean, they have an excellent dentistry program at APL," Cornell added with a friendly tone.

William slowly turned his head toward his passenger. "Cornell, when was the last time you utilized the dental services at APL?" William requested in a low, narrow tone.

Cornell, taken slightly aback by the question, looked closer into William's eyes.

"It was just last week," Cornell added.

CHAPTER 20

William slammed the breaks and veered off the road. When the car came to a complete halt, William smashed the side of Cornell's temple, rendering him incapacitated for a few minutes. William then reached down with his left hand, retrieving a familiar pair of pliers and began probing the young man's mouth.

Mac came through the door of his apartment with a half-eaten buttered roll still hanging from his mouth.

Coffee and a buttered roll weren't on everyone's top breakfast consideration. However, living in New York, the buttered roll holds a much higher relevance than most people could ever realize. Part of Mac's daily routine was to talk with fat Al Barone downstairs at the deli, grab coffee and some eats, and get the lowdown on what really happened in the metropolis as he slept with her hotness.

Al spent thirty years in the midtown morgue. As he would say, "I just know things, and even though my clients are quiet, they speak volumes."

He didn't have much time to kick it with Al this morning. However, there was one story floating in the white-collar circle that flagged his interest. Apparently, there was a kidnapping at some think tank in Maryland. The strange thing was that this story was on every damn channel. Somehow Mac knew this piece of information was important. Unfortunately, it would have to wait.

Right now, the hot blonde would have to wake up, get cleaned up, and find some clothes. They have a meeting scheduled at noon at the Schwartz auditorium at NYU. The anticipation of this meeting was growing within Mac's mind, and the conversation he had earlier with the field supervisor was leading him to deeper and more intense areas of thought.

Major had called him last night with the 411 on Gregory. According to everything out there, he was a straight-up guy and, for the most part, could be worked with. Of course, when you got right to the bottom of the full Monty, this guy was a politician, and that was that.

"Baby, it's time to get moving," Mac said as he rolled into the room.

"I'm up, I'm up," Magen said with fright and confusion.

"Magen, I need you to be honest with me! I picked up on something this morning that might be important, but I need you to be fully straight with me," Mac said as he kneeled in front of the bed.

"Mac, the drama is killing me. Get it out, my man," Magen said playfully.

"What do you know about a facility in Maryland called the Apple Physics Laboratory?" Mac added evenly.

CHAPTER 21

The question laid Magen out like a lightning strike. The playful manner was gone; a baffled and stunned Magen sat searching for words. The cat was out of the bag; the expression on her face gave away the fact that she was more than familiar with APL. There really was no reason to start lying; however, she needed to tread lightly. National Security had nearly pulled her clearance for asking too many questions about that fucking building. She had her ass reamed out in the worst way by Gregory that week.

As she thought the current scenario through, a smile slid across her hot sexy mouth. Mac was impressed; less than forty-eight hours in her world, and he had penetrated into some sensitive areas surrounding this case. Not to mention the significant penetrating that went on in this bed last night. She was glad he was here now, with her. She needed to come clean with him; holding anything back at this point would be ridiculous. There was also a part of her that wanted his trust and affection.

"The building is in Laurel, Maryland. From the outside, it looks like one of any thousand factories throughout the Delmarva Peninsula. The brains from Haskins have been running the show down there for over fifty years. They work hand in hand with NASA, so everything is up there now. Hubble, weather satellites, spy satellites, and now they even have this monster called Swift. They say that this mission is all about bursts of gamma rays, yada yada. The truth is if they ever turned this thing on Earth, how do you New Yorkers say, *forgetaboutit*."

"You obviously have some history with this place, and I am thinking that this is a good time to lay out the information and take a clean look at what you know and what your thoughts are. The fear that I have is that when I asked you about the lab in Maryland the first thought that came to your mind was how you were going to avoid telling me the truth," Mac said evenly and with intense serious affect.

"I know you may think that, but it wasn't that simple," Magen broke in.

"I know there is more to the story," Mac added with apparent suppressed anger.

Magen averted her eyes from him instinctively; historically that was how she dealt with confrontational behavior, not that she was intimidated by Mac. It was simply that she didn't want to say anything that would crush Mac's fragile male ego.

"Maybe what we should do is start from a point where you feel comfortable. It is clear to me that something about that place has you questioning my information clearance," Mac stated.

"Are you finished?" Magen added with obvious attitude.

"Am I finished? No, Magen, I am just getting started, and I desperately need your help," Mac pleaded.

"Mac! Know one thing, I am not your enemy. What you can't see from your pedestal is that I have been down this road and it almost ruined me. Eight months into my first year, I found a connection between two missing scientists and the security team at APL. I pressed it with my superior and was nearly court-martialed! It was worse than you could imagine. They made comments like threat to national security! They took my dad off his base and questioned him for hours about organizations I was involved in. It was horrible, and you bet your ass I backed down and moved on. I know you put a few dots together and think you're going to walk through the gauntlet and come out without so much as a scratch," Magen said with slight malice. "Well, good luck with that, camper," she said with her obvious mocking tone.

"Can we talk about the details of what you were dealing with when you hit the bureaucratic wall?" Mac said in a far less aggressive tone.

"Fat," she said without skipping a beat.

"Fat what?" he added with a puzzled look.

"That is the common denominator through the past several years of my investigation," Magen said as she shook her head and waited for the laugh.

"I am not really following you," Mac said with that same puzzled look upon his face.

Magen sat Mac down and initiated the timeline of events that she had pieced together over the past three years. She reached into her suitcase and pulled out files complete with medical records and photos. The crime scene photos dated back prior to World War II. Some earlier data came from paper clippings from both the *London Times* and the *Boston Herald*. Her research was well constructed and alarming, without judgments or opinions. The facts spoke for themselves, and the data was indisputable.

According to the information in front of him there was a distinct pattern surrounding the executions of over ninety physicians and scientists from twelve separate countries. All of them had deep involvement with obesity studies in one form or another. There was extensive diversity among the grouping. Some were involved with the studies of the current epidemic that was currently gripping the planet; others were working in the private sector with pharmaceutical companies looking for alternative fat supplements. There was even a televangelist whose platform was convincing thousands of people to avoid fatty foods, claiming it would help them find Jesus.

According to the news reports, he was struck by a lightning bolt on a sunny day outside Galveston, Texas. One of the strangest elements surrounding these cases was the brutal nature of these deaths. There were several decapitations, electrocutions, and a full assortment of vivisections, both outer extremities and internal organs. Mac was drawn to one case where a Chinese scientist was said to have bite marks over 30 percent of his body. The teeth marks were listed as "Of Unknown Origin."

Magen summed it up with the statement that "fat was the common denominator. The proof could hardly stand up in court, but you could map out the truth with little or no imagination."

Where her theories began to run into trouble was in the motivation. Why would anyone go through such extreme lengths as was laid out before him? What was it about obesity that created this scenario? There must be more to this picture than what was being identified.

A deeper concern is how something like this could go on for so long, without being picked up on someone's radar. Magen continued to ramble on about each case. Mac slowly began to disconnect; the information was coming too fast, and he was unable to process the data.

"Wait! At some point, you had to take this to your superiors. What did they say to all of this?" Mac blurted out.

Magen stopped cold midsentence and began to straighten out her paperwork connected to the case. She was obviously considering her words carefully. Agent Cummings took a long deep breath and turned to face Mac. "I know you are feeling the same way any rational person would. How does this case get past motive?" Magen added sheepishly.

"So, they're not even reviewing the evidence. That doesn't make any sense!" Mac said with surprise in his voice.

"I am a joke at the bureau! They have no problem looking at my tits whenever I walk into the room, but they laugh at me whenever they're together. They call me the chubby chaser!" Magen added with self-loathing.

"The chubby chaser!" Mac said with a smile.

They both started laughing out of control, and for just a few seconds, the nightmare was tolerable. They came back together in each other's arms in the unmade bed, and after kissing her hard and long, Mac turned to her and said, "We need to make them listen."

Magen said nothing as she rolled Mac on his back and made him submit to her hot, wet mouth.

CHAPTER 22

Interstate 95, New Jersey

"What the fuck!" Cornell screamed as he woke up in the passenger seat bleeding from the space where two of his back molars used to be. The ringing in his left ear was a direct result of the shot he took to the temple. He sat in the chair, trying to make sense of the predicament he now found himself in.

"Mr. Dean, I really don't understand what your story is, but I am not the bad guy," Cornell said with an empathetic tone.

Bill Dean briefly thought to explain the situation to his new friend, and then changed his mind due to time restraints. He fished into his pocket to retrieve the two teeth that he had removed from the man.

"Here, I defused them," William said in a matter-of-fact-tone.

"Are those my teeth?" Cornell said with some visible surprise.

"Look real close," Bill said intently.

As the two teeth rolled into Cornell's hand, he glanced at them briefly, not fully understanding what he was looking for. His primary concern was the bizarre behavior from the man next to him. Cornell had been a huge fan of the accomplishments of William Dean; this made this whole situation surreal.

What was his issue with teeth? he thought to himself as he raised them to his eyes.

Then he began to see something that just couldn't be possible. There was a distinct pattern of wires starting from mid tooth and leading out through the bottom root. There was some real confusion running through his head as to why someone would even think to do this. There was also relief that the man with the gun next to him just might not be as crazy as he initially thought.

"What is this in my teeth?" Cornell asked, holding them under William's nose.

"That, my friend, is an extremely sophisticated high-frequency tracking device," William responded.

"Is there a reason why someone would place this nasty thing in my mouth?" he asked with a puzzle tone.

"It's not who you are. It's all about where you work and the control that a certain group of people need on you," William said with a hint of anger in his voice.

"It's that Haskins bunch, right?" Cornell added.

"That's very perceptive of you," William said with some surprise.

Cornell wiped the blood from his lips with the back of his sleeve then looked out his window. It was hard to process what was going on. The intuition that he had carried around with him since he was old enough to think told him all along that something was not right with that Hopkins pack. He knew all of them, not on a personal level, but they all stood out almost in an awkward way.

Many times, he would walk into rooms where they would be standing around talking. They would stop cold, sometimes midsentence, and they would always sport those phony smiles. There was a time he had considered the possibility that the whole bunch of them were homosexuals. Not that it overly concerned him regarding their persuasion on that matter. It was just that he had difficulty fitting their behavior into who they were. He thought it only natural to at least try to understand the people around him. In the end, he had written them off as supreme nerds. He had spoken to other people at the campus about their weirdness, and the bottom line was that they really knew their stuff. Most folks thought of them as a genius pack; their contributions to physics were revolutionary, to say the least. It had been said many times that they were the future of the company. When he heard things like that, it made him uncomfortable. Deep down, that intuition he got from his mother told him something wasn't right with them.

What was happening now was something that he would never have considered.

Are they involved with some form of terrorist cell? What in God's name are they after?

His thoughts began to wander back to William and the gun he was holding in his lap. William Dean was absolutely panic-stricken, and that was the worst of it. Cornell was always a big fan of the bleeding man at the wheel. He had never seen him with this kind of stress. However, even after having his hardwired teeth yanked from his skull, he still felt trust for this man. Trust was something that Cornell never gave easily, especially to gray-haired white people.

"Mr. Dean, what the hell are they up to?" Cornell asked.

"I don't know what they're up to, but I do know they have been killing people, and it has been going on for some time," William said with obvious stress in his voice.

"How long has this been going on?" Cornell said with elevated fear in his voice.

"A long time," William said quickly, not exactly ready to explain something that he was struggling with himself.

"You're avoiding my question, Mr. Dean," Cornell added, as he lowered his eyebrow in Bill's direction.

"After having a brilliant CIA operative investigate the data, I am currently under the impression that this has been going on for three or four decades, maybe more," Bill said painfully.

"That's not possible. Some of these assholes aren't that old," Cornell said with confusion in his voice.

"How did you know about the Hopkins crew?" Bill asked.

"They never quite looked at me the right way!" he said with some ease.

"I am not really sure I fully understand," Bill said with a puzzled tone.

"You will never truly understand what I am talking about, and that's all right. Being a black man in this field, you get used to the way white people look at you," Cornell said, almost without any real emotion.

"It's not something good or bad. It is just what it is!" Cornell went on. "Most people you run into during the course of the day have some level of feeling, whether it has to do with the daily events or things at home, all people feel something, but not these guys. They are consistently ice-cold every damn day. It's almost impossible too," Cornell added with a chilling tone.

"These unfeeling assholes may be responsible for the assassination of nearly 75 people in several different countries," Bill added with a low melodic tone for effect.

Cornell didn't flinch from the bomb dropped at his feet; he simply looked out the window at the Susquehanna River. He thought of his children and the continuous pain from his jawbone. For a brief moment, he indulged in some minor self-pity, then snapped back. He thought of his faith and how important it was to fight evil in the world. Flying down Interstate 95, he thought of just how different his day was unwinding since he walked into the building.

He was beginning to get a grip on his fear, and he felt his backbone sliding back into place. Cornell lived for the love of his wife and children, and he was remotely sure that they were going to be contacted sooner than later.

He felt it was important to control the situation.

"I need to contact my wife and I really don't want to give away your location. What do we do?" Cornell asked in a solid tone that left no room for argument.

"Cornell, I have done everything I could possibly do to cover my tracks. And even with everything I laid out there to confuse these fucks, I know that they have me tracked on satellite," Bill added without hesitation. "So feel free to use my phone. This isn't a covert operation," Bill added.

"Bill, you would never make it as a kidnapper," Cornell said, attempting some levity. "Oh, by the way, do you have a clue as to where we are going?" Cornell asked as he took the phone from Bill's hand.

"There is a doctor in charge of the case out of Washington. His name is Gregory, Dr. Timothy Gregory. That's our destination today, Cornell," Bill said evenly.

"Do you trust him?" Cornell asked.

William Dean really didn't need to ponder the question put forth by Cornell. He had known Tim Gregory since his freshman year at Princeton. They were never close and, for the most part, traveled in different circles. He always felt there was a mutual respect between the both of them. However, they did have moments through the years where their academic competition became heated. After leaving college, they both excelled in their respected fields. He knew that Dr. Tim was involved with some of the highest forms of evil on this planet. So, the question regarding trust was not relevant at this point. What he needed was a monster to kick ass on the other monsters.

Tim Gregory was the meanest of the monsters, or what you might call the devil you know.

"There is absolutely no trust to be had at this point of the game, but he's our guy," William added with a sense of clarity.

"Good enough for me, Mr. Dean. It may be time to punch the beast," Cornell added with newfound conviction.

"I believe you're right, Corporal Clegg," Bill enunciated as he pushed the gas and pinned the needle. "May God have mercy on our souls," Bill stated as the Chevy cleared 110 miles per hour.

CHAPTER 23

Mac and Magen pulled down by Washington Square Park, en route to NYU. Magen had won the coin toss in front of the hotel and was now doing the driving. They felt very easy with each other, considering last night's throw down. For both of them, there were brief moments of guilt early this morning that didn't last too long. Mac stared out the window at the park he had known all his life. The elm trees broke the sunlight and made Mac squint, even with his new Serengetis. Magen spoke on about her last visit to NYU and how difficult the parking was in the area during the week. Mac listened with half an ear; his thoughts drifted to the early day running through this park. He was once told that more than twenty thousand people were buried under the park. Years later, he validated that claim when he busted a local historian who had made his wife part of the history.

"What's this Gregory guy look like?" Mac asked.

Magen had to give this some thought; she had worked for Tim for some time and had been hearing about him for the most part of her life.

"Tall, good-looking, clean, and confident. A little like you," Magen said with a smile.

Mac smiled as he looked out once more over the park. *The years had been good to his park*, he thought to himself as Magen moved into a parking area.

He opened the door of the rental, and the smell of dirty-water dogs hit him square in the face. He scanned the area and located the source of the boiling hot dogs.

He was tempted for a moment, then decided against it. You just can't eat any damn dog in this town; you need to tread lightly. All it takes is one bad bite in this city, and all could be lost. Mac had his regular dirty-water dog wagon over by the big park entrance on the Upper East Side.

He never got sick, the quality was always consistent, and best of all, the sautéed onions were always fresh. Mac regained his focus and joined Magen on the sidewalk. The college was busy as usual, small groups spread out all over the building. The old feelings of his college days were running through his mind. It wasn't this school, but it could have been; he recalled the way he felt on campus. Back then, he had it all figured out. There was pure clarity then. It only took a decade before he realized how fuckin' ridiculous he was and how pointless his point of view really was.

He scanned the crowd once more looking for his target, and there he was. Tall kid pretending that a cop wasn't walking in his direction; he was most likely holding a bag of something. He just worked too hard to protect his front right jacket pocket. Mac couldn't help himself and stopped about two feet away, turned in the young man's direction, and dropped his eyeglasses to the bridge of his nose. His gaze was icy and solid, and the youngster was obviously becoming uncomfortable.

"I guess I'll catch you later," Mac said as he looked straight through the student.

The group all started to move toward the park; however, the young student hung on for a second more. He said nothing, but his eyes spoke volumes. He then pushed off to catch his friends without even a glance back.

Magen walked back and asked, "What was that?"

"A gift that I missed back in the day," Mac said.

They stood in the lobby talking with security when Magen grabbed his arm and motioned him to the flat screen on the wall.

There was too much noise in the lobby, but you could easily read the bold letters at the bottom, MURDER AT APPLIED PHYSICS LAB, MARYLAND.

Mac moved to the television and at the same time pulled out his Blackberry and speed-dialed the office. Magen scanned the area for the television remote and saw nothing. She grabbed a chair and slid it over then reached up and turned up the manual volume. An extremely plastic public relations woman by the name of Helen Worthington was playing down the murder of a delivery person by a long-term executive.

CHAPTER 24

A picture of the man was posted alongside the story line. Magen placed her hand over her mouth, and the frame of horror that Mac caught in her eyes spoke volumes. Magen kept looking in the face of the man on the screen; the disbelief she was feeling had Mac fully intrigued.

"Mac, this is a major player down there. This is a spun fairy tale," Magen added with conviction.

"Weren't we talking about this fuckin' place this morning?" Mac added with a half question.

Magen heard the words coming from his mouth; however, the data was not being processed. Her thoughts were running wild, and although the puzzle was still jumbled, she knew this was important. She was thinking that in the end when she broke this case open, it would be right here that the worm turned. What she just heard on the television was an absolute fabrication.

Two years ago, she spoke at length with Helen Worthington regarding her findings; she lied then, and she was lying now. This was an act of desperation; something had happened, and a cover-up was in the works.

William Dean, a killer of a delivery person and now missing in action. The thought of this was so far-fetched, it could only be the act of desperation.

This guy was a team player down there, and when I pressed him about time frames, he didn't even want to give me the time of day. He dismissed me on more than one occasion, she recalled.

SEEDS OF THE GRAY

Even though he was a prick, she still never considered him to be involved in anything related to this case. William Dean was a Boy Scout, and most important at this point, he was an honest person with a family.

"Mac, we need to get the fuck out of here!" Magen said with strong urgency.

"That is not an option! I need you here."

The statement came from a tall well-dressed Caucasian man who more or less just appeared.

"Mac, please let me introduce Dr. Timothy Gregory, the name at the bottom of my paychecks every two weeks," Magen added mildly. Magen stood in front of this casual man and began to plead her case for immediate action away from the school.

The tall man listened to Magen with the air of confidence that could only mean he knew something. Dr. Gregory moved to Mac and extended his right hand. "It is my pleasure, Officer MacDonald," he said graciously.

"You seem to know something that we don't. Will you enlighten us, please?" Mac said gently.

"Always the cop, Officer MacDonald, is that it?" Dr. Gregory added with a slight bit of attitude.

"Oh, by the grace of God almighty and the pressure of the marketplace, right?" Mac snapped back.

"I heard that you are on the sharper side of the pencil box," Gregory added then paused. "This is a good thing. You will need it," added the smiling doctor.

"Why do I feel that you are dancing around my question?" Mac said evenly.

A smile spread across the section chief's face, showing a near perfect row of teeth that would make a dentist weep. He looked at the two in front of him and then scanned the area. He reached into his pocket and pulled out a pack of Marlboro reds, and from the pack he pulled what looked like an antenna. He motioned to Mac, running the device up one side of his body and then down the other.

"Is that what I think it is? Did you get that at James Bond School?" Mac stated with genuine surprise.

"James Bond is kind of cool, but in reality, the English can't make a tee time. This puppy is state-of-the-art from Korea, and those people know their shit when it comes to mini spyware. There is even room for a few smokes, if that is your preference." As his hand left Mac and moved toward Magen, a faint tone began to emanate from Magen's pocket.

"What the fuck!" Mac let out.

Magen was totally blown away, looking from Mac to the section chief. "This is a joke," she snapped.

"Empty" was all he said as he placed his finger on his mouth, motioning them both to be quiet.

Magen pulled everything she had in her front pocket and held it in front of all three of them. The section chief narrowed it down to a small red plastic coffee lid plug.

Dr. Gregory snatched it and took it right over to the garbage and tossed it.

"Where did you pick that up?" Gregory asked with little to no surprise.

"Maybe an hour ago at Starbucks on the Upper East Side," Magen said in a confused tone.

"It is amazing just how deep this network runs and how diversified they are. Fuckin' Starbucks!" Gregory added with amazement, shaking his head.

"You said 'they.' Who exactly is they, Dr. Tim? What is it that you are not telling us?" Mac snapped.

"I know that you're slightly out of your league, and that fact is rapidly tearing at your systematic cop brain," Gregory spewed with obvious discontent.

"Kiss my ass, you silver spoon preppy. Just go against every fiber of your being and tell us the truth," Mac snapped.

"Why, is there something you learned at the academy that can help us with this?" Gregory stated mockingly.

"Are you kidding me, you dick? I don't know what your issue with cops is, but I could only imagine that mouth of yours walked you into an ass beating," Mac spat back.

"Are you two kidding me with this bullshit? Is this some type of joke? People are dying, and you two are having a cockfight!" Magen screamed.

"I must apologize for acting so inappropriately at this junction," Tim Gregory stated with unmistakable embarrassment in his voice.

"Now can we get back to your statement about them, and who they are?" Mac stated without any malice from the previous conversation.

Gregory hung his head down and inhaled deeply. "I never really had a fix on who they were. What I do know is that for some time, all roads have been leading back down to Laurel, Maryland. The Apple Physics Lab has popped up on all radars. The problem has always been the protection that these geeks afford themselves. It has been hailed as the temple of information, and to even attempt to violate said temple was considered in bad taste, not to mention extremely bad for one's career. They are highly connected in the deepest circles. We are talking about a relationship of one of the leading health-care facilities in the civilized world and the American space program. These people barricade themselves with insanely high-ranking friends. Now I am not saying that these folks are above retribution, or not accountable for those acts committed. The problem we have been having over the years is presenting the cases to the various district attorney offices and other legal authorities. We find the facts have been so far-fetched and bizarre that we come off looking like assholes.

"This shouldn't come as any surprise to you, Officer MacDonald. Your people have been down this road," Dr. Gregory added.

"I'm not sure I understand what you mean by 'your people'!"

"My intel has you as a close friend to one Paul Major, recent retiree of the NYPD," Gregory added, all Fed-like.

"What would Paul Major have to do with what is going on with this shit?" Mac responded with a stunned look.

"In 1977, he was the arresting officer in a triple-murder case, all three lab techs out of Columbia University. Never made it to trial. The whole thing blew up when your friend told the grand jury that he watched the perpetrator walk through a wall. He kicked the door down, finding three dead by massive coronary and the bad guy holding a syringe of vitamin K. The grand jury most likely would have made some type of move. Then, in comes Alan Dershowitzcum, ready to take on the police force for defamation of character. The DA folded before the liberal bloodsucker's briefcase hit the table. Your buddy walked up to the lawyer and flicked him right in his hooknose. The bump is still there today.

"The case died right there in that very room, and your pal rode a desk for the next two years. That asshole walked right out the door with that piece-of-shit attorney. The strange thing after that was there was never a sign of that son of a bitch after that day. There is an old file back in Langley that says your pal did him Jimmy Hoffa style and the body was never found."

Gregory closed his story with a shrug of his shoulders. "For years, I couldn't stop wondering about that bump on Dershowitzcum's nose. I should have known," Mac added, making light of story.

The unfortunate truth of the matter was that he stood in front of this prick agent, desperately trying not to urinate in his own pants. He had known Paul the better part of his life, and there was a closeness that had been achieved. The strongest block of trust he knew would never be laid to waste by this dick. It was something that he didn't want to display to anyone, especially Dr. Gregory, but he really felt the need to get away and make sense of it.

Mac's Blackberry sent out a loud ping. The office! A much-needed distraction.

"Yes, I have been trying to reach you," Mac barked at the young officer. "I will be meeting up with you within two hours. I am in possession of an unknown object. We are receiving radiation feedback from the item. I need Bill Lange standing by when the item arrives at the lab. Are there any questions?"

"No, sir, I have it all," said the young officer.

"Young man, I can't stress just how important your ability to get this done in a reasonable amount of time is to my case," Mac pleaded in an almost evil tone.

"I will not let you down. Watch for me in twenty minutes," cracked back the enthused young officer.

The line went dead, but Mac kept the Blackberry to his ear for a few brief minutes. He considered making that call to Paul, but he lost his thought trail and didn't want to open this up on the phone. He needed the eyes to get to the truth.

Magen walked up to Mac and started discussing the content of the pending lecture. The medical terms didn't mean anything to him. Magen would have to interrupt most of the data. After reading about 10 percent of the format, Mac asked Magen if it was totally necessary for him to attend.

Dr. Gregory turned quickly on his heels to confront Mac. "You're here for a reason. Make no mistake about it. This is important stuff, and we are pretty sure that the key to what has been going on with this case centers on what these scientists have been working on. We have been working this one for a long time. There are files in Langley that date back before you and I were born. This has been my primary for the last seven years, and let me be really clear, we have never been closer to understanding the who and what to this puppy. At 1800 hours yesterday evening, all active NASA satellites repositioned their focus up and down Interstate 95 from Laurel, Maryland, right back to the Lincoln Tunnel. I think the bad guys are looking for one Mr. William Dean. They're making him out to be some snapped executive. I know this guy, and I'm not buying it," Gregory said with confidence.

"One question! Why do you think this guy is heading to New York? Why not head to Virginia? It would be a cleaner ride."

"I can't figure that!" Gregory's loss of confidence was apparent.

"Unless he had some reason to think that Langley was, in fact, compromised?" Mac said, fishing.

"I am not ruling out anything at this point. The truth is that most likely there have been internal elements protecting the bad guys from the light of day," Dr. Gregory added with a hint of shame.

"You say that Dean and you have a history and he could be heading in your direction?" Mac asked, half knowing the answer.

"I can't see him going down that road, but anything is possible," Gregory stated.

"I think we shall know soon enough, but as for now, we have a lecture to sit through on fat, right?"

"I take it that Magen has given you her rendition of the fat theory as the primary element," Gregory added with some hesitation.

"It's solid data and well researched, and I'm not afraid to say that it scared the shit out of me," Mac stated.

"What about motive? You're a cop. You can't get past the big piece of fact," Gregory said aggressively.

"Motive is based on reality. What is going on here may not be fully based on any reality we can understand," Mac chimed with his best philosophic tone.

"What the fuck have you been smoking? Do you hear yourself?" Greg snapped.

"You're not fooling me with the crazy-story act. There is some solid and scary stuff in that folder. The worst of it to me is that I know there are some powerful, evil sons of bitches that are behind this. My guess is that you also know this to be right, and that's why you need to punch holes in Agent Cummings's findings. The technological advancement that I have seen over the past seventy-two hours has me convinced that there is government involvement at the highest level. For all I know, you could play a role in all this. It could be your job to throw us off the right trail. There has been very little over the past few days that ring with any reality that I can sink my teeth in," Mac laid out to Gregory without any hesitation.

"Interesting choice of words, Detective," Gregory added, and motioned them to the door.

CHAPTER 25

> I met a man who said he didn't believe in God. It wasn't long before I realized he believed in nothing!
>
> —A stone in my backyard

The big room back at Laurel, Maryland, was as quiet as it has ever been. There were seven individuals in total, all Haskins alumni, two on each door and five at the table. The two at the door were both from research and development. They were wearing their isolation scrubs, complete with hairnets and face shields. This made the situation even stranger than usual. It was bad enough to have an executive meeting called at five o'clock in the morning.

Then the room occupants began to dismiss the department heads that were not Haskins connected. The staff was becoming highly confused and suspicious. Within twenty-four hours, the facility had become the stage for both a homicide and a kidnapping, and now bizarre meetings at the crack of dawn. There was a sense of desperation from the Hopkins crew. Not that they were showing outside emotion, but they were obviously isolating themselves.

Without any emotion or communication, two of the five proceeded to the center of the room and placed several steellike balls on the floor at mathematically identical placements. There was an immediate response as the steel balls began to pull light from every inch of the room. Light began to bend in direct correlation with the positioned devices. For a slight moment, there was a void of both light and sound.

As the light arched, it began to diminish a shadow and began to take a detailed form. Then there was a blink of the bluest light imaginable and warmth that seemed to emanate from every direction of the room. When full focus was restored, there stood a gray human-like creature. The others moved closer as if to provide aid.

A striking middle-aged woman walked from the table with what appeared to be a basin of water. The gray received the basin and slowly poured the contents over his head. As he completed the task a strong muscular human form emerged, stunning, beautiful, and as close to perfect as physically possible. He stretched his hands and arms and blinked continuously as if to get used to his new skin and adopted form. He was standing naked, attempting to gain balance. The others remained in a circle, allowing for proper depth perception to be achieved. As the alien completed his transformation, it was obviously noted that the proportion of his genital area was extremely out of place. The head of his semi-erect circumcised penis swung very close to mid knee. It was also apparent that this alien was different from the others in the room. The first telltale sign was when he finished drying off the fluid, he turned to the table, and as a large grin spread across his face, he said, "It feels so good drawing Earth air. Who the fuck has a cigarette?" He blasted with what appeared to be a strong New York accent.

The others in the room didn't really know how to respond, but it was clear that the new arrival was in charge despite his youthful appearance. Clothing was made available to the young leader as to his specifications. He utilized the steel balls to bring himself up to speed on the last hundred hours. As the data was being processed, he barked orders as he walked. Within thirty minutes, he had set up a press conference for both media and staff. He wanted the first plane out of some Maryland airport to LaGuardia, New York, directly after the conference. He presented a lot like a politician but looked very much like someone out of a Hollywood miniseries.

His race was difficult to gauge at first glance. You would think Caucasian; however, there were features that might be consistent to either African or even Asian. One of the most shocking points that stood out with our new visitor was his air of complete confidence, practically cocky. However, there was much more than a young man's arrogance; there was charm and a heightened sense of emotional being. The deficit that was so apparent in the rest of the office gathering really was emphasized by the over-the-top drama demonstrated by the recent arrival.

The response from others in the office also defined the new member as significantly different from themselves. It wasn't initially clear if the new arrival held some higher status or the reaction was based on fear. If asked to describe the reaction of the gathering regarding the new addition, the word "uncomfortable" would come to mind. The behavior and language was not an accident on the part of the new member. He was fully aware of the response and feelings he was drumming up in the others. It was as if he really didn't care or he thought himself better.

The young individual was now sitting among the gathered staff members as if he had been there all along. He had three computers open in front of him and two other forms of communication devices that were sending mathematical equations practically at the speed of light. His green eyes were rolled back in his head, and a thin membrane was stretched across his eyeballs, much like a shark. Then as fast as the data download accelerated, it stopped dead.

He stood up, turned to the others, let out a sigh of relief, then added, "That will wake your ass up in the morning."

The door opened up, and in came Helen Worthington. "Cain, it's so good to have you back. It has been an absolute madhouse," Helen pleaded.

"Helen, I watched you earlier during the morning teleconference, and, honey, you were absolutely brilliant," Cain added.

"I don't know about that. I really feel like I have been flying by the seat of my pants since two in the morning," Helen stated, acting like she was about to drop.

"I have always loved the seat of your pants, flying or not," Cain added with a devious smile.

"Shannon Troetel from CNN bushwhacked me at the tail end of the conference. She's not buying a word of it," Helen said flatly.

"That's okay because we are not selling today. This one is on the house. I will deal with Shannon on my own," Cain said with a touch of evil in his voice.

"Like I said, really glad you're back," Helen concluded.

"Well, Helen, I am not going to lie to you, I always feel good when I get back home," Cain said with a wide smile.

"Are you ready for showtime?" Helen asked with a nervous giggle.

"Ready as always, little lady. Let's put this puppy to sleep," Cain said, and led them through the door.

They walked out to the lobby where they were met by a sea of lights and cameras. Cain ran his hand down the length of his cashmere coat and straightened out the collar. Helen pulled herself back slightly to give a vantage point where Cain could position himself for a fast response and an easy getaway.

The noise level in the lobby was ridiculous, and it was painfully obvious that this crew cared only about the story and little to nothing about the players. Cain raised his right hand and motioned several times for silence in the room.

The crowd fell first to murmur, then finally to silence.

"Good morning, ladies and gentlemen! My name is Alexander Cain. I am the legal representative from the Haskins EAP program. We have been working with William Dean for the past nine months here at the Laurel facility and in my office back in Westminster. I have monitored the events over the past twenty hours and have been in touch with both the authorities and my superiors and have been requested to discuss the nature of my involvement regarding both Mr. Dean and Mr. Pierce. These two gentlemen have worked together for the past twenty-three years. Sometime last year, they engaged in an anonymous relationship of a romantic nature. It is currently our belief that something went wrong within that relationship!"

The press conference erupted into an explosion of sighs and gasps, then came the questions; nothing was making any sense.

"So, we are not dealing with an actual kidnapping, is that right?" voiced a young reporter holding a microphone.

"We are not sure what we are dealing with at this time," Cain said in a manner that indicated that they, in fact, knew full well what was going on, but chose to be discreet.

"Mr. Cain, this is a love triangle that has gone bad, is that what we are being informed of today?" asked Scott Spano from the *Washington Post*.

"It appears that this is the most likely scenario. Mr. Roy Glover, the pizza delivery employee, has also been discussed in my office over the past few months," Cain added as he clarified and finalized his fabrication.

Cain answered several more questions, staying vague to a fault. As the press conference began to wind down, Cain began to monitor the majority of the press members breaking from the pack and heading for the exit. He also kept a mental note of the few who were staying with the story. They would need to be dealt with at a later time. His fabrication began to fall into line exactly as he reviewed it in his mind only minutes earlier. He knew it was a little bit of a gamble to present this type of story out to a pack of press. The press corps could have gone the opposite direction with this onion and really gone full circus. His theory was simply that the big players like the *Times* and the *Post* really didn't want to wrap themselves up with the nature of a homosexual love triangle. When the *Times* started to break ranks from the pack, soon the others began their departure.

As Helen noted earlier, CNN was hanging in with obvious skepticism. That would have to be handled immediately; he briefly licked his lips at the fine-dining potential. He announced to the remaining press corps that he needed to meet with the authorities regarding current events. As he walked to the hall, he noticed Helen was frozen and pale, and he then realized that he had given her no notice to the story change. As he moved in her direction to pass her en route to the office, she slowly turned her head and looked him directly in his eyes.

Regardless of the sheer panic that he saw in her face, he couldn't help his desire to rock the boat just a little. Cain paused for a second then leaned over to her ear and said, "Helen! It was a timing oversight. I should have briefed you prior to this meeting, but please don't break into a panic attack in front of all these people. It would be hell to explain." Cain smiled.

Helen did her best to force a smile through her obvious astonishment.

As Cain moved off the makeshift platform, he indulged a quick glance toward the CNN reporter Shannon Troetel. She was moving quickly through the diminishing crowd with a microphone in her hand. As he took his second step off the platform, she blocked his passage to the office. She put the microphone under her arm and then produced a black-and-white photo from a folder she was holding. She held it directly under his eyes. "Do you recognize this photo, Mr. Cain?"

Cain took the photo in his hand and lightly smiled at her. He recognized the face immediately; it was Grigori Yefimovich Rasputin. It was Christmas 1916, and the man standing next to him in the photo was all too familiar; he went by the name Alexi then. Four days after the photo was taken, Alexi would rip the penis and testicles from this fraud of a holy man, and eat them in front of him as he screamed in horror.

"I think I remember the photo from somewhere," Cain said as he handed the photo back to Shannon.

"Do you recognize the other man in the photo?" Shannon pressed.

"My strength has never been with Russian history. Is there something I can help you with?" Cain added as he motioned to leave.

"I met you seventeen years ago at a fundraiser for President Clinton. You most likely don't remember me. You left a lasting impression on me. There was something so interesting about you. Then over the past two decades I kept finding photos of you from all around the world, some dating back over a hundred years. When I saw you tonight and as young as you were back then, I said to myself, *Holy shit!*" Shannon watched his eyes as she spoke for some reaction.

"Young lady, do you even hear the words coming from your mouth? You have me thinking the same thing. Holy shit, there is a crazy woman who thinks I'm a hundred years old," Cain said in a humorous manner.

"I know what I am saying sounds crazy, but I also know that I am right about you. I have not said anything about you to a soul. Who would believe me? So, Mr. Cain, I have made first contact. The ball is in your court. I believe you have the ability and the technology to find me if you want me!" she added with a provocative look.

"The lengths some women will go to for an exclusive! Do you see that gentleman in the blue shirt?" Cain said as he pointed to one of the Haskins team.

"Yes!" Shannon added.

"Well, he's from planet Whatchamyass. Could you give him your cell number? I would read your mind, but I broke my antenna coming through customs," Cain joked then turned on his heels and departed. He didn't look back, but he could feel that she was beginning to question her position on Cain's historic presence. He thought to himself that things were not going to get better. The Internet was spreading information faster than they could contain or control. He knew if someone started to do some real research, they would shit an extremely large brick. The things he had seen in this world were unbelievable. He felt sorry for the new crew who were here now; they didn't understand what fun was or how to obtain it. That was the problem with these fuckin' clones; they were two-dimensional thinkers in a three-dimensional world. If something was going wrong, they only knew one way to deal with issues, limited thinkers. This whole thing was blowing up for the sole reason that these assholes couldn't think one step ahead of their actions.

We have spent centuries cultivating this planet.

Cain thought of his own seven thousand years that he had personally invested on this rock.

He didn't talk about it much, even to his own line. He was proud of what he had accomplished over the past centuries. He loved Earth in a strange way. He enjoyed the deception and the feeling of being the great gardener of this planet. That was the real high for him as he moved through the world playing with humans like windup toys. The only drawback about being in this world was the fuckin' skin suit he walked around in; it just felt so disgusting. He checked the time on his Blackberry and rolled out the back door; the car was ready. NASA had arranged for a jet to be fueled and ready at the south gate of Andrews. He was four and half minutes ahead of schedule time, enough to stop for smokes.

CHAPTER 26

Schwartz Hall, New York
10:00 a.m.

"Good morning, ladies and gentlemen, I welcome you to NYU. My name is Dr. Sidney Gotlieb, and I am going to take a few hours of your time to talk about a subject that is near and feared by my heart—the epidemic of obesity in America and how we respond to this great tragedy!"

There was a pause as Sidney scanned the room.

"I notice that only half the room managed to raise an eyebrow at the word 'tragedy.' The others leered at me with a look that said, 'You better do better than that for my time.' Time is a major player in the realm of obesity. Not the only key, but definitely a major player. We are going to talk about the biggest health issue facing America today! I am going to talk about humans as a species and how we got ourselves in this situation. I am going to talk about the role our government plays in the health and safety of its people and what they are doing or aren't doing. You are going to ask me questions! I really want to hear from the students because it is my hope that one of you out there catches the obesity fever and helps us out of the big boy pants we have eaten ourselves into. We are going to touch base on how we look at fat people in our everyday lives. It is my deepest wish that after this conference, you are going to really start to notice that you are in the middle of a war. I can imagine that many of you have never even considered thinking of excess weight as a war, but hear me out today.

"What if I told you that as you sit here today, your hard-earned tax dollars are working on repairing the damages this epidemic has produced? As a matter of fact, if I was able to cut a check to everyone thirty-five years and older for your tax contribution, we would be spinning out of here at the end of the day in brand-new Corvettes, billions and billions every year right out of your pockets. This epidemic negatively affects every man, woman, and child in this country. America is ground zero for this silent plague that has the body count potential greater than cigarette smoking, alcoholism, and crack cocaine combined. Did you hear me when I said combined?" he stressed. "Am I getting through to anyone in this room?" His eyes panned the room. "At this point, is anyone asking themselves why we are not hearing about this every day? You may come up on the sporadic news article. *20/20* did a weak piece on teen obesity not long ago. However, you're bright people. You know how the news works. Who died, who cried, and, most important, who lied! Obesity doesn't sell, so you really don't get the full story. Currently, our children are fatter than they ever were, and there is no sign of relief in sight. The numbers are astounding and absolutely frightening. We will touch base on them in a bit, but I would like to get to back to the concept of time. Time, as I mentioned before, plays a major role in obesity. Let's break that down.

"Scientific data estimates that the universe initially went boom 13 plus billion years ago. Our planet is estimated at 4 plus billion years of age, due to the shifting plates. It was only 250,000 years back that the Homo sapiens first climbed down from the trees to eat a little grass somewhere in mid-Africa. Another 150 years, we start finding Homo sapiens in the Middle East. It was only 18,000 years ago that our version of human ancestors arrived in the Americas. We can trace our first stable settlement in the Americas to 8,000 years back. Now, I need you to understand that when I say 'settlement,' it's not like what we worked our way through this morning to get here.

"These limited cities were more or less large gatherings of confused humans. They were too paranoid to live under the wild conditions of the times. Later, communication became more structured and useful, and things slowly got better. Of course, being humans, we had to throw in the occasional war and sacrifice. More than likely it is our line of human ancestry that killed off the Cro-Magnon man. That's just how we roll." Dr. Gotlieb continued, "Now it was only a little more than 5,000 years back that some damn fool turned the wheel. Now, we're rolling right along. It is not too far from there that we started agriculture and the mass production of crops. This is a huge piece of the puzzle. I want to spend some time on this! We can trace the first sapiens back 250,000 thousand years, but mass production of food only 5,000 years. Are we starting to see where I am going with this? Now the concept of hunter and gatherer didn't stop 5,000 years ago. A large portion of this country continues with both mercantile and some minor farming, but there are still some hunting and fishing pockets. In many cases still seen in aboriginal cultures, the males did the hunting, and the females did the farming. May I take a moment and thank the ladies, not only for putting up with our running out of the house with the old hunting story, but also for saving our miserable butts from absolute extinction.

"As time went on, a shift began to take place, and we began to work the Earth much harder than our efforts to kill for food. This is pretty amazing, if you take a moment to think about it. We could never make up our minds on anything as a species. However, when it came to our method of food intake, we reached consensus almost overnight. The population grows, and large pockets of humans spread throughout Africa, Europe, and Asia. Food and animals are the primary trade elements. Grains and spices led to fruits and vegetables, and you all know the rest. Now, when it came to the Americas, things rolled out much differently. We developed in a much different way than anywhere on the planet, and at a much faster pace. The immigrants that first settled this land were driven, many of them expelled religious zealots. They utilized trading posts and general stores. When they spread out of the cities, they found a land as rich as one's mind could hardly fathom. Buffalos spread for miles, without any real natural enemies, so they would basically shoot them, skin, and serve up their own hides. The Native Americans had a most excellent relationship with the land and the bounty. They killed what they could use for food and clothing. When the Europeans came and annihilated everything in their path, it literally broke the spirit of the natives. The white man came and learned what they could about farming and hunting patterns from the natives, and then realized they couldn't live with them. Well, maybe not all, but that's another conference.

"Then something amazing happened. Gold turned up in the Midwest. When there is gold, there are people, and they came in waves. So now we have new farming methods for the settlers, combined with countless people driven by the dream of newfound wealth. The soil in the Midwest was ideal for farming, and before long, the hardworking American farmer was building barns and silos to house their overflow. Food surplus was a new concept to a people who had dealt with plagues and famines for thousands of years. Then, something took place that would change everything regarding the delivery of food and its availability. In 1916, the first self-serve convenience store opened its doors, the Piggly Wiggly. I couldn't make that up even if I tried!"

Dr. Sidney Gotlieb reached over to a nearby table and grabbed a remote. As he pushed the power button, the screen behind him lit up with a map of the United States with the states sectioned off.

"Behind me is a map of the states in the year 1900. The average weight for a college age male at this time was 133 pounds. The average weight for women at this time was 122 pounds. In the year 2000, men plumped up to an average of 166 pounds and the ladies up to 144 pounds. It gets worse. In 1985, only eight states could claim 10 percent obesity. Twenty years later, twenty-five states could make that claim, and here they are."

As he turned with the remote, large red shading began to spread over the southern states.

"Oh! It looks like the Bible belt has been praying over some ribs and biscuits," Gotlieb joked to short bursts of laughter from the crowd.

"Now! The amazing thing here is the correlation between weight gain throughout the region, and the spread of these self-serve produce stores. Here, we highlight the rise of these markets, and you can see that they follow a pattern. Money, supply and demand, and easy access is the formula that set America up for an overnight fat ass. I wish that we could turn this conversation in a positive direction. Unfortunately, that is truly not the case. You are educated people. I don't need to bore you with the details. It's all around us. This is why our president's health plan will crumble like a handful of blue cheese over bacon and baked potato. We are a fast-food nation, and our children's idea of exercise consists of sitting in front of high-tech video games with a remote control. If you have ever had the sad honor of watching them in action, it is pretty scary. Our government puts warning labels on them to alert parents that there are suggestive themes and bad language, and maybe some nudity, but what should go on the label is 'Put it down and run away.' I view all this stuff, PlayStation, Xbox, and all the other mind-numbing amusements, as simply legal crack, and the addiction is horrific. The direction that today's youth has taken is extremely self-destructive and isolating. Their bellies are stretching to epic proportions. Mark my words, twenty years from today, we are going to see a spike in obesity-related depression, the likes of nothing we have ever imagined. Now, I am not the smartest man in the world by any stretch of the imagination, and I have no issue in reading the writing on the wall. So, I find it really hard to believe that I am the only physician that is arriving to this obvious conclusion. Our government seems to have some idea of the pending wave of bacon grease. The wife of our president seems to have taken up the flag of healthy eating of the American children. Is this a coincidence? I think not! I fully believe that her husband's health-care plan will tumble down the feeding trough the moment that taxpayers realize they've been taken for a ride.

"Now hear me out, you and I are under attack every single moment of every day. The market forces want you to do two things in this world. First, they want you to be happy. Secondly, they want you to consume!" The doctor emphasized the word "consume" for effect. "So if you follow the logic, the obese person is doing exactly what is outlined by our society. This begs the question, where is everyone, and what are we doing to counteract the incoming storm? I remember a few years back, Governor Schwarzenegger was all over the tube, motivating all the kids to get the hell off the couch and just do something. Then that went away, and you want to know something that really twists my melon? Granted it was a lame attempt, not too much thought went into the program, but believe it or not, it worked, and the kids listened. I have seen the numbers, and I was stunned. Schools got involved, parents, even the spineless media gave it some airtime. Imagine if we let it ride and got some of the *High School Musical* heroes to jump on the bandwagon. Wow! Things could have really become interesting. We were throwing terms around like 'epidemics.' We were scared, and then we found something that could help, only to shoot it down. I wonder about things like that. Don't you?"

Dr. Gotlieb paced a little back and forth; he reached out for his remote and pressed a series of buttons. Behind him, the map of the United States began to fade away. It was soon replaced by the word "Pharmaceuticals" in large black letters. Sidney reached out for his bottle of water then took two quick hits and returned the bottle to the table.

"We live in a pill society. We have a pill for everything, red pills, pink pills, blue pills, and everything in between. There are thousands of pills for the stomach, hundreds for the heart, and if you have a headache, you can get a bigger one trying to navigate through the endless choices. When it comes to obesity, your choices are narrowed down to two medications that have been suspect at best. The first, a cute little item out of the Merck/ Pfizer bag of tricks and said to be a real breakthrough. Unfortunately, that's not really the case. The name of the med is known as Rimosinion, and most people know it as Acomplonua. It started out of the gate in European trials with some real promise. Then it all went wrong. Anxiety levels started to spike. Depression among the trial subjects was unbearable. Suicide numbers were off the charts, and not just for a small percentage of already depressed individuals. This med was turning happy fat people into angry, violent, depressed fat people. I bet the US armed forces are taking a real close look at this little beauty!" Gotlieb stated with some fear in his eyes, "However, it most likely will never hit the US market.

"Now! We do have something out there that is showing some positives for our obese brothers and sisters. When I say obese, know that I am talking about those who have a body mass index or BMI of 30 percent or greater. The name of the med is Sibutrutune, and it's simply a nonaddictive amphetamine sold over the counter under the brand name Ollie. The downside of this puppy is something known as fecal urgency and, my favorite, good old-fashioned explosive diarrhea. Now if you are motivated and can get past that funky stuff, you still have to face the reality that the pounds seem to come back with a vengeance. In summary, we are not really anywhere closer to reversing the process of weight gain than we were thirty years ago. This scares the hell out of me. I have to ask myself what is going on. I mean, we are really smart people. Look what we have been able to do with HIV/AIDS. It was once a death sentence but not anymore. How about our work with Ebola? Hell, we cloned a sheep in Scotland, and we grew body parts in petri dishes. Not to mention nanotechnology and the endless possibilities down that road. What about the gains we have made in the study of embryonic stem cells? Holy smokes, don't people realize that this is the Finnegan pin to long-term space travel for all humankind? I feel I am losing some of you, so please let me clarify my last remark. Earth basically is a large rock floating through space, and space is a cold, pointless, and wonderfully scary place. Stuff happens out there. In the life span of our magnificent planet, we have already sustained meteor strikes that killed 99 percent of every living thing on this round fragile globe. We really shouldn't be waiting for the next strike. The long-term focus of

NASA and other valuable programs should be to get us on the move. The catch is that the closest possibility is over two hundred plus years away. Now! If we pulled together three hundred of our smartest scientists that the planet has to offer and then got them into the best possible physical shape with the thought of sending those out on a deep space mission to the closest alternate galaxy that we estimate could possibly sustain life, they would arrive absolutely retarded and deformed, if they had the common sense to arrive at all. Inbreeding with the limited number of subjects and the given time parameters would be devastating. The only real hope for mankind lies in stem cell research. It is amazing that this issue plays host to some form of ethical battlefield.

"I apologize for straying off from our primary subject. You really need to stop me when I start deviating," Gotlieb stated to additional laughs from the crowd. "The point I was trying to make before you let me interrupt myself is that we are fighting against our very own feeble genetics. Well, this brings me back to the body that is designed to store fat, so the fact that we have difficulty processing the weight is not fully surprising. The fact that we have been spinning our wheels for decades is disturbing. Earlier, I said that our president's health plan would fail. Please let me tell you why. Throughout all 2,600 pages of a well-attended document, it makes no room for the direction mankind is developing. In fact, the detail of the document is practically blind to the reality of what is happening throughout this country."

Mac had been paying close attention to what Dr. Gotlieb was talking about. He had been waiting for a chance to present a question but found it quite difficult with the good doctor's continuous rambling.

Finally, an opening appeared, and he couldn't refrain any longer.

"Dr. Gotlieb, I have a question that I thought you might assist me with," Mac interrupted.

Dr. Gotlieb narrowed his eyes to see the three people sitting near the back of Schwartz Hall, "How can I help?"

"You seem to be extremely knowledgeable regarding the subject matter. Maybe you can help us with an issue that has been keeping me up as of late!" Mac added.

"Yes!" Dr. Gotlieb returned impatiently.

"Who would profit the most from keeping the wheels of progress from rolling in the right direction?"

"I am not following you, sir," Sidney said.

"My father is sir. My name is Lieutenant Robert MacDonald of the NYPD, and I am currently investigating the death of one Aaron Goldstein. I am also pursuing the deaths or disappearances of an additional 102 scientists working along the same line!" Mac said, as if reading from a cue card.

"Is this a joke?" Dr. Gotlieb proclaimed with nervousness in his voice.

"I wish that I was! Getting back to my original question of who could benefit from slowing the process on the battle of obesity…"

"Hold on! I would have heard if that many of my colleagues went missing or were murdered," Dr. Sidney added with a suspicious tone.

"The time frame extends from the end of World War II 'til present day," Mac stated.

"I really am not sure how to respond to that statement. Aaron Goldstein was a dear friend of mine, and a brilliant young man," Dr. Gotlieb said with a hint of genuine sadness.

You could hear a pin drop in Schwartz Hall as the discussion came to an abrupt halt. The seventy-four people that were present were fully stunned and engaged in what was being discussed. Both Magen and Dr. Gregory were in shock that their case was being aired in an open forum. The conference had truly taken a strange turn toward the surreal. Now it was apparent, this train was not going to get back on track. Dr. Gotlieb moved to the table and grabbed the remote that he had put down earlier and then shut down the conference. He apologized to everyone in the hall and then moved to the exit. He announced that full credits would be awarded to all participants. There was no protest from those present in the hall. Several people stared at Mac as they made their way from the room.

Gregory was berating Agent Cummings apparently for her inability to control the situation and her new partner. Mac stood for a few seconds watching the crowd file from the hall. As he prepared to turn and support Magen during her tongue-lashing, Dr. Gotlieb emerged from the exit area. He stood briefly looking at Mac and then motioned him to follow him to the back area.

"Let's go!" Mac interrupted.

"I think you need me to do the talking. We have heard way too much out of you this morning," Dr. Gregory blasted as he walked past Mac.

"You okay?" Mac asked Magen as she stood to follow.

"He just can't appreciate your slash-and-burn tactics, but it gets me hot, you sexy bitch," Magen stated.

"Oh, baby! Daddy likey," Mac said in his best sexy voice.

When he arrived in the back area, Gregory was on his third set of apologies. Being a cop, Mac couldn't help but to instinctively evaluate the room.

He quickly noted that Sidney's hands were shaking. Then he realized that his eyes were glassy and swollen. Something was not right with this situation; Dr. Gotlieb was not the type to rattle to this degree.

"You have something to add to this puzzle, don't you?" Mac said bluntly.

"I think that I do! However, it dates back to 1952. My father could possibly be part of this situation," Dr. Gotlieb added with obvious tension in his voice.

"What was his full name, and what country was he working out of at the time?" Magen said as she unfolded her laptop.

"My father's name was Abraham Gotlieb. He was working out of Israel in 1952, but that's not where he went missing from. We were on vacation in Negril, Jamaica. I was six years old, and I remember it as if it was yesterday," Sidney reflected.

"I have nothing on Abraham Gotlieb in my database," Magen motioned to Mac.

"There is more to the disappearance that we need to talk about! I know this is going to sound crazy, but you need to hear it," Gotlieb pleaded.

"There's not much you could tell me this week that I would have a real problem with. It has been beyond insane," Mac proclaimed.

"I was on the beach running up and down, trying not to let the water hit my feet. I saw my father. He was no more than twenty yards away. I was smiling directly at him when he took him away."

"He took him?" Dr. Gregory chimed in.

"I know that I was a child all of five, but I know what I saw! There was a black man standing on the water, not in the water but on it," Gotlieb stated with obvious sincerity.

"On the water," Tim Gregory muttered with his eyebrow lifted.

"I know it sounds crazy. I sat in front of a therapist for the next decade who slowly but surely convinced me that the whole thing was some form of memory suppression," Gotlieb continued.

"Go on, Dr. Gotlieb, please," Mac pleaded.

"My father was snorkeling. He lifted his head out of the water into the face of this man, and then they were both gone," Gotlieb stated with a flat effect.

"So they just vanished into thin air. Is that what you're saying? Or were they sucked into the water?" Mac pushed.

"Not into the water, not up, or sideways, just absolutely gone," Gotlieb concluded.

"What type of work was your father involved with at the time of his disappearance?" Magen asked.

"He was working on healthy food substitutes for the Israeli Army, extending the shelf life of perishables," Gotlieb recollected.

"Let me say this, Dr. Gotlieb, I don't know if there is an actual connection with the current case. To be honest with you, I am not sure of many things right now." Mac paused for a moment and thought of what the good Dr. had to say.

The memory of a young boy is and always will be questionable. Maybe the therapist was right. He could have been blocking out the horrific demise of his father, for all he knew.

However, what if there was truth in what he saw? What about the transmitter from the coffee container? How could they possibly operate with that level of technology and not show up on someone's grid? How does NASA work into this equation?

More importantly, how does Agent Cummings's theory work itself into this scenario?

Part of me feels that I am getting closer. The other part feels that I should stop while I'm ahead. There is something that I am missing! The motive is starting to point in the direction of slowing the process in the fight against people losing weight. Why in God's name would any organization want people to be fat? What am I missing? Is there a pharmaceutical company that is benefitting from the growing obesity problems in this country? This is worldwide, so how could they possible coordinate so much activity, and for what gain?

Mac ran his hands through his hair and ruffled through his pockets for a smoke. Then he recalled that he stopped months ago.

Really bad timing, he thought to himself.

CHAPTER 27

I think that my education at NYU has come to an end. I don't see Dr. Gotlieb adding to this story or assisting us any further. I need to get that biodegradable transmitter back to Bill Lange. Then I need to find William Dean!

"Dr. Gotlieb, I will have someone from my department talk with you about the work Dr. Goldstein was doing. I want to apologize for interrupting the conference!" Mac stated as he turned on his heels.

"Good luck, Officer. I will write up a statement regarding Aaron's work. It will be available in a few hours. If there is anything else I can do to aid you on this case, please feel free to contact me through the school," Dr. Gotlieb explained and sunk into the desk chair and stared at the wall.

Mac exchanged numbers with the doctor and met up with Magen in the hall. Dr. Gregory was nowhere to be found. Mac was slightly surprised and a little relieved. He needed to get to a phone and set a few projects in motion.

"Where is Mr. Charming?" Mac said with a smile.

"He walked outside. He was having trouble getting reception on his phone," Magen explained.

"I really want to get out of here. We are wasting time in this place, and we don't have time to waste," Mac said with some level of seriousness.

"You are on to something, aren't you?" Magen spoke with a level of surprise.

"No, not even close. If I were you, I would be the first to know, but we need to put a few things into place," Mac emphasized.

"What about Gregory?" Magen asked with little enthusiasm, fully knowing the answer.

"We have to go. I really want you with me," Mac offered softly.

"You got me, cowboy," Magen said with a smile.

As they moved quickly down the avenue, Mac broke out his cell and called into the office. He was rolling and he knew it. Mac could feel when he was in the zone.

He knew exactly what he needed to do.

CHAPTER 28

He thought to himself how convenient it was that this guy William Dean was coming to New York, and that he didn't have to drive down to Laurel, Maryland. He really wanted to put a tail on Gregory; if this guy came up to meet with someone, who else but Gregory would he be looking to contact.

Finally, a voice came on the line.

"This is Lieutenant Robert MacDonald. I need to get in touch with Officer Steven Rodriguez," Mac barked.

There was a brief pause as the operator attempted to find Steve. Time ticked by as Mac's mind raced with all the points he needed to deal with to effectively work this case. The anxiety related his ability to position people where they needed to be was draining for him. The cutbacks in staff were constantly creating delays within the department; it was an ongoing battle.

The accountants and bureaucrats were running the department, and with the help of some greedy lawyers, it was a wonder anything was ever done. The courts were ridiculous and backed up to the point of breaking.

As his thoughts circled around the internal cancer within his department, a click came on the line.

"Steve! As fast as you can, get someone over to NYU! You are looking for a Fed by the name of Dr. Timothy Gregory. He runs about six feet, maybe two hundred on the weight. Gray suit, expensive, phone strapped to his ear. Where is Lange? I have something that he needs to look at. All right, I am on my way!" Mac said, then shut off.

"Are we heading to One Police Plaza?" Magen added as she got into the driver's seat.

"Oh, shit!" Mac roared.

"What is it?" Magen jumped.

"Gregory has the transmitter," Mac said flatly.

"No, he doesn't," Magen said with a smile as she held out her hand displaying the item.

"You da woman," Mac stated.

"You know it," she added.

CHAPTER 29

Lincoln Tunnel, New York

The wheels screeched on the Chevy as he leaned into the gas pedal, coming off the final turn of the Lincoln Tunnel. William knew the satellite capabilities that were available to his new enemy. Although the Chevy was his only means of transportation, the car stuck out like a sore thumb, and it had to go.

He glanced over to Cornell who was currently lost in his own thoughts.

They had rambled on about the events of the past few hours through most of the trip. William was not sure about Pierce's stance on the enemy not being from this world. He did realize that some of what was going on was way beyond the capability of any technology available today. The thought of extraterrestrial involvement was puzzling.

Why would an alien race come to this planet and infiltrate APL and NASA?

What would be the possible gain for a superior race to come here and act this way?

The more he wrestled with this issue, the stranger his questions became. He needed to get his mind back to the tangible realities that could be dealt with.

What I need most is to get rid of the car, he thought to himself.

The tunnel was dark and troubling; even with the artificial lighting, the Lincoln Tunnel always seemed dreary. He never considered himself claustrophobic, but he could actually feel the ugly wash over him like a molasses blanket after ten feet in that hole.

William really started to feel the panic roll in; all he wanted to do was get out of there. However, his intellect told him nothing good was on the other end of this tunnel. He needed to get downtown as soon as he got out of the hole. He had a much better chance losing the car down by the Battery or one of the warehouses off the pier.

Speed was going to help the situation immensely. This is the only advantage I have at this point, he thought to himself.

The second he hit the turn, it was balls out; that was the smart way to go. Even if they were waiting at the mouth of the tunnel, he could catch them off guard. They would need a chopper to keep up with this old pig, and even that could be a problem in downtown New York.

"Pierce, it's time to buckle up," Dean said with cool precision.

"What's going on?" Pierce snapped.

"We are about to make a leap into light speed. You may want to strap up," William Dean added.

"Oh, Lord, please bless this ugly ride and my beautiful black ass," Pierce chanted in his best preacher voice, hands lifted to the sky.

"Amen," Dean added.

In low gear, the big block didn't have the menacing sound that one might think. It was coasting now in first gear with a low hum coming from under the hood. William had the vantage point to see both sets of lights, so he could time the light just right.

The yellow light flipped on the southbound avenue.

Dean's hands were white and bloodless from the hard grip on the wheel; he pressed the clutch deep into the floor. His right foot found the gas pedal, and he began to bring the massive Detroit engine to life.

When the light changed, William sidestepped the clutch and sent the wheels screaming like Lucifer's chariot. Smoke filled the street, and New Yorkers were running in all directions. The rest of the cars in the area were frozen and stunned with the scene before them.

Finally, the already hot tires found the black top and gripped on like gunmetal magnets. The Chevy blasted forward like a bullet out of a high-powered rifle.

William was on the clutch; shifting into second, he could feel the beast respond, and it felt good to him. When he reached the end of the block, he glanced down at the speedometer and saw the needle danced past seventy.

Cornell was coming out of the initial shock of the past few seconds. His face was pasty and his eyes were wide; slowly he began to breathe, and that led to hyperventilation.

There was a feeble attempt at discussion from Cornell in between deep breaths. A yellow cab not really paying attention jumped out on the avenue.

William, fully aware that he wouldn't be able to avoid hitting the cab, braced himself for impact.

At the last moment, the cab saw the Chevy bearing down on him and jerked the wheel. The Chevy clipped the side-view mirror and both door handles, but didn't slow the momentum of the vehicle. The people on the avenue up ahead were in a panic state as they watched the ugly black car heading toward them at one hundred plus miles an hour.

It was the roar of the engine that was so out of place, even in the city that never sleeps. Dean knew that he wouldn't be able to keep this up for long without killing both Cornell and himself. As he went through the fourth intersection from the tunnel, he began to consider options.

He had just passed a subway entrance and thought that it would be a safe place to be, considering the capabilities of those tracking him. The amazing thing was that he had now covered nine full city blocks without touching the brakes. Luck was something that he would welcome with open arms, without question.

Cornell was starting to wind down, and finally was able to find his voice. "Please stop this, William," Cornell pleaded.

"Hang in there, Mr. Pierce. We are putting some real distance between us and the bad guys," Mac yelled through the adrenaline.

"Mr. Dean, I don't think these things are going to track us down," Cornell said with an easy manner.

"No, why would you say that?" William yelled over the screaming engine.

"These things are waiting for us somewhere. That's just how they think," Cornell added with the same easy manner.

"Waiting for us!" Dean said slowly.

"Oh, yeah!" Cornell said.

"Of course, they are!" William said as he eased off the gas.

The thing to do was act without purpose, William thought to himself. *Pierce was absolutely correct. It didn't matter how I was getting somewhere. It was all about where I was getting. If I run down Agent Cummings right now, they will be right there waiting for me. I will be killed, and so will anyone I come in contact with. She is going to come to me somehow. Then we can work on a plan.*

Up ahead, he could see a different subway platform, and he thought to himself, *Time to be spontaneous.*

He slammed the brake on the beast, and the top-heavy car fishtailed all over the road. When the car came to a full stop, he turned to Cornell and yelled, "Let's go. We don't have much time."

"Not much time for what, William?" Cornell asked.

"We need to fall off the grid!" Dean said with a new level of confidence.

CHAPTER 30

Fort Meade, Maryland

Cain made the left off Route 175 and pulled up to the gate at Fort Meade. The back of the limo was comfortable, even with the advanced computer system that spread through the entire length of the vehicle. Cain was able to monitor the retrieval efforts of one William Dean throughout the full Eastern Seaboard.

There were several computers designated for communications from his operatives from Laurel, Maryland, and New York. Directly to his right was something much different from any available computer in the market. This utilized a laser-based hologram system that identified the programmed humans that they had cultivated over the past seven centuries. Cain had the ability to activate several thousand individuals in Manhattan alone. He could see what they see and manipulate their responses. However, even this technology had its limitations, and Cain knew that half of New York was underground.

This is what he was doing at Fort Meade; few people were aware of the outstanding computer capability available at this institution. For the past decade, they had been putting the final touches on the world's most sophisticated space-to-planet tracking system. The component of this device that intrigued Cain the most was the infrared capabilities.

The technological genius that created this device came straight from the Laurel facility. It was pitched to Congress as a device that would be able to monitor cave activity throughout Afghanistan and

Pakistan, and possibly find the cleric bin Laden prior to his dishonorable death. They jumped all over it, and even strapped on some pork on it to boot. Of course, how could you find someone who really doesn't exist? This species is absolutely disgusting when it comes to what their leaders slam down their throats, and what they actually go for.

He recalled the last time he was here and how the security was not this aggressive. Today there were soldiers with M-16s, dogs, and barriers, most definitely a product of the post-9/11 world.

The biggest issue for Cain was that there was a line, and that was something that he simply could not tolerate.

Before he could complain about the possibility of waiting, a three-star general appeared at the gate. Cain could see some brief discussion, and then soldiers started to hop like crickets. The outgoing drive was opened, and the steel barriers were lowered into the ground. The limo eased past the gate slowly and then came to a full stop.

The limo door opened, and General Frank Nieves slid in and faced Cain.

His face was stern and chiseled; he stroked his right hand down the full length of his uniform. Cain had never met this soldier, but from the looks of him, he was anticipating some "tough guy" bullshit. Then to his astonishment, the good general began to speak with the most feminine, over-the-top gay voice that he had ever heard.

Cain was stunned and speechless.

The general made Liberace sound like John Wayne; Cain did everything he could to keep from laughing out loud.

"Mr. Cain, I received a call from the Pentagon this morning and was given strict instruction to provide you with carte blanche through the facility," General Nevins said as if welcoming him to the party.

"I know that this must seem highly irregular, but let me assure you of the necessity," Cain began and then was cut off.

"Oh, please, I welcome the distraction. I mean, really, there's a war going on, and I am wasting away in Maryland," General Frank added.

"Your cooperation will not go unnoticed, General. You are doing your part right here in Maryland," Cain stated with raw emotion as he laid his hand on top of the general's wrist.

"Thank you, Mr. Cain," the general added as he began to look at his new guest in a different light.

"Oh, well done! I commend your pains, and everyone shall share in thy gains," Cain said out loud.

"Macbeth," General Nieves offered.

"It never ceases to amaze me how soldiers love their Shakespeare, and he was such a gentle boy," Cain pondered out loud.

"All good soldiers have that same gentle boy down deep," Frank said with intended feeling.

"Well put, General," Cain stated with a simple calm as he pulled up to the communications building.

General Nieves had been so involved with the conversation that he had not noticed the level of computer hardware that was spread through the limo. He considered himself somewhat of a geek, but there were several units in the vehicle that he could not identify. He stood staring at the setup, trying to determine the function of the hologram device. He didn't want to appear over interested or suspicious of what he was seeing. However, he knew this was big; who was this guy, and why was he here?

The Pentagon doesn't throw their weight around unless there is an absolute threat to national security.

"General, I am going to need the Cyclops room for twenty minutes without interruption," Cain said as they walked up to the entrance.

"I was instructed to give you free reign of the facility. However, this is slightly more than I anticipated," General Nieves stated with a startled look.

"General, I am not here to upset you! I am here to save lives, American lives," Cain said with strong conviction.

"I understand, and I have my orders. It's just that the Cyclops room is the highest level of security on the campus," the general said with reserve.

"What can I do to make you feel at ease with the situation?" Cain added with compassion.

"I don't think there is anything. It's most likely my own paranoia," the general disclosed.

"I am not in the feelings business, General, but I need you on board, so I need to know now if this is going to be a problem," Cain pushed.

The general took all of three seconds to respond with exactly what Cain expected.

"Oh, no problem here, Mr. Cain," the general responded.

Cain turned on his heels and walked through the front door with the general in tow. Several of Cain's men were following with equipment. The room went silent as the entourage entered, seven men deep.

The front guards jumped to attention as if an automatic switch went off. The several civilians in the room started to back against the wall as the crew came through. There was a brief moment of real confusion in the hall; however, they recovered quickly.

Over the past few years, they had been on high alert on more than one occasion. The drilling and mock disasters had put them in a heightened state of awareness.

The general moved the pack of matching suits to the long hall on the left.

"The elevators can be found down the hall, on the right-hand side," the general alerted the men.

Cain and the general, along with three other men, jumped in the first elevator; the rest of the crew caught the next. Cain reached out and pressed the button marked 4B, then stepped back.

"How did you know what floor the Cyclops room was on? Have you been here before?" the general asked with a puzzled tone.

"I have been here many times over the years, General," Cain said flatly, not trying to appear to be hiding anything.

"I have been here for over a decade and have never laid eyes on you. When were you here?" he asked.

"That's classified, General, but let me assure you, I have been in this building before you arrived, and during your tenure," Cain stated.

"Do you guys know who shot Kennedy?" the general tried to make light, feeling uncomfortable.

"What makes you think he was shot at all?" Cain offered.

The general began to laugh and then stopped, realizing that nobody else was laughing. The doors opened, and Cain stepped out first, motioning to the secure area that housed the Cyclops Central Intelligence Satellite. The Cyclops is a low-orbit laser-guided satellite with infrared technology. This is the best of the best of what is available within a thousand miles of the Eastern Seaboard.

The general moved to the front of the team, removed his badge, then swiped it on the door lock. The wall slid across, displaying a computer station. The general placed his hand on the monitor pad, then his left eye was scanned. Instantly the wall split, revealing a room of military personnel and computer geeks. Two of the primary operators were in their early twenties.

Cain stepped up to the center platform and cleared his throat of two full days of smoking Camel non-filters.

"Good afternoon, everyone, my name is Cain. I know this is going to sound extremely odd, but I am going to need everyone in the room to leave for twenty-three minutes," he said evenly and with strong confidence.

"Is this some kind of joke?" Major French spoke up with a terminal look in his eyes.

"This is the least funny thing I will say today, so listen really carefully. I need twenty-three minutes," Cain returned with equal aggression.

"General, this is most irregular, and I have seen no notification from the field office ordering us to relinquish control of Cyclops," Major French stood his ground.

The general walked to the center of the room and produced a letter from his right front pocket. He announced in front of the room that the letter was from the secretary of state. He handed it to the major who took it slowly. He recognized the letterhead immediately; he had received several over the past few years and knew it was legitimate.

"Twenty-three minutes! Let's go, gentlemen," Major French managed through gritted teeth.

As they filed out the door, Cain's men took the operating positions as they had practiced their whole lives. They took to the most sophisticated technology available on the planet as if it was a Sega video game.

He placed his hand on the general and ushered him to a chair in the back. The general barely felt the needle with the neurotoxin and quickly went to sleep.

CHAPTER 31

Cain took center stage as if he was Captain Kirk of the starship *Enterprise*.

He sat facing the large screen, wringing his hands with a grin on his face that could only be described as shit eating. It took all of three minutes to position the satellite and another two to adjust the series of lenses.

It would have taken the Fort Meade team an hour to achieve this.

On the big screen, the city entrance of the Lincoln Tunnel was clearly displayed. Not only were the vehicles identifiable, but also, the infrared imaging allowed the viewer the ability to distinguish the number of passengers.

"Okay, let's back it up. I need a little wider angle," Cain requested.

"Yes, sir," echoed one of the minions.

"A few more seconds, and there, out of the tunnel. Eyes open!" Cain blasted.

"Black Chevy, inside lane, forty-seven degrees," announced one of Cain's men with little to no emotion at all.

"Showtime," Cain exalted to the odd looks of the others.

"I can hack into the street surveillance camera system and monitor the vehicle's movement throughout the city," stated one of the visitors.

"That will not be necessary," Cain returned.

"I don't understand," responded the confused visitor.

"They will not be in the car long enough for that to be of any real significance," Cain returned.

"How could you possibly know that?" asked the youngest of the visitors.

Cain stared briefly at the young one, not with evil intent but just enough to make him uncomfortable.

Just then the black Chevy jumped off the corner, spilling smoke all over the street. The men turned to look at Cain who was smiling ear to ear.

It was quite important that Cain had requested the wide angle on the satellite; a tight view could have been problematic with all the smoke.

They watched as the Chevy blindly flew down the avenue. The heat from the vehicle and the smoke made the infrared useless. All Cain could do was to watch the events unfold before his eyes. He fished into his blazer pocket and removed an unfiltered smoke, stuck it in his mouth, and lit it.

He pulled deep on the smoke then requested that the room smoke detector be disengaged. The black car was moving at a high rate of speed when another yellow vehicle jumped out on the avenue.

There was a minor collision, and the men at the operating positions turned to Cain for direction.

"I hate those fuckin' cabs!" Cain said as he shrugged his shoulders.

Cain stood up and stepped on the butt of the smoke; he glanced at the screen then looked over at one of the men who had been guarding the door.

"Let's set it up!" he said with authority.

The bigger of the two men placed a stainless steel case on the table. He then drilled through the combination and stepped back as the plasma hologram began to take shape.

Light began to dance around the room, and it was difficult to watch the center of the device. The clarity of the light was intoxicating, but not to the visitors in the room. Other than Cain, the others stayed focused on the Chevy flying down the avenue.

"He must be doing a buck twenty down Ninth Avenue. That's just not right!" Cain said with a hint of respect in his tone.

Cain put on some dark glasses, glanced at the big board, then held his hand toward the device. He was immediately bathed with a blue light that covered him from head to toe. The light seemed to have a purpose and direction, giving it the indication of intelligence.

Cain seemed to be drawn in to the light as if there was a union of the two emerging. He was breathing heavily and seemed euphoric, but the smile never left his face. The connection between Cain and the sphere of energy had created a dual mind or level of consciousness.

Cain now had the ability to reach the other visitors and the humans who had been cultivated by seed implants. He could drill down to anywhere in the world and connect with the minds of both his species and those infected. He locked into a young black man named Derrick Simms who was working for Verizon, nineteen feet above the ground, manipulating cable wire.

The bucket was unsteady, but Cain's eyes focused just in time to see the black Chevy blast through the intersection. He could see people running and screaming and the roar of the Detroit engine. He had merged out several times, but it was always strange when he materialized on the other side.

Cain reached down and touched his jacket; he could taste the breakfast burrito from McDonald's that he finished forty minutes ago, and yet his new body was back in the Cyclops room.

He looked back up in time to see the Chevy lock up its brakes. The vehicle fishtailed from one side of the street to the other; the driver worked the wheel like a master, and Cain was impressed.

"Soaring high above the breezes, going anywhere she pleases," Cain began to sing as he lowered the bucket.

The vehicle came to a full stop, and two men leaped from the car and bolted toward the subway.

Cain's extension was more than a thousand yards away from the subway entrance; this was inadequate. He needed to slide out but was having issues finding a proper host.

He was able to find a visitor and initiate connection.

Jimmy Ling was mixing shrimp and garlic sauce when he felt the connection begin to take over. The rest of the thought process was Cain pushing the change and liking it.

Jimmy was still there, but it was Cain's eyes that now scanned the room.

As he stood in front of the burner, his vision intensified as well as the rest of his senses. He leaped the counter without effort and then made the motion to leap through the large plate glass window.

He thought, *Only in the Big Apple could I get away with this!*

He stopped himself, and that was significant in the transformed state; control was most difficult.

Cain knew that he was in full violation of all planetary protocol and that some explaining would be forthcoming. The majority of the human race was extremely comfortable with the concept that they were alone, safe, and isolated in the universe. Cain recalled his early teachings as a young offspring regarding the reasoning behind any host planet involvement.

He knew the proper procedure and the reason why policies were diligently protected. However, there was a part of him that wanted to wake the human race up. Cain had made several trips over the centuries and had really strong feelings for the inhabitance of this planet. This was a place of amazing wonder and terrifying irony. He had helped shape this world and had gained high prestige among the council of his planet.

Many thought of him as slightly unstable and partly infected by the emotional instability that was an overwhelming side effect of this planet. Fortunately, several of the primaries of the council knew of his sacrifice and what he has been able to achieve on this planet. The contribution that he had secured over the years has provided nourishment to generations of his kind. Several planets had started high development over the past few decades, and now the troubles here on Earth were creating questions.

There is great pride taken by the council in the harvester's ability to stay undetected. It was that final thought that froze him right before he hit the plate glass window. Cain took a deep breath and looked out the window in time to see William Dean and a black man running for the subway entrance. Cain was finished with Jimmy and quickly slid to the only available seed that was within range at the station.

Jimmy fell to one knee and let a good part of his breakfast cover the plate window. Fully transformed back to human form, Jimmy wiped his mouth and looked over his shoulder at his two coworkers. Their eyes were full of fear and total amazement. Jimmy smiled, showing a row of broken, mashed teeth, much less threatening than seconds ago.

"If you never ask, I will never have to tell you!" Jimmy said in flawless Cantonese, then walked out the door. The two cooks went back to work without a word between them.

CHAPTER 32

Molly Kleinberg took the subway early Friday morning for the past twenty-seven years for a sit-down breakfast with her daughter. She loved the independence that so many of her friends no longer had. Molly would leave her apartment in Kew Gardens, Queens, and make the change at Jamaica for Manhattan.

Her daughter, Lauren, always offered to pick her mother up; the gesture was always declined. However, whenever she discussed her day, the conversation would start with "She made me take the train again," in her best *victimese*.

Molly, now seventy-nine years of age, kept up relatively good health and enjoyed her weekly visits.

Her daughter, on the other hand, called the visits the weekly terror session.

Nothing Lauren did was ever good enough for her mother. Her children were damaged, and the restaurants she chose were always inadequate. This might sound like a horrible situation to most, but it worked for them. Molly had just turned the page of the *Reader's Digest* when she found herself rolling up the little magazine and grinding her teeth to the point that her bottom plate snapped.

Oh my, Molly thought as she leaped at the black man running through the subway doors.

Cain slid in the nearest seed closest to the direction where William Dean was moving. When Cain reached total awareness within Molly's body, he struggled with both vision and balance.

He initially wasn't aware that he had landed in the body of a near eighty-year-old human female. She was not capable of reaching Dean as he came through the door. Fortunately, she was able to spring out of her bench seat and latch on to the right leg of the black man who was running with him, digging her teeth into the muscle of his right leg.

Molly wouldn't be able put up much of a fight with her teeth, seeing as how they had been gone for the past seven years. The bottom dental plate that had just snapped was now protruding out of Molly's neck, and blood was running out of both the mouth and nose.

The black man who was now immobilized turned and looked straight into Cain's eyes.

Cain saw absolute terror in those eyes, and it only motivated him to dig in deeper.

One of the positives that Cain noted was long, thin fingers and nails on the human female that he was now digging deep into the skin of the aging black man. Cain could feel muscles snapping in the back of the female, and he knew it wouldn't be long before he would have to slide out and find another host.

As the flailing man started to focus his kicks on the top of the woman's head, Cain utilized all of her available strength on defense. All at once the female's body was jerked off the screaming man; through the bloodied hair, he could see William Dean.

He had grabbed tightly and ripped her from the floor and off Cornell.

Cain could see William Dean ball up his fist and land it hard on the bridge of the human female's nose. There was shock wave back at the Cyclops room, and Cain was thrown five feet across the floor. Cain, shaken and severely disorientated, managed to bust out a hearty laugh.

"Now that will wake you up in the morning," Cain cried out in his own voice from the floor.

Cain crawled from the floor and braced himself against one of the monitor boards. The crew at the boards didn't seem too concerned about their leader. The younger member felt it was necessary to remind Cain that the system has a fail-safe and if there were ever a loss of consciousness of the seeds, there would be an instant rejection.

"Yeah, I remember that was an issue. When do you think we can get around to fixing that?" Cain said with some mild cynicism.

"It's a fail-safe system, sir. If it didn't initiate reject protocol, you would be extinguished," the young one added with some nervousness in his voice.

"How long until we can reboot? I need to get back out there," Cain added with authority.

"I can have you ready in several seconds. However, you will require a living host," stated the larger member who was frantically working on the system.

"Last known coordinates, I need them up on the board," Cain belted out.

"They have left the train and have entered the underground system. We are unable to track by conventional means," responded the visitor on the primary board.

"What about the blood trail?" Cain snapped back and waited through the pause.

"The Cyclops attempt has failed. There is only limited penetration from the device, and they have exceeded depth capacity," responded the primary.

"Well, that's a wrap! Our time here is up, and we need to regroup at city office," Cain said with indifference.

Cain's consciousness returned to his new body, and as he stood up, there was a feeling of something off. Cain reached his hand to his face and wiped a droplet of blood from the corner of his mouth.

He stared at it for a few seconds and then turned to the younger team member and said, "There seems to be several changes to the seed collector that I am not aware of. Please find the time to brief me!" Cain stated.

"Yes, sir!" the member stated.

CHAPTER 33

New York Subway

William Dean was huffing and puffing by the time he and Cornell hit the bottom of the stairs. There were hundreds of people coming and going, and they really were not concerned about two men running. Only New York.

Cornell stopped Dean and made him slow down to take a rest. He also started to put money together for the subway in order to get through the gate without any difficulty. They kept up a pretty good pace and hit the platform just in time to catch an incoming tube heading uptown.

Dean was through the double doors first, and his eyes quickly scanned the crowd, looking for anything that didn't look right. Cornell was right behind him talking about the direction they were going and why, then the screaming started and all hell broke loose.

Dean turned to see an old woman, her face full of blood, raking her hands around Cornell's neck. Cornell was able to break the hold; unfortunately, she had now dug her long nails into his calf muscle. Initially, he was caught off guard and terrified by what he was seeing. Then it dawned on him that this was "them" getting closer. Dean jumped on the old woman, grabbed her by her hair, and laid her out with a bone-crushing punch from his free right hand.

Silence filled the subway.

He could feel his knuckles crashing through her brittle cheekbone. He could also feel all life leave her body, and that it was time to run.

"Cornell, it's time to move!" William shouted.

"Are you kidding? Half of my leg has been ripped off," Cornell snapped back with extreme panic in his voice.

William took off his belt and cut a piece of T-shirt from under his coat jacket, then made a makeshift field dressing. He was able to get Cornell to his feet, but the wound was really bad, and it needed attention. William knew that forward progression was the only thing that would save them; staying put was a critical mistake.

The sophistication that these people were capable of was astounding. William thought of the old woman in the train as they moved down the platform.

There was something in her eyes that was haunting to him.

There was a total absence of self; it was as if she was possessed. Who would be able to reach into the mind of a random person and turn them into that zombie that he just destroyed. This was so far above what he was ready for; at his age, it was ridiculous. He should be painting the sail house down in Annapolis, not running through the shitty subways of Manhattan.

William carried Cornell for at least a thousand yards before Cornell let out a scream that told the tale. William picked up his friend and made for the service stairs that fed back out on the avenue.

Cornell pleaded for his new friend to stop and put him down; every movement was causing unbelievable pain.

"Four blocks from here is St. Vincent's Hospital. We can make it," William pleaded.

"Not a chance! Leave me here and get the hell out of here," Cornell begged his partner.

"I can't do that," William said in a harsh tone.

"I am done, Bill. Please forgive me, but you have to go now," Cornell roared through gritted teeth.

William Dean once carried a man for sixteen miles across a frozen Korean wasteland; now he couldn't make four blocks, and what made it worse was that he was responsible for Cornell being here in the first place.

He was in such turmoil about this situation that he stood above Cornell, weeping tears on his bloody leg.

"Cornell, I am so sorry that I dragged you into this. It was just that I was so damn scared, I was rolling without a plan," William said as he sought forgiveness.

"Enough! You need to get moving. This is only the beginning, Mr. Dean. Thank you for letting me in. I always knew they were damn aliens," Cornell said with a slight smile.

"I can get a car and come back!" Dean ranted with a high level of desperation.

"I will be fine! Now please get the hell out of here," Cornell pleaded.

William Dean took one last look at Cornell and started a fast walk down the block. The pit in his stomach was screaming from both hunger and what had transpired with his friend.

The Central Intelligence Agency had several drop spots in Manhattan; six blocks down and two over was one of them. He knew that he could arrange an audience if he could make the time parameter at the Slaughtered Lamb Pub on Fourth Street.

He took a second to bare a slight smile at the thought that he was heading to a place called Slaughtered Lamb.

The CIA was always trying to emphasize that they had a sense of humor. Having a long history of being just a bit too intense, they took every opportunity to show the lighter side.

William struggled with the concept that the people he was running to might be compromised as well. He had no idea how deep the deception ran. The only thing that was for certain at this point was that he needed help.

The second focus that was running through his mind was how he was going to present this to an agent, who, most likely, was listening to the name William Dean for the past twenty-four hours.

What was he going to say to this man that wouldn't sound like absolute insanity?

Every government agency on the planet must be seeking him out. He needed to find out what was being said before he put himself in harm's way.

William caught sight of a pay phone and fished in his pockets for change. He dialed the home office of the New York Federal Bureau of Investigation. An automated voice came on, initially giving him directions on how to navigate the system.

After a few seconds, a female voice came on the phone.

"Hello, you have reached the science department. How can I direct your call?"

"Tom Kenna, please," William asked.

"One moment, please, who's calling?"

"This is his brother Michael."

"Transferring you now," the voice trailed off.

"Tom Kenna, how can I help you?"

"Tom, whatever you do, don't say my name out loud," William Dean pleaded.

"Who is this?" he demanded.

"I played wide receiver at Annapolis in '71," William hinted.

"Oh, that receiver. Martin, where are you?" Tom snapped with new focus.

"I need to know how hot I am," William asked.

"My friend, you're Elvis hot. There are rumors flying that you have sold out to the Hongs," Tom said with an air of disbelief.

"Some really bad people are doing a job on me," William started then was cut off.

"I think I met one of the BPs at 0600. I was given a poly first thing this morning regarding any dealings I had with you," Tom went on.

"Why are they connecting me with the Chinese?" William asked, seeming confused.

"The whole thing is total bullshit, and everyone knows it. What have you gotten into?" Tom inquired, trying to be careful to not change the tone of his voice.

"Do you think it is safe to connect with the Central Intel?" William asked, half knowing the answer.

"That would be a big no, my friend. Most likely fatal at this point of the game. Friends are few and far between," Tom continued in the same monotone voice.

"Recommendations," William snapped.

"Leave New York ASAP, if not sooner," Tom pleaded.

"You don't know what it took to get here. Leaving is not a viable option," William stated as if a line in the sand had been drawn.

"There is a female agent working a subway killing right here in New York. She put out a blanket e-mail hoping to connect with you. Her name is Magen Cummings. Don't know her. What I have heard is hot but crazy. She works for that prick Tim Gregory out of Virginia. I think you know him," Tom went on.

"How can I find them?" William asked.

"Well, I think that should be easy. They are looking for you. All you have to do is get caught," Tom said with ease.

"Is she working with the locals?" William asked, grasping at straws.

"Yes! They have been on the news. Mostly him, concerning the subway killing. He's Lieutenant something. You need to get to a TV. It's almost noon," Tom trailed off.

He hung up the phone, scanned the full length of the block then continued on his mission to reach the Slaughtered Lamb.

He needed to find this woman.

His friend pointed him in the direction of the noon news. He realized that he was real hot out here, and most likely the noon news was going to confirm that.

William pulled some cash out of his pocket and walked up to a brim and shade vendor. He purchased a knockoff pair of Oakleys and a Yankee cap. He knew that he looked absolutely ridiculous, but for some strange reason, he didn't draw that much attention in the village.

As he entered the Slaughtered Lamb, a high-pitched wail lit both of his years. One of the props howled like a wolf, and he jumped out of his skin. A young magnificent girl, whose breasts defied gravity, greeted him with perfect white teeth glowing like Christmas lights. He declined the table and motioned to the long bar where sat three or four small gatherings of office coworkers.

The news started with Mayor Bloomberg talking about Veterans Day, much hand shaking and penis kissing from the top pimp of New York. Then it came; William and Cornell in a series of photos from the past two years. Some of the photos were doctored, creating the illusion that their relationship was up close and personal. The caption that ran at the bottom of the screen was GAY LOVE TRIANGLE LEADS TO MURDER.

William listened closely to the story that the PR rep was rolling out. Alexander Cain was the name of the designated speaker. There was something about him that was really familiar, and a very uncomfortable chill ran straight down his back.

CHAPTER 34

It was the eyes! William thought to himself.

He remembered those eyes somewhere back when he was a kid. He also realized that he looked into those eyes twenty minutes ago when he pulled the deranged old woman off Cornell.

This is the enemy, he thought to himself with the feeling of both fear and relief.

At least he now could put a face on the evil that had destroyed his life within three hours.

William sat watching the overhead flat screen as people he knew were interviewed. William caught eye of the bartender as she surfed by the crowd.

"Hi! What can I get you?" she said.

"I would like two fingers of the MacCallens, no ice, please," Mr. Dean requested with some degree of proficiency.

"Coming right up, sir," shot the young, perky girl.

William scanned the room, trying to make sense of things. His scotch was taking the edge off the day. Knocking back twelve-year scotch on an empty stomach was unadvisable, but effective. He had to admit to himself that the story and the cover was genius. At first, he didn't understand the homosexual reference. Then he began to see the clarity of the move; people really love drama. It's prime-time soap opera right smack in the middle of the afternoon news. People will buy this hook, line, and sinker.

Their mouths will drop to the floor; they will shake their heads. Some will feel validated by the thought of homosexuals involved in such tasteless behavior. The reality is that this is what we have come to expect; who knew it would come to this? The youngster on the television continued to say the words "homosexual" and "love triangle"; it cut deep into his soul. It was about self-respect, and it meant something; to think that people he loved were hearing this.

He never had an issue with gay people, and actually was so proud of some of his friends who had come out. So, he felt slightly guilty to be angry with this young accuser. The man Cain continued to spin his story with such passion that William was slightly impressed with his lying ability. If this were being said about someone else, he would fall for it also. There was a moment of hopelessness that rolled through William's head, a rare occurrence.

The gripping fear was rolling around in his head, and there seemed to be no real way out of his present situation. He needed to get help for Cornell; he should have made the call from the pay phone.

His thinking process was off its mark. His best bet was to borrow a cell phone from one of the patrons.

Scanning the people at the bar, he caught sight of an older gentleman standing alone, enjoying the afternoon constitutional. He looked to be that perfect individual who wouldn't mind lending his phone for some alcohol-soaked conversation. William placed his glass on the table and was about to make the move when he saw her.

She was magnificent and glided like a goddess through the Lamb. Her hair was dark like the wings of a raven, and it flowed with her every move.

William felt all the anxiety and fear drip out of his body. He thought to himself, *It is amazing what a beautiful woman could do to a man.*

As she moved in, he noticed the tone of her skin and how absolutely perfect it was. She was all Italian, mostly Sicilian, and her dark eyes could start and stop world wars on a dime. She saw him staring and she smiled, and that was it; William would gladly sell his soul to hold that smile in place. She was in her midforties, but her breasts would still be the envy of any college-age female.

Then William realized she was coming toward him.

He was so overcome by her that he only now realized how out of place she was in the Slaughtered Lamb. The only thing he could do was to act cool and hope she didn't notice his worship face.

"William Dean! My name is Phyllis Capaso. I am the Manhattan field supervisor for the National Security Agency," a voice from the angel at his right side proclaimed.

"NSA, what are you people doing here?" William responded with shock and dismay.

"We actually have been watching you and Mr. Pierce from space," responded the beautiful woman with a slight giggle.

"From space? Do you mean by satellite?" William shot back with some agitation growing in his voice.

"At 1800 hours, NASA was ordered to shift the *Magellan* freedom satellite from Eastern Europe right down Interstate 95. That is within the borders of the United States of America, and that is our sandbox. The first question I have for you is what have you done to upset these bad people? The second question is who are these bad people that have the ability to manipulate this country's highest level of security and are involved with this?" Phyllis probed.

"I take it that you know who I am, and who I work for," William began to explain.

"William Dean, director of operations, APL, Laurel, Maryland. I have an extensive file on you," Phyllis stated.

"What would you say if I told you that there is an internal group within the APL complex with ties to NASA, Army, and Air Force, and did I mention they are powerful?" William said in a matter-of-fact manner.

"It would make sense, but still very scary. Who runs the show?" she asked quickly.

"No idea, but there is a connection to Johns Hopkins," he added.

"The hospital," she added with surprise.

"I know how all this must sound to you. I am struggling with the facts and motivations," William said in an apologetic tone.

"Where is Mr. Pierce?" Phyllis requested.

"He's close by, and he needs immediate medical care. He was attacked by a senior citizen two hours ago on the subway," William began to explain and then was cut off.

"A senior citizen attacked you on the subway. Is that what you are telling me?" the field agent snapped.

"I know this must sound crazy. She possessed abnormal strength and was clearly fixated on causing damage or slowing forward progression," William said as he attempted to explain.

"I have a car ready to roll outside. I wouldn't trust this to the local authorities," Phyllis explained.

"Let's move!" William stated.

CHAPTER 35

Second Avenue Subway Entrance Side Alley

Cornell lay in the alley half covering his body with newspaper, trying not to think of the growing pain. He considered making a move out of the alley, but fear kept him from taking that leap. The blood loss had not stopped completely, but William did a real good job on it. He was worried about his friend and knew that his path was dangerous, and that trouble was closing in on his heels.

The ground was cold and damp from the night; not much sun was able to reach back into the alley. He could hear people walking and talking; cars and trucks were on the move. Then he heard brakes lock up; there was a delay, and then a car door opened and closed.

Slowly, footsteps were heading in his direction; he thought it was a good thing that the feet were not running. Through hazy eyes, he saw sandals and black pants; as his eyes moved up, he could see an Indian gentleman with a friendly smile.

"Good morning, Mr. Pierce, my name is Alfred Balbo. It is my great pleasure," announced the middle-aged Sikh.

"How do you know who I am?" Cornell said with some resistance.

"I have been summoned to retrieve you and care for your wounds, my good sir," Alfred proclaimed.

"Mr. Dean came through, knew it," Cornell said through foggy eyes.

"Again, it is my great pleasure," responded Alfred as he looped his arm around the injured man and picked him up like a child.

Cornell grimaced in pain but happy to be leaving. He gazed at the face of his savior and noticed the turban and the red dot on the forehead; he knew the dot was known as the pottu or the third eye. The turban indicated that he was a man of respect; his turban was utilized to hide the hair that was a gift from God and should never be cut. It was wrapped around his head in a spiral form, held in place by the well-designed turban.

Cornell leaned off the chest of the man to see the direction they were heading as they cleared the alley. A yellow cab sat in the middle of the avenue, still running. The big man opened the back door and then with real gentleness placed Cornell in the back seat of the cab, and off they went.

He was fading in and out.

He took his last bit of strength lifting his right arm to the back of the seat to see and held his hand to the glass. "Thank you for coming for me."

The man at the wheel said nothing.

Cornell made a feeble attempt to get the driver's attention and then fully lost consciousness and slid to the back of the cab, wondering if his friend was safe.

CHAPTER 36

One Police Plaza, New York

Bill Lange was waiting in the interrogation room with sweaty palms when Mac and Magen rolled in. Mac had called ahead and informed Bill that he possessed a transmitter that could be the most advanced piece of equipment he had ever come across. That was enough to send Bill over the edge. He ran down to the office without blinking. The film that the lieutenant produced yesterday had his mind wheeling; if this were even close to that level of advancement, he would not be able to stay away.

He had spent the last thirteen hours reviewing that piece of film that Mac sprang on him.

The Road Runner, what was that about? he thought.

What was the connection or message that was being sent?

Or was it just a gag?

The character itself was known for its sheer elusiveness. Was that the statement being made here? That they were impossible to catch, and we were similar to that coyote who never wins?

It was a stretch, but it had a ring of flair, and maybe that's a starting point.

They thought themselves an organization with unbelievable tech sophistication, that they felt an air of superiority. Why else would they plant that distortion in the film that they knew we would monitor at some point?

It was meant to be seen.

As Bill sat there scrambling these theories through his head, he knew that he was reaching. However, Bill realized that none of this made total sense.

Mac and the blonde could possibly fill in the blanks.

It was at that moment that both Mac and Magen came through the side door. Bill Lange jumped from the fake leather chair like a schoolboy excited about a new program. His palms were sweating, and his eyes were fixed and dilated; he was high on the possibilities of what was happening.

"Finally, I have been sitting here for the past thirty-seven minutes. What could be more important than what you have in your possession?" Bill exalted.

"Bill, I take it that you have been waiting for this little puppy here," Mac reveled as he handed Bill the transistor device.

"Holy mother! I think it has silicone and aluminum properties, but I need to take it to the appropriate lab for analysis. I can run up to MIT and break it down in forty minutes. What do you say, Mac?" Bill Lange begged.

"I place this in your hands, Mr. Lange. I need answers as soon as humanly possible."

The rest of what Mac was saying trailed off as Bill bolted for the door, fully caught up with his new toy.

"Do you think Bill is excited?" Mac said to Magen.

Magen turned with a smile and laughed slightly as Mac continued down the hall. They needed to follow up with their superiors and work out the probabilities of just where William Dean would be heading.

The smart money was on familiar faces here in New York.

Dean must know two thousand people in this city, she guessed. However, he was not the type to endanger anyone for his own skin; he was a full-blown Boy Scout. He would look to place himself somewhere away from the people he cares about.

The line of thinking was considering that he was still alive and still running. He has some really bad enemies rolling down his back.

The more she thought of the probabilities, the more she feared for William Dean. If he was still on the run, then he is truly lucky.

As these thoughts raced through her head, she reached into her bag and pulled out her iPhone. There were six messages left on her phone, all from Gregory; she had turned off the ringer and forgot to reengage it.

"Shit," she said out loud. She quickly fumbled with the device and was able to connect with Dr. Gregory who was furious and was having difficulty containing his anger. Magen did her best to explain what had happened but was cut off in the middle of her sentence.

"Enough! William Dean made a phone call to a college friend twenty-seven minutes ago. He was en route to the CIA tipping house known as the Slaughtered Lamb on Fourth," Gregory belted out with a high degree of tension.

"Is there anyone en route to intercept Mr. Dean?" Magen requested.

There was a momentary pause on the line as Gregory placed his hand over the phone and barked instruction at someone in his office.

"I have two agents at the facility and three others combing the area. No sign of subject," Gregory stated.

"There is a second individual named Pierce who is currently with Dean. Was there any sign of him?" Magen asked.

"Nothing coming back from those on the scene. I really think you need to get involved with the area sweep. The car was located several blocks away right next to a subway entrance. However, we clock him making the call two blocks from the car. This could mean one of two things regarding his behavior. First, he never went into the subway, or he jumped off at the first stop. There is something else that you need to know. There was a woman murdered on the G train that passed through that area at the time in question. The intel that is being acquired indicates that William Dean may be the killer," Gregory went on with the details at a pace that was similar to a hummingbird on meth.

"I am rolling out the door. Can you send me everything that you have on the data I have missed?" Magen requested.

"Downloading to you now. I am also sending you a file on all old contacts that we have been able to identify," Gregory disclosed and hung up the phone.

Magen threw her phone into the bag and turned down the hall. She needed to grab Mac and get downtown. Her heels were really loud as she boogied down the corridor.

Dean was still alive and right here in New York; it was time to get in this game. Dean was the key; he knew something, and they were hunting him down.

They had to get a hold on him before he disappeared, or worse.

This was as close to any form of break on this case. This whole killing story is not even close to what is considered a possibility. It must be a dummy story released by the bad guys to aid in the pursuit of Dean's capture. Dean really doesn't have much time before something bad happens.

I have to put my hands on him soon, or this case is going to slip into the abyss of no return. I would have to start all over again from the beginning, and I am not ready to go backwards. Mac had no idea what was going on out there, but there really wasn't time for a briefing. He would have to be informed on the way. *Where the hell had that man disappeared to?*

These were the thoughts that raced through Magen's head as she went room to room looking for Mac.

Mac slowly removed his Serengeti sunglasses, and his jaw was slowly creeping south.

"William Dean is wanted for the murder of an old woman from Queens," he said with immense confusion.

"There was a boatload of eyewitnesses that identified him from the photos that we have circulated," Corporal Cleg from communications began to explain.

"This makes no sense at all," Mac exhaled, running his hands through his hair.

"Apparently there was a violent struggle between the woman and Pierce. Several of the witnesses identified Dean kicking the woman several times in the face, killing her," the corporal continued.

"All I hear about this guy is extreme Boy Scout. We're not getting the full story," Mac stated.

"There were two blood types taken from the scene. We are running it to APL to identify if it's a match for Pierce," the corporal went on.

"This is crazy. William Dean didn't stomp an old lady from Queens to her death on the C train. It just doesn't happen like that," Mac expelled, shaking his head.

"There is one other thing that was picked up during initial interrogation of the witnesses," Cleg revealed.

"What would that be?" Mac snapped.

"A young attorney from Malverne, Long Island, stated that Pierce was unable to move on his own accord, and that Dean needed to carry him from that point on," Cleg concluded.

"Well, that would really slow down the progression," Mac said out loud.

Cleg turned on his heels and slowly paced toward the door. Before he could reach out his hand, the door busted open and Magen stood there, wide-eyed and hyperventilating. She wanted to leave immediately and really didn't want to get into any conversation regarding the new developments. It was at that moment that Mac realized that she was fully briefed by her own people and her intel was most likely superior to his own.

Mac stood up, grabbed his coat, and walked past Cleg as he joined Magen out in the hall. She was moving fast and really motivated, he thought, to initiate some dialogue, but her eyes stopped him cold. She was on to something, and time was of the essence.

"Let's take my car," Mac suggested.

"William Dean made contact with a college friend a little while ago, and he was en route to a pub known as the Slaughtered Lamb. This is a well-known CIA point house, and we now know that he was at the building less than ten minutes ago," Magen stated with real tension in her voice.

"How the hell do you know all of this?" Mac snapped.

Magen pulled the hair from her face to reveal a transmitter in her ear. "I have been receiving live feed from one of the agents on the scene who has been conducting interviews with some of the patrons," Magen explained.

"How the hell do I get one of those toys, and where are we going?" Mac added with a sense of giddiness in his voice.

"NYPD budget does not cover these toys, and we are moving toward the Slaughtered Lamb in hopes that something develops," Magen continued as she intensified her pace.

"You have someone in the building now, and there is no sign of Dean, so why are we heading in that direction?" Mac questioned the logic.

"One of the patrons at the Lamb stated that Dean was escorted out of the building by a middle-aged female that was dressed to the nines," Magen announced.

"Wow, the plot thickens, and there must be a reason why we are not feeding that information to every police officer in the city," he said with obvious sarcasm.

"I am pretty sure I know who picked him up. There will be no reason to put out an APB, but maybe a shoot-on-sight order," Magen added with a hint of evil.

"Hey, I know that tone. Could it be that you don't like this lady?" Mac said with a smile.

"Her name is Phyllis Capaso. She works for an internal structure of the National Security Administration, and we do have a slight history," Magen said bluntly.

"Now you really have me rolling. Who is the honey?" Mac said with a hard smile.

"Honey she's not, and she has a terrible habit of getting in the middle of my investigations," Magen echoed with a hint of intense bitterness.

"Magen, I am getting the feeling that you may have issues playing with others," Mac said in a joking manner, but regretted it the moment the words came out of his mouth.

Magen rolled her eyes in Mac's direction, shooting him a look that made him feel extremely vulnerable. He quickly turned away, really not wishing to see that side of her. Magen thought about the long-term issues that she had with Phyllis over the years. She really didn't want to drive a wedge between Mac and herself over the anger she felt for Phyllis.

Magen took a deep breath and put on her best smile as they both got into her car. She turned to Mac and started to unravel the tale of their history.

Phyllis made her look really stupid a few years back when she was getting close to Dr. Mazza. From what she learned later, Phyllis had picked up on the fact that the FBI was about to move on Robert Mazza's old house, and the NSA swooped in and snatched him. Of course, she fully denied any underhanded activity and stated that Magen's deductive reasoning was faulty and amateurish. It wasn't long after that, the company cell phone she was using turned up compromised during a random sweep. Again, full denial from the NSA, but it was obvious to everyone involved that the only agency with probability and gain potential would have been the NSA. There have also been several interceptions of documents, all related to this current case.

"I have feelers out to several agencies throughout the world. They send me files and new cases that flag for common trends like obesity, animal mutilations, and other bizarre incidents. One of my contacts called me last year and confided in me that he was approached by Phyllis to copy anything that was being sent. He was paid an awful lot of money for the copies. I can imagine that she most likely has been shadowing my total investigation, possibly under orders, but it could be her own private investigation. Most likely she has caught wind of the investigation and thinks there could be something there.

"It really sucks when you spend years making a case where there was nothing and then find someone is rolling up your ass, looking to benefit off your hard work," Magen said with deep feeling.

"The more I learn about the government that has been watching out for my best interest, the deeper I fall into a state of full-blown depression," Mac added with a smirk.

"I am sure that within your agency, there are deceptions and scenarios that go all the way to the top," Magen stated.

"You are most likely right about that, but power will and always has corrupted the greedy," Mac added, attempting to be comfortable with the conversation.

"That is quite profound of you, Robert. Are you trying to make me feel better?" Magen added with a slight smile.

"I hope that later we can work on that 'feeling good' possibility, but I have an idea about intercepting William Dean," Mac added off the cuff.

"Now you have jolted my interest on two levels. Please let me in!" she said with a sexy smile.

"Let's turn the tables on Phyllis and her hot self. True that New York is a big town, but it's my town. This woman would not be able to just stay in any old dwelling. My guess is she is in one of three hotels that would be acceptable for a woman who requires the finer things in life," Mac stated his deductive theory.

"I can't even tell you how high your stocks just went up. If this pans out, you might have just secured yourself a happy ending tonight," Magen whispered in her sexiest voice.

Mac smiled as he reached in his pocket for his cell phone. If there was one thing he could do better than anyone else, it would be to find someone. Being a cop in New York was hard and sometimes extremely stressful. However, there were fringe benefits. New Yorkers, with all their complaining and whining, knew that their ass was grass without a superior police department. They look out for the law in this town, and Mac has had almost two decades of making connections with the inner motor of this city.

In this city, the doormen at the five stars are masters of the information game. They can and do get their hands on anything and everything at the drop of a dime. They network within their own little circle; what one knows, the others know.

If she was the kind of woman that Magen described, then she could only be in a handful of locations. Unbridled vanity could only be satisfied in one of the house's endless fantasies, and if this was the path she took, then she's mine.

As Magen listened to the ongoing dialogue that was taking place between several agents in the field, she thought about the connection that had developed between Mac and herself. He was really a good man, and they seemed to be in short supply as of late. Magen thought of the sex last night and smiled. She was not a stranger to the touch of a man, not to say that she was a whore or anything, but it was good between them. They were in tune, and maybe both slightly fearful of each other, and that felt good. There were no lies between them; there really wasn't a need for that.

No representatives were necessary; they were able to be themselves, and it was so peaceful and beautiful. This case has been consuming for every aspect of her life, and the loss of her husband is always close in her subconscious mind. It made her feel good that she still had that part of her love that she could still share.

She stopped herself midsentence because she knew where the thought process was going. Magen felt herself asking the questions about the end of the case and what will she do. However, she knew that she needed to stay in the here and now. Magen knew that she had a tendency to overanalyze her relationships. This time the best practice was to take it as it comes, and not to get caught up with the what-ifs.

CHAPTER 37

Some days I look at a girl and think, *Wow, I sure would like to date her.* Other times I wonder how her head would look on a stick.

—Some random American serial killer

Brooklyn Navy Yard

Cornell slowly opened his left eye; it was damp and cold with deep seething darkness. He was able to slowly make out some objects in the dark. There were engines, huge copper-laced carbine engines maybe twenty feet high. They had long been abandoned as were the rest of the buildings in the area.

He kept as quiet as possible in hopes that he might hear something out there in the darkness. There was something out there, maybe twenty or thirty yards past the window that was slightly open, and that was forty feet away from where he was lying.

Something was rocking; it had to be water.

Pierce shifted his leg, anticipating sharp pain to roll up his flank. He was really surprised to find that his leg had been attended to in the most professional manner. He must have been given a local anesthetic because he felt no pain at all. His hands were bound, and he was attached to a recoiling cable that provided him with one meter of mobility.

Cornell slowly elevated himself to a chair that had been placed there purposely. He initiated a body inventory and quickly found two puncture marks at the fold of his right arm. He didn't know if he had been drugged or if possibly something else had been injected into him. The dampness was uncomfortable, and although his leg felt better, the old building made him nervous. He was always uncomfortable in old buildings.

He had grown up on Monument Street in Baltimore; there were old buildings wherever your eyes fell. He avoided going anywhere near them back then, because bad things always happened in those places. His eyes were starting to adjust to the absence of light.

He thought of calling out to see if there was anyone in the area, but then thought better of it.

Time was slipping by, and Cornell was not sure of just how long he had been awake. He started to nod, phasing in and out of consciousness, and then he began to hear noises that were deliberate. The initial noise was almost like uneven footsteps, and then labored breathing. As Cornell narrowed his eyes to peer into the darkness, he began to smell something overpowering.

Then like a flash of lightning, yellow eyes opened right in front of him, maybe three feet from his face. Fear ran through Cornell's body like a hurricane wave; he forced himself to breathe. The animal was enormous, and the breathing was louder, as if it was preparing to strike.

Cornell couldn't break his stare on the animal's eyes; he wanted to jump out of the way, but he was frozen. Tears rolled down his face, but he wasn't crying; his body was shaking from top to bottom. As much as he tried to stop, it was pointless; he was gripped by absolute terror. The animal moved from side to side, positioning its weight from right to left. It made little to no sound, only deep breathing. Cornell began to pray some in his head then some verbal; it was mostly garbled. The beast took a step back but continued its focus on Cornell's face. Cornell began to calm down, and his brain started to function again.

He looked hard at the face of the animal, then it dawned on him that this was one of them; this was a being from another planet.

CHAPTER 38

He had caught a fraction of a glimpse back in the lounge at APL years ago. He had forgotten just how beautiful they were. Back then, he only saw a side view of the face, but these beings mostly run five hundred pounds.

Cornell regained his sea legs and stood up slowly, not wishing to aggravate the being. As he reached full extension, he took in a deep breath; he wondered if this animallike being could smell the fear on him.

Caution was never one of my strong points, he thought to himself as he contemplated communicating with the alien.

"I don't know if you can understand me, but how in the world do you condense that body into a human form?" Cornell asked timidly.

The multicolored lionlike being tilted his head and slowly stood up. He presented much like a human in posture, not like an animal standing on its hind legs. It moved closer to Cornell and appeared to evaluate him, then moved in and peered deep into his eyes.

"You have been on our warning list for nine years. There have been others with the ability to bend their vision around our camouflage," it said in a deep, scary voice with a touch of English accent.

"I only saw it once a few years back. I thought maybe it was my imagination," Cornell added with a hint of sadness.

"Mostly it is humans with dark eyes, sometimes green but never blue eyes," the being acknowledged as if he was trying to reason through their faulty system.

"You seem to know me. Have I ever met you in human form?" Cornell probed.

"I arrived yesterday to track down your new friend Mr. Dean, and let me say I can't thank you enough. I love this nutty rock. Please let me introduce myself. I am Cain, and it is my extreme pleasure," he added with a nightmarish grin.

"What is it that you beings want on this planet?" Cornell asked sheepishly.

"Mr. Pierce, we have been cultivating resources on this planet for over seven thousand years. I myself have been enjoying the fruit of this vine for most of it," Cain added, still grinning.

"Not to be rude, but just how old are you?" Cornell asked.

"I have been transformed over seventy-three times, and I know you have no idea what that means, but let me just say nine years ago, I was in a different body," Cain said with an air of superiority.

"Why are you beings working at the Physics Lab?" Cornell continued.

"You have so many questions, don't you?" Cain's attitude seemed to change. "I have only one question for you, Mr. Pierce. In what direction was Mr. Dean going?" Cain drilled as he moved in closer.

"I really have no idea where he was going. I really don't think he had a plan or a destination. I was under the impression that he was going to find someone here, but he didn't confide," Cornell answered openly as his fear began to escalate.

Cain moved his face closer, smelling Cornell; his eyes narrowed, and the catlike whiskers folded back against his large face.

"Then why is that I need you alive, Mr. Pierce?" Cain said with absolutely no feelings.

"Mr. Cain, I can't stop you from killing me, but I really can't help you," Cornell offered as if coming to grips with the fact that he had reached the end of the road.

"Very honorable, Mr. Pierce, I will be sure to tell Mr. Dean of your valor prior to ripping out his heart," Cain stated as he emphasized his grin.

Cornell didn't respond; his head slumped down, and the realization that he would never leave this room began to creep in. The alien was evil, and he knew that now. This one was different from the others; he was much more complex, and unlike the others, he was emotional.

Cornell tried to think about what he could do to use that to his benefit. The others back at APL were really stiff, cold, and unfeeling. He thought that there must be a reason why this one stood out, and maybe that was something he could use. The being backed away and started pacing the immediate area; its eyes were focused on the tired black man hunched in the chair. There was something in those eyes that Cornell recognized from his many years surrounded by intelligent whites; it was the inner feeling of superiority. It was then that Cornell thought there might be the possibility of changing his bad situation. It was his experience through his life that there was that vanity; there was impending ruin. Cornell thought to himself that he needed to be careful, but he really needed to engage the beast.

"You spent several hours together on the highway. There were discussions and scenarios. I find it hard to believe that names were not mentioned," Cain tested.

"I don't owe William Dean anything. He kidnapped me, pulled some teeth out of my head, and shortened my life span," Cornell snarled.

"He what?" Cain snapped.

Cornell realized that he had opened Pandora's box, and nothing would be able to take that back. The trick now was not to backpedal at this point, and follow the thought process.

He felt it hard to believe that they weren't on top of this, what they thought was going on with their tracking ability.

"Pulled the very teeth from my head, told me I was being monitored," Cornell went on as if he was clueless about events.

"You want to be very careful about your next series of words. Were you being monitored?" Cain demanded as he laid his index talon on the lower optical orbit of Cornell's face.

"Please! I don't know what he found or what he was looking for. Not much of anything was really making sense," Cornell pleaded as if afraid and unknowledgeable.

"Open your mouth," Cain snapped.

"Why do you want me to open my mouth?" Cornell pleaded.

"I said open your mouth before I rip your jaw from your skull," Cain snapped in a ferocious, angry tone.

Cornell slowly opened his mouth, now slightly fearful of the intensity in Cain's voice. Cain reached out and grabbed Cornell's face and applied enough pressure to open the jaw to its maximum range. He examined the empty holes in the mouth where Cornell's molars had been the day before. The pockets were fresh, and they were filled with dried blood. Cain stared hard at both holes for some time, and then he pushed Cornell back into the chair.

This thing was really angry, and that was totally confusing; why the agitation?

Dean was wrong about the teeth; Cain's people had nothing to do with this.

CHAPTER 39

He seemed visibly shocked that something was going on in their world that they were unaware of.

Then the others began to roll out of the dark, all of them in human form and obviously subservient to this Cain thing; he was barking and snarling, and they were reacting to the commands. One of the minions came directly over and bent from the waist, his face inches away now that he could smell rotting, decayed meat.

"Open!" it said with total absence of emotion.

Cornell opened immediately and let the being do its examination that was thorough and lengthy. Cain moved quickly back to his position less than a foot away. His speed was violently quick; he practically pushed the other being to the floor. He reached out and dug his talons into various sections of Cornell's skull. It was the thumb that punctured his lower cheek; that created the most pain. Cornell let out a grunt from the pain, not what the beast expected, but he was holding fast to his pride.

"I will not tolerate deception on your part at this juncture, Mr. Pierce, so I will ask you only one time, who do you rely on for your dental affairs?" Cain drilled into Cornell's face.

"My dental affairs!" Cornell laughed. "Are you an English alien?" Cornell said, taunting the large being.

"Is that your final answer? Well, survey says your dental work was in vain," Cain's voice boomed as he snatched Cornell from the back of the neck and slammed his mouth on the cold cement floor.

Cornell made some minor pain-related noises and then spat out the remainder of his broken teeth. He rolled on his back, lying on the floor, dazed and battered; there was blood streaking down both sides of his face. He gazed up at the smirking Cain who stared down at him as if he was food.

The blood that was dribbling out of his mouth had changed the alien's focus almost instantly. The others were circling in from the darkness; now there were six in total.

Two began to change instantly right in front of his eyes. Cain himself began intensifying his gaze, and then a thin film slid horizontally, much like a shark. Then, like a shot, he regained his composure and let out a noise that cut the room in half. The others retreated, some back to the dark.

Cain began to make his own change back to the humanlike form that shielded him from the world.

Cornell tapped his finger to his chest, counting out the time it took to make the change. Nineteen taps, and there, before his eyes, was a slightly good-looking motherfuckin' white boy or half brother.

Cornell stared at the young man before him, and then began to laugh, slowly at first, then much more profound. He spit out some of the pooling blood in his mouth between laughing fits, and then turned to Cain with the look of disapproval on his face.

"Look at you, a true wolf in sheep's clothing," Cornell taunted.

Cain smiled and thought over the analogy, realizing to himself just how dead-on that was.

The black man was trying to penetrate him; what was he thinking?

The bigger question was who was responsible for implanting tracking devices in this human?

They would need to have the full staff of APL evaluated right now. Why in the world would the supply supervisor be targeted, unless the dental office at APL is responsible?

Cain turned to some of the minions behind him and started barking alien tones and clicking sounds. There was movement in the dark, beyond Cornell's line of sight, but he assumed that some of them were on the move.

Cain reached out his hands and snatched Cornell off the floor and swung him hard into the chair.

"I get the feeling that you are attempting to provoke a negative response from me," Cain said with a large Cheshire cat smile.

"You're different from the rest of the robots, aren't you, Cain? Why is that?" Cornell probed.

"You're very perceptive, Mr. Pierce. Tell me what else you have looked into."

"That posse of yours is way too stiff and empty with no real emotion. You just don't fit in!" Cornell continued.

"They're clones, first or second generation. Thomas and I, on the other hand, are something totally different," Cain said, devoid of even a shred of humility.

"What are you, really?" Cornell probed at the alien through bloody spittle.

"I am a Gray, with the ability to slide," Cain stated as if he was talking sports.

"I don't understand what that means. Please let me know what the hell is going on," Cornell pleaded.

Cain smiled slightly at the bleeding man in the chair, then turned and grabbed a fold-up chair and placed it on the inside of a meter from Cornell. The back of the chair was facing Pierce as Cain straddled it and folded his arms then began to deliberate.

Pierce knew that this monster wanted nothing but to talk about events that were unfolding.

CHAPTER 40

"First, you need to understand that space travel is a nightmare, no way around it." Cain laughed.

"Do you have a ship?" Cornell asked.

"There is a ship. It currently is out of this universe, so we utilize ionized gates for short intergalactic transport with help from your magnetic field," Cain went on as if Cornell could follow.

"What are the gates?" Cornell probed.

"The gates allow for the converted energy to travel and focus into tight beams. One would hate to come through the door with one's asshole on top of its head." Cain laughed out loud.

Cornell did his best to force a smile through bloody teeth, but it was hard to follow this random language and terminology.

"Anyway, that's how the clones come into the picture. It takes centuries to move back and forth. The last time I stepped on this planet, Ronald Reagan was running for the presidential nomination. Now you need to understand this. I am not a clone. As I told you before, I am a Gray!" Cain stated with a great deal of pride.

"What is a Gray?" Cornell probed.

"The Grays are the second religion of the universe," Cain said with that air of superiority.

"Religion, as in God?" Pierce speculated.

"Our race doesn't have such a patriarchal sense that most humans view their God, but in a much more pure, spiritual alignment," Cain continued.

"So, what was the first religion?" Cornell asked.

"The architects, of course. Where do you think all the water came from on this floating rock?" Cain responded as if he was stating the obvious.

"I know you're trying, but I'm having trouble following you," Cornell said in an apologetic manner.

"We connect with the divine during the feed, and it is the most natural, beautiful event your human eyes has ever beheld. The universe is made of God, all things are connected, and when we take in the feed, we take the divine within," Cain was in the zone now.

"What are you feeding on that is so beautiful?" Cornel asked, half hoping not to hear the answer.

"We have been feeding on your race and others for centuries, Mr. Pierce, and that is only the beginning. We work really hard to make you better," Cain stated with the reverence of an ice cube.

"You're making people fat so you can eat them, aren't you?" Cornell implied with horror in his eyes.

CHAPTER 41

"How the hell do you make people fat? That is something they do all on their own." Cain laughed.

"What are you things doing in this world?" Cornell probed.

"Although we can't fatten the calf, we are capable of slowing the progress of weight loss with some simple setbacks," Cain proceeded.

"You're killing scientists that can make a difference, afraid they might cut into your feeding habits," Cornell stated through wet, bloody lips.

"You are just way too informed for a supply clerk, aren't you, Mr. Pierce?" Cain's eyes lit up like Times Square.

Cornell realized as soon as it came out of his mouth that he had sealed his fate. This monster would never even consider his exit from this room. He was angry with himself for allowing his emotions to overrule the common sense that had always been true to him. It was difficult for Cornell to remain objective and emotion free in the face of this twisted, crazy half animal.

His brother Lionel had died not three years ago from type 2 diabetes; he struggled with his weight all his life. All his people suffered from the decisions that this thing has made to keep his plate full. He thought of young black women walking around like cows, and his grandchildren who were gaining weight every year. The deeper his thoughts went, the greater his anger grew. At first, he considered leaping at the source of so much pain and poking its eye out.

Unfortunately, he knew it would be a useless endeavor; this thing moved way too fast.

Maybe if he could work the nail clipper out of his back pocket and lure Cain into his face, he could take a shot at that eye.

Cornel slowly started to shift his hands toward his back; shifting the weight from his right cheek, he could feel the steel clippers.

"You know what is going to destroy you, Cain, and your pack of carbon copies?" Cornell spewed through bloody lips.

"No, please enlighten me, Mr. Pierce. What is going to destroy me and my peeps?" Cain responded with a tone of pure amusement.

"It's you and your lack of any decency. It will be your undoing," Cornell taunted the large visitor.

"During your trip to this city in that gas-sucking cart, you most likely killed hundreds of smaller residents of this planet! You eat a variety of additional residents of this planet on a daily basis, and you talk to me of decency. I acquit your human race no greater than a carbon-based infection that is sucking the life force from this rich planet!" Cain barked at the bleeding man.

"You tell yourself anything you want, you fuckin' freak. You're just a larger parasite no better than us," Cornell pushed.

The rage was obvious in the eyes of the nightmare that was now moving toward Pierce at alarming speed. Cornell reached into his back pocket and snatched the nail clipper as fast as he could. With his thumb, he flipped it open, and with one fast motion, he targeted the closest eye of the angered alien.

As Cain placed his hands on the chair, he caught sight of Cornell's hand honing into his eyeline and immediately snapped open his large jaw. In a flash, Cain's razor-like teeth snapped off Cornell's hand mid wrist.

In less than a second, Cain had retreated back to his initial point. He fully realized why the human was taunting him the way he was, and he was slightly embarrassed.

The warehouse was filled with agonizing screams of the handless Cornell. As he clutched his blood-spurting stub, he lifted his eyes to see the lurking Cain spitting out a blood-soaked silver nail clipper.

The minions caught wind of the fresh blood and with lightning speed began to roll in. Cain barked a high-pitched wail, and snack time was over. Cornell quickly took off his belt and utilized it as a tourniquet.

Cain finished chewing and wiped at his lower jaw. There was some grumbling from the underlings, and it wasn't pleasant.

CHAPTER 42

Cain looked long and hard at Cornell trying to rationalize killing him, but he knew that he could possibly still have information that might help. Cain turned on his heels then barked some orders at the others. He then disappeared into the dark shadow against the back wall and was gone.

Cornell tended to his bleeding arm as he noticed one of the younger ones moving in his direction. Fear initially gripped Cornell as he felt the visitor approach. He turned to see the young alien staring down at him; there was something in his hand. He managed to clear his thoughts long enough to really focus on the kid and wondered just how old this one was.

"Are you a clone, young man?" Cornell asked.

"No, like Cain, I am also a transfer, four journeys, nowhere near the longevity of the Cain," the younger alien went on.

"The Cain. Is that what he is referred to by your species? That sounds as if he is held in high esteem. Maybe that's the reason for his obvious arrogance."

"There are those from our world who consider him a hero or a prophet. He holds one of nine seats on the Council of Light," the young Thomas continued.

"The Council of Light, what is that?" Cornell probed.

"There are over two thousand known planets that are known to support various intellectual humanoid life. Some that you could not even conceive and in the middle of all of that there is a governing body that attempts to keep order through continued communication. The arrangement is much like your United Nations but on an infinite scale."

How is it that Cain finds himself on this council? What gives him this power?

"I personally find him a bit brutal and fascist at his core!" Cornell stated.

"I would never make excuses for the things that he does, and I have seen him do some unbelievable things. However, he has the honor of being on the Council of Light for having the constitution to make the kinds of decision others could never make. Then again, you are not alone in your feelings that Cain's methods may possibly be unsound!"

"What is it that you have in your hands there?" Cornell probed.

"This is Yelena, as we call it. On occasion, we do find our ultraviolet protection damaged and we utilize this to speed the healing and avoid infection. Please," he said as he handed Cornell the small jar.

"Thank you," he said as he took the jar.

He began to rub the contents on the traumatized area, and within moments, he began to feel relief. In a matter of seconds, skin began to form around the violated area.

The pain was totally gone now, replaced by a numbness that was easy to deal with.

The alien started to walk away, not looking for an outcome or a response. Cornell had way too many questions to let this one walk away.

"What is your name?" Cornell asked, trying to keep the conversation rolling.

"I am Thomas," said the younger alien.

Yes, of course, you are. Why should you be anyone but? Cornell thought as he considered the religious similarity.

"When we are in sleep mode during our trip to this world, we are programmed with a full identity, name, profession, even memories," Thomas explained.

"Memories, like a past life?" Cornell asked.

"No, not life but lives. Wherever one of us has gone, the new arrivals know the way. You could drop me in any town on this planet, and I would be able to find my direction without too much difficulty," the young one boasted.

"That must come in handy. I get lost driving in DC on a weekly basis."

"It's your system that is highly suspect. It creates its own problems. The engineering of your transport linkage is ridiculous and to an outsider almost purposely confusing," Thomas voiced his feelings like an angry tourist.

"I see that you have given this a lot of thought." Cornell forced a smile.

"I have an engineering background, and my IQ is not measurable by your standards, so when I look at things, I am always considering improvements and possibilities," Thomas said without skipping a beat.

"If you focus on improvements on a regular basis, you could make yourself crazy on this planet," Cornell suggested.

"Yes, it is difficult. You are a strange people. You accept mediocrity as if it is common practice. I don't know if you think of these things. The most amazing thing to me is that almost all of you live a lie and are quite fine with that," Thomas stressed.

"We live our lives to the best of our abilities. We try to raise families and find that right person to spend our time with," Cornell explained.

"You are delusional and think like a peasant. The truth is that a fraction of the human host holds the majority of all the resources," Thomas pontificated.

"Money and resources isn't the goal of all of us here on Earth, although one might not fully grasp that," Cornell pleaded his case, not sure if he believed it himself.

"Spoken like a true peasant and a product of your own media lie machine," Thomas taunted.

"You seem to have deep feelings regarding this planet's resource distribution," Cornell said with a bit of sarcasm.

"I find it amazing that semi-intelligent beings allow the dysfunction to continue century after century," Thomas stated with profound disgust.

"What I find amazing is that as old as your culture is, you sound much like our teens of today," Cornell said, feeling the connection with this Thomas.

"That makes total sense actually. The revolution must start with them," Thomas said with some ease.

"Why is that?" Cornell shot back.

"Your society is designed to emasculate males as they exceed twenty years of age, and your females struggle with a sense of purpose," Thomas stated with conviction.

"There are many societies and traditions throughout the world, and many hold females to the highest standard," Cornell engaged.

"I am speaking specifically of the United States. It is here that the revolution must begin because this is the source of the plague," he said without skipping a beat.

"Thomas, I think I understand your point of view. What I find amazing is that you have this feeling at all," Cornell said with some surprise for emphasis.

"Why is that, Mr. Pierce?" Thomas shot back, almost startled.

"Your views indicate that you have feeling and even compassion for the beings of this world. This I find most interesting. It would be like me caring for the outcome of a cheeseburger," Cornell said flatly.

"Well, maybe I like cheeseburgers!" Thomas said with an ear-to-ear smile.

"You are most interesting, Thomas. Where has the Cain gone to?" Cornell asked with a quick snap in hopes of a faster response.

"Cain's business is his own, but if you must know, there are several in this room much in need of a feed. If he doesn't return soon, all hell will break loose, and the red vino leaking from your damaged paw is creating quite the stir," Thomas stated with a slight change in his demeanor.

"This creates a bit of a situation, and to think I was hoping that Cain wouldn't return," Cornell added with a hint of sarcasm.

"Just goes to show one must be careful of what one wishes for!" Thomas smiled and winked.

CHAPTER 43

ADHD isn't something new. There was a time you either possessed it or you were the lunch of a larger animal.

—Unknown

Mac pushed on the gas as he turned down Fourth Avenue; the wheels in his head were in hyperdrive. He couldn't help but think that he was missing something. Like a stepchild left out in the rain. That's the curse of detective work. You spend countless hours second-guessing your prior moves. Then you start rolling your potential errors through the puzzle board.

Magen was sitting closer than before; she was talking, but Mac was unable to pick up most of it. He was in his element sailing through the city he loved. He began to think about Dean and what he was doing. He must be really tired; that drive from Maryland was not that long, but really boring. It was that damn New Jersey Turnpike; it was really high on the boring meter as any stretch in this country.

The way he figured things, this was an older man running hard; he would need to get some rest. This Phyllis babe would have to find some place for him to relax.

Then it hit Mac like a brick; it was the chick Phyllis that was the key.

He was tracking the wrong person. William Dean was the package; the real mark was the woman. She would need to have some real creature comforts that would not be able to be had just anywhere. Mac pulled off to the side of the street in front of Fourth Street deli. Magen looked at Mac with a stunned look, thinking that he was getting something to eat.

"Tell me everything about the habits of this CIA operative woman that has been playing you," Mac stated with a sense of urgency.

"She is not playing me!" Magen shot back defensively.

"Please, I need to know everything that you know about this bitch. It's really important," Mac pressed again with the same sense of urgency.

"The woman thinks she is a goddess. The bitch uses her looks and her body to get the things she wants," Magen continued as the light went on in her head.

"What does she need to survive? Could she be living in a sleazy hotel?" Mac was fishing.

"No way! That would be totally beneath her. She needs silk and room service and, most important, well-prepared sushi," Magen stated as she began to follow the thought process.

"This is the way to go. She's the key, not Dean. It is her vanity that's going to help find them in this city," Mac explained.

"I must admit that I am really impressed. If we had time I would rock your world, but you have the rain check, big boy," Magen teased in a dripping hot voice.

"Don't threaten me with a good time, woman," Mac added with enthusiasm in his voice.

"Now that you have me thinking in that direction, she was fairly quick to pounce on Dean at the Slaughtered Lamb. It leads me to believe that she might be close," Magen considered.

"That puts her midtown, maybe three to four major players that could handle the needs. The sushi could always be taken in. However, the Four Seasons has a Japanese import that stands alone."

Mac grabbed his phone and started to dial his go-to guy over at the Four Seasons. Stan Wilson was the top honcho at the Four Seasons; all things ran through him. Some people called him the real mayor of New York, and no fart was released without his clearance. He operated the building like a king in his castle. He was most likely connected, but he was always able to keep his face out of the papers. He was well-liked by guests and staff alike, and in today's market, that was not an easy task.

If there was anyone in this city that could find this bitch, it would be him.

They met years ago out on Long Island and developed a pretty good relationship. For a brief second, he debated making the call; he never felt good about using his friends for anything. However, if there was ever a time to draw on a marker, it was now. Mac placed his phone to his ear and listened for the ring.

"Stan Wilson here! How can I help you?" an all-business voice chimed in.

"Hey, player! What up?" Mac shot back.

"Mac! What's up? You don't usually call me during the day unless you have been shot or you're worried that I'm about to be," Stan probed with a worried tone.

"You can lighten that sphincter right about now. I need a favor," Mac added, going right to business.

"Mac, you're family. Whatever I can do for you, just ask!" Stan's tone changed like a flash.

"There is a high-end female rolling through the five-star CIA, currently rolling with an older Republican. They are really trying to stay incognito, but it's over-the-top. The woman is a sushi connoisseur. Most likely room service is hopping like Mexican jumping beans, bottled water only."

"I will put my ear out there," Stan stated after a brief pause.

"I really appreciate anything you can do," Mac said with sincere respect.

"I will talk to you soon. My cousin Aldo just rolled into town," Stan disclosed.

"Say hello. Talk to you soon." Mac ended the call.

Mac smiled as he put his phone away, then his face started to turn in the opposite direction. He started to realize that Stan was worried about his phone being compromised. Maybe this is something that he should be concerned about. He got out of the car, opened the trunk, and pulled out a vinyl case. Inside was a transmitter sweep. He first used it on himself and found nothing. Then he passed it over his cell phone.

The device lit up like a Christmas tree.

He called Magen out of the car and started to roll the wand over her. The earring on the left side of her face began to ring. Then he placed her cell phone on the hood of the car and swept over it, and again, the device lit up.

"Lose the earring. It seems to be tainted," Mac implied.

"What made you evaluate for the bugs? Were you being paranoid?" Magen asked with some shock.

"The conversation that I just had with Stan was odd at best. He was sending me a code regarding our girl's whereabouts."

"You know where she is?" Magen snapped.

"She's in room 4A at the Four Seasons, but the fact that he relayed that to me in code indicates that he is worried about others listening in on his phone."

"How do you think that our phones were compromised since Schwartz Hall at NYU?" she inquired with a puzzled look on her face.

"The only time my phone was out of my pocket was back at the office, I plugged it in my charger," Mac thought out loud.

"The Penn Plaza offices are highly secured. It would be almost impossible for someone to penetrate and fix our phones," Magen said with limited confidence in what she was saying.

"I have seen the impossible come across the table more than once since I met you. The question is who had access to both of our phones?" Mac pondered.

"The earrings that were tampered must have been compromised in the past few days. They were in my case at the hotel," Magen reflected.

"I am beginning to think that your friend Phyllis has you on a short leash, and it's time to flip that script," Mac stated with enthusiasm.

"The CIA would need several levels of clearance to operate against local authorities. Even Phyllis has parameters that she needs to work within," Magen stressed.

"Let's sweep the car, pull all the hot wires, and pay our little angel a visit. I want to test a theory," Mac stated.

CHAPTER 44

Mac and Magen spent the next twenty minutes sweeping the car; six separate microphones were located throughout the vehicle. One was the actual radio volume control on the radio made in China, two were from Japan, and a long blonde hair in the back seat that he believed was an Israeli product.

Magen disarmed each device and put everything in a bag on the front seat. Mac turned the vehicle around and motored to the back entrance of the Four Seasons Hotel.

Magen got out of the car and walked through the internal garage, quickly identifying two agents sitting in their car, obviously not trying to hide their presence. They were half asleep and really not focused; they were most likely a monitoring detail. Watching Phyllis all week must be taking its toll.

Getting past these two was not going to be much of an issue. The real test is going to be what is past the first floor. The fact of the matter is that the CIA has the package and Dean is of major value; they just won't let them walk in and escort him out. He would need to actually want to go on his own free will.

Mac circled the parameter and identified several potential government personnel. He connected with Magen back behind the kitchen, then explained his recon of the front of the building. She pointed out the lazy twosome in the Crown Victoria who were less than two hundred yards off the pool entrance.

"So, are you about ready to make this thing happen?" Mac said with enthusiasm.

"We didn't come here for the Asian chicken. Of course, it is quite good here," Magen added, making light of the situation.

"You can roll right into the Garden Bar. You will most likely draw attention being as hot as you are, but you look like you belong there," Mac added, letting his cop side show.

"Where are you going to be through this siege, and how are we going to connect when we get into position?" Magen pressed.

"I am going in through the kitchen. They know me. Stan and I go back a spell, and he's the closest to family that I have."

"What's our contact point?" Magen continued.

"You hit the Garden Bar. Order something trendy, maybe a strange martini. Take a few minutes, flash those blues. I am sure someone will be drawn in," Mac went on as if he was back in Desert Storm.

"What's the point of me hooking up with someone at the bar?" Magen asked with confusion in her voice.

"These people have a point person at the bar, and they will be looking for someone alone, not interested in a connection. As soon as you make that connection, excuse yourself to the bathroom, hit the stairwell to the fourth floor," Mac went on faster now, paying close attention to detail.

"You will be there when I get there, right?" Magen pushed.

"I will be there, but remember 4A, the stairwell is on the left-hand side. We can do this." Mac touched her face and turned toward the kitchen.

CHAPTER 45

Magen walked around the corner and right into the front door; the doorman opened the door and tipped his hat and flashed a smile. Magen moved gracefully without asking for direction as if she owned the place and knew exactly where she was going.

Taking Mac's advice, she arrived at the corner of the bar and asked the bartender for the martini menu. Deciding on the Godiva chocolate martini, she removed her coat, displaying her magnificent breasts and well-sculpted body. The males in the room immediately took notice, and a few ladies. Seconds later, as on schedule, a young attorney arrived at her left side with a confident smile and a line of shit that had been practiced in the mirror for months. Magen did her best to act interested as the youngster rambled on about his growing importance within some law firm with too many names to ever remember. Her forced smile was making him nervous and provoked him to trying harder. She looked into his eyes for a few seconds, and his comfort level fell to pieces. Magen glanced up at the English wall clock and turned to the young man and excused herself.

The stairwell was right where Mac said it would be, and she was able to access it without complication.

Mac entered the back door carrying an empty banana box that he had picked up right outside the door. He quickly surveyed the area and spotted the point person about twenty-five feet away. The guy's back was to Mac, but he could see that the suit was no lightweight. He was pushing easy 220 pounds with minimal fat. Fortunately, the guy was going to town on a large plate of meatballs and spaghetti that Stan had placed in his face seconds ago, anticipating Mac's arrival.

Stan looked up long enough to motion his eyes to the service elevator, then dove back into idle conversation.

Mac grabbed a white coat and made his way out the service door to the elevator. As he approached the doors, the elevator opened up, and two housekeeping people walked out, not even giving Mac a second look. He walked into the service elevator and hit the button for the fourth. He waited for a brief moment, and the door slowly closed. Mac took a deep breath and began to remove his coat. A chill ran up his spine, and that concerned Mac deeply; he had been in countless situations and always trusted his inner voice. He knew deep down that something was wrong.

He felt that it could possibly concern Magen.

He had never been down this road with someone he cared about. He kept telling himself that she was a trained professional and she was better off than he was. The other end of his emotional field was just telling him that something was really wrong. The door opened to an empty hall; in front of him were two brass plates on the wall indicating rooms one through twenty to the right, and twenty-one through forty to the left.

He stepped out into the hall and was stunned not to see anyone. The standard protocol was to at least have a detail outside the room. He heard the stairway door open and turned to see Magen slowly creep out. The nervous smile on her face told the story; she was feeling the same way.

"I am feeling that this is just about too easy. What do you think?" Magen said as they moved toward the door.

"This is beyond strange," Mac added.

"There are protocols that we need to follow in this type of operation, but they don't seem to be too interested in standards of any kind," Magen initiated the line of dialogue mostly due to nervousness.

"I have not felt right about this since I walked into the elevator, but we didn't track this guy down to walk away from this door," Mac said firmly.

"You are so right about that," Magen stated with conviction as she reached out and rapped three times hard on the door.

They glanced at each other for a brief moment, drawing courage from each other. Mac managed a slight smile in hopes to ease the immediate tension. There were a few seconds of silence, and the pressure mounted before some noise was heard from the other side of the door.

Magen exhaled in Buddhist fashion to calm the mounting adrenaline. She had practiced yoga for years, and if there was ever a time she needed to draw on that teaching, it was now. Mac, on the other hand, reached behind him and massaged the handle of his Beretta for security, and that seemed to work for him just fine. The door handle twisted and turned slowly counterclockwise and began to open.

CHAPTER 46

The first thought that ran through Mac's head was *The door isn't even locked.*

They have been expecting company, and this was a walk-in. His gut feeling was always dead-on; he knew at that moment things were going to get really strange.

"Hi, Magen, it's nice to see you, and you must be Detective MacDonald. Please come in," Phyllis said, clearly not remotely fazed by their arrival.

"Thank you!" Mac evenly returned, realizing the scenario was far out of his hands. As they entered the room, there was a sense of calm that was unexpected. The entrance room was small, well lit, and cold. There were electrical devices and wires everywhere you looked; this was a home base.

Against the bedroom door stood the meanest Marine gunnery sergeant on this side of hell. Mac could tell from the stripes and colors that this man had seen action in every corner of this planet. The fact was that if he didn't want you to pass through the door into the bedroom, you weren't going.

Phyllis picked up some fruit off the cart near the door and took a slightly healthy bite out of a large beautiful strawberry. There was a hint of juice that rolled down the right side of her face. She gracefully lifted her index finger and caught it midstream. Mac began to understand the tension between her and Magen; this was one sensual woman. Mac turned and caught the eyes of Magen who was shooting cold daggers right through Mac's very soul. This was the first time since they met that Mac could honestly say he felt sheer terror; he immediately diverted his eyes.

Phyllis grabbed a state-of-the-art frequency device and ran it up and down both Magen first then Mac; nothing was identified. She smiled and then motioned them toward the bedroom door. The Marine turned his back and opened the French-style doors and then stood aside.

The room had been converted into a conference room with several video flat screens organized throughout the room. The large walnut table was filled with several representatives from organizations around the world. Mac instantly recognized one of the suits from television; he was a major player at Homeland Security. His name was Bersin, maybe Alfred or Alan, he couldn't be sure, but he was a personal friend to the Speaker of the House Nickalosi.

Phyllis began introductions, not necessarily by importance but to those closer to her. The gentleman to the right was introduced as Ehud Barack; he was involved with the Israeli intelligence. He nodded his head slightly and then pushed his glasses back on his face. There was a second that I thought he wanted to engage in some form of dialogue but restrained himself. Phyllis then motioned toward Mr. Alan Bersin, and Magen stepped up and admitted that she was fully aware of both him and the gentleman to his right. That was Juergen Stock, the Homeland Security station chief of Europe.

Mac started putting the players together and began to get a sickening feeling deep in the pit of his stomach. The man to the far left was obviously a priest; he walked over to Magen first and introduced himself as Father John DaTonne. He introduced himself as a canon lawyer from Rome and the personal emissary to Cardinal Balone. Mac was not sure what all that meant, and he guessed it was written all over his face, because Magen turned to him and whispered, "He's from the Vatican!" she said with confused desperation in her voice.

"Homeland Security, the CIA, and the Vatican, oh my!" Mac joked, hiding his feeling of inadequacy.

William Dean stood up and walked up to the Vatican rep and Magen, and began to introduce himself. Magen stopped him midsentence and reached out and grabbed his hands and began to unfold the tale of the past twenty-four hours.

Dean looked really spent; the past two days had taken its toll.

Mac sat back and took in the scene; this was something that he had not factored in. He turned and reviewed the video unit at the base of the table and realized that it was a direct feed into the Interpol office in Berlin, Germany. He then began to scan the rest of the feeds in the room and began to understand that this was ground zero for the most powerful organization on the planet. He turned back at the moment that William Dean reached his hand out at Mac and then began to thank him for his diligence in staying on target to track him down. Mac shook his head and held on to his hand for a few more seconds. Mac locked eyes with Dean and motioned to the electronics in the room and the photos on the wall.

"I take it by the video feed coming in from the nine different countries that I can identify, we need to sit down and have a briefing," Mac said with conviction in his voice.

"Yes! I can only imagine what you and Agent Cummings must be thinking," William Dean stated as he scanned the room.

"Please have a seat. We need to bring you up to speed on what is taking place. This is going to take some time. Can I get you anything?" Phyllis asked like a gracious host.

"I would love some water. I had one of the street hot dogs, and I believe the primary ingredient is salt," Magen requested with a hint of nervousness in her voice.

"On the way, Magen. We are still waiting for another party to arrive," Phyllis said as she headed for the refrigerator.

"I can't help but notice that the live feed at the far end of the table is from China. Now the last time I looked, we were having extensive communication problems with them?" Mac laid out the observation in the form of a question.

"We have made great strides within the past few hours that I thought would be impossible in my lifetime," Bersin said with unbridled enthusiasm.

"My research has covered the western hemisphere and a good part of Asia, and I have found countless patterns in both. I have no data at all from China, but I would love to speak with someone who has been monitoring this phenomenon," Magen requested, looking to enhance her data.

"This would most likely be impossible. Our communication is fragile at best," Bersin chimed back quickly.

"Forgive me, but I am getting the 'pink elephant in the room' feeling," Mac announced, letting his New York out of the box.

"Aliens are here, and apparently they have been here for some time. It is now coming to light that their intentions are questionable at best!" Barack snapped back, also not a fan of the subtleties.

"They seem to have a strong interest in creating obesity, or at the very least preventing any individual from halting the epidemic that is obviously running its course," Magen chimed in, testing the waters of how everyone fully understood the situation.

"Everyone at this table is familiar with your research. It is the only reason you and Lieutenant MacDonald are sitting at this table," Phyllis announced with some regret in her voice.

"The important thing here is that the data you collected initiated several other collaborative investigations worldwide," Juergen Stock said firmly.

"I am assuming that several theories are being entertained at this time. Have there been any additional findings that we are privileged to?" Magen requested.

"With the cornerstone of your research, we were able to run two decades of missing persons from countless databases around the globe," Stock kept on, almost in a praising light.

"We identified something outstanding last month that I am willing to share with you because I believe you are responsible for unveiling the darkest secret this planet has ever seen," Phyllis stated with pure admiration in her voice.

"Thank you, Phyllis, that does mean a lot to me," Magen responded.

"We identified missing females over the past two decades with a particular obesity chromosome outnumbered other missing females six to one," Phyllis read from a computer.

"What you are saying, I believe, is that this new information would indicate the strong possibility that harvesting is a prime motive," Magen stated almost in the form of a question.

There was silence in the room as everyone began to look at one another. There was an air of discomfort that filled the room. The two men from Homeland Security began to click together and several Bluetooth devices began to light up the room.

The Israeli gentleman had several conversations going at one time via computer. Mac looked around the room in sheer amazement of what was going on; he snapped a quick look at Magen who was also a bit stunned. Mac began to reflect on a case he followed in his first year after making detective. It was a four-hundred-pound sumo wrestler from Japan who came over to do an event against a crazy wrestler named George the Animal Steel. Unfortunately, the big man was a no-show; the tape they had was confusing. He was viewed walking into his room just before nine at night, and that was the last they saw of him. At the end of the day, they thought that Yakuza snatched him up and snuffed him out. He remembered saying to himself, *How does a monster of a man just disappear?* A chill ran up his spine as he thought of these things ripping the flesh off the big man. Mac thought of the far wall at the station filled with three-inch binders full of lost and missing people. He remembered the milk cartons in front of his Cheerios all those mornings. The thought of eating bloody meat was rolling through his head when his thought pattern was broken by a buzzing.

CHAPTER 47

The Blackberry in front of Phyllis began to vibrate and move counterclockwise. Instantly, Phyllis picked up the phone and placed it at her ear then paused for a moment. She confirmed with the party on the other end and clicked off the phone. She stood up and announced to the group that the individual that they were waiting for had, in fact, arrived.

Mac immediately knew she received the same call when Magen and he arrived. The place was hardwired beyond anything he had ever seen. The thought that these people had gone to such lengths made him extremely uneasy.

Phyllis stood up and started to motion toward the door, fully aware of a new arrival. She was practically reaching for the door when a loud, pronounced knock silenced the room. Phyllis greeted the older gentleman at the door and ushered him in. Mac sized up the man as a longtime player, possibly the Marines or Green Berets. He had been out of the service for a long time, but he was still in deep. The lines on his face told the story of countless service to his country. By looking at him, you wouldn't think that much; here was a guy you could pass on the street and not think too much of. Mac could see through the camouflage that this man worked a lifetime to develop.

"Good afternoon. My name is Robert Kingston. I have worked primarily for the United States for the past thirty years. Since 1999, I have been working as an independent for several of the agencies that are represented here today. Two years ago, I was contracted out to monitor some irregularities in spending at Applied Physics and to locate one Dr. Mazza who had disappeared with property and documentation belonging to Apple Physics. I have been directly reporting to Mr. William Dean for the past twenty-two months. I have a presentation that may shine some light on what is actually taking place. Please bear with me as I organize the facts that I have uncovered primarily within the last two weeks."

Robert Kingston reached in his worn leather binder to remove eight-by-ten photos. Phyllis started to communicate with the techs that were scattered throughout the room. She then pulled an easel from another part of the room and presented it to Robert. He nodded to Phyllis as he began to place the photos in a pyramid formation. Mac noticed immediately the photo of Aaron Goldstein that he placed at the bottom of the pyramid. Phyllis spent some time barking orders at the computer geeks in the room, making sure they were getting everything. Mac could see that this guy was a total professional and had been in this position in the past. He didn't appear nervous or out of his element, just doing his job. He had finished placing the photos in the sequence that was desired, and then turned to Phyllis to acknowledge that he was, in fact, ready to proceed.

Phyllis quickly snapped at the techs to be ready to not miss any of the information.

"Ladies and gentlemen, please let me conclude my research, and then if there are questions, I will gladly comply if I am capable," Kingston stated.

"Yesterday morning, I met with Mr. William Dean on the grounds of Apple Physics. I informed him that my trail was leading back to that very building." Kingston continued, "When I returned to New York, I learned that shit had hit the fan in a big way," surprising the panel with his verbiage. "As soon as I found out about the bomb going off in Maryland, I contacted the NYC branch of the CIA and arranged an interception of Mr. Dean. Now the data." Kingston turned and laid his finger on Dr. Robert Mazza.

Kingston began his tale with his pursuit of a half-German, half-Italian physician named Mazza. The information was designed to be impartial and nonjudgmental. However, it was obvious that the good doctor was one twisted motherfucker. His thought process was beyond sick and scary. The thought that this satanic shit ball was most likely in the fuckin' city made Mac sick.

The good doctor was really good at staying one step ahead of the operation team that was on his ass.

The reality was that he was too good, and he was not really that capable of the level of avoidance that he continued to demonstrate. It wasn't long before it became apparent that the good doctor was being assisted with information from someone or some organization that was extremely knowledgeable and connected.

Kingston began to relay in detail the process of what he did to counteract those working against him.

It began slowly with disseminated bad information over a period of time to several agencies. It wasn't long before he realized that it was the information itself that was being intercepted. He took himself to a spy and security store in Bayside, Queens, and purchased a micro frequency detector and started with his cell phone. After that, he began to review people and places he came in contact with.

Soon, a pattern began to unfold; the closer he got to law enforcement personnel, the higher level of frequency was being picked up on the device. Then he started doing interviews, first with local authorities, then with low-level government officials. It was then that he found the dental connection.

He paused, took a breath, and told the room that nine weeks ago he went down to the basement and pulled the back molars out of his head. He notified the team that everyone in this room had been screened and cleared. He announced to all that he met with Mr. Dean and discussed information that triggered a negative response.

"I know from Mr. Dean's dental records, that I was actually able to download from the Internet, that he in fact is not compromised. However, within the last few weeks I have upgraded my detection equipment and was able to pick up some strong readings in his presence. Please let me say that I had no idea that my tactics would put Mr. Dean in danger. The fact of the matter is that Applied Physics is ground zero for a massive web of incoming information. My meeting with Mr. Dean had two parts to it. First, I needed to assess his involvement, if any, and second, assess the grounds itself."

"I knew it was strange for you to request a meeting by the pond, but I thought you were just being paranoid," William broke the rain of information.

Kingston managed a slight smile, then returned to business. The information he had collected was compelling and outrageous.

He told the story of Aaron Goldstein and how he was murdered and why.

CHAPTER 48

He pointed to a photo of a retired city cop who was being manipulated by the outside force that appeared to be at the core of the crisis. Then he broke out some photos of what appeared to be humanistic lions; the film was grainy and weak. This was most likely from an ATM or some other low-level security camera.

Kingston laid out some wild scenarios of their functional ability and depth of strength and intelligence. Mac looked at Magen, who, for all intents and purposes, was frozen in disbelief of what was being laid out before her.

He leaned over to her, grabbing her hand, to provide some comfort or support. Magen jumped at his touch and then realized that it was him; she reached out and squeezed his hand.

The investigator continued with his understanding of the situation. Once he established the connection with the Johns Haskins community, the rest really fell into place.

Apple Physics, several branches of the FBI, even Central Intel, are infiltrated.

There are countless governments throughout the world that are compromised.

The more Kingston went on, the deeper the onion unraveled; they were everywhere. All the points had been systematically covered; everywhere you turned, it was impossible not to trigger the source. They operated on multiple levels, universities, science communities, and, of course, the hospital systems.

Kingston pulled a vial from his pocket and extracted several items, coins, buttons, and a small lock of human hair in a clear plastic envelope. He explained that he had collected several hundred bugs over the last several months, some ranging from the size of a coffee cup, to the smaller devices he spread on the table. Mac could tell that he was overly impressed by their capability; the admiration was starting to become apparent. Magen stood up and placed the coffee plug on the table, next to the others on display.

"I know you didn't want interruptions, but I was handed one of these today at Starbucks," Magen said as she returned to her seat.

"That's a new one! This was handed to you randomly at a Starbucks?" Kingston returned with real interest.

"My regional guy, Dr. Timothy Gregory, ran a wand over me early today and found that I was being monitored," Magen confided.

"That is astounding. I can't help but wonder what it was that triggered them to flag you!" Kingston pondered aloud.

"I have been wondering that myself. I paid cash. It wasn't like they flagged my card," Magen continued, still puzzled.

"I find it hard to believe that it was simply random," Kingston returned with a puzzled look.

Kingston paced in front of the table, thinking about Magen's claim regarding the random tagging. He was struggling with the whole concept that it was some form of coincidence.

Mac began to scan the room, not because he had lost interest, but it was something that cops do. He began to notice the wire harnessing that was spread throughout the room. Initially, he thought it was the setup for the several computers that were spread through the room. Then he realized that the leads ran through the room and connected to one centralized box close to the middle of the floor. Mac never considered himself an electrician, but he did have some working knowledge of the fundamentals of electricity, and he started to piece together what he was seeing in front of him. They were sitting in a room that was frequency proof. Like a large electric bubble that they could let anything out, but nothing come in.

Mac started to look at the players in the room and began to realize that they were not planning an offensive against the enemy; they were hiding, and they were scared.

Kingston pointed to a photo of an older white-haired man named Dr. Carl Mendelson. The doctor was a former professor of zoology at Weber College in Idaho. Apparently, he had been doing some intense field research of migration patterns of certain bird species when he made a startling discovery.

As part of his research, he began routine dissections to identify the parts of the brain responsible for both memory and navigation.

Dr. Mendelson sent a thesis and research data to the Smithsonian three weeks ago. He had located a calcified seed behind the skull of several of the birds. The more he looked, the more he found; the package he sent to the Smithsonian had 125 individual seeds.

"The significance of this meant nothing to me three weeks ago. However, now that we are aware of the alien ability to isolate frequency and monitor the lowest of bands of sound detectable, this data is highly important.

"Since the information came to light, there have been several additional finds where these seeds have been identified. Twenty-three additional species of migrating birds had been identified globally. There are other animal species found to have these implants. We were amazed to find a school of herring off the coast of Iceland that was emanating a similar frequency."

"Birds and fish are being tampered with for what purpose?" Mac chimed in, slightly confused.

"Well, that was a complete mystery until this morning, when a young man straight out of MIT laid out a highly acceptable theory."

Kingston walked back to his easel and quickly turned it around and began to draw symbols on the back of the page. He explained that they were having real difficulty understanding what was going on. Then this young man stepped up and told the science team that they were thinking like two-dimensional humans on Earth. The only way they could remotely understand the motivation of an alien race would be to contemplate their vision from space.

When they put that philosophy in the mix, it became clear that an advanced race could, in theory, devise a methodology of bouncing a frequency around the entire planet at will. Satellite capability is always limited by the shape of the Earth.

Kingston spoke of the long search for bin Laden and how cave rats in Afghanistan were able to time the Earth's rotation in order to avoid satellite lock on. He admitted that they weren't fully clear on the extent of exactly what these seed capabilities were. The possibility that these frequency levels are being utilized to cause harm or even to the psychological manipulation of humans is a reality.

"We are way out of our league with this technology. We have only scratched the surface of what they can do."

There was something that Kingston wanted to close with, but it was obviously troubling for him to even talk about it. He gripped the back of the chair to the point where the blood rushed from his knuckles. He paused briefly, and then he announced straight into the camera that there was a new development from one of the designated labs.

CHAPTER 49

It appeared that the seeds passed from one generation to another; at least it had been identified in certain animal breeds. That was something that Mac really needed to process; initially, he couldn't understand the significance, and then he began to see why Kingston was hesitant.

The only reason that these seeds would need to transfer to offspring would be for long-term global control. The deeper Mac's mind went, the clarity of the situation began to take shape.

This is important, he thought to himself. *It has to be.*

The only question that remained now was just how long the gardeners had been sowing the seeds.

Mac had spent the majority of his life enduring Catholic school, so it came as no surprise that his thoughts turned to God. He had struggled his whole life with the concept of an omnipotent force controlling the universe. However, when he found himself in dangerous situations, he often asked that God provide comfort and assistance. He always considered himself a reasonable individual, and being a rational person, he considered that the Bible was more or less a template of proper behavior.

He had taken several college courses during his school years and felt that he was fairly informed. He considered that the Bible was written centuries after the death of Christ, that it was written by man, and he knew that man will always be a fallible beast, more wrong than right.

As a younger man, he came across a story of Horus, the Egyptian sky god. It was apparent to him that the story of Jesus was a direct descendent of Horus, the son of Osiris. Horus was father and son, or father, son, and Holy Ghost. Horus was also born of a virgin mother and known to have the power to heal. The similarities of both Horus and Jesus are remarkable and compelling. He also struggled with the similarities to Mithras and Apollo. The most significant piece of the puzzle came when he learned that the story of Horus was written three thousand years prior to the birth of Jesus. So now he was faced with some real hard truths about the world he is living in, and all he could think about was the faith he didn't know he had.

Mac took in a deep breath and tried to clear his mind. The information that was being laid out was emotionally draining, at least for Mac. He scanned the room and saw the same desperation on the faces of everyone there.

The only person who didn't appear shaken was our Central Intelligence host; she was more or less going through the motions. It dawned on Mac that she really didn't get worked up about anything that was said today.

That is not normal, he thought, *unless that everything that is being discussed was no surprise to her.*

"That is where we stand on the intel at this time. Are there any additional questions that I can attempt to answer now or follow up on?" Kingston concluded as he ended his presentation.

"Has anyone reviewed the tissue samples at the Department of Infectious Diseases?" Magen requested.

"I am not aware of any current investigation, but I can make a formal request with the *New England Journal of Medicine* and not draw too much attention," Kingston responded.

"Since the HIV epidemic, they have been cataloguing millions of tissue samples from several countries. It could be a good place to start if we wish to establish a time frame of these frequency seeds," Magen suggested.

"Noted. I will send the e-mail as soon as I close today. I should have some preliminary data within twenty-four hours," Kingston finished.

"So where do we go from here?" Mac threw out to test the waters.

There were a lot of inhales and exhales as the tech guys began to scan the room, finally taking their eyes off the screen.

Not a word was spoken for a long period of time. This was the moment of truth, as Mac saw things. There was a real problem taking the next step. This wasn't anything that you could jump into and expect an expectable outcome. As Captain Kirk would say, "We are entering uncharted space."

The only difference was we don't have the Enterprise *ready. Truth be told, these visitors could stomp us out like an anthill, and we wouldn't even know what hit us. The flip side of this is if we sit around and do absolutely nothing, then our fate will truly be sealed.*

Mac could read the helplessness on the faces of the people who are trained to make global decisions; this was unlike anything one could prepare for.

As Mac continued to scan the room, he noticed that once again Phyllis was inappropriately relaxed without the anxiety that the rest of the room was feeling.

He looked over at Magen to see if she was picking up on the Phyllis phenomenon.

She wasn't processing the room; Magen was off in her mind trying to make sense of the situation. Mac could see the wheels rolling in her head, and her facial expressions were running back and forth from puzzlement to disappointment. He waved his hand in front of her face, startling her back to real time. She stopped long enough to force a smile and squeeze his hand.

"There really was no way of confronting this situation. We are simply in the phase of data collection," Kingston narrated.

"We have more theory than fact. At this time, our goal right now is to process what we have and look for vulnerabilities," Kingston continued.

"Have we identified any of the visitors that we could possibly isolate and interrogate?" Mac requested.

"We have identified one of the primaries that we consider a new arrival," Kingston continued as he pulled a photo out of his bag and passed it. "This, we have identified as one Cain, we have absolutely no data on this visitor even remotely connected to APL. Yet, here he is at the press conference standing with some highly respected corporate personnel."

He spent some time describing William Dean's mental break as if he had firsthand knowledge of the situation.

"This may sound crazy, but I met this guy about forty years ago, and he was slightly older then," William Dean broke in with distress in his voice.

"Are you sure it's the same guy? Forty years is a long time to remember," Kingston challenged.

"He shook my hand the day I was hired," Dean snapped back. "I know this sounds crazy. We spoke, he told me that he was at Woodstock the week before, and he had dropped acid as Jimi Hendrix played 'Star-Spangled Banner.' You don't forget something like that when it comes from your operations chief," Dean stated as he began to recall more of the event.

"Operations chief! That is significant!" Kingston turned to one of the computer guys and raised his hand.

"I am on it, boss!" the young tech guy shouted back.

Mac, always being the cop, watched the faces of the people in the room just to see the tension that they were feeling. Anyone with reasonable intelligence would be visibly upset with the subject matter. So, he was intrigued by the sight of Phyllis, who looked more nervous about what was going on.

She was biting her lower lip and rubbing her hands, but she wasn't upset about the subject matter; we were digging too deep. That was interesting to Mac because that indicated that she was most likely working a separate investigation.

The question now was, was it Phyllis who was working the case or was the CIA working an investigation?

"Found him," the young tech shouted out from behind the computer.

CHAPTER 50

"Mr. Cain, chairman of the board at Jane Haskins, announces that ground to be broken in Laurel, Maryland, on joint venture with NASA will initiate Applied Physics Facility," the tech read from the computer screen with limited emotion.

"Wow! That's really him," Kingston stated with noted disbelief in his voice.

"Mr. Dean was right about him or it appearing much younger forty years ago. How is that possible?" Magen shot out as she emerged from the informational explosion that they had all been through.

"We are dealing with a race of beings that far exceed our capability on every possible level. We are children to them!" Kingston stated with obvious anxiety in his voice.

Mac instinctively began to realize that Kingston's statement was being directed toward Phyllis. There was more going on here then met the eye; he had been feeling it since he walked in the room. There was a second investigation going on, and the CIA was involved.

That makes sense, he thought.

This is how these people ran their lives. Trust absolutely no one, and always have friends on both sides of the fence. The question was just how much did the CIA know in addition to what was being dropped on them today?

It would be almost shortsighted if he was to think that they were uninformed about the visitors. The Central Intelligence Agency would be the first line of defense an opposing force would need to get past in order to stage this type of penetration.

If I were to set up a clandestine operation against any of the major powers on this planet, it would help to establish a sentinel position within a monitoring agency.

Mac realized that he wasn't sure about any of this and that it was based on only possibilities. However, he had known that this Phyllis was all wrong from her first phony smile at the door.

The CIA that he has been aware of since he was a child never played it straight. As a matter of fact, historically they went out of their way not to play it straight. So, it would only make sense that they were positioning themselves for the game of the millennium.

From the way Kingston was responding to the new data, he was picking up on the double-dealing. This could be a perfect opportunity to split the herd and clean the room.

"I am getting the feeling that the CIA may have entered into a separate investigation. What's your feeling on this, Mr. Kingston?" Mac said aloud, making sure that everyone in the room heard him clearly.

"Well, I am not the person to answer that question, Officer MacDonald. Possibly Ms. Capaso could enlighten us!" Kingston snapped.

"I am simply an intermediate in this situation. I answer to a higher authority!" Phyllis pleaded, giving a significant performance.

"This is the wrong time for that kind of cop-out. We are in some real deep shit here!" Mac chimed in.

"Please, Phyllis, I know that we have had some differences in the past, but this is a time when we really need to come together," Magen pleaded.

"I am given a template to follow by my superiors. I am not the enemy. I am just doing my job," Phyllis stated with less enthusiasm.

"Ms. Capaso, I am quite aware of the assholes who sign your check, but if you don't come clean about what they are working on, I might just shoot you for doing your job!" William Dean responded through gritted teeth.

CHAPTER 51

"Easy, Bill!" Kingston stepped in, fully realizing the last forty-eight hours may have put William over the edge.

"I kidnapped a very decent man two days ago and most likely delivered him to his death at the hands of flesh-eating aliens. This shit will not fly," William Dean announced with a high level of anxiety.

"We are going to work this out, Bill. Take it easy!" Mac said evenly as he placed his hand on the distraught man.

Phyllis moved to the chair in the middle of the room and slowly sat down, looking from Magen and back to Dean. She placed her head in her hands and began to take deep breaths.

William sat back down in his chair, not taking his eyes off the woman in the middle of the room.

She then lifted her head and stared flatly at the camera section in the corner. Phyllis stood from her chair then reached deep down for the dignity that was under direct assault. Her hand motioned to the tech guys who were turned facing her, awaiting her response to the accusations.

The crew turned to their monitors and began to shut down the connections to the outside parties still online. The lady fixed her hair then brushed her long thin hands down the front of her dress. When the last light of computer connection went off, she turned to William Dean and put her hands together as if praying.

"At no time were we looking to place you in harm's way," Phyllis initiated.

"Please, I really understand the game I was playing it before you were born! What's going on?" Dean stated.

"Two years ago, during a routine investigation, we came across a closed file that belonged to Agent Cummings," Phyllis continued.

"What? You stole my research, you snake," Magen snarled.

"I wasn't responsible for the theft. However, it did spark an internal investigation that uncovered the visitors' presence, and you should feel good about that," Phyllis stated.

"I think I would have felt better if Mr. Dean shot you, but thank you!" Magen returned.

"I can understand your anger, but this is the world we live in, and I can't change what has happened. However, I can make this right if you let me," Phyllis pleaded.

"Make this right! Is that what I am hearing from you, Ms. Capaso? There is no making this right!" Dean stood and spoke in her face, not yelling but venomous.

"Well, then you people need to make up your mind. You can stay angry or just let me fill in some of the blanks," Phyllis stated.

"Ms. Capaso, you will have to forgive us. We are really quite disgusted with you and the people you represent. However, the things you know in that twisted mind of yours are the things we need to know," Mac clarified.

"Officer MacDonald, you really have no idea the world we live in. Lies are the currency we use to provide you with the illusion of safety and protection," Phyllis explained with true passion.

"I don't doubt what you are saying is true. I just wish you all would just stop playing this fuckin' game!" Mac shot back with an equal amount of passion.

"Too late! If we weren't playing along, you would be speaking in Russian or Chinese!" Phyllis snapped.

"Please let us stop the political shuffle. These things never really reach a middle ground, and we don't have time to play this game," Magen announced.

There was a moment of silence as everyone agreed that time was of the essence and they needed to move on with this.

Phyllis started to unwind a tale of epic proportion, and as she continued, fear was escalating. Apparently, Alexander Cain is the priority focus of several investigations that the CIA has underway. They have documented his presence in over three hundred historic references. His presence dates back as far as recordable time, and there are some theorists that feel he is shaping events that have long-standing effects. He can be linked to the courts of kings, both English and French, and his counsel has been respected. Recently, a photo came to light that places Cain with the czar Nicholas and Rasputin in the final days of their lives. There are countless photos of him with some slight differences, but him with world leaders throughout the centuries.

The CIA had been waiting for him to show up on the grid; they have been monitoring for his face and voiceprint on every point of the globe. The moment they caught him on an internal camera from Laurel, Maryland, they went crazy in Langley. Within three hours, they sent in an agent with journalism credentials to a press conference where he spoke of Mr. Dean's affair with a male supply clerk. Unfortunately, she was reported missing early this morning. She had six separate transmitters on her person; they all went south at the same time.

The idea was to make contact and open a potential dialogue with the designated visitor and see where that would take things. Mac couldn't help but think that this was a total act of desperation. He knew those evil fuckin' assholes just threw that girl to a proverbial wolf, without any real hesitation. He couldn't help but think that they murdered that girl to test the waters.

He began to consider the point of view of the Central Intelligence Agency and really struggled with the philosophy. Mac was really getting uncomfortable; the situation was bleak. He turned to William Dean and asked, "Mr. Dean, you seem like a reasonable person. Can I ask you a question?"

"Anything I can help you with," Dean shot back.

"The implications here are mind-boggling. Do you think the CIA did the right thing sending this girl in to die?" Mac said with a defiant air.

"I think I understand where you are coming from, Officer MacDonald, but the last time I looked, the NYPD had some dark element connected to its name," William added with a matter-of-fact tone.

"Good point! Thank you, sir. However, we don't send our own into the belly of the beast," Mac stated firmly.

"Officer MacDonald, I have always thought that American police in general are isolating and, for the most part, work against the people they serve the most," William said with just a little sadness in his voice.

"I think we are just going to agree to disagree on that," Mac said with a hint of a smile.

"Your moral high ground is admirable, Officer, but I assure you the beings that we are dealing with have no way to gauge your superiority," Phyllis blasted as she grew tired of Mac's disdain.

"This is really getting us absolutely nowhere! You will have to forgive Officer MacDonald. He still has a soul," Magen barked directly in the face of the surprised Phyllis.

"Wow, Magen! It's so good to see you get your feisty up!" Phyllis smirked.

"The hostility within this room is alarming, and the sad reality here is that in our present state we don't stand a chance!" the canon attorney DaTonne chimed in with genuine agitation.

The room went painfully quiet as the leaders within the room began to realize the priest was absolutely correct. The way things were going, they were going to get hurt or worse.

The beings that they were dealing with were advanced, organized, and extremely lethal. They had been living among us for centuries that we know about, and their capability for deception is evident. The humans, on the other hand, are afraid of shadows that they are not even sure are there. The worst of it is that they hate one another and there just isn't enough time to pull the players together.

Mac sat and pondered the harsh reality that he was faced with, and being a lifetime cop, he knew that he needed to break this down. The way he saw this unfolding was in two directions: a long drawn-out IT war, or a swift frontal assault. They didn't have time or the ability to play their game. Their only real chance was to penetrate the hive and either take down the queen, or bag one of the drones and squeeze the truth out of it.

It was at that very minute that Mac knew what needed to be done. He leaned over to William Dean and said, "You mentioned earlier that there were several underlings at the building in Maryland. Do I have that right?"

"Six that I know of. They all hang out together really tight, all Hopkins grads," Dean said with a slight puzzled look.

"Do they leave the building and go to separate homes, or do they go to one place when they leave the lab at night?" Mac probed.

"Oh, I don't know!" Dean began. "Wait! I know the answer to this. They have separate homes!" Dean shouted.

"You seem really sure!" Mac smiled.

"Dead sure. I had to do a survey three years ago. I bought several of the homes myself to keep employees within twenty miles of the facility," Dean stated with newfound passion.

"Do you know where they live?" Mac asked.

"Four out of the six, yes, I do!" William Dean added, starting to see where the conversation was heading.

CHAPTER 52

"Hold the phone, cowboys. We really don't want to tip our hand rushing into some slightly planned excursion," Phyllis chimed in as she picked up on the dialogue.

"Is the CIA ready to go with an alternative plan, or is there something else that you folks are up to?" Dean waded in.

"The agency is currently fact-finding at this point. There is a significant deficit in information, and my superiors would like to be patient and cautious." Phyllis stumbled a little as she stated her organization's position.

"Ms. Capaso, is there anything else that you are not telling us that might aid in the understanding of our current position or retrieving Mr. Pierce?" Dean asked as he picked up on the hesitation.

"You bet there is!" Mac snapped. "I have only known you for about forty minutes, and I can't believe you are such a bad liar, considering the people you work for," Mac said with a smile.

"Excuse me!" Phyllis snapped. "I have no need to account to you on any level."

"The only thing that makes any sense to me is the possibility that you are afraid and you want us to have the information, but you have only been given partial clearance on the information you can provide us," Mac stated as he pondered the situation.

"That is some fine deductive reasoning, young man!" William Dean said with an air of surprise.

"Please let us in the game, Agent Capaso. We are just spinning our wheels without it," Mac added with the slight feel of compassion.

The woman, who was really beautiful, scanned the room and sat down with the look of pure defeat. Mac looked deep in her face and realized he was dead-on with his analysis of her situation. Magen moved over to her and started to talk slowly with her back to him. He could tell from the look on her face that whatever Magen was saying was having a profound impact.

It was at that time Mac became increasingly aware of the Israeli who was reviewing papers and purposely disengaging himself from everything that was going on within the room. Phyllis was also working really hard not to look in his direction.

Then suddenly, as if it was scripted, the Israeli stood up and walked to the computer access panel and flicked the switch. The full line of computers and cameras all went totally silent, as did those in the room. The man walked slowly to the middle of the room then grabbed his case and placed the papers he was working on carefully in the file section. He turned to Phyllis and those gathered around her. His face was drawn and somewhat defeated; however, he remained calm as he addressed the room.

"I will take my leave of you now. Please don't be too hard on Agent Capaso. She has been under strict instruction to limit her dialogue," the man began.

"Why would you people go through all of this, leading us here, this room, only to give us limited information?" Mac pleaded.

"Old habits die hard. Trust has become such a foreign concept, I apologize! Please, Agent Capaso, provide them with the answers that they seek," he finished and walked through the door.

"I think it is safe to say that Elvis has left the building," Mac jested with nervous humor.

"What exactly was it that you people have been holding on to that was so damn important?" Dean probed.

"I was given permission to provide information on a need-to-know basis," Phyllis said with tears welling up in her eyes.

"I wish I could provide you with comfort and understanding, but I am so disgusted with you pack of lunatics," Magen added with cold distain.

"I follow orders! That's what I do. That is how you survive in this business," Agent Capaso picked up as she finished her statement.

"What gives, Phyllis? What is so sensitive that you people needed to waste two hours of vital time?" Magen requested.

"The United States government currently has in its possession part of what we believe to be one of their transportation devices!" Phyllis initiated.

"You said part of the machine. I take it that it's not working," Mac probed.

"The Russians also have a similar machine. However, they have denied this fact, and we have not been able to compare both units," Phyllis continued.

"Does your intel confirm the potential of their unit working?" Mac asked.

"No, they are having the same issues we are, configuration and power source," Phyllis continued.

"Where is the American unit being stored at this time?" William Dean probed.

"Currently the unit is being housed in an underground bunker ninety miles outside of Las Vegas in a location know as Groom Lake," Phyllis stated after a brief moment of hesitation.

"Groom Lake. That's Area 51, right? I'm right about that, Nevada, right?" Mac scrambled with excitement.

"That is one of the names that the facility has been called. Most recently the nut balls have tagged the place Homey Airport or Paradise Ranch," Phyllis stated.

"Well, I guess they weren't that nuts after all. They knew that something was wrong out there!" Mac shot back at the glaring agent.

"I could secure temporary passes for any government installation if you think it would help," she offered.

"Well, I don't think flying out to Nevada could help our situation, considering the device is nonoperational," William Dean stated.

"I am simply trying to provide you with the full access of governmental facilities!" Phyllis concluded.

"I think our primary focus is best served to attempt to locate Mr. Pierce. If you could help with that, it would be most appreciated," William Dean motioned, still concerned about his friend.

"From what we have been able to piece together, the man was assisted into a yellow cab outside the train station. That cab was lost from detection as it entered Brooklyn," Phyllis stated.

"I can't ask anyone to join my personal crusade. However, I will need to make my way to Brooklyn. Can intelligence assist me we with any additional manpower?" Dean requested.

"We have several agents mobilized in the Williamsburg section, concentrating on warehouse areas and abandoned dwellings," Agent Capaso stated.

"I would like to assist with their efforts," William Dean requested with passion in his voice.

CHAPTER 53

Cornell snapped out of some light sleep that he allowed himself after his conversation with Thomas.

There was a high-pitched sound of air brakes releasing pressure after coming to a full stop.

He was totally isolated and blind in the dark, so he could only imagine a truck pulling up, with someone fully unaware of what was going on within this building. Thoughts raced through Cornell's awakening mind of the dangerous possibilities of someone coming through the door at that moment. He contemplated several different scenarios that would assist him to make contact with the driver of the truck. The unfortunate truth was that there was nothing he could do. If the guy came through the door, he could scream and warn the poor bastard, but it would be too late. If this guy even stepped through that door, he is toast; there was nothing that he could do to change the outcome.

He stopped his thoughts and considered the flip side of the situation. There was a possibility that the trucker was one of them and maybe they had found Mr. Dean. He was angry with himself for not even thinking about Dean since he came to this place; he only thought of himself. That was not his nature; he was a Christian who cared for others. It was being with these things that screwed up his thinking.

His thinking came to an abrupt halt as a lever was pulled somewhere in the building and a series of lights flashed on. He turned around to see several of the aliens moving slowly toward the front door, and then there was the sound of another switch. The light hurt his eyes, but he was happy to have the lights on; the darkness was working on him. The room was filled with light, and for the first time since his arrival, he could make out the full content of the room. There were three large engines all in a row toward the back of the warehouse. He didn't understand their purpose or what they could possibly be used for.

Steel and iron sheets were in several different locations; again, he couldn't understand the purpose. Everything looked old, but the facility was clean; he wondered about the dust and who cleaned the place. He counted seven people in the room, all males around the same age. They all had a very similar look to them. It wasn't a physical similarity; each individual was different. Two of the visitors were of African descent; the others had European features. Thomas had some Asian quality but not fully.

As his thoughts were focused on the visitors, he heard the double doors open and voices; fear gripped him. A young woman walked through the doors wearing what appeared to be a tour guide uniform. She was extremely good-looking and well proportioned. She was followed by a dozen older individuals who were busy taking photos and listening to their pretty guide.

"The building was utilized by government agencies as far back as 1945. The Bradley Tank was assembled in this very building, then loaded into ships across the street," she started her performance.

"What's that smell in this place?" snapped one of the tourists.

"During the Vietnam War, the factory was utilized for helicopter assembly weapon research. It was finally decommissioned in 1974," the woman continued.

"Why in God's name are we here? This is not part of the tour," an older gentleman announced.

"This is the warehouse section of the building. In the factory section, they worked on the guidance system for the Black Hawk helicopter," she continued.

"This is ridiculous. You're not even listening to us!" shouted an older man in a Red Sox cap.

"I assure you, I am listening to everything you have to say," she said with an air of arrogance.

"Then why are we here?" he snapped back.

"Oh, you're here for lunch!" she said coldly.

CHAPTER 54

Fear gripped Cornell as he began to see what was unfolding in front of his eyes. He held his breath as he watched the visitors close in on the tourists. The guide began to unbutton her white blouse to the absolute astonishment of the people in front of her. Her white lace bra sat perfectly against her light brown skin. She reached behind her back and with precise movement, she unhinged the light fragile garment that fell to the floor. Her firm supple breasts pointed high, the simple perfection of her nipples was breathtaking.

Cornell knew it was a designed distraction as he watched the others complete their own disrobing. His eyes locked with Thomas who was taking in deep breaths, and then the change began. In seconds, Thomas completed a full metamorphosis from an average male into what could only be described as an eight-foot wolf god. The narrative really didn't do justice to what he was watching. These beings were canine like but nothing like the human ideal of canine. There was a blank, flat look in the eyes of all canines that was truly the opposite with these beings.

Here was a high-intellect marker present accompanied by brutal superiority. Cornell felt dizzy and slightly nauseous; he wasn't sure why, but the illness intensified when the beings began to change.

Thomas moved past the young woman and reached out toward the older man, who had initiated flight mode to escape his fate.

The being that was Thomas caught the man at the midway point near the base of his spine. With one crisp yank, the old man was crippled and paralyzed for the last few seconds of his life. Then, there was a crushing noise that could only be bones separating from cartilage.

The room was now gripped in mass hysteria; smiles turned to high-pitched screams.

The young guide had fully transformed, and with one quick motion, she sprang off the floor then ricocheted from the ceiling. Her talons found a nine-year-old boy mid chest and ripped him from the hands of his screaming grandmother. The rest of the visitors had joined the feast, and within seconds, the room had become one large blood spray.

Sunlight beams came through the window, and the mists of fine blood were easily identified. Cornell had to force himself to look away; he kneeled behind the chair and held tight to his ears in hopes of drowning out the screams. Then he realized that one of the screams was growing closer to him. He removed his hands and stood up in time to see that a middle-aged woman had broken free of the carnage and was lumbering toward him at a blistering pace. He realized at that moment that her left arm and shoulder were missing, and blood was shooting from her wound. Every step she took forced more blood from her broken body. She had made it six feet from Cornell's position and then fell to her knees and looked directly at him.

"Please," she sputtered through tears.

A light brown visitor pounced down on her back with enough force that her right eye evacuated from her skull. The alien licked it from the floor and dragged her limp body back to the central area where the chaos was all but ended.

Now there was just the sound of eating with the snap of the intermittent bone. Cornell realized that he was standing in a puddle of his own urine. He slowly sank back to his knee and began to weep like a child. He had lived through two tours of duty during the Vietnam War, and had witnessed horror of an epic proportion. However, this was more than he could bear; his stomach and head were both struggling to deal with the event. He thought to himself how fortunate that his belly was empty because there no way he could possible hold food down.

The slaughter was over, but the visions and screams still echoed in Cornell's head. He slowly pulled himself together, first focusing on his thoughts and then on his hands that were shaking uncontrollably. He held both hands out in front of his body, then practiced rhythm breathing. After a few seconds, the calm began to wash over him; he had reached a point where reason began to even out his thoughts.

Then he realized that Thomas was standing in front of him, fully transformed back to the human form.

Cornell looked up to see a blank, flat expression on his face. He was confused by Thomas; he had never seen anything like the horror show of two minutes ago. However, Thomas sat there almost perplexed by Cornell's emotions.

Cornell smiled slightly as he regained his composure, not wanting to show any weakness to this being.

"I can tell you there are no other life forms within the known universe that leak from their eyes when they are under distress," Thomas said flatly.

"Well, I guess that makes us unique!" Cornell added with a slight smile.

"Carbon-based life forms are far from unique. there are planets throughout the universe that are littered with them," Thomas stated.

"Then why are you here, and not having a full-blown picnic on one of those planets?" Cornell asked.

"The natural resources on this planet are through the roof. You have no idea how rare that is," Thomas began.

"I find myself desiring to return to your planet, not only for the feast but the freshness of the air and water. You people have no idea of what a miracle you have under your feet," Thomas continued. "But, the most important thing to us is you're Rollers. Few planets can support the existence of that breed distortion." Thomas smiled.

"Rollers, what are they?" Cornell asked with confusion.

"They are those who walk among you with excessive weight!" Thomas stated.

"I guess you people don't have to concern yourselves with being politically correct," Cornell said.

"I don't understand what it is that you are saying," Thomas seemed puzzled.

"In my world, it is considered in poor taste to make fun of overweight people," Cornell attempted to explain.

"That is human nonsense and extremely dishonest. You isolate these people and make their disorder worse. No matter, guilt or no guilt, it all tastes the same," Thomas stated with his attempt at humor.

"You might be right, Thomas. I must admit that I tend to shy away from obese people as a rule," Cornell pondered.

"Have you ever asked yourself why, in some cultures, the Rollers are revered and in others they are treated like lepers?" Thomas seemed puzzled.

"They make us uncomfortable here in the land of plenty. They are the negative possibility for most of us."

"The negative possibility, imagine that," Thomas stated as he shook his head.

"The reality is that you beings are responsible for the current epidemic, and the Rollers are designed for your harvesting needs," Cornell stated.

"That is not totally accurate. I know that you think we are the axis of evil, but we are not alternating anything that wasn't already in the mail," Thomas clarified.

"Your boss filled me in on your little project here on Earth. I don't know why you feel a need to sugarcoat your actions," Cornell taunted.

"I need to justify absolutely zero to you, meat bag, and your attempts at provoking me are starting to annoy me," Thomas stated coldly as he turned and walked away.

CHAPTER 55

Sometimes there is a good reason that some roads are less traveled!

—Voice of the lost

"We just received a call from Langley. Apparently a meeting is taking place here in New York, at the Four Seasons Hotel in a modified safe room," one of the visitors related to Cain.

"Who is at this meeting?"

"We have learned that the CIA, NSA, Vatican counsel, and several local authorities are in attendance," the visitor stated with limited emotions.

"What the fuck is a modified safe room?" Cain screamed as he grabbed the apprentice's windpipe.

"They are effectively jamming any signals from entering or leaving the room!" the stunned visitor pronounced through his painful throat.

"I think we can stop looking for Mr. Dean at this point. Assemble everyone in the area," Cain commanded as he released his grip on the younger visitor.

"Why do you wish to end the search? We believe we are making progress," the visitor asked.

Cain looked at the being for a few seconds and then retrieved a nickel-plated Beretta from his waist and shot the being in the face.

He wondered how they had been able to maintain their stealth existence for as long as they had with lack of critical thinking.

He recalled his last visit to Earth and the level of professionalism of those in charge. There was something really wrong here, and these were truly dangerous times. He began to concern himself with the dedication level of his superiors. His initial thought was that Earth had moved from the guild's primary status list. Possibly, they had taken their eye off the prize; however, they did send him back after the first sign of trouble.

The fact that human authorities have been busy digging into Gray business is highly unfortunate. He smiled and thought to himself that something needed to be done to stifle the momentum of forces working against his project.

Those involved needed to understand that they were so far out of their league that they resembled children playing with matches. Cain felt anger dripping over his heart, and he embraced these emotions with great relish. It had been some time since he felt these feelings pulsing through his body. His home world had become a tiresome place filled with peacekeepers and naturalists; decisions were hard to come by. He had to work many favors to return to this planet.

He estimated that he could be at the Four Seasons Hotel in less than twenty minutes. He needed help from several areas, and instinctively he knew how to respond to this situation.

Cain's eyes began to fluctuate between black and yellow due to his increased rage.

As the others began to move closer, not fully understanding why he eliminated the team member, they were presented with a stunned look. Cain was indifferent to their confusion and was fixated on business. He began to bark orders to everyone within earshot, and they were falling over themselves to hear the plan.

CHAPTER 56

"I want a full grid around a ten-block radius. Central point will be the Four Seasons Hotel," Cain barked.

"We have initiated a full lockdown of one kilometer, and we have established partial penetration of the room," one of the Haskins visitors responded.

"How were they able to isolate themselves from our surveillance?" Cain asked with surprise in his tone.

"They are utilizing a primitive electro bubble that is reversing our signal. Not bad for their level of technology," the aide stated with respect.

"We need to identify the human who designed the room. He is way too informed for my liking," Cain instructed.

"He will be identified and terminated, sir, if that is your specifications," the aide said nervously.

"Oh, no, there will be no terminations on this trip. I want these collaborators captured and dissected. I will retrieve every speck of information that they are holding in their little monkey melons." Cain's tone intensified.

"There are two primary teams converging on the Four Seasons at this time. The alpha squad is awaiting a go for extraction," the aide continued.

"Move fast. No one in the room should be injured. Are we clear?" Cain snapped.

"Yes, sir, they have their orders. We should be there in less than seven minutes," he continued.

"I want the room disassembled, and all the communication devices that are salvageable, I want to know who was on the receiving end of every word that went out of the room. Let's go," Cain barked.

The Four Seasons was quiet; the clock on the wall indicated that it was just past midnight. The doorman was slightly confused by the shadows that passed on his right, and then even more profound, there was a strong stench that now permeated the night air.

The man was now in a heightened sense of awareness. He had seen something; he just wasn't sure what it was. Then there was a dull thud from behind him; he reached behind and felt his head, and when his hand came back around to his field of vision, there was a large clump of hair and blood in his hands. His sight faded, and he died before he fell to the ground on the red carpet of the finest hotel in New York.

The front door of the Four Seasons shattered and splintered glass in every direction. The dark shadows now came into full view of both the patrons and the staff that had the misfortune to be present in the lobby. Screams filled the air as the beings laid into a group of four who were leaving the restaurant.

The concierge quickly picked up the phone and began to dial. He instinctively glanced up to see a wolflike figure moving at him from the ceiling at incredible speed. The being's large right talon caught his arm above the elbow. His arm with the phone attached fell to the floor like a prop from a cheap horror film. He tried to scream, only to have his face smashed with enough velocity that his lower jaw was severed.

A night janitor who watched the events from the open stairwell down the hall panicked and closed and locked the door. As he turned to take the stairs, the door exploded, and there stood an ominous being that was panting like a rabid canine. The stunned man raised a broomstick and poked the being in the left eye. As the man ran from the scene screaming in broken Spanish, the being hit the floor and began to wail like nothing on this Earth.

Back in the lobby, the screaming had stopped as the two other beings took to the stairs four at a time. The wounded alien who then realized he had now become a liability to the mission made his escape from a partially open window twenty feet off the ground entrance. It took several leaps up and then sprang to the building across the street. It was out of full view within seconds.

CHAPTER 57

"There, in the lobby!" the young red-haired man at the computer yelled with sudden shock riddled in his voice.

"Who's in the lobby?" Magen responded, not wanting to consider the obvious.

"Abort!" Phyllis screamed as she joined the techs at the control board.

"The red and blue switch," the tech yelled in Phyllis's direction.

"Where should we go?" William Dean called out in desperation.

"The room across the hall is one of ours. The fire escape leads to the back alley. Ho now!" Phyllis said through panic tears.

"We're out of here!" Mac said as he grabbed Magen's hand and led her to the door.

As Mac and Magen moved through the front door, they were stunned to see several soldiers in full riot gear. Mac didn't recognize the emblems on the uniforms or the weapons they were carrying. He thought that was strange, but in that moment of flight, it wasn't his priority. He wasn't fully sure of what was moving in on their position, but he could see the terror in William Dean's eyes. He didn't see the man as someone who would spook all that easy, so something was on the way, and it was bad.

They were ushered toward the door across the hall, but Mac wasn't having any of that; it was time to change lanes. He grabbed Magen's hand and moved her past the door, with only minimal resistance. They hit the door to the stairs at the same moment the room they had just left lit up like the Fourth of July. Mac could hear the roar of the magnesium, and the light filled the entire floor.

They were torching the whole room, he thought to himself.

On the other side of the door, the noise was still buzzing in his ears from the room explosion. Then he began to hear a much different sound working its way up the stairs at an almost impossible pace. Mac directed Magen to the stairwell leading upstairs; after they had taken a few steps, Mac second-guessed that decision, feeling that it would have been better to take the sure escape route down the back.

They had made two flights when all hell broke loose downstairs; first, the door exploded, and then countless bullet rounds echoed through the building. Then as fast as it erupted, the event ended with only silence. Mac could hear some strange sounds coming from the stairwell; he really didn't want to hang around and get the details. He considered getting off the top floor and then taking the service elevator down to the kitchen. Then he thought that if the whole building was under siege, then the best option would be to hit the roof and call for backup.

He reached the roof door and realized that he was totally out of breath; he turned and looked at Magen who was smiling at his fatigue.

"I plan to give up smoking for Lent," Mac joked with Magen.

"I hope not. I really like the taste of tobacco in your wet mouth, and there is a sexy element of a man smoking," Magen said with a provocative flare.

"Really, to think of all that money I spent on gum," Mac snapped back, not knowing if she was serious or not.

He was surprised to find the roof door open; hotels in the city were very protective of the security of their high points. As a cop, he knew that 10 percent of the suicide rate in this city is made up of tourists. Their most common method is long falls, primarily from one of our many fine bridges, but the number one suicidal destination here in the Big Apple is tall hotels.

All this was rolling through his head as he pushed the door open, only to stare in the face of a young, good-looking man in an extremely expensive suit.

CHAPTER 58

Cain continued to bark orders to the penetration team, as he navigated himself into position to jettison from the helicopter. He nodded to the pilot and his team leader, and in one quick motion, four of the visitors, including Cain, stepped out into a brisk and windy New York evening. The fact that they were hovering the Huey 120 feet above the hotel didn't seem to concern them in the least.

As Cain sailed through the air, closing in on the roof, he connected his thoughts with the ground team who had already neutralized the lobby and were now proceeding to the safe room. The four of them came down on the roof within three feet of each other, and the landing was flawless and gentle.

One of the aliens immediately began to scale the outside wall heading down to the target room. The others fanned out to access the several exits. Cain reached behind his neck and straightened out his collar that had become disheveled during his descent. It was at that moment that the door opened, and there stood a highly surprised man and woman. Cain recognized the woman from his debriefing prior to his transport back to Earth. The man he didn't recognize, but he reeked of human authority figure; from the clothing he was wearing, Cain guessed local.

"Agent Cummings I would like to introduce myself. Alexander Cain, at your service," Cain announced while waving his hand for effect.

"I have heard quite a bit about you over the last twenty-four hours. It is my pleasure," Magen returned greetings, desperately trying to keep her composure.

"The young gentleman with the Beretta tucked into his waist, I apologize, your name escapes me," Cain added with an evil smile.

"Bob MacDonald, New York's finest, and please don't apologize. I understand you're from out of town!" Mac responded back, having trouble taking the youngster in front of him seriously.

"Oh, that is funny. I believe that I am starting to like you already, Officer MacDonald." Cain smiled.

"I grow on people and apparently everything else," Mac snapped back, attempting to cover his fear with humor.

"You and your friends have hurt a lot of people. I have been tracking your assassinations for several years," Magen stated with an accusatory tone.

"Well, we all have a job to do, my young friend. Where is William Dean?" Cain said coldly.

"Listen, Mr. Cain, I am sure you could find Mr. Dean on your own. Why don't we sit down and attempt to reach some kind of understanding about what you folks are doing and why?" Mac asked nicely, slowly moving his left hand toward his waist to retrieve his Beretta.

"If that weapon leaves your waist, you will never masturbate the same way again. Are we clear, monkey boy?" Cain stated as he moved with incredible speed to position himself less than an inch from Mac's face.

"Clear as an unmudded lake!" Mac returned as he slowly moved his hand away from his waist.

"I know that fight-or-flight mechanism is kicking into overdrive with your human brain, but please let me assure you that either option would be futile," Cain stated with clear authority.

"So where do we go from here, Mr. Cain? I am sure that your focus right now is containment," Magen said, attempting to appeal to his superior intellect.

"I think we have moved past the point of containment. You should see the lobby of this place," Cain stated with a bit of a childish giggle.

"Whatever has happened down there, the agency can clean it up. Not saying it was right, but there are no options off the table at this time," Magen added with growing concern for her safety.

"There is no way I can determine what information left that room or who has access to it," Cain pondered as his face moved from Magen and Mac.

Mac's brain raced as he considered making a run for the back stairs. He wondered if this thing could read his mind. He was confused about the Beretta he had tucked in his waist; how did it see the type of weapon from ten feet away, from behind his shirt?

This average-size young man in front of him posed no real threat, and Mac felt that he could overpower him. His concern was now for Magen; how he could keep her safe if he was to make a move on the alien?

Mac had all these thoughts rolling around his head when he saw a shadow move from the far line of his sight. Mac turned to see the being in its raw form walk from the shadow. He could feel the muscles in his chest constrict as the being came within striking distance.

There stood an absolute magnificent creature; Mac estimated the visitor at seven foot six. the weight was hard to establish due to the fur, but it was easy to guess that it was over four hundred pounds. Fear gripped Mac, and he could feel Magen's hand gripping his own hand to the point where there was no blood left in his digits.

Cain seemed even smaller with the giant standing next to him; the shoulders were stunning. Mac couldn't take his eyes off the being; he felt fear, but there was something else that he didn't understand. There was something reassuring about the being, and then Mac realized that the visitor resembled an actual Thunder Cat, a cartoon from his youth. Of course, the being was canine in nature; possibly it was the build and the superiority. Mac was stunned by the movements of the big beast-like creature; even with its great size, the agility was amazing.

"I sense that the sight of my big friend has your heartbeat accelerating. No reason to be upset. Please let me introduce Thomas, my second-in-command," Cain said with random calmness as if this was a dinner party.

"I am pleased to meet you both," Thomas stated as he gently laid out his massive paw, talons withdrawn.

"Officer MacDonald from Queens, New York. It is a real pleasure to meet you," Mac said as he laid his small hand in the twenty-inch palm of the giant before him.

"Agent Cummings, it is my pleasure to meet you. You have been the focal point of a multitude of policy changes since the year of the rat." The giant bowed with his hands at its side.

"Thank you! I am picking up an accent from your speech. Is your background Hispanic?" she probed.

"You have an extremely good ear. When I am not in my normal phase, my identity is Latino," Thomas added with respect in his voice for Magen's ability.

"Is there accent training involved with your insertion into your human role?" Magen continued to probe.

"Agent Cummings, you have already caught us. Why are you still interrogating us?" Cain laughed as Thomas joined in.

"Don't take it personally. This lady just will not stop believe me," Mac said out loud to the chuckles of everyone on that roof, except Magen.

"That's funny halfway across the known universe, and the male species can't help being stupid," Magen said without any fear of reprisal from the visitors.

"Let me please apologize, Agent Cummings. No offense was intended," Thomas came forward and raised his hands as if to plead forgiveness.

"So, what are we doing? Where is all this going? We don't have a chance against the pack of you and your friends," Mac asked.

"Where is this going?" Cain responded then continued, "Let me tell you where this was going. We were coming down here to eliminate everyone connected to that room," Cain said with minimal emotion.

CHAPTER 59

"That is pretty scary, Mr. Cain!" Magen said, constantly reminding herself that the child in front of her was a savage narcissistic psychopath.

"I stepped out of a helicopter twelve minutes ago and floated down over this city and felt a great truth roll over me," Cain began as he paced the roof, "That truth is that I love this city. I have always loved it. Do you know this area was called New Amsterdam?" Cain asked, not really looking for an answer.

"There are four Grays on this planet, one female in China, another in Russia, and both me and Thomas here in the States. The rest are clones or biotechs," Cain continued.

"The other Grays are connected directly to me when they want to be. The sense I have is that they are all feeling the pending threat," he went on.

"There is no threat from us?" Mac responded with stress in his voice.

"I need to arrange a meeting with the decision makers of this planet, more specific, the NSA, CIA, and possibly some degree of local authorities. I will leave that up to your superiors," Cain began to speak louder as the helicopter began to circle the building.

"It sounds to me like you are considering some level of truce between our species and your own?" Magen asked.

"I know all this must sound absolutely strange to the both of you. All things shall be revealed in due time. Please work on the arrangements," Cain was close to shouting at this point.

"We need to know the whereabouts of one Cornell Pierce. Is the man injured?" Mac snapped back to being a cop now, realizing that he wasn't going to die on the roof of the Four Seasons.

"Please work on the meeting. I will be in touch. Mr. Pierce is alive and will be returned," Cain finished.

At the close of Cain's last sentence, the giant behind Mac blasted off the roof and, in seconds, was closing in on the helicopter. Cain smiled at both Magen and Mac and with effortless grace followed the giant.

Like a rocket, he snapped off the roof; they could both feel the air suck away from the area. Magen took two steps forward, being pulled by the vacuum created from the alien departure. Mac watched the helicopter as it sailed out of sight, struggling to piece together the events of the last several minutes.

He reached out and grabbed Magen's hand as she was being sucked forward. She thanked him then began to straighten her hair and clothing that had been ruffled. Mac turned from the helicopter to look at Magen who looked stunned and amazed. He contemplated saying something funny and off-center but restrained himself. Magen really didn't look like humor would be well received at that very moment. Mac released his grip on her arm, realizing that he was still holding her.

Mac had lived in the city for most of his adult life, and being a cop, he had seen some of the worst that the city had to offer. However, even through all the madness, he still was able to compartmentalize the majority of the events that were placed in his path. This was way beyond anything his brain was able to deal with. He watched as the copter trailed off over the Kosciuszko Bridge, and he held his eyes for a few minutes more.

Then there was cold silence. Magen was lost in her own thoughts, and Mac didn't know where to start.

"Well, that was really something. I don't think I have ever been that afraid of someone that young and pretty," Mac began, mostly to hear words leave his mouth and promote breathing.

"That alien was talking like he wanted to make some kind of deal, am I right?" Magen asked with obvious confusion.

"Yeah, he wants to have a sit-down with the brass," Mac continued, not able to stop the slapstick comebacks.

"Mac, are we actually going back to Gregory and Phyllis to set up some kind of cosmic council?" Magen continued to run the scenario through her head.

"At least you are working with people who are open to the possibilities of extraterrestrial involvement. My captain would shoot me on general principle if I told him what went down here," Mac stated.

"I am still trying to wrap my head around what really did go down here tonight," Magen said as she looked back toward the direction of the helicopter that was now long gone.

"Aliens in New York, what are you having a problem with?" Mac kept going, unable to stop.

"We need to find William Dean and the rest of the people that fled the room a few minutes ago. They could be hurt or worse," Magen announced as she began to regain her composure.

"Well, from the sound of the sirens down on the street, I think it's safe to say that all hell has broken loose," Mac added as he peeked over the building's edge.

"We need to get down there and connect with our people. Please, let's get off this roof," Magen said as if she had enough.

"Right behind you. This roof has seen the last of me," Mac stated as he held the door for Magen.

CHAPTER 60

Cain and Thomas walked into the warehouse, not concerned with the blood and bones spread throughout the staging area. Thomas stepped over a shredded torso, avoiding a long spreading bloodstain, deeply concerned about the Italian shoes he had recently purchased. On the back wall, there was a row of racks loaded with electronic products. Cain moved a wall receptacle to the left and entered a series of numbers on an LCD keyboard. He took a step back, and within seconds, the shelves began to fold away from the center, revealing a steel door. Cain then stepped in front of the door and waited as the retinal scan aligned directly in front of his face. There was a pause, and then the door popped open. He reached out, opened the door, and Thomas and he entered the room that was wall-to-wall with the planet's most sophisticated computer systems.

Some of the components were not from Earth but were integrated to enhance the system's functioning ability. Cain and Thomas sat in the two chairs facing the primary board; the chairs were taken directly from the retired space shuttle. Thomas was able to secure them from eBay under a dummy company connected with the Smithsonian.

They attached several leads to the side of their skull and throat then began to manipulate the boards throughout the room with their thought patterns.

On the big board to the right were the images of two individuals; one female oriental named Sonja and another older man with strong facial features named Nickolas Putin were staring at Cain.

Sounds similar to humpback whales began to echo throughout the room; the dialogue was easy and relaxed at first, then slowly escalated. Cain was the facilitator, that was easy to see; however, the Russian gentleman Nickolas was also impressively vocal.

One thing that was absolutely clear was that they all wanted to stay on Earth. The issue was the method that Cain had chosen to reveal some truth to the human authorities. They had followed a long line of pioneers who lived a standing code to exist only in the shadows, to be only ghostlike. Now a meeting that would expose the truth that they had worked so hard to conceal worked against everything they have established over the centuries.

Cain was respected among the Grays, but this was a violation of great significance. The hesitation and fear filled the dialogue, but Cain was firm that in order to meet the desired end, a partial truce needed to be obtained. He explained that a penetration into their existence had already occurred, and there was an attempt to clean the event; however, this attempt was a complete failure. They were able to make some connections regarding their activities; they are aware of their tracking procedures through the use of migrating wildlife. They were able to piece together patterns surrounding the deaths of countless scientists.

There was a gasp from the two on the wall. Cain continued to explain his plan, and the three others listened closely with only minor interruptions. Cain spoke of the superiority of the Grays, the duty and honor of the four still remaining. His pride was evident, and it was shared deeply with others. Thomas began to clarify the events that took place at the hotel; he spoke of the host of agencies that were involved with the improvised room. Although the room itself was primitive, it was effective; obviously some advanced thinking went into the construction.

"It is clear they have a fundamental understanding of our tactics and ability. The level of understanding is unclear, but I feel that it is safe to say they have a working knowledge of our mission. I understand the apprehension of those germinated from the one true seed. However, I see only one viable course of action. The humans are confused and afraid. This is the perfect time to penetrate and come to terms that we could all live with. I will miss many things from the Zen, as I know we all will. I often find myself dreaming of the Red Oceans of the Flow, during the passing of the three moons. I leave an extension of myself on Zen; he is close to my soul. There is strength in his talons. We all have connections there, yet here we are seeking our own interest and glory. Earth has been our home, for me at least."

"Young Thomas, we feel your passion for what you speak. All of us have something on this planet," Nickolas began in broken English that was not too difficult to follow. "The problem here is complete exposure. There are four of us against a full planet of neurotic carbon-based life forms," Nickolas half joked.

"I understand this goes against everything that we practice as a superior species," Cain volunteered.

"That it does. However, we feel that it is the right time to make the leap," Nickolas admitted.

"We are in full agreement. I have to acknowledge that the council is unaware of this activity. After this meeting, we will sever all ties with the Zen and its inhabitants," Cain finished his discussion to a cold silence.

"Are we all to present ourselves at this meeting, or will one of us be representing the alliance?" Sonja asked as she broke her silence.

"I am open to discussion regarding how we should proceed with this meeting. I am greatly aware that it impacts us all," Cain stated.

"Cain is the only one who has been identified in human form. I believe the safest course of action would be to move slowly with the integrations, possibly hologram the initial contact," Sonja suggested.

"I understand your hesitation. However I will be attending in form, I can make arrangements for three interactive holograms," Cain reported.

"That would be acceptable and prudent," Sonja stated.

"I am in agreement with that plan. We will await a time and place and additional information," Nickolas added as he and Sonja faded from the plasma screen.

"If you wish for me to attend this meeting, I am ready to stand by you," Thomas volunteered without hesitation.

"That is honorable, Thomas, but this is something that I want to engage myself. The others are right to be hesitant. These are fearful creatures, and the safe play is for one of us to initiate the dialogue," Cain said boldly and without reservations.

"You will be totally on your own in there. What happens if they attempt to damage you?" Thomas asked with genuine concern.

"The possibility does exist that they may attempt some degree of challenge. I have considered that scenario," Cain stated, flatly shaking his head with indifference.

"Then I guess that it would be better for the rest of us to be outside to mount an attack or retrieval," Thomas stated.

"We will work out the communications when I am in the specified location. Believe me, I don't want to be caught in there with my ass hanging out if something goes bad," Cain said through pockets of laughter.

CHAPTER 61

Mac and Magen walked through the wet smoke on the first floor, only to enter a bloodbath in the lobby.

The carnage was horrific.

The electrical cords were pulled from the ceiling which started a fire in the front lounge, setting off the sprinkler system.

Now the once beautiful lounge of the Four Seasons resembled downtown Baghdad. The emergency service people were running from victim to victim, frantically trying to save lives, having minimal to no success at all.

There was a large team working with the concierge in hopes of stopping the blood loss; they had secured the arm in a cooler of ice, the blood loss was significant, and as much as they tried to revive the aging man, he continued to be unresponsive.

Several of the guests that were attacked on the initial assault were being placed in black body bags. For the couple who were celebrating their fifty-first wedding anniversary, the decision to come to the Big Apple from Bangor, Maine, was nothing but misery.

The smell was overwhelming in the lounge; even the fire department personnel were covering their faces. So, he didn't realize Dr. Gregory was in front of him until it was too late. The anger in his eyes was apparent, but there was some relief when he saw Magen. He filed that away, and then began to see other familiar faces parading in through other parts of the hotel.

William Dean stood against the wall half asleep; he has been through too much for a man his age. Mac found himself feeling really bad for the old guy; he felt he was an honorable guy, and they're hard to come by nowadays.

One of the techs was slowly scrambling out the door, not paying any attention to the carnage that laid about his feet. He spotted Mac and did the old double take; his eyes told the tale of surprise, but he just picked up his pace and walked behind the cops at the door.

There was no sign of Phyllis or several of the others; he wondered if she was torn limb from limb, or possibly worse. Then Mac's eyes caught sight of the Jewish spook who left the office prematurely. He was standing among the crowd eating what appeared to be a gyro; it was wrapped in foil, so it was hard to distinguish. Mac smiled and thought how nice it would have been to have Mr. Sneaky Ass out on that roof a few moments ago.

His concentration was broken by Dr. Gregory who had turned around and began to bark, "What the hell is going on here? This is your idea of a quiet operation? What the hell happened here?" he demanded through his handheld handkerchief.

"Well, Tim, we made first contact with an alien force, and as you can see, they didn't come in peace," Mac stated, holding back a deep desire to slap the superior.

"Well, that's not going to the press. This was a terrorist attack. I'm going to need a guest list!" Gregory shouted to the aide who was not far behind him.

"Terrorist attack. That the best we can do? You are going to have half of New York in a panic mode," Mac responded.

"I am open to a better plan. If you have a superior idea that doesn't include men from Mars, please let me in," Gregory pushed.

"Let's say it was a gas main explosion in the lower garage. That might work, but several people did see the beings in action," Magen chimed in.

"We can run with that. Let's get a dummy gas team in here!" he barked again at the aide.

"You people are crazy. This is the Four Seasons, and forty people must have seen what went on here," Mac stated in a challenging tone.

"There were sixteen people screaming about giant cats when we arrived. They are being processed as we speak. The press will go with whatever we tell them to run with," Gregory said with the authority he possessed.

"That's just madness. You can't contain this. The truth will come rolling out from somewhere," Mac continued to push.

"You're right about that. Shit, I might leak it myself. Just another conspiracy theory with no one really listening," Gregory finished with Mac turning and walking off.

"Damn, that guy is a dick. How the hell do you work for that tool?" Mac pressed Magen.

"I really don't work for him. I work to protect the American people from forces working against them," Magen said with a big smile on her face.

"Who are you kidding? I think you might be in shock," Mac said as he looked closely into Magen's eyes.

"I think you're right. Take me back to your place and fuck me," Magen said without any real emotion.

"You're a mind reader. They teach you that at the academy?" Mac joked as he began to lead her to the door.

"You must be out of your minds if you think you're walking out of here without a full debriefing," Gregory had circled back and was blocking the two from the exit.

"Who are you kidding, Tim? You have had us bugged since NYU. You know exactly what took place on that roof. We will be in tomorrow," Magen said without any doubt.

"We still have too many questions that can't wait until the morning. You know the drill," Gregory pressed.

"You have a microphone on me. Are you out of your fuckin' mind, you motherfucker!" Mac growled as he reached out and grabbed the man by the shirt.

"Mac, let him go. I really want to get out of here," Magen pleaded as she clutched his arm.

"What gives you the right to tag me, you dick!" Mac stated as he slowly loosened his grip on the agent.

"Your station commander signed off on you after Goldstein was pasted by the C train. Your ass is mine, sonny Jim!" Gregory said coldly as he stepped aside.

"Let's go. Something tells me we have a long day tomorrow," Magen grabbed Mac as she pushed past her senior.

CHAPTER 62

Biting deeply into human flesh must suck for the first few seconds!

—The hungry

Cain sat back against the uncomfortable bench seat of the subway and let the rhythm of the train relax him. He was strong and firm with the other three tonight, but he was concerned about the meeting that he committed himself to. He didn't need to take this dingy, smelly subway, but he loved watching the people; for him, it never got old.

There was a raw emotion that he enjoyed deeply presented by these New Yorkers; they feasted on life, and he respected that. He had lived many lives in many cities all across this planet, but it was here that he felt the most at ease.

He watched a young woman who was most likely on her way home; her small son was in tow, and he was a handful. Cain guessed that she was of mixed descent. There was Afro-American evident in her features, but there was also Latino and possibly some Germanic; regardless, she was magnificent. Cain thought that she would be a queen if this were a thousand years earlier. Humans would have gone to war for her then died without hesitation or question.

He missed those days; honor was the only thing that mattered then. They were not too strong on intellect, but they meant what they said then. The child of the young lady spent a good portion of time meeting most of the people on the train. Most humans become uncomfortable around small children; it is something that happens slowly over time. A side effect of the civilized society, as humans develop their intellect, the youth become highly prized and taboo to the stranger's touch and attention.

They have come a long way from working farms and labor houses, where the little darlings were exploited and brutalized. Cain thought about his own extensions living throughout the universe, and the difference they have made in multiple galaxies. He considered how they would be affected by his decision to stay on a savage middle C, inhabited by carbon-based life forms. He felt some of them would be devastated and others would laugh.

The council would react with a negative response. *I would be deemed a trader, and my assets would be seized. It would be a decision of finality. They could possibly send someone to retire me.*

As Cain reflected these outcomes, the small child had worked his way to his own personal space. He stared at Cain with that slow processing gaze the human children possessed in endless quantity. Cain reached out to the child's ear and pretended to extract a fifteen-centimeter stick of red candy. Cain loved to chew on this crap; he often wondered why adults left these products for the offspring.

"How did you fit that into your ear?" Cain joked as he looked at the mother not so much for approval, but he was interested in her.

"I didn't have that in my ear. You put that there!" the child smiled and stated, not fully sure of his assessment.

"Say thank you, Joshua!" the mother stated firmly in an attempt to train the child in basic etiquette.

"Thank you!" he said with some reluctance.

"You didn't have to do that. It was very nice," the girl professed as she moved to the seat next to him.

"It's all good. My name is Alex!" Cain said as he reached out to shake her hand, using his index finger to gently probe the pleasure center nerves between her thumb and palm.

"I'm Cleo, and you have met Joshua," the girl said as she looked oddly at Cain.

SEEDS OF THE GRAY

"What is it? Do I have something in my teeth?" Cain joked.

"No, you just seem really out of place, rolling uptown on the subway at this hour. You from out of town or something?" Cleo laughed, but her curiosity was evident.

"I'm too white for this train, is that what you're saying?" Cain smiled as he attempted to make her uncomfortable slightly.

"Well, you are slightly pale, for this side of town," Cleo smiled as she rolled back at Cain.

"I like to live life on the edge, so where are you coming from?" Cain asked, feeling very positive about the direction of the conversation.

"We were visiting the useless father of this one, over on the Rock." Cleo's facial expression changed as she thought about her cross to bear.

"What is the Rock?" Cain asked, but was fully aware of the term; he had some history in that Afro-American stud locker.

"Riker's Island. The asshole got jammed up. Now he's doing a nickel, and they have him down from Attica to stand trial on something else," she went on, becoming increasingly disconnected in her eyes.

Cain knew that look, and he began to feel the pain she was pushing down. His intuitive nature was highly sensitive to human thought process, a side effect of centuries of interpersonal involvement. He anticipated her reaction and soon realized there was a hole in her world the size of some galaxies.

Cain estimated the age of the offspring at thirty-nine and one-fourth months from womb exit. The child was too happy and undisciplined; this told Cain that the child was most likely educated without the male parental figure for the majority of that time.

Cleo continued to discuss the issues surrounding the downfall of her man; deep down, she knew he was lost. Cain realized she most likely never had the chance to unload the mountain that had become her life to anyone. Cain really didn't mind the dialogue; however, he determined he only had two or three stops to connect with this beauty. The child somehow migrated to Cain's right knee and seemed comfortable. Mom really liked the fact the young offspring was relaxed in his hands.

"Cleo, take a leap of faith. Come to dinner with me. And you can even bring that short boyfriend of yours!" Cain requested, turning on the charm.

"Dude, you don't even know me. How can I say yes to that?" Cleo stated with a look of confusion on her face.

"Well, if you're afraid of the pale face, I understand. I know that I am a bit scary!" Cain said as he put his fingers up to his face like fangs.

"You don't scare me. In a strange way, I think you're cute, but there's an awful lot of pain in your eyes for someone so young," Cleo said as she looked deep into his face.

"Wow, that is amazingly insightful. For one so young, you must be familiar with that same brand of pain," Cain said slowly as he recovered from the reality shot that the young girl laid on him.

"I am on my own, and life has given me some sucker punches!" Cleo shot back.

"So, I know this Asian place on the West Side, best springs on the planet," Cain stated with raw enthusiasm.

"Miss Saigon on Eighty-Ninth, is that the place you're talking about?" Cleo probed with obvious interest.

"Yeah, that's the place! I love those rolls. Please come with me?" Cain pressed, turning on the charm with just a little bit extra.

"I do like those rolls, and Joshua needs to eat, but this isn't a date. You get me, right?" Cleo voiced with little to no conviction.

"Oh, no, I'm not talking date. I don't even like you!" Cain said with a big smile reaching across his face.

"I can't believe I'm doing this. I must be out of my mind," Cleo stated as she shook her head, letting the actress in her present disbelief.

"I am so glad that you're crazy and brave, but mostly beautiful beyond belief," Cain stated as he softened and slightly gloated as he watched her start to soften as well.

SEEDS OF THE GRAY

Cain reached in his pocket and fished out his cell, hit a quick series of digits, and was soon connected. He requested to be picked up outside the Seventy-Second subway entrance, and then clicked off the phone. He looked down at the child who was remaining calm on his lap to the joy of both the mother and the rest of the passengers.

Cain wet his finger and twisted it into the child's ear, making a high-pitched squeaky noise. The belly laugh that came from the child filled the subway car, and reminded Cain why he was making the decision to stay here. He could tell that he was working the child up, and that could possibly get ugly, so he quickly changed direction. He moved to calm the child, and then slowly pulled out a silver fifty-cent piece from the child's ear. The amazement of the newfound coin stopped the small boy in his tracks.

Cain remembered the day he won the coin in a poker game with John Lennon and three other drunken roadies on a train heading south out of Seattle.

He still struggled with the concept that so many humans still worship that bully. The truth is that all too many of the human hero figures are far from who they are and their place in history on so many levels.

The train began to decrease in speed; Cain could feel the subtle downshift from the conductor. He smiled and then turned to the young woman, lightly touching her hand.

"Let's go. If I don't eat something soon, there will be hell to pay," Cain stated as he made the move out of the chair, holding the child's hand.

"Why are we getting off here? If we go two more stops, we could shoot across the park," Cleo asked with some obvious confusion.

"I know you don't know me, but I am asking you to trust me. I will not let you down, Cleo," Cain said with his most sincere expression.

"You are one strange individual, but I am in. Let's go," Cleo said as she grabbed the hand of the young boy and waited for the train to come to a complete stop.

"You are an amazing young lady. You must have a good intuition about people. Have you always been that way?" Cain asked with newfound interest.

"Since I was a young girl, I have had feelings about people that others don't see. In your case, I feel something special and unique," Cleo said softly and with deep reflection.

"Your mother is really special, little Joshua, did you know that?" Cain smiled as he bent at the waist, placing his face inches from the child's endless smile.

"I know that, and you're really special, too, aren't you?" the small child stated simply as he placed his arms around Cain's neck.

"Not like your mom!" Cain smiled outwardly, but internally he was shocked by the statement.

Cain pondered the journey through the history of this planet and recalled many of the humans that he had come in contact with tended to be in touch with something extra. He wondered if it was the natural progression of the species or was it some deeper connection the planet. Alexander the Great was this way; on more than one occasion, he would state things way beyond his twenty-three years. Then there were the times when he would start talking to the wind. Cain would recoil in shock when the wind answered back; he thinks about this often.

There was something so magical about this planet and its inhabitants. The majority of the humans that survive on this planet are simple and pointless; however, he would be lying to himself if he didn't recognize there was something extraordinary happening with a small population of the population.

One of their leaders, Kennedy, was capable of processing information at a rate nine times faster than the average human. Sixty years ago, he recalled meeting a monk in the mountains of Tibet who was able to see through the Gray projection technology. The old man turned to Cain and said in an ancient language, "Was your journey long, old one?"

There was also the Egyptian that ran screaming when they saw him, mistaking him for one of their evil demons, Apophis. Their brains are like those of children, but there is substantial development in the wind. The question is where is all this going to end?

"Joshua is special, isn't he?" Cain asked with confidence of a question he already knew the answer of.

"How do you mean that?" Cleo shot back with stunned confusion and some slight fear of the recognition.

"He can see deep into me, much deeper than the rest of the sheep. I take it he gets that from you," Cain explained.

"The looking glass is strong in the boy, much stronger than me. He tends to be more like his grandmother," Cleo freely confided in Cain.

"Does it always work that way? I mean, are these things passed on, or do they skip generations? I know I am full of questions. Can't help myself. I just find it fascinating," Cain relayed, his passion evident.

"I wish that I could tell you. I would love to understand this thing myself. My mother didn't have it, but my nana lived her life around it. Back then in the South, it was all right," Cleo attempted to explain without sounding spooky.

"When you look at me, what is it that you see?" Cain probed.

"It's not what I see. It's what I don't feel. There is an aura surrounding you, shades of the most intense colors. I can't tell what that's about, but I know you mean us no harm," Cleo explained, but it was difficult.

"How about you, little man? What do you see when you look at me?" he asked with an easygoing smile.

"French fries and a cheeseburger and a warm car that smells good," the young one chimed in without skipping a beat.

"Now you're talking, but do you want to hear something gross?" Cain said with a twisted scowl.

"Yes, yes, I do," Joshua shouted and jumped up and down in place.

"I like mayonnaise on my cheeseburgers," Cain said as if he was deeply ashamed.

"Wow, that's nasty," Joshua screamed and gestured as if he was about to vomit.

"I have to agree with Joshua. That is big-time nasty. Must be a white thing," Cleo added as they stepped onto the platform.

The second they came within sight of the escalator, Joshua took off like a shot, with his shouting mother on his heels. Cain took a few seconds to think about what was about to take place over the next few days. The girl and child had been a fantastic distraction for him. He really didn't want to think about the meeting that he had requested or the many variables that could seal his fate.

He was not comfortable with the concept of reasoning with his food source. The human race was prone to impulsivity and poor decision-making; there were no guarantees down this road.

It was useless to ponder these things at this point in time, he told himself. The young woman had gained on the special toddler and turned and gave Cain a look that could only mean *Are you still sure about taking this child out in public?*

Cain began to laugh at her fear, and then closed in on the two; he hoisted the hyper child in the air, and spun him around like a top. Laughter erupted from deep within his young belly. Cain did enjoy his ability to connect closely with children, and this was one exceptional child.

As they moved through the subway exit, Cain spotted the limo off to his left, then started to motion Cleo in that direction. The lights and sounds from the city were in full effect tonight, almost like an awakening from a dream. Joshua instinctively reached out and grabbed his mother's hand; to Cain's surprise, Cleo looped her arm under his and moved her body closer. Cain smiled as they walked about twenty feet, entwined like a family, hard to believe they met just moments ago.

Cain stopped suddenly in his tracks right in front of the limo and seemed to be frozen. Cleo and Joshua didn't know what was going on and looked at Cain with confusion. He turned and looked deep into the eyes of the beautiful female that was obviously alarmed at his behavior.

"What is it, Alex?" Cleo asked.

"Everything is just perfect. Please get in!" Cain motioned toward the long black limo that was sitting in front of them.

"You kidding, this is you? Are you for real?" Cleo stated with shock in her voice.

"Queen Cleo, your chariot awaits," Cain opened the back door, and grabbed Joshua and hoisted him into the limo behind his mother.

"This car is so big!" Joshua said and laughed as he was being thrown in the back seat.

"Now we can sit back and relax and go get ourselves something to eat. What do you think?" Cain said as he settled into the back seat.

"What do I think? I think your white ass has been holding out on me! What is this, are you rich or something?" Cleo asked with a suspicious tone.

"Well, money is not an issue in my world. I come from a long line of inventors, and we are comfortable. I haven't been holding out on you. It's just a car, Cleo." Cain was helping her calm down by minimizing the situation.

"Just a car? There are three televisions in this bitch. I am not used to this," Cleo said as she motioned her son away from the electronics.

"He is fine. There is nothing in here that can't be fixed," Cain stated as he reached out for her hand and held it gently.

"Any more surprises you have up your sleeve?" Cleo asked, but she seemed to be calming.

"Oh, the night is still young, my fine princess. This town is ours," Cain opened the roof window and lifted Joshua and himself up and started to sing along with the music on the radio.

"Get down here, you two. Are you trying to give me a heart attack? You could get a spanking right along with this, young man," Cleo yelled as she smacked Cain on his ass.

"Don't threaten me with a good time," Cain continued screaming out of the roof.

"Please get in here, Alex!" Cleo stated.

"Yes, dear, I am sorry for my bad behavior," Cain stated as if he were a small child.

"I like you in here right next to me. Does that work for you?" Cleo said to him as she wrapped her arm slowly around his.

"That more than works for me, and may I say that you look so beautiful tonight?" Cain whispered and kept his eyes locked on hers.

"I haven't eaten anything yet, and I have butterflies. You making the move on me, Alex?" Cleo stated openly.

"Yes, I believe that I am. Can't help myself. It's been a while since someone showed me my heart," Cain said softly.

"This is the coolest car I have ever seen. Look at the TVs. I want to live here!" Joshua yelled as he jumped around the back of the limo.

"Where can I take you, sir?" the driver had rolled the window partially down and requested directions.

"We're going to Soho. Take us to the Bann. I just had an overwhelming desire for Korean," Cain announced with extreme enthusiasm.

"Soho. You took the subway all the way up here, just to drive all the way back down. Are you having a moment?" Cleo asked, but not really concerned.

"Sometimes you just have to go with your gut, and my gut is telling me it's time for civilized food," he continued with raw vigor.

"You're kind of cute when you have a bone to chew on, aren't you?" Cleo said with a big beautiful smile.

"What do you mean by that?" Cain asked with a big smile.

"You get hyped when you're hot for something. I can see it in your eyes, and it's nothing bad, cute," Cleo said gently.

"So, you think I'm cute?" Cain asked hoping for a positive response.

"Yeah, you're all right, in a pale kind of way!" Cleo smirked.

"This is it, up on the right, see the blue light? Thank God, I am starving," Cain stated as he hugged his new friends.

"Me, too, I could eat a horse, but I need to tell you a secret," Joshua whispered as he leaned into Cain's ear.

"What is it, little man?" Cain whispered back.

"Well, first, Mommy really likes you," Joshua began.

"I really like her also. She smells so good!" Cain shot back with a laugh as Cleo pinched his butt.

"I also need to tell you there's a big, bad lady in that restaurant and she hurts people," Joshua confided to Cain.

"Yeah, don't worry about her. I would never let anything hurt you!" Cain said softly, absolutely stunned by the child's ability.

CHAPTER 63

Magen grabbed the shaking hand of Officer MacDonald and pulled it close to her. He began to regain his composure and focus on the woman he had grown close to in a very short period of time. She smiled at him and moved her body closer.

Mac was devastated, and as much as he tried to compartmentalize the events of the evening, his thoughts always circled back to the hotel rooftop. Magen was keyed in on the struggle that Mac was experiencing; she was dealing with her own internal battle and not sure what help she could contribute. Mac could feel her division and worked to pull himself together so he could be supportive. His mind just couldn't let go of the alien vaulting off that roof and connecting with that helicopter. The strength and precision of that act defies all possibility. The reality that this being was on a superior level was hard to get past, but he was too tired, cranky, and in severe pain.

Magen's phone rang, and they both came to a stop; Mac could see raw intensity in her eyes. His thought of some sleep had just been washed. She clicked off the phone and stared at the device for a few moments before turning to Mac.

"That was Kingston. He said we need to go to Lynbrook, Long Island. There seems to be more insanity to this development," Magen stated, feeling just as tired as Mac.

"What is it? And please don't tell me that we need to drive out to the damn island," Mac asked. However, he wasn't sure that he wanted the answer.

"He thinks that Dr. Mazza may be reconnecting to the home he grew up in. He was doing some unauthorized research with children, never made trial, bolted," Magen began to explain.

"I don't remember the name. Was it a Fed issue or a local problem?" Mac asked, still trying to recall the case.

"He was working with NASA and some other government agencies. They said he was utilizing fetus DNA of aborted children to build stronger soldiers or giants. It was prior to the cloning in Scotland, so the whole thing never got dragged into the spotlight. I remember seeing him on the news, thought to myself that this was one bad guy."

"What kind of person can hold a dead baby in their hands and chop through it like veal shank?"

"They traced him to his mother's house on the island, but missed him," Magen continued to unfold the story.

"How does this tie into an alien springing off the roof of the premier hotel in Manhattan?" Mac struggled, trying to make the connection.

"I have no idea, but Kingston wants us on it, and he seems to have a serious beat on what's going on, so I am going to find this nut, and I might smash his face."

"I don't even like this ass wipe, but all of a sudden I am worried about him," Mac said with a slight smile.

"I don't blame you. I would love to find and hurt this animal!" Magen stated with venom leaking out between her words.

"Can't believe I don't recall this one, and it happened in my backyard. Half the force is from Long Island, friends and family," Mac said out loud.

"Like I said, it wasn't that big of a story back then. I was in Washington at the time. I remember the ops guy talk about the guy. He gave the spooks the creeps, and that's not easy to do," Magen stated.

"Is this guy a real doctor, or is he more scientist with the tag doctor?" Mac probed, trying to get a better understanding of the history.

"I don't have the full dirt on Mazza. What I do know is that he has a history of questionable experimentation with children, infants, and mothers," Magen began to explain, but her negative feelings were visibly obvious.

"That's pretty fucked up, and he works for our government?" Mac said with a sad tone.

"He works for several governments, and is protected by most of them. It's my guess that's how he gets away from capture time after time," Magen expressed her theory.

"If you're right about the 'guardian angel' scenario, then we are taking a ride for nothing, you know that, right?" Mac needed to state the obvious in hopes that Magen realized the futility of this journey.

"I know you think this a wasted trip, but I think this Kingston guy is playing by his own rules, a ronin, and that could just be the break we need," Magen said with great intensity.

"You know something, you're starting to give me hope. Let's get Dr. Mazza!" Mac joined in on the enthusiasm that Magen had in abundance.

CHAPTER 64

My Delta KI name is Titus.

—Noise from a day in May

Dr. Robert Mazza walked the trail through the Tanglewood Preserves many times. He often thought of those who died here along these very trails during the early days of the Revolutionary War.

Few people realized that this small little ten-acre strip of land underwent a full-day battle that in the end came down to hand-to-hand combat. Today his intention had nothing to do with the past; his goal was to find one of the many young children who played in this area. He wasn't too proud of his actions when it came to his addiction to children. He was intelligent and fully understood the chemical imbalance that caused him to act in the manner that was slightly embarrassing.

Today he needed a child to feel their warmth and innocence.

After he fed his addiction, he would somehow coax the little darling back to Mom's house. The babies needed to feed. The police were still combing the area, so he would need to act quickly and be painfully cautious. He has been so distracted over the last few months; he knew he screwed up big time leaving the Seeds unattended. Not that he gave the man in the park a second thought. The firm had assured him that there would be no autopsy performed on the victim.

He didn't give it a second thought; if the firm said it would be dealt with, then it was a done deal. Robert allowed himself a minute to contemplate what would have happened if the right forensic physician got a hold of the body. He quickly let those thoughts skate away as he heard footsteps coming through the woods.

A young boy was approaching; he was in a baseball uniform complete with a yellow cap. Dr. Mazza became extremely excited with anticipation. His sickness was balling up in his throat, and his first words came pouring out like lava.

"Hey, slugger, how was the game?" Mazza said in a friendly voice.

"Good" was all the youngster could muster as the startled look began to dissipate.

"I am so glad you came by. I lost my keys in that group of trees over there. Could you help me find them?" Mazza pressed the young boy.

"Mister, I have to get home," the little ballplayer said as he began to motion away from the adult.

"I understand, but I really need some help. There's ten bucks in it for you," the doctor stated as he waved the bill like a flag at the youth.

"Ten bucks, what do I have to do?" said the eager youngster eyeing the money and the potential that came with it.

"I threw my keys up in the air, and they got stuck in the tree over there. I am years from climbing any trees, but I bet you could get it," Mazza rolled out the lie he had used many times before.

"I can climb any tree in these woods, better than any of my friends," the child boasted.

"That's the spirit. Let's go!" the doctor motioned.

"How did you throw your keys in a tree? That's silly," the young man started to process the story a little too late.

"This is the place. I am going to need for you to take off your clothes, my little one!" Mazza said flatly, but his tone meant business.

"You're out of your mind, mister!" The child now gripped with fear began to move past Mazza.

SEEDS OF THE GRAY

"I don't think so!" Mazza said as he grabbed the child and flung him to the ground.

"Why are you doing this?" the child called out now, crying and shaking with fear.

"I can't help myself. I am sick, but that's really not important," Mazza stated as he motioned toward the child.

"Go fuck yourself!" the youngster yelled as he rose to his feet with an egg-size rock in his right hand.

The young pitcher cocked his arm like 120 times he had done earlier that day; the rock left his hand after a full windup. It had gained seventy miles an hour right before it blasted on the bridge of the older doctor's nose.

Mazza let out a yell that could be heard a half mile away.

Both nostrils shot blood, and instinctively his hands gripped the damaged area. The doctor found himself on the floor of the woods with the wail of a high-pitched siren surrounding his skull from all sides. He opened his eyes in time to see the back of the young ballplayer running at top speed through the brush; pursuit would be futile.

Mazza reached his hand back for the ground to regain his balance. He was able to get to his feet, hand and shirt covered with his own blood. He could hardly see with his eyes filled with water. As his senses began to come back around, his anger grew. He knew that it was time to move, and these woods were no longer safe hunting grounds for his needs. The worst of it was that his children would not be eating tonight, and that could be tragic; they needed meat at all costs.

Rage filled his heart and pumped through the pain; he was moving fast now, not quite running, but a good pace was achieved.

He could see his car and didn't hear the police, although he knew that snot-nosed kid was running straight to an adult. The area would be covered with police in a matter of minutes; there was no time to spare. As he fumbled with his keys the reality of the situation was firing through his already charged mind. His children could not go another night without a feed; he needed to deal with this.

He made a left on Peninsular Boulevard; this would take him into Hempstead, Long Island. If he were to find dinner for the kids, it would be here. Regardless of what the little shit tells the authorities, they wouldn't be down here looking for the perpetrator. Mazza had rolled through this area many times over the years. Hempstead was a good place to find drugs, guns, and the occasional prostitute.

Today could be salvaged if he could find someone looking for a fast dollar. There's a strip club down the main drag that attracted the finest people; that's the best thing that he could come up with, so it had to work.

Mazza pulled the car to the side of the road, and for the first time since the woods, he took a moment to breathe. He pulled the rearview mirror down to take a quick look at his face.

Blood was all over his face and his shirt; he needed to make some changes, or no one would come near him.

He pulled out a water bottle from the back seat and attended to his face, and found a shirt in the trunk. As he got himself together, he formulated a plan, keeping things really basic—find dinner and go home.

CHAPTER 65

Mazza rolled out to Front Street and started his search. It didn't take long for him to come across a few ladies of the evening.

His new plan was to roll around the block, then park halfway down the block until the pack of them broke up. He needed to isolate one of them, and that would be the end of it. He could get the woman in the car, take her back to the house, or choke her to death in the back seat.

As he turned the corner, a black dude in his forties walked in front of the car, holding some electronic devices. The doctor tapped the brakes and was about to fly past him when he recalled his purpose and what he needed to do. He did a fast survey of the middle-aged man; from his clothing and poor hygiene, he guessed that he was a drug abuser. He considered the possible danger of letting this guy in the vehicle.

Unfortunately, there was no time to play it safe. Mazza put on a big smile and rolled the window.

"Hey, is that a GPS system? Been looking for one of those!"

"Listen, my name is Ronald. My friends call me Rondo. You can ask anyone out here, I have quality items and I stand behind my goods," Ronald finished his script and smiled back at his new mark with two rows of brown and broken teeth.

"I really need one of these. How much for the GPS, bottom price?" the doctor said, baiting the man.

"Hey, my man, what happened to your face?" Ronald asked, pretending to have some interest.

"I wish I could say something clever, but I bumped it on the fridge. Really, how much do you want for the GPS?" Mazza threw out the lie with no hesitation and kept the druggie on track.

"They go about 300, but for you, 125, and that is a deal," Rondo stated in a tone that indicated that the deal of the week had just been announced.

"Rondo, my good buddy, the wires are stripped in three different places. Someone pulled really hard on this device." The doctor played the haggling customer out of habit; he was simply enjoying himself.

"My man, are you playing with me? This is a quality product," Rondo said in full action, now prepared himself to walk away.

"Now a hundred bucks would be a fair price. What do you say about that?" Mazza said as he dangled the carrot.

"You have cash on you?" asked the entrepreneur ready to make the deal.

"No, I never travel with cash. I guess you're not taking a check?" Mazza asked in a tone that echoed with comedy.

"There's an ATM around the corner. I could cut through the projects and meet you out front," Rondo tried to help the process along.

"Listen, jump in. I don't live too far from here. I'll run by the house, pick up the cash, and take you back," Mazza said as he opened the car door and climbed in.

"Say what, why you don't run home and get the loot and come back?" he shot back, a little surprised by the offer.

"No problem, see you in a while!" Mazza said without missing a beat.

"Hey, if you're good with me taking a ride with you, we cool?" Ronald said as his greed had gotten the better of him. The thought of his one hundred dollars driving away was too much for him.

"Jump in. I'm a few minutes down the road. I don't understand what the issue is. This is just a business deal, right?"

"Not too many people ask me to get in their car. Most of my business is done right there on that block!" Ronald glanced back in the rearview mirror and pondered his bad decision but then let it go.

"You're not a vegetarian, are you, Rondo?" Mazza asked out of the blue.

"Not me! Shit, that is some crazy shit there, humans walkin' around like rabbits, and what is that tofu thing?" Ronald shot back, not so much asking the question but making a statement.

"I don't know the appeal. I understand it to be processed soybeans. To be honest with you, the shit never passed my lips, I did try once, felt like snot on my tongue!" The good doctor continued the small talk until he made the left onto the block where his mother's house was located.

"This is a nice area. You live here?" the man asked, eyeballing the homes in the area.

"My mother lives here. I have a work area in the basement, and I own two homes on the next block over, little getaways. Anyway, you want to come in?" Mazza asked without any tension in his voice, even though he was highly anxious.

"No, I'll just chill. Don't be too long," Ronald shot back now, fearing that his new white business partner could be a homosexual.

"Okay, no problem, I'll be back before you know it," Mazza stated, and off he went.

The interior of the car was hauntingly quiet; Ronald thought that the combination of a quiet street and a quiet car made for a silent scenario.

As Ronald tried to work through the sound of his confused thoughts, two people jogged by and looked straight into the car where Rondo was sitting; the smaller of the two men looked back several times as if the black man sitting on the block was going to change color.

"Just keep lookin' back. I'm sure the black man is gonna go away," Ronald said under his breath as he smiled and waved at the jogger.

Several minutes had passed, and still, Mazza had not returned to the vehicle, and Rondo began to feel it. He began to reconsider his decision to follow this ass into the house.

Then the negativity began to slide into the brain, that deep what-if negativity. Ronald began to torture himself with the possibility of his new friend's change of mind. Then he considered that something was wrong in the house; maybe the money was lost and he was looking for it?

Ronald then began to think about the bench warrant that was put out on him last summer from his son's mother regarding some money he owed her. He thought about the jogger; maybe he called the police on the black dude sitting in the car on an all-white block.

He reached down and pulled back the door latch; it popped open. Ronald got out of the car; his patience had reached the end, and he needed to make this deal or move on.

For two or three seconds, he sat against the car; deep down, he knew he was making a poor decision, but he let it go. He took the first seven steps that came to a fork where he could go to the front door or pull right and go around back. He paused for a few minutes, remembering what the freak said about living in the back. He turned right and, with a quick pace, started for the back.

The last thing he wanted was for some nosy crackers to stick their glass balls out the window and see some black cat rolling through the yard. Ronald turned the corner to see a set of stairs going down; he paused to take a breath. Then down he went to the bottom and stood outside the door, peeking through the window.

Unable to see anything through the curtains, he reached slowly out for the handle of the door. He was sweating and struggling with the decision to proceed, but turning around to go back to the car was counterproductive. Ronald gripped the handle and took one last second, stared up at the sky, a behavior that he repeated when he was nervous. He entered the basement apartment, softly calling out for his new friend.

CHAPTER 66

Immediately he could smell something that resembled the hospital he spent some time in last summer. As he looked around, he realized that this wasn't an apartment at all; it was a laboratory. Ronald then saw Robert at the counter across the room with his back to the door, shaking some fluid in a glass beaker.

"Is this some kind of joke? I am roasting my ass off in that shit box. You got my fuckin' money?" Ronald pressed the issue after seeing Mazza in no apparent hurry.

"Rondo, my friend, are you taking any medication?" Mazza asked without even turning around.

"What? I am not taking anything. Are you taking the GPS, or are we done here?" Ronald was able to get those words out when a sharp pain came from his calf.

Ronald instinctively backed against the door and looked down. There at his feet was a small girl with milky pale skin and eyes darker than midnight. It was then that Ronald realized that he was unable to move.

There was a new taste in his mouth that seemed foreign. Panic gripped him at his core. He didn't know what was going on; his breathing became erratic.

He began to slide down the wall, unable to maintain his balance; all muscle tone was lost.

The young girl was now joined by a boy.

A brother, most likely, Ronald thought.

The girl removed her hands from her face, revealing a row of saber-like teeth. Ronald made an attempt to scream, but only air came; he felt consciousness slip away and then darkness as the paralytic took effect.

Right before his eyelids closed, he watched the two little monsters dig their ugly teeth into the fleshy part of his upper thigh.

There was no pain, and some part of his brain was happy about that.

CHAPTER 67

Magen got off the parkway and followed the sign toward Lynbrook, Long Island.

There were cop cars flying in both directions. Mac knew something was really wrong. He couldn't help but think that crime was no stranger to the suburbs. He always imagined that people were close out here; you knew who your neighbor was.

He wondered how this mutt Mazza was able to operate in this type of area without someone pulling the plug. As he pondered the many questions about this freak, Magen reached back behind the seat to her communication center and ripped off an incoming fax.

It was a newspaper clipping from Kingston.

She spent a few minutes reading the clipping and then handed it over with anger in her face. The paper clipping told the story of a man who was killed in a park a block from their destination. The manner in which this man was killed was gruesome, bones broken and ripped from his body.

The article is leaning toward some dog pack, but my guess is that we didn't get this from Kingston for shits and giggles.

He could see from the look on Magen's face that she fully believed that Mazza had a hand in this tragedy. Mac realized the possibilities of them rolling up on Mazza after countless attempts by several agencies was slim. He was actually enjoying the downtime with Magen; he was even able to get some winks when they hit the Belt Parkway.

They were close to their destination according to the GPS; Mac flicked the release on his gun holster and removed the Beretta. He popped the clip and surveyed the ammo and released the safety.

Magen glanced over and took a deep breath, then let it go, feeling herself relax. No matter how many times you made a move on a suspect, it really never got easier. There was always the anxiety of the unknown, the possibility that something could go wrong.

You would like to tell yourself that you are just going into the house to make an arrest on some wacky scientist. Unfortunately, that kind of thinking could get you deader than shit. Every time that weapon came out, the odds of someone dying just escalated.

He thought to himself, *It's that one time you relax that all hell breaks loose.*

As he was thinking his approach through, Magen jerked the car to the side of the road.

"Is this it?" Mac announced in a soft, low voice.

"Three houses up on the right, blue car in the front," Magen stated as she reached for her handheld cell phone.

"Why are we down the block? I would think the sooner we charge the house, the better our chances," Mac questioned, trying to plead his case for a preemptive strike.

"I need a plate run. New York, Victor, Harry, Charlie, 1132. Thank you," Magen said into her phone.

"You Feds are so by-the-book sexy!" Mac said with a sarcastic ring.

"Excuse me?" Magen practically screamed into the phone.

"What is it?" Mac snapped, surprised by her reaction.

"There is a 'do not proceed' order on that plate number, meaning that we cannot move on him," Magen said with confusion in her voice.

"That is not an option from where I am sitting!" Mac was starting to get heated, and it could be felt in his tone.

"There's an unmarked pulling up behind us," Magen announced as she caught his approach from the rearview mirror.

"What!" Mac stopped cold. This was the last thing in the world he expected.

"Roll down your window. He's on his way!" Magen said as if she was talking into her sleeve so the officer would not be able to see the communication.

"Good afternoon, folks, I received a call from one of the neighbors stating that there were some strangers sitting in a car. You don't look strange," the officer said in jest.

"It's all relative!" Mac joked back, displaying his gold lieutenant badge. Magen also presented identification.

"I take it back. This is strange. Why is a federal agent and city brass sitting on my little slice of heaven?" the officer asked with actual concern.

"We were about to bum-rush the white house over there, but someone seems to be concerned with probable cause," Mac said as his gaze rolled slowly over to Magen.

"I can only think terrorism would have two agencies working together," the officer stated but hoped he was wrong.

"There could be a monster in that house, a real-life monster," Magen told the officer and convinced him that she wasn't kidding.

"That white house over there with that tan Honda out front?" the officer asked.

"That's the one. A doctor twisted beyond belief," Mac added.

"About an hour ago, I got a 911 that some young boy was almost raped a few blocks away. That car in front of the house is a close description to the perp's car!" the officer stated.

Both car doors opened at the same time. Magen went to the back of the vehicle and popped the trunk. She put on her Kevlar vest, and pulled down the FBI tag. Her father loved his .45-caliber; it was the gun she grew up with, and the one she reached for today.

The officer picked up his walkie-talkie and was about to call in for backup when Mac grabbed his hand and motioned for him to hold on. Magen walked up to the two cops and could see the confusion in his face.

"I know you play by the book, I respect that, but we feel that this doctor has been tipped off on more than one occasion, so please give us a few minutes," Magen pleaded, placing her hand on his shoulder.

"I tend to roll by the book, not ashamed of that, but there are times when the book needs to stay in the Crown Vic!" the officer stated as he tossed the walkie on the seat of the car.

"Glad to have you on board, Officer...?" Mac said, fishing for a name.

"Scott Devine, protect and serve, and every chance I get to crush the windpipe of some child molester, game on," Officer Scott said as he removed his glasses and withdrew his Glock.

"Game on! I love it. Let's get this prick!" Mac stated as he and the others moved on the house.

"Stop behind his car before we proceed to the house!" Magen called out as they double-timed toward the house.

"What do we need to wait for? Time is critical with this guy," Mac stated as he crouched next to Magen.

"I really wanted to check the engine for heat, see how long the car has been sitting here," Magen pleaded her case as she reached to feel the front end of the vehicle.

"What are we working with?" Mac asked, not taking his eyes off the house.

"Oh, Mac, you can fry an egg off this side panel. He's in there," Magen stated as her emotional level escalated.

"Most of the homes in this area have basement apartments, with a separate entrance," Officer Devine informed the two.

"We are going to need you on that. Please do not enter the dwelling on your own. Just cover the flank!" Magen directed the officer.

"Yes, Agent!" Officer Devine responded as he prepared to charge to the back.

"Ready, Mac?" Magen asked with loaded anticipation.

"Born ready. Let us do it!" Mac snapped as he rolled toward the house.

As if they had worked together for years, the three law enforcement professionals moved together and were in position in moments.

CHAPTER 68

Mac and Magen stood on both side of the front door. Magen announced that federal authorities were at the front door, and the door needed to be opened immediately.

Mac gave a three count and kicked the door open.

The house was quiet and vacant; the furniture was covered with plastic. The first floor gave the impression that no one had lived here for some time. They had found the door that they assumed led to the basement. It was locked with several strong locks from both sides; they realized that their only way to gain access was from out back. They circled around the back to find Officer Devine with his gun drawn on the back stairs.

"Anything?" Magen asked as she came to a stop in the backyard.

"Not even a sound out of the basement. Spooky," the officer whispered.

"Well, we are not getting any younger. Let's do this," Mac announced.

Officer Devine stepped in front of Mac and Magen and held up his hand. He wasn't trying to secure credit for a possible arrest; he had thought this out. The only way this could go down legally was for him to take the lead into the dwelling and be accompanied by these two off-duty officers.

The front of the house didn't matter, but taking the next step and entering the back apartment is a whole other story.

"You know it needs to go down this way. Let's go," Officer Devine declared and motioned down the steps.

"Take it slow. This is one nutty fuck!" Mac stated as he turned to see a shaking Magen at the top of the stairs.

"I'm good!" she said before he could say anything.

"Then we have a job to do, right?" Mac stated.

"The door is open," Officer Devine stated from the bottom of the stairs.

"Mac, I don't like this!" Magen said with a tone that stressed caution.

"Take it nice and easy, Scott!" Mac advised.

"Police, we are entering the home!" the officer called out loud enough to be heard throughout the house.

The officer pushed the door open and immediately covered his nose to the stench that permeated the room. Mac, who was directly behind him, heard the gag reaction from the officer, prior to realizing the smell for himself. When it hit, Mac stepped back; the smell of death was not new to him. He cautioned Magen to hold her ground. Unfortunately, it was too late as she had stepped into the back door with her gun drawn in trained anticipation.

She quickly began to gag and back up herself. The room was absent of light; some thin blue rays were entering from the far window, but were of no help to their current position. He kept his eyes front; with his left hand, he fumbled around for a light switch. He found it and flipped it up, without any result even after several attempts.

The officer had produced a standard-issue military flashlight and turned it on. The blood was evident almost instantly; it was all over the walls, tables, and mostly the floor.

As their eyes adjusted, they could make out what appeared to be a fabricated prison cell, and on the floor was a man. As they moved in on the area, they could make out two hands holding the bars. As their eyes trailed down, they could see that both legs had been eaten away from the bone.

There was clothing, muscle, and tendons ripped and thrown throughout the area. The young man's backside was also eaten away from the body; his anus appeared to be puckering with blood bubbles that were popping and spraying red droplets all through the makeshift cell.

Magen quickly moved toward the door after just a few seconds of viewing the horrific scene.

Officer Devine began to look close at the face of the pale face of the victim, when without warning his eyes shot open.

"Holy shit! He's alive, he's alive! We need a medic!" Devine called out as he backpedaled across the room.

CHAPTER 69

"Easy, I think it was just some kind of muscle memory."

"Help me!" The dying man gurgled through foam and blood that was dripping from his face.

"Jesus H. Christ, he is alive. How is that possible?" Mac stated.

Magen gagged as she felt the vomit rise up her throat; she reached for her phone and wobbled toward the door.

Devine and Mac regained their sense of stability and joined the dying man. His eyes were closed again, and there seemed to be no additional movement.

As they moved in closer, the pile of clothing to the right moved slightly, the over-vigilant officer noticed it first. His first thought was that possibly he was just being fearful and paranoid.

He motioned the light over in the direction and shined his light right in the face of what appeared to be a small pale black-eyed child. The strange-looking child who was covered in blood and meat parts began to change shape.

He looked afraid and shocked, but slowly motioned over to the officer.

Scott looked up at Mac who was still studying the man in the cage and was unaware of the presence of the child. Officer Devine looked back at the child who was now within arm's length. The mouth of the child slowly opened, revealing a row of needlelike teeth soaked in blood; it was then that a thin membrane flipped over the child's eyes, much like a shark.

The officer began to shake as horrific fear gripped him deep; the flashlight in his hand began to shake.

The hit came so fast that initially Devine was unclear of what happened, until he reached for his face and found that most of his nose and top lip were totally missing.

Mac had caught the tail end of the strike and quickly raised his gun and fired several shots from the Beretta. The small figure that he was firing on had moved with unbelievable quickness and was now heading toward Magen's position.

The noise that came from the being had exploded within the small room. When Mac thought of the noise later, he could only describe it as glass being scraped across a blackboard.

The being hit one table and sent wood in every direction; it then hit the bottom of the back door and went through it like butter. Long wooden pieces and splinters instantly filled the air.

Magen had managed to get off three shots, hitting nothing but drywall. As their eyes were focused on the basement door, the window behind them at the back of the house exploded as something flew through it with unbelievable speed.

The blood was spraying from the officer's face, and it was hard to contain due to his rolling and screaming on the ground. Mac did what he could to attempt to help, but Scott was beyond reason with pain. Magen was on the phone calling for help and chasing the childlike animal through the backyard.

Mac was able to find the lights on the far wall of the laboratory and flicked it on.

It was then that he could see the absolute carnage.

CHAPTER 70

The room was a laboratory with state-of-the-art computerized machinery. The first thought that ran through Mac's head was the words Magen had said about the good doctor having help.

You just don't pick this equipment up at Best Buy or anywhere else commercially. The blood against the white sterile environment was so ghoulish and unnerving. Mac grabbed some paper towels and returned to the wounded officer, who had now slipped into shock from both trauma and blood loss.

He was able to pull the man's hands from his battered face, but needed to look away after seeing the damage.

Magen came running back into the door, winded, and gasping for breath.

"How is he? I can hear the ambulance," Magen was able to get out between long deep breaths.

"He's in shock! Whatever that thing was took half his nose and the top portion of the lip," Mac explained.

"I can't believe this. Three shots at point-blank range and I hit absolutely nothing. The paperwork is going to be unreal," Magen said out loud after contemplation.

"Paperwork. Hell, they could pull my badge after this clusterfuck!" Mac said as he ran his hands through his hair in agitation.

"It was a child, you know, that thing I chased through the yards!" Magen said with deep sorrow at the reality.

"Did you get a chance to see what flew out the back window, or were you too busy with the craziness in here?" Mac asked, still trying to put that part of the equation together.

"Yeah, they met together two yards down. I was kind of far away, but it looked like a young girl. I know that sounds crazy," Magen said, slowly recalling the facts.

"A girl, are you sure?" Mac said with obvious confusion.

"No, Mac, I am not really sure about anything. It was dark in here, bright out there. My eyes didn't adjust!" There was frustration in Magen's voice.

For the first time, Magen began to look around the room, and the horror of the scene really set in. She forced her face away from the bleeding officer and the dead man in the cage. Magen began to look over the equipment that was highly advanced for a basement lab.

She noticed some of the safety checks were still on one or two of the items. Then she found what she was looking for; one of the stickers read "Applied Physics LLC," and it was signed off three weeks ago. This was the key she was seeking for; the aid that this guy was receiving was coming right out of Apple Physics.

They have us running around in circles. Someone really doesn't want the doctor caught. Kingston sent us here, because he knew that we were the only people on earth that would move on him. This equipment tells the full tale. The people we work for are the same people that are protecting him. Really didn't want to consider this or maybe didn't want it to fall this way.

Magen took out her iPhone and started taking photos of dates, stickers, and the equipment. She was moving as fast as she could to secure as much information as possible before the local authorities arrived. She began to pull files from the drawer and lining the pages up in blocks of four, and continued snapping photos as fast as she could. She located two laptops and began to wrap them in some towels to take to the car.

Mac watched what Magen was doing, and his first thought went to his old friend Bill Lange; if there was anyone who could get the info off those computers, it was him.

He thought to himself that he really needed to get out of this house. The face of that small yellow-eyed creature was haunting him.

The officer in his hands had faded into unconsciousness. This was the best-case scenario; his screaming and shaking was unbearable.

The paramedics came through the door like gang busters ready to save the world. However, after surveying the surrounding scene, they lost that fired-up look. The younger of the two sat down in a chair close to the alloy cage and stared at the dead man with the missing limbs.

CHAPTER 71

The senior man turned the officer over, and let out a wail.

"Scott, can you hear me? Jesus, help us!" the man screamed as he recognized his friend.

"He has been down seventeen minutes, lost a lot of blood, took a bite from a really big dog. He may need a rabies workup!" Mac began to rifle off the series of events, slowly realizing that this was a small town and they were a close bunch, but had never seen this level of brutality.

"Are you telling me a dog did this?" the paramedic yelled in disbelief.

"Shot right out that door, and a second one went through the window behind me," Mac related as two additional local police officers entered the room.

"Is that one of ours on the floor?" the first officer demanded.

"It's Scott Devine. Half his face is missing. They're telling me it was a dog. I don't like it," the paramedic claimed.

"Who are you two? And what the fuck happened?" the officer began but then caught sight of what was left of the man in the cage.

Mac produced his badge, and then Magen followed with her FBI credentials.

Mac could see that confusion was gripping the officer as he was attempting to piece together the crime scene. The young paramedic began to vomit and retch at the side of the cage. The scene had fully overwhelmed him, and he hit the breaking point.

This prompted his partner to instantly go to his aid, leaving the bleeding officer unattended on the floor. Mac motioned to the second officer who was at the far end of the room; he noticed the sergeant stripes and began engaging him with the drama that had just taken place. It was then that Mac noticed that the officer was clenching something in his left hand; one of the safety stickers was visible at the base of the thumb.

Mac stopped unraveling his tale and quickly motioned to Magen to retreat out the back with a fast nod of the head. Magen was still dealing with the trauma of a few minutes ago and didn't catch the cue. Mac acted as if he was fully wrapped up with the wounded officer, keeping pressure on the wound and keeping his head elevated. However, he was keeping the eyes in the back of his head on the sergeant.

He was watching him close as he removed not only the stickers but some of the documents as well.

He was one of them, or he was being paid, and after some thought, that made the most sense because he was far from a professional.

We need to keep an eye on this one, and Magen has to snap out of it. This is ridiculous.

The paramedic moved back to the downed officer, and that was enough for Mac.

"Agent Cummings, I need a minute!" Mac stated with some authority in his voice.

"Yeah, I need to take a moment out of this basement. Today really sucked!" Magen stated as she snapped out of her daze.

"Yes, you do. Please follow me!" Mac requested with some sarcasm noted in his voice.

"Mac, what's up? You sound heated?" Magen probed as they walked through the basement door.

"First, you need to snap out of the daze you're in. I know what happened here today was severe, but the sergeant down there peeled those labels off the jars you took photos of," Mac began.

"What? You saw him do that?" Magen responded with shock that instantly put the day's events behind her.

"Several of the safety stickers and four or five sheets of paper just got liberated into the guy's pocket," he explained.

"So, what do we do? Should we move on the guy, call him out?" Magen said with aggression.

"Bad plan! That could go real bad on so many levels. We need to see where he is taking that paperwork," Mac stated, looking for a confirming response.

"What if he is simply being paid to destroy the data, and has no intention of delivering the lab notes?"

"That is definitely a strong possibility, a chance I think we need to take."

"You know that I am with you, Mac, but we need to get the hell out of here. I got a text about ten minutes ago. They set up a meeting with Cain. We have nine hours."

"That didn't take long for them to put that together. We need to roll out of here," Mac agreed as he pulled out his phone.

"Who are you calling?" Magen asked as she watched him pull his phone.

"I know a city cop who lives two towns away. I am going to put him on the three stripes downstairs," Mac confided as he connected with his old friend.

Magen grabbed her coat and had some limited conversation with the primary on the scene.

The detectives were en route, according to the officer.

The last thing she needed was to be drawn into a scenario where she would have to explain herself to a roomful of local dicks; that conversation could be nine hours alone. She handed the primary her card, and hit the door.

Mac was already in the car.

They were both pretty much covered in blood, and other fluids that were unmentionable. They hit the gas and didn't look back; Mac sat back in the passenger seat and closed his eyes, trying to make sense of the past hour. He glanced over at Magen to find her in tears.

He was taken aback at first, then realized that they really didn't know each other long enough for him to judge the reaction. He placed his hand on the back of her neck, and slowly began to rub. She did her best to control herself; he could feel her stiffen up, ashamed at her vulnerability. He stopped his massage and retracted his hand, turning his body to face her.

Magen had regained her composure and turned her swollen eyes to the man she had become all too close with. There was really no need for words; everything had already been said.

Mac reached out his left hand, gently took her right hand off the steering wheel, holding it gently in his, and said the only thing that would provide any comfort, "Baby, we will roast that fuck one day, I promise!"

CHAPTER 72

Cain opened the door of the restaurant and let Cleo and the boy in.

They were quickly seated by a middle-aged Asian man who overcompensated for his limited English with a silly face full of smiles.

Cain caught sight of Mike, the fat woman who owned this place; she was gracefully waltzing through the place. Her deep laughter could be heard throughout the building; it was a show just watching her.

She caught sight of Cain and stopped dead in her tracks; the laughter stopped all too quickly.

She did her best to hide the fear and regain composure, as she continued her waltz over to their table. Cain's eyes never left the woman's face as she rolled on over. He imagined himself leaping over the table and eating the fat monster in front of her staff and patrons.

Cain glanced down at the boy and could sense the agitation.

"Mr. Cain, it is such an honor you have returned to the Bann, and who are these delicious people?"

"Cleo, Joshua, I want you to meet the Soho dragon lady, Mike," Cain introduced the large woman as if they were old friends.

"They are delicious. I love them!" The large woman laughed and reached out to touch Joshua, who recoiled defensively.

"Young Joshua has the sight, and he sees the darkness flowing through your swollen body," Cain said with a gruesome smile.

"Really, that is crazy. Tell me you play with Mike, Mr. Cain?" the large woman said with a hint of fear spilling from her trembling lips.

"Oh, Mike, you know better than that. I don't play with my food!" Cain said with that same evil smile.

The big woman turned on her heels and quickly moved away. Cain watched her as she gracefully rolled down the aisle; then she glanced back. Cain looked over to Joshua who was watching her closely. He thought it was odd how deeply he was focused on her. He wondered about his gift and how it worked.

Cleo seemed to be connected in some to way to Joshua's thought process, like some electric current flow that they are both tapped into.

He pondered if this was some form of new gift or possibly an old gift that has lain dormant for centuries. He leaned down slowly in front of Joshua and actually saw the connection snap off.

Cain smiled at Joshua as he saw him start to come around.

"Welcome back, young man. Could you tell me what the big lady is thinking right now?" Cain asked with a boyish tone.

"She is making a phone call to a police officer named Bobby MacDonald. She is afraid of something from outer space," Joshua said with real confusion connected what he was feeling.

"Guys, I will be back in a flash. Order whatever you want," Cain said as he got up from the table.

"Alex, tell me what you like before you go," Cleo said.

"Sweetness, I want you to order for me, if you don't mind. I have a feeling you are going to do well by me," Cain said as he left the table.

"I really like Mr. Alex, Mommy. He makes me feel all right," Joshua said randomly without any reasoning.

"I do, too, baby boy! What do you want to eat?" Cleo asked, not even considering her answer.

CHAPTER 73

"Mike, I want you to put that phone away for the next hour. Officer MacDonald can wait to hear about my menu choice!" Cain said as he walked up to Mike who was fumbling with her phone.

"Mr. Cain, you startled me. I wasn't going to call anyone," Mike stated through trembling chunky lips.

"That's a really good idea, because if the police roll in here while I am eating, I will rip the arm from your body and kill any family you might have with the bloody stumps," Cain said as his eyeballs turned totally bright red.

"I'm turning the phone off now, Mr. Cain!" Mike said softly as she felt the urine release into her pants and the sharp pain run down her left arm.

"I am so glad, Mike. How's the Peking duck tonight?" Cain said with a long wide smile, emphasizing his four-inch incisors that were slowly fading back to normal size.

"Duck, best in city. We friends. I take care of Mr. Cain tonight," Mike said, shaking like a leaf.

"Excellent, so glad we had this little talk," Cain said as he turned to return to the table.

"Best duck in the city!" Mike called out with a forced laugh as she scrambled away.

Dr. Mazza was in the fetal position at the bottom of the closet, crying and sniveling, anticipating the authorities' arrival.

He waited and waited, but nobody came; they saw the children and still not even a knock on the door.

The coward was able to pull himself together long enough to fish for his cell phone in his pocket. He rose to his feet and slowly opened the closet door and walked to the window. He peeled the curtain back and watched the forensic team going in and out of his lab.

His fear began to turn to cold anger; they were in his mother's house. His children were missing, and they hadn't returned to the designated key point. They were out there afraid and confused; this was not in the contract.

The bitch promised there would be no American authorities in my mother's house. She lied! he thought out loud. *I have years of research in that damn lab, light-years away from anyone else. Now look at what they are doing to my stuff. This is wrong, and that bitch is going to pay.*

He put the phone to his ear, then took it away and looked at it. Then he hit the speed dial.

"Helen Worthington, how can I help?" the current and acting chief of Applied Physics answered.

"You people said I would be safe. They are ripping my lab apart, and you people said I would be safe!" Mazza screamed into the phone.

"Dr. Mazza! Where the hell have you been? I have sent two teams through all three houses. Where have you been?"

"I am afraid. I was hiding in a closet," Mazza started to explain, but was quickly cut off.

"Doctor, listen to me! Where are the children?" Helen probed.

"They are pulling my lab to pieces. All my research is gone," Mazza was rambling at this point, totally lost.

"Doctor, you need to hear me! Where are the children?" she stressed, pleading at this point with a more intense tone.

"They are gone. They were frightened, and they ran away, and you told me we were going to be safe!" the doctor was crying and screaming at this point.

"Gone where? Where? What are you saying, Doctor?" Helen said in disbelief.

"My angels are lost, alone, and confused. You said that we were going to be safe, protected, you said!" the doctor kept repeating.

"Listen, there will be a blue van pulling up in front of your house in seven minutes. Get in it," Worthington stated and abruptly hung up.

The doctor stared at the phone for a few seconds as a multitude of thoughts raced into his overactive brain.

Dr. Mazza raced through the house, pulling files of any real significance from every corner of the house. He started to create a large pile in the middle of the living room floor of files, computers, and feeding compounds for the children. He rushed into the kitchen and started to unload blood vials out of the refrigerator. He packed up everything and continued to run through the house, thinking about the secret stashes he had developed through the years.

He turned into the babysitting room; it was named after the Secret Service guys that would sleep there when things got rough. He thought to himself, *Where the hell is that fuckin' bunch now when I really need them?*

He kicked the closet door that was slightly ajar, but it popped open. There hanging on the bar were two MAC-10 machine guns. Mazza stared at them for a little while, thinking that it might not be a good idea just to leave them alone. Then he reached out and grabbed the closest one and pulled back the slide to chamber the round.

He continued pulling things together from all areas from the room. He strapped the MAC-10 around his shoulder and took a long trench coat out of the closet and put it on, concealing the weapon under his left armpit.

He also packed clothing for the children in hopes that they would find them somewhere. Mazza filled his arms with the items from the floor and began to transfer them to the garage. It took three trips, and then he heard the hum of an engine; he hit the button on the wall and paused at the garage door.

Before the door reached the peak, Mazza caught sight of dark slacks and shoes standing in front of the van.

He waited until the door went all the way to the top.

There stood Garrison, one of Worthington's mercenary flunkies; he thought that just didn't add up.

"Garrison, why are you here? I need help with all these bags. Put the blue ones up front!" Mazza barked although he still felt uneasy about Helen's main puppet being sent on a gofer mission.

"You don't need those variables!" Garrison stated as he withdrew a small-caliber pistol with a silencing device attached to the barrel.

"You're joking, right?" the doctor stated with a confused tone.

"The joke is over, Doctor!" the man said as he leveled the pistol at the skull of the scared man.

CHAPTER 74

"Go fuck yourself, shit heel!" the doctor yelled as he spun the MAC-10 out and began to spray the area in front of him.

The first bullet that was fired left Garrison's gun and quickly evaporated the lobe and a significant portion of the doctor's left ear.

The one shot was all that was allowed as the long solid burst from the MAC-10 shredded through Garrison's face.

The soldier's camouflage shirt was now a blood fountain.

Mazza double-timed out the back of the garage, leaking blood in every direction from his mangled ear.

He hit the back door and practically flew through it, screaming as he ran. The large soldier was unable to hold the small weapon after the bullet ripped apart his face and chest.

As Mazza retreated into the garage, he put his back against the side wall that was hidden from the street. He waited to hear the door open from the van; the second man must be coming to kill him.

Mazza stood with his back against the wall for about thirty seconds. The stress was too much for him; he could no longer control his crying. Still, no sound came from the van; Mazza had reached his breaking point. He pulled the slide back on the MAC-10 and ran from the garage with his weapon pointed at the van window.

When he reached for the door of the van, his tension came to an abrupt halt.

He could see that the driver was very much dead. During the exchange with Garrison the driver caught a stray in his left eye.

"A lucky shot, sorry!" he said out loud and dragged the balding man from the van, leaving him facedown in the driveway as he reversed the van and sped off, waving to the neighbors as he went.

Cornell woke from a small nap to see Thomas walking through the door without Cain. He thought that to be extremely strange, this being the first time he had seen one without the other.

Thomas stopped and looked over in the direction of his position, and then went through the double doors. Cornell scanned the room, attempting to get some idea of the time; it was hard to determine with the tinting on the top windows. He knew the nap was not long, but he slept hard; the exhaustion of the day finally caught up with him.

Thomas reappeared and slowly walked toward the small holding area where Cornell was sitting. He stood over Cornell with a slight smile that faded in and out, as if several thoughts were circling in his brain. He reached out his left hand and nodded for his good arm. When he had retrieved the arm, he quickly undid the Teflon lock and handed the arm back to the nervous Cornell. He glanced down on the arm and looked closely at the wounds that had developed under the shackle. Being a diabetic, he knew that these wounds needed to be cared for soon.

The smile returned to the face of Thomas.

Cornell was trying to put the chain of events into context and the change in the big man's behavior. The fact that Thomas was not only being civil, but there was some apparent concern in his dark eyes.

"Come with me. Time to get you right, young sir!" Thomas said, sporting that same wicked smile.

"Have I outlived my usefulness, Thomas?" Cornell probed but kept his composure all the same.

"If I was to kill you, I would be picking you out of my teeth long before now, so come with me," Thomas stated without any room for rebuttal.

"I have no information that is of value to you. Torture me if necessary, but it would be useless."

"That's good to know," he stated as he dragged Cornell into the computer room.

"What the hell is this place?" Cornell shouted, the fear getting the best of him.

Thomas grabbed Cornell and forcefully placed him in one of the cockpit chairs. Then straps were pulled out from behind the chair; Thomas was fast and moved with incredible agility. He then secured Cornell's damaged arm and began to look really close to the tissue carnage. He spent some time putting together some chemicals and then turned to Cornell and began a slow purposeful walk in his direction.

The evil thoughts that raced through his mind were making him nauseous and frightened. He found himself thinking that this alien was going to dip his painful stub into acid or whatever chemicals he had mixed up.

Thomas placed a foam cylinder from the damaged area sticking out a foot, then secured the device to his arm, not saying a word through the process. He then added the chemicals, slowly pouring them into a hole in the foam. The device was connected to the several computers that were far beyond his comprehension; even the language was foreign.

Cornell began to feel sensation from within the foam, not painful, but really odd. Thomas was monitoring several dials on a specific device to the left. It began to heat up. Cornell began to say something, but the alien interjected in a booming voice, "Don't move! If you like the use of that arm, then I suggest you listen to what I am saying."

Thomas laid it out there like there was absolutely no wiggle room on this one.

"It is starting to burn, Thomas. This could be a really good time to tell me what it is you are doing here?" Cornell pleaded.

"Just don't move! I am doing some repair work. Cain has something going on, and apparently your well-being has increased in importance!" Thomas said as that mocking grin returned to his face.

"So, this is going to help—" was all Cornell was able to get out before Thomas stopped him.

"Mr. Pierce, for some reason, when you talk, you move your hands, both of them. In your case, it is more than just slight. Some humans can't talk without moving their arms at all. We can't rhyme or reason with it. Regardless, things will work out so much better if you stop talking!" Thomas stated with little to no emotion at all.

Cornell stared at the alien as the heat still continued to increase. He had to dig deep to find the trust or faith in what this alien was saying was true. This was extremely difficult, knowing full well that this being would have no issue at all eating his flesh right down to his bone.

The concept of trusting that this savage being had his best interest at heart was borderline comical. Yet there he sat grinding his teeth as the pain and heat intensified, sending waves of electrical blasts straight up his arm. He gazed at Thomas, whose expression was flat and emotionless. He could have been scrambling eggs or flipping pancakes; either way, his vacant expression was intimidating.

The pain then began to level off; the building intensity had stopped. Then a slow wind down from the machinery could be felt throughout the room. Before long, the heat and pain was not only bearable but also subsiding.

Thomas looked at the reading that was being displayed on the wall of computers. Throughout the whole process, Thomas continued to present with his cold, flat effect. At no time was there any indication that the procedure was of any value.

After several minutes of silence, Thomas turned toward the chair with a device that could only be described as a miniature light saber. He reached out and grabbed the foam bubble connected to Cornell's arm; it had solidified over the past minutes. Thomas began to cut the contraption first on the topside and then on the bottom.

Cornell could smell smoke, and even though there was no pain, the sight of burning material accompanied with the smoke was unnerving. Thomas had finished utilizing the device and then glanced with a slight evil smile at Cornell!

"Ready?" Thomas said as his evil smile intensified.

"Am I ready? What am I ready for?" Cornell stated with obvious confusion.

Thomas then smashed the cocoon-like contraption on the table with considerable force.

Instinctively, Cornell recoiled his arm away in an attempt to protect his already damaged arm.

It was then that he saw his hand was now back.

His eyes widened as he looked upon the miracle in front of his face. Tears began to well up in his eyes as he realized that it was, in fact, his own hand. He identified a scar that he received as a child between his thumb and forefinger.

He had cocked a BB gun on the meat between those two fingers, resulting in a lifelong scar. There it was along with other spots and hair groupings that he had come to recognize as his alone.

How in the world had they been able to make this happen? Cornell thought of all the kids coming back from the Middle East with lost limbs. What an amazing technology this would be in the hands of one of the military hospitals.

Cornell looked up at Thomas who was moving toward him with new devices; he recognized the blood pressure cuff, and some kind of oxygen-reading device, but he didn't recognize the third thing.

"Thomas, I don't know what to say to you. I don't know if you even realize the gift that you have given back to me!" Cornell said.

"Mr. Pierce, I am fully aware of my actions and what it means to any being to have a limb restored. I want you to realize that I am just following the orders from Mr. Cain. The boss wants your hand back on, and so the job is done!"

Thomas finished with his tests and then walked to one of the underlings and made some reference about him, then began to walk off.

"Thomas, are you saying Cain ordered this?" Cornell called out.

"That is correct. What were you thinking, random act of kindness?" Thomas stated as the evil smile resurfaced.

"So, I am now a bargaining chip?" Cornell yelled.

"Of course, you are, why else would you be breathing?" Thomas finished and walked off.

CHAPTER 75

Mac sat back in the passenger seat as Magen drove; he looked down at his hands and noticed that his effort to remove the blood wasn't very effective. He glanced out the window as the car entered the on-ramp to the Southern State Parkway.

He wondered what these people would think if they became aware that there was an evil here beyond their comprehension.

Mac began to allow himself a moment to relax, as the last few days began to catch up to him. They had only gone a few exits when Magen's phone went off.

She lifted it to her ear and began to talk. Mac was hardly paying any attention as sleep was starting to roll in, until she let out a meaty "Are you kidding?"

Mac immediately jumped back into the game as he watched her face turn from shock to determination.

"What is it, now?" Mac stated with some frustration in his voice.

"Multiple shots fired and two men down a block away from the house we just left," Magen said as she headed for the closest exit to turn the boat around and get back to the scene.

"This is crazy. Was anything else said, and who is calling you with these updates?" Mac probed as he began to wonder how she was able to stay updated on these events.

"Gregory has the whole Eastern Seaboard monitored for any related activity. He is plugged into everything you could imagine!" Magen stated, keeping Mac in the loop.

"Were they able to identify the men down, or am I jumping the gun?" Mac asked, trying to dig for additional information.

"The locals weren't even on the scene. He did say that a half dozen frantic 911 calls were intercepted, and some of them were pretty outrageous, but that's all we have so far," Magen stressed as she buried her foot to the floor and turned on the external siren.

When they arrived at the scene, there were two marked and one undercover in front of the house. The neighborhood was buzzing as people lined the street.

Mac and Magen walked up on the scene with their credentials out for the ready. Mac quickly walked up on the body to determine if it was the doctor who had possibly become way too much of a liability.

Magen moved right in on the detective who was standing in the driveway. Mac began to read the scene and follow the chain of events that he had done many times before.

There were several shells scattered all along the driveway, indicating that the gunfire was heading toward the garage. As he moved closer in that direction he could see more shells on the floor of the garage; these were of a larger caliber. These were small and fat, possibly .45 caliber; with the way the shells were spread apart, the only thing that made sense in his mind was MAC-10. He poked his head out to take one more look at the body on the lawn. The whole scenario began to unfold as his brain worked to put the pieces together. His eyes caught a splash of blood on the garage door track.

He stepped closer to the droplets and then slowly started to step back, looking for additional blood. Nothing was visible and that he thought was odd. Mac squatted like a baseball catcher, just to get a better perspective. He began to notice that there were several areas that were disturbed, as if someone had run a rag through.

Someone was cleaning up the tracks, and not really doing a great job. Mac followed the questionable areas out the back door of the garage, only to run face-to-face with the sergeant from the doctor's house.

"I need you to turn around and get back in your car!" the tall officer said to Mac.

"Just looking over the crime scene. We are both on the same side, right?" Mac said with a slight air of sarcasm in his voice.

"You and your friend have absolutely zero jurisdiction here, and you need to leave, now!" As the officer voiced his demand to Mac, two other officers began to circle in, glaring at Mac.

"Well, I believe that I have learned enough here, gentlemen!" Mac stated as he turned and walked through the garage, only to find Magen in a shouting match on the front lawn.

"Have you lost your mind? I have every right in the world to be here. I am in the middle of a high-profile investigation. You are impeding that investigation! Do you hear me, Officer?" Magen's voice continued to escalate as her anger grew and she searched for a badge.

"I don't give a shit about your bullshit high-profile investigation. If you are still on my crime scene in the next five minutes, we're going to have a real problem!" the detective stated between deep drags from his filter-less smoke.

"What is going on here?" Magen declared with obvious confusion in her voice.

"Come on, Agent Cummings, we have a deadline to meet!" Mac said as he began to pull Magen to the car.

"Mac, what are you doing? These assholes are playing games!" Magen shouted loud enough to be heard by a good part of the neighborhood.

"It's a cover team. We need to leave fast!" Mac said softly under his breath.

"What do you mean?" Magen said, now fully confused about the events.

"That sergeant that we ran into at the other house was in the backyard cleaning up a blood trail!" Mac told Magen as he held the car door for her.

"What did he say when he saw you?" Magen asked.

"He made it clear that I was not wanted on his crime scene. There were several swipe marks where blood spatter should have been!" Mac explained as he fished in his pocket for his iPhone.

"What are you doing with the phone?" Magen probed.

"Your doctor friend is wounded, from the small splatter that I was able to find. I don't think it's all that bad. However, he's a doctor, and he is going to deal with this gunshot even if it is only a flesh wound!" Mac began.

"So, if I was wounded in Long Island and half the world wanted my ass on a silver platter, where would I go?" Magen began to follow the reasoning.

"Are you capable of accessing Google Maps on that computer of yours in the back?" Mac asked as he began to run through possibilities.

"I might be able to do better than that. There is a think tank back at Langley, and these geeks live for this kind of thing!" Magen said with a long smile.

"Well then, let us unleash the geeks!" Mac stated with increased enthusiasm and purpose.

CHAPTER 76

"We believe that Dr. Robert Mazza has been wounded, possible GSW. He has fled these coordinates thirty minutes ago, and he is currently driving a dark-colored van!" Magen spoke into her phone, entering every shred of information she considered pertinent as she made the right at the end of the corner.

"Just slow down when you get to the yellow house!" Mac stated as he pointed to a house six deep on his right.

Initially, Mac considered popping out of the car and talk with some neighbors if he could backtrack and look without being noticed. Unfortunately, he wasn't alone in his thinking process; uniforms and plainclothes were all over the area securing the full block. No doubt they were looking to isolate and control any and all information leaving the scene.

He motioned for Magen to speed up! Magen picked up quickly on the events unfolding. Her brain was racing with the possibilities of where the wounded doctor went or where he would feel safe. He most likely would be concerned about tending to his injury. He would be too smart to go anywhere near a hospital.

He might consider a nurse's office at one of the local schools or one of the pharmacies in the area. He would need to conceal any bloody clothes; that would be a priority for him. Mac sat back in the seat with a pensive look upon his face. He turned to Magen who was deep in her own thoughts.

"What about the local hospitals? He would want to patch himself up, don't you think?" Mac said, really just to open a dialogue but not convinced of the possibility.

"Not a chance. He would rule that out immediately, but I agree he would want to deal with his injury. I was thinking that he might want to slip into one of the local schools, nurse's office, maybe even a vet's!" Magen offered, also unsure of her decision.

"I could really use an aerial map of the area. It would really give me an idea of countless possibilities," Mac stated with agitation in his voice.

"That I can make happen. Pull out the computer out of the back and let me enter the data," Magen said as she grabbed the cell for support.

"It must be nice to have endless resources to catch the bad guys. You Feds crack me up with this shit," Mac said, half kidding with the woman he become immensely friendly with.

"American tax dollars at work, but we do on occasion get results," Magen voiced with an air of pride in the agency that had become her home and family.

"Wow! This thing is working pretty fast. Is there a way to show points of interest?" Mac asked, trying to narrow down the good doctor's options based on the information that he had already compiled.

"Run a C-14 program in addition to satellite profile. Include everything of a medical nature. I also want exit points from the area with probability equations factored in," Magen continued to bark orders into the phone.

Mac sat back in wonder as the current screen came to life with street names and key points. Anything that was remotely connected to medical significance was highlighted in red. Mac was able to use a point-free pen to draw possibilities from both the lab and the area where the shooting took place. He noticed that physician offices were outlined throughout the screen, and there were many of them. As he drew the line, he quickly noticed that they were intersecting with several of the highlighted high-level targets. He took in a deep a sigh at the reality of the unlimited possibilities that a somewhat intelligent man could have at his disposal.

He thought that Magen needed to be looking at this; she has had a history with this animal. If anyone could put this puzzle together, it would be her with the best possible insight.

Mac asked Magen to pull over and take a few minutes and review the grid. Magen looked over into Mac's eyes and saw the desperation and frustration. She pulled the car to the side of the road and began to decipher the data.

She quickly saw what was frustrating her new partner; there were just too many scenarios for Mazza. She began to think like the injured doctor, as painful as it was to try and crawl into the head of such an evil fuck.

She spoke into the phone requesting the removal of all the local physician offices, thinking that he wouldn't risk that. He was sneaky, and would be looking for a safe haven without collateral damage.

All the hospitals were eliminated; he knew the security would too heavy. Mac sat back and watched the grid clear; his trained mind began to see things much clearer. As they sat there breaking down the neighborhood, Mac watched two Crown Victorias roll by slowly.

It was the local boys, and they were looking for the good doctor also, and maybe even keeping a closer eye on the Fed.

Mac let it go and returned his focus to the grid on the computer. Then he caught sight of one of the listed soft targets, Community Abortion Clinic, just two miles from their position; it stood out and triggered Mac. He used the laser pen to show Magen, who caught it and made the connection instantly. She started the engine and sped off like a rocket.

CHAPTER 77

"It made absolute sense. It had all the requirements that he would need, and it was all low-profile," Magen stated with newfound enthusiasm.

"It's still a shot in the dark, but damn, it just sounds like him!" Mac responded.

"We have company. Three cars back, not doing a real good job at being discreet," Magen said with some mild concern.

"Yeah, they have been running around us since we left the cleaned-up shooting. They just want what we want, but their motivation is most likely someone else's agenda," Mac stated with conviction.

"I think I need to bring a team in and put this to bed! We are not going to be able to successfully extract him without help," Magen stated as she reached for the phone.

"Tell me how long would it take a team of spooks to get mobilized? This is Long Island. You're not in Virginia anymore, Dorothy," Mac asked jokingly, but considering the time frame.

"For all I know, they're on standby at Kennedy Airport. Might even be out there in Islip," Magen stated, knowing how her people operated, but got back on the phone to confirm.

"I am dying to know where these locals are getting their orders from. Can't get it out of my gut that there is so much more going on!" Mac said as he continued to process the last two days.

"I was wrong. Two teams left LaGuardia Airport almost twenty minutes ago. Their ETA to us is within ten minutes," Magen said with regained energy.

"Wow! That couldn't come at a better time. I really think we are on to something with this clinic," Mac stated with conviction.

"Hope so. I am going to drive around a little, try and lose our friends. Bet you dinner I can shake them in less than ten minutes!" Magen said to Mac with a competitive grin.

"I don't know, these locals know the area, and they like to drive. I have ten on the locals!" Mac shot back as he fished a ten-spot from his pocket and laid it on the dashboard.

"Game on. Oh, ye of little faith," Magen said as she buckled up.

"Go for it. Would love to lose that money," Mac pushed.

Magen saw the light begin to change from green to red, and slowly began to drift to the left. Those following began to drift in the same direction. Just in case Magen was to make a fast left, they would be well positioned.

There were more or less twenty cars in the general vicinity, some flanking Magen to the right, some to the left.

A split second before the light changed, Magen slammed on the gas and pulled the car all the way to the right, knowing full well she could make the right on red.

Horns were blasting from all sides now, and the cars behind Magen quickly hit their brakes. The local police were pinned three cars deep, and all they could really do was watch Magen make the right turn practically on only two wheels.

Before the Crown Victoria got to the corner, Magen had made a series of rights and lefts. Mac was holding on for dear life, doing his best not to show any fear. There were several close calls; he didn't mind the close ones with the other cars, but the close hits on pedestrians really shook him up.

Magen was in the zone, years of training and not having the opportunity to show her stuff. Mac looked over and could see the absolute elation on her face; she was letting go of the insanity of the day, and Mac was slightly envious.

After a half dozen rights and lefts later, Magen slowed and pulled the vehicle behind an oil truck blocking the vision from the main artery two hundred yards away. They sat for a few seconds as Magen regained her composure.

"I am pretty sure we lost them. I believe that ten-spot belongs to the victor!" Magen boasted as she reached her hand to grab up the cash.

"Hold that thought, Ms. Speedy Gonzalez. I guarantee these locals will be in front of us or behind us within forty-five seconds," Mac stated, holding his Swiss Army watch in front of Magen's face.

"That would be highly unlikely, but I will bite!" Magen stated as she watched the second hand.

"Behind us, two blocks down, is that a Crown Vic sticking its nose out of the block to the right?" Mac pointed out with still twenty seconds to spare.

"Holy shit! How is that possible? I left that car in the dust," Magen snapped with disbelief.

"They are keyed in on the car. Either the computer or maybe you have a LoJack system on board, really not sure," Mac stated.

"Or even worse, maybe they have someone filtering them the same satellite imaging!" Magen considered, not buying the computer scenario and the government LoJack system is deemed classified; she would have major difficulty accessing that puppy herself.

"Well, that would really suck, but to be honest, it has been really hard to decipher the good guys from the bad guys since you hit on me at the pizza parlor!" Mac smiled at his new friend, but there was real truth in what he was saying.

"There is no doubt about that. This whole thing has me in a constant state of shock, but I am really glad you're here with me!" Magen placed her hand on Mac's arm.

"It has been unreal. Magen, you really are special to me, and I know we have all of forty-eight hours together, but I have not felt this close to a woman for a long time, and I like it!" Mac said through heavy breathing. He grabbed her arm and pulled her mouth to his, and for those few seconds, the world just went away.

"So, what now? These monkeys are all over us and seem to be able to track our movements fairly well," Magen probed for a solid plan.

"It is time to bag this twisted fuck. His own people have turned on him, he's running, and he's scared!" Mac was clear on the how, but it was all riding on the outside chance that he was at this clinic.

"I can have one of the teams run interference with the locals and then put the second on us as backup?" Magen offered.

"That sounds like a plan. Agent Cummings, I believe it is time to rock and roll!" Mac smiled as Magen slowly backed up the car, threw it into drive, and literally jumped on the gas.

The engine screamed as the tires spun with insane purpose. Smoke rose up from the bottom of the vehicle like a B horror movie. Then the government-issue shot down the block like a bullet.

The Crown Vic had already made the turn to pursue, but had an awful lot of ground to make up. Magen came out on the main artery sideways with tires screaming. Mac knew she really just got lucky that she wasn't by oncoming, but luck was something they would need plenty of over the next half hour.

Magen was barking instructions into the phone for the teams to be perfectly clear on their assignments. Mac looked at the GPS and saw that they were three minutes off the primary site. Mac began to yell out instructions, rights and lefts so fast that spittle began to fly from his mouth.

Magen did her best to follow his demands and try and secure the location prior to their arrival.

The first team was already in place. Magen turned to Mac and said, "They are using tranquilizing darts. I am guessing that call came from orders outside our team. What the hell is going on?"

"Magen, come on, you are not that naive. The line between the good guys and the bad guys has vanished when that thing bolted off the hotel roof," Mac added with humor only because he knew that he was so far over his head.

"I am not naive, just hopeful that there are still some good guys," Magen said in a loud voice as she hit another sharp right, following Mac's direction.

"Two blocks up on the right, green building. That's it!" Mac shouted.

"I got it!" Magen said as she reached down and grabbed the emergency brake and pulled it straight up, sending the car into a violent spin to the right.

"Holy shit! Please don't kill me!" Mac screamed.

"No worries, we will just dock the ship and go collect our package," Magen said as the tires slammed against the sidewalk, and they both opened the doors.

CHAPTER 78

There was a chain-link fence on the side of the building; Mac removed a long coat from the back seat, then he threw it over the barbed wire and began to help Magen over the fence.

He didn't have to help too much; her training had served her well. She was up and over the fence in a flash.

She hit the ground and drew her gun in one fast motion. Mac was right behind her; his Beretta was locked and loaded. They crept down the alley, keeping close to the wall for a sense of security.

The first thing that Magen noticed was a torn-apart red bag waste spread throughout the whole area; she saw little pieces of aborted fetus remains, and then the smell hit her nose and she gagged. Mac was focused on the noises he was hearing from the roof, and was unable to put together the carnage of human remains at his feet.

From Mac's vantage point, he saw the doctor first; at his leg was one of the savage children. It looked at Mac and snarled, baring teeth-like razors the size of fingers.

Mac was frozen momentarily at the sight of the nightmare that the doctor had created.

Magen raised her government-issue and took aim at the abomination next to the doctor.

The wounded doctor quickly spun around and let out the last spray from the MAC-10. The burst sent most of the bullets high, except for one that hit Megan, grazing her shoulder bone. The hit twisted her body around three times before she hit the ground.

Mac raised his Beretta, but before he could get a shot, two darts hit the child and one hit the doctor in the throat.

The child let out a screech that could be heard from miles away. The second child came to aid the other, only to catch several darts on different parts of its body. There were several seconds of spasms, then the child went down, falling on top of the doctor who was also down and lifeless.

Both of Magen's teams were now all over the scene.

They began to triage Magen immediately, and then tended to the doctor. They handled the children much differently; they had planned for their extraction and stood ready with zoo equipment. Canine transports and protective devices were utilized for the two subhuman children.

There was absolutely no discussion with Mac; these guys moved with total precision and had everything wrapped up in minutes. The locals made no attempt to interfere with the heavily armed federal team.

An ambulance pulled to the mouth of the alley, and two paramedics ran to Magen, already aware of what to expect and the type of wound that had been sustained. Mac began to break from the shock he was in and moved quickly to Magen's side; he was intercepted by an older man in a suit who seemed to have appeared out of nowhere.

"Lieutenant MacDonald, my name is Agent Savel. I have been looking for you!" he said with a big smiling face.

"Looks like you found me. Excuse me," Mac stated as he continued his steps toward Magen, even though he was aware that this wasn't going to fly with this guy.

"She is doing well. Took one in the shoulder, knocked the wind out of her, some blood loss, but should be on her feet in no time," Savel said as he slowly walked behind Mac.

"Who are you, and why are you so forthcoming with information?" Mac turned with new interest at the suit on his heels.

"Easy, son, I told you who I am! You have been through a lot, I get it, but I am also the guy in charge! Agent Cummings is going into that ambulance then to a helicopter nine minutes away. Finally, there is a jet sitting at Kennedy ready to take her to Andrews. Are you heading back to the city, or are you taking a ride back to Maryland?"

"Really would like to go with her back to Andrews if we can make that happen!" Mac stated, with a hint of apology in his voice.

"Better get going, train's leaving the station, son!" the older man pointed to the ambulance that was getting ready to load Magen in.

"Thank you!" Mac said with confusion in his voice, but put out his hand just the same.

"We aren't all assholes," the older agent offered, seeing the hesitation in Mac's eyes.

They both smiled as Mac jumped in the back of the ambulance.

CHAPTER 79

Cain woke up to the sounds of horns and sirens; even though they were forty-four floors high, the sounds of the city were still present. He pulled back the satin sheets and eased his way out of bed, careful not to wake Cleo.

He pulled the penthouse curtains back and sat there, taking in the city in all its glory. The lights and faint sounds from this far up gave Cain the sense of superiority as the rest of the world seemed slightly smaller and quite insignificant.

He had become highly impressive when faking his sleep phase. The human being required seven to nine hours of sleep over a twenty-four-hour period. He understood that this was necessary for them to maximize functioning at their peak performance. Cain found it amazing that these creatures spent a third of their lives shut off.

He had spent some considerable time practicing the sleep phase; he enjoyed the meditation aspect of it and felt it calmed his rapid mind.

The pending meeting was keeping his brain highly sensitive.

Finding the child was brilliant, he thought to himself.

He had no doubt that the humans would be extremely defensive, especially after the hotel fiasco. Their ability to capture him would be a priority of theirs; that he would need to abolish immediately.

Human thinking would be drawn to the potential upper hand, which could be an issue for him.

The child was the key to his safety; he would need to bluff his way through. His ability to utilize the child to stay one step ahead of the human plan is going to be extremely important. He would be able to keep Cleo busy with a day of shopping and pampering that only New York could provide. The little one would love the game and the whole excitement of what is going on!

Cain thought to himself that this might have all types of holes through the plan. However, it was time to surface and make arrangements for the future of the mother planet; they had enjoyed a long stealth existence of maneuvering through the shadows of this planet. Too much damage had come to light over the past seventy-two hours.

There are bodies being processed by multiple organizations. By now they identified some strange DNA. He wondered what was going through the minds of these puzzled scientists with limited information. They knew that they were looking at DNA of some form of subhuman being. Of course, they are only given some limited data, teased by their superiors.

The labs must be a ball of confusion, all those tightly packed strands of DNA pulled from the saliva of the mutilated bodies from the lobby. It would take this species decades to do anything that could be dangerous to them. By then, many changes will have come and gone and what they hold would be insignificant.

He turned to look at Cleo in bed; in the warm dim light he could make out the lines of her gleaming body. Stunning was all that would come to his mind. Her breasts were full, not damaged at all from the years of breastfeeding that the little one required. They were still perfect and well framed. The curve of her back reminded him of the rings of Salvo, a B-class planet he had lived there also a thousand years ago.

Cain cherished these moments of quiet where he could reflect on the line of time he had traveled. There were endless events that circled his head, and he tried to formulate a manageable time frame. He realized that he wasn't capable of placing time with events; there was just too much. He had lived among countless humanoid colonies over the centuries, and here he sat trying to pull a puzzle together that had endless pieces. He laughed to himself just for a few seconds and then went back to his plan for the meeting later that day.

He felt the slight trickle of unease as he began to think of the task before him. Cain's race of beings paid extremely close attention to the messages from the body. He believed that he was communicating with the divine, and that caution would be prudent.

He was alone now; Thomas and the others were back in Maryland making departure arrangements. Mr. Pierce would be whole again by now, and that would be his olive branch to open the meeting. Offering Mr. Pierce back alive and undigested would buy much credibility with the authority figures.

Cain thought of Mr. William Dean and his ability to stay alive with so much rolling against him. He thought of that female agent on the roof of the hotel; she had information that was impressive. He was taken off guard by that reality. Cain knew that they could fold up the whole show on Earth and just be another conspiracy theory. The seeds would break down and eventually liquefy within a matter of months. He considered that without electrical current that was being coordinated through their system, the seeds would be rejected by their host quite fast.

He wanted to stay, and that would take some doing; after all, this was still just a savage planet. He knew that the humanoid population that inhabited this rock was just a stone's throw from living in caves and defecating on their living room floor. He felt they had moved past the point where they could self-destruct and terminate their own life cycle, but not by much.

The truth is that the human experience is waiting for the next crisis, and that's how they roll!

He knew all this and still wanted to be part of this crazy ride.

Cain knew his life was going down this road the moment he stepped out of the transport and smelled the air. He knew he was back on this rock and staying. There was nothing out there for him; he knew this and was firm on his decision.

Deep down, some of the council also knew he would stay if he ever got the chance to return. He could see it in their faces when the order came down from command that this was the last time they would look upon the being of Cain. For some of them, that was all right; enemies are impossible to avoid in his world. For the few close friends, there was that mix of joy and pain to see someone you love get what he needs. However, you know that it will mean never seeing the being in one's life cycle.

Cain stood there at the window looking down, running all this through his mind. He reached out and put his hands on the glass, feeling the cool large plates. He really did love this place and felt a spiritual pull to be here, and that he couldn't fight. So, they were just going to learn how to live with the three Grays and deal.

He smiled to himself as his thoughts drifted back to the two on the roof. The female agent said something that indicated some higher knowledge of him; this was interesting to him. It amazed him just how much enlightenment had taken place on this planet over two decades. He was puzzled with the look in her eyes. It wasn't fear; it was confirmation.

That would assume that her reasoning was confirmed at that very moment.

She knew that he existed, and depending on how long she had been investigating, such an unpopular reality that moment was her "You see, I am not crazy" moment.

She would need to be there at the meeting; that would need to be unconditional.

Cain sat at his computer and began to compose an e-mail outlining the terms of the meeting, nothing outrageous, and he knew they would not be able to follow it to the letter; however, it was a beginning.

He finished and returned to the beautiful body fast asleep in his bed. Cain slid under the sheets slowly, twisting his body in the most impossible position. He stared at the ceiling for only a second, then closed his eyes and considered every scenario that could face him in the following day.

CHAPTER 80

Magen was resting peacefully and able to make a fairly decent account of herself through the whole ordeal. Of course, there was a complete disconnect of any thought that the second the bullet caught her shoulder and spun her around like a top. The sheer force of the impact just took all the oxygen out of her chest, and her body simply responded by shutting down.

The good side was she was already complaining about being in the hospital and had been requesting her weapon. Mac slunk back in the recliner and found some sleep that he needed so severely. These hospitals can often be a symphony of sounds with bells and alarms. This didn't stop Mac from crashing like he hadn't slept in years.

Magen watched him for a while, trying to make sense of the day. She was thinking of the two little demon children and how they looked with the tranquilizer darts all over their little bodies. She didn't want to think of them as demon children, but they were altered and ferocious.

Magen allowed herself a minute to think about what laid in store for the two altered children now that the government has them. The thought of it made her sad; they would never be free again. For all she knew, they could be dead; the science ghouls could have felt they were too dangerous to study. The sound that came out of the female child when she was darted in the face was something she will carry with her the rest of her life.

Magen looked over at Mac and wondered what would happen next; she could be transferred and not see him for long periods of time. The thought of that troubled and upset her.

Since the loss of the love of her life, there was no one who got through to her sexually; could she just walk away? Did Mac want her in his life?

As she puzzled with this, Magen looked up to see three dark trench coats. Not Feds. *Spooks*, she thought, and one was pushing a wheelchair.

"Good morning, Agent. If you're up for it, you have an open invitation to the meeting of the century. Interested?" the man pushing the chair announced.

Magen looked puzzled at the three and realized she knew the elder man to the right. Vance Rider, one of the most decorated agents in the history of the agency, a Congressional Medal of Honor recipient. His picture was on the wall at the headquarters.

This is a strange choice of chaperone from the powers that be!

"So, where are we going?" Magen asked.

CHAPTER 81

"Your first stop is a departmental debriefing, and then you two are off to a sit-down dinner with an out-of-town guest at a quality restaurant right here in New York," said the man holding the chair.

"Out-of-town guest, I like that! Can I ask who you are working for?" Magen probed.

"Agent Cummings, you are fully aware of whom we work for, and you know why we are here. Your presence has been requested as well as Officer Sleepy MacDonald here. This is one you don't say no to," the tall man said with a blank expression.

"Requested? Who requested our presence at this meeting?" Magen asked with noted confusion in her tone.

"The out-of-town guest that you met on the roof of the newly decorated Four Seasons has sent an e-mail requesting that Officer MacDonald and yourself, along with two others, attend a dinner conference at a public location to be determined in four hours and nine minutes," the tall man said.

"Our conversation wasn't that long or profound. This is not making any sense," Magen stated.

"You must have said something that had relatively a high amount of impact, or we wouldn't be here!" the man stated, visibly growing tired of the conversation.

"Really not sure what I said, but you're right about one thing!" Magen began.

"That would be?" said the tall man.

"This is not an invitation you pass up on. Mac, wake up!" Magen yelled as she slowly got herself out of bed.

"What are you doing?" Mac shot back as he climbed out of a much-needed sleep.

"We need to get out of here, and we need to do that now. Can you help me put my shirt on?" Magen stated as she began to rise from the bed slowly.

"What the hell are you talking about? Where do you think you're going?" Mac snapped back as he was distracted by a noise behind him.

"These are the maids, and they're here to clean the room!" Magen joked through the pain.

"We don't have ugly maids in New York. Just ask Strauss-Kahn. What gives, gentlemen?" Mac continued on the joke line but was instinctively concerned.

"The individual on the roof has invited us to dinner. Apparently, we made an impression!" Magen continued to joke through the pain. Even though the bullet was removed, the trauma to the area was sobering; copper casing will do that.

"What! The leaping lizard has invited us to dinner, and we are going?" Mac said as he turned from the three silent men.

"I have been following the handiwork of this thing for years. Nobody believed me, and they thought I was a joke. I have to go!" Magen laid it out there.

"So, this is about pride! You know what they say about pride. Why can't you let the old jarheads deal with that thing?" Mac attempted to appeal to her intellectual side.

"Mac, we have been invited to meet with an extraterrestrial being, and you are fighting this? What is it?" Magen asked.

"Did you not see those bodies in the hotel lobby? We're not playing with the 'phone home' ET. These are cold, calculating killing machines!" Mac's voice began to rise to emphasize his point.

"I can't let this one go! I am going to this meeting. I am compelled to do so. Please come with me," Magen pleaded as she pulled the curtain and finished pulling her shirt down over her sore shoulder.

"I have no desire to face this thing again. It is pushing my Irish luck to face the devil a second time on his invitation, sorry." Mac was finished, really clear about his decision.

"Mac, I haven't been this close to anyone since..." Magen paused unable to continue.

"I really do care about you, Agent Cummings, and part of me understands why you need to do this. I'm not going anywhere. Try and understand my point!" Mac said as he turned for the door.

"Walking away is not possible. The request is for the both of you to attend this meeting," the tall man said as he released his grip on the wheelchair.

"Slim, I'm a New York City police detective. How are you going to tell me what I'm going to do?" Mac said in his best "tough guy" voice.

"If I have to, I will take this vial out of my pocket and have these two gentlemen hold you down as I drug you and carry you to this meeting. Then I'm going to punch you in the face because I don't really like you, but you will make this meeting," the tall man said as if he was talking to a child, slowly and with purpose.

"I guess we are having dinner, honey!" Mac said with a smile, fully realizing the gravity of his situation.

CHAPTER 82

Cain opened the door of the limo and began to emerge into the sunny morning. He was being extra careful not to step his new Italian shoes into anything that could be problematic. He looked back at Joshua and told him he would be back in a few minutes. The child looked up from the television and smiled at Cain.

"I know! Can I have some soda?" young Joshua asked.

"What did you eat for breakfast?" Cain shot back with all the concern of a hovering parent.

"I had pancakes and sausage with juice, but that was a while ago," Joshua proclaimed.

"Just wait a little. We are going to a restaurant later. Don't ruin your appetite," Cain finished as he closed the door and proceeded into the bank.

"Mr. Cain, please let me assist you!" the young director said immediately as he saw Cain enter the door.

He motioned Cain to the stairs that led to the vault. Cain gave no hesitation and followed the young man to the basement, then stepped aside as the man began to open the vault utilizing a series of keys and code numbers.

The noise from the large steel pins retracting filled the room. The young man utilized a fair amount of strength to open the door. Cain thanked him and proceeded into the vault as the young man began to close up behind him.

The strong smell of coffee permeated the vault. Thomas and Mr. Cornell Pierce were having breakfast at a round café table in the center of the vault.

"Good morning, Thomas! Mr. Pierce, how are you feeling today, all ready to go free?" Cain said in a friendly voice.

"I was wondering why I was having my coffee in a bank vault," Cornell shot back.

"I am sorry that we are not out in the beautiful sunny day, but I just wanted to fill you in on the events of the day. Is that acceptable?" Cain had pulled up a chair and sat comfortably in front of the aging black man.

"Please tell me what you need from me," Cornell said without any real conviction.

"Nothing at all. I am taking you back to your people this morning, and all I am looking for is that you allow me to do just that!" Cain probed as he gestured his hands for a response.

"I am not following you, young man!" Cornell stated, somewhat confused.

"All I want to do is take you back. I don't want to chase you, and please don't throw yourself out of the vehicle. Are you good with that?" Cain asked.

"I will not run, and I am too old to jump out of a car. I could break a hip." Cornell smiled at the alien.

"Yes, I saw how old you and Mr. Dean are when you rolled into this town." Cain narrowed his eyes.

"That was pure adrenaline. I have been in pain ever since I was dragged into that damn car. I'll do the right thing!" Cornell confirmed.

"Excellent. I have a limo outside. Please finish your coffee, and off we go," Cain said as he turned to Thomas.

"Well, all right!" Cornell said as he turned back to his coffee.

"Thomas, may I have a moment with you in the conference room, please."

Thomas and Cain walked to the back of the vault which appeared to be a wall of safety deposit boxes. Thomas placed a key in the central box and gave two full twists to the left. The deposit boxes began to fold away like stacked cups. Cain and Thomas stepped into the adjoining room that was filled with electronic devices that were unrecognizable.

"This will all have to be broken down and scrapped. Everything that can be traced to this century will need to be totally destroyed," Cain stated as he scanned the room.

"I have started the dismantling process back in Brooklyn, and we are fully pulled out of Maryland and Virginia." Thomas began to unravel the evacuation procedure.

"How about California? Have we started the pullout process there?" Cain asked.

"We are a little behind out there, but by the time that you're finished with the meeting, we should be fully extracted." Thomas's confidence was evident.

"Thomas, you have done an excellent job, and have served me well since my return. I would like to keep some resources here in New York, just in case!" Cain found a second to recognize the commitment of his young apprentice.

"It has been my absolute pleasure. I wouldn't change a thing," Thomas said with full sincerity.

"There is still time to change your mind if you wish to stay. I can make that happen," Cain offered.

"I have thought deeply about staying, but I have connections with those on Zen who would be negatively affected," Thomas added with sorrow.

"Very well then, I will take my leave of you at this time." Cain pressed the bridge of his nose against that of Thomas's; they parted and left the room.

"For the feed!" Thomas said with deep pride.

"For the feed!" Cain returned.

Across the street from the restaurant where the meeting with Cain was scheduled, a multitude of authorities were in the process of briefing both Magen and Lieutenant MacDonald. They were brought up to speed on the request made by Cain to have Magen, Robert, Mr. Dean, and anyone else that was necessary to approve a truce.

They were given instructions to meet Cain at the midtown restaurant at noon.

The Central Intelligence Agency was working in congruence with NSA and Homeland Security. They had totally taken over the restaurant and had substituted their own people right down to the chefs.

As Magen scanned the room, she was amazed at the high level of communication gear that was spread throughout it. She recognized most of the devices, but several were above her pay grade.

There were two agents working with the four who would be present at the table. Microphones and cameras were in place throughout the restaurant, but that was only the beginning. The scientists that were consulting felt that the alien was utilizing some form of cloaking device, and the power source of that device could be radioactive.

Censors were placed on the extremities of all four of those chosen to sit down for the meeting. There were X-ray devices at all the entrances and exits. Infrared monitors were sitting next to standard camera monitors. They were educated on what they were trying to establish during this meeting.

At this point, they knew that several high-level government agencies had been infiltrated and compromised. However, they didn't have a clue on the level of penetration. The agencies looked at this as a fact-finding mission, and at no time were there to be any aggression toward this extraterrestrial being.

They needed numbers and just how long they have been operating on the planet. They were fully aware of Magen's file and were highly interested in the reasoning of why they needed to manipulate obesity.

Magen was shocked at just how well versed they were with her file.

As Magen continued to listen to the instruction of the agent in charge, Mac caught sight of a separate team off to the side placing photos on a growing section on the wall. He slowly moved out of the group and approached the group who were so busy, they didn't even notice his slow and calculated inspection.

"Officer MacDonald, it is good to see that you survived the hotel siege. How are you?" the Israeli Ehud Barack appeared at Mac's back.

"You do get around, Mr. Barack. I recognize some of those faces on the board. What gives with this?" Mac probed.

"Apparently, there has been an exodus taking place throughout the world. Since early yesterday we have had endless reports of people missing. From high-ranking officials to office clerks, and it is not letting up. We have a count of close to four hundred, but if this continues at this pace, we estimate well over two thousand." Barack educated Mac on the development, but didn't seem too surprised by the events taking place.

"So, you think these people were alien plants that have been operating against us! Damn, I just don't get it," Mac stated.

"What are you having issues with, Officer MacDonald?" Barack asked, slightly puzzled.

"It seems an awful lot to give up. If they are as smart as I think they are, they could have hid the identity of these operatives and kept us guessing indefinitely," Mac said with confusion in his voice.

"Your ability to think critically and outside the box is truly above your local authority status. You are absolutely correct. This is a fact that can't be overlooked," the Israeli stated with new respect for the officer.

"I take it that you have already developed a theory for this behavior?" Mac probed.

"Indeed, I have, sir. I believe that this alien that we now know as Cain wishes to stay here on Earth!" Barack said with deep conviction.

"Why go through all this trouble with the evacuation of this planet for the sole purpose of staying?" Mac was struggling with the thought process.

"Why, indeed. That is, as you Americans say, is the sixty-four-thousand-dollar question!" The older gentleman was convinced that this was the true path of events.

"Maybe his hand is forced due to the fact that his cover is blown!" Mac thought out loud.

"What does it mean that his hand is forced?" The Israeli seemed confused.

"Well, we all have a code we follow, to some degree. Maybe he was sent as a fail-safe, and it didn't work out." Mac began to roll out his theory.

"So, what you're saying is that the minute their existence was compromised, they set into motion this pyramid of denial by eliminating all the layers of their network." Barack began to follow the same thought pattern.

"Wouldn't that make more sense than just one alien orchestrating this whole event for his own twisted fantasy?" Mac smiled.

"This is rational thinking, but I still think that this Cain is not without surprises. I feel it coming," the Israeli said with feeling.

"Well, we should start to find the truth very soon. As crazy as this is, I must confess that I am really excited about the possibilities of this meeting. This creature could have been alive during the Civil War, Lincoln's time!" Mac stated with newfound enthusiasm.

"I admit that there is a jealousy I possess towards you and Agent Cummings. I would kill to have a seat across from this being for just a moment. You speak of past presidents. I believe this being could have known Jesus or the pharaohs of Egypt," Barack's voice hid no emotion.

"Wow, this is too much. Maybe you would like to take my position during this encounter. I am starting to get nervous," Mac requested as his breakfast began to rise in his throat.

"I would indeed, sir. Unfortunately, this is not my destiny. Like youth, it is wasted on those who can't really appreciate it!" Barack patted Mac on the shoulder and walked back to the board.

Mac watched as the Israeli joined the white coats at the table, suddenly feeling very alone and vulnerable. His eyes caught the several military operation people filing quickly into a side office for their own briefing.

Mac was able to recognize some of the cases that they were transporting. He knew sniper rifles when he saw them, standard-issue.

The thought of all those scopes pointing at my table this afternoon is going to be troubling.

CHAPTER 83

He looked over at Magen and thought even after being shot, she was still beautiful.

She seemed to be transfixed on the briefing, and occasionally she would grimace and rub the top of her shoulder.

He needed to touch base with his superiors and inform them of what was going on and get an update on the good Dr. Mazza.

Mac grabbed one of the military guards and asked for a private phone so he could contact his office. The young man looked at him as if he had three heads.

"Sorry, sir, this facility is on full communication lockdown until after the scheduled engagement!" The young soldier waited for a few seconds for rebuttal and then turned and walked away.

Mac realized that he was just too tired to argue with these people. What he needed to do was to get this thing over with and get some sleep. The office was going to be pissed, this big of an operation going down in the backyard with no warning.

Mac walked over to where Magen was sitting and slumped down in the chair next to her. She broke her thought process long enough to glance his way and flash that big smile.

Mac smiled back with less enthusiasm.

The conversation he had with the Israeli agent was still running through his brain. He asked himself if he considered this a big opportunity or was the fear he felt justified. Barack really put the hook in him when he thought that this being could have possibly known Christ.

Mac had not really taken time to think this out, but reality was creeping in. He had been born Catholic, Irish and Scottish lineage; there was never a doubt about the savior. Every day of his education was spent in Catholic school, even college.

It was then that he realized that it wasn't the being himself that was putting fear in his heart, but the possible truth it represented. The concept of an afterlife gave him hope, and the thought of losing that filled him with real dread. Then he remembered the lawyer from the Vatican that was in the hotel safe room; they must be thinking the same thing.

The public could never know of this being's existence.

He began to consider the domino effect that it would take place if knowledge of this Cain was leaked. Mac looked around the room and counted almost fifty people working in this room alone; there are others in authority that aren't even here.

How in God's name would all of this be contained?

Then he started to see something sinister through his cop brain. Could they realize that this was not containable, and were strictly going to attack the leak at its source? Wikileaks is going to feast on this nightmare; he could see Julian waxing his brilliant little carrot at the thought of this actually taking place. Or maybe at this point maybe nobody really cares; this could be just too big to be believable.

He thought of the first time he kneeled and prayed to Jesus. His father was hospitalized after a union strike got out of hand. He had taken a real good blow to the head; the doctor was worried about intracranial bleeding. He had never seen his mother so scared; it frightened the living shit out of him. His mother grabbed his hand and rushed him off to the chapel at St. Luke's and said, through dark stained eyes, "Listen, that is Jesus and he knows everything, and he will help your daddy pull through this, but you have to have faith, so pray!"

That was his first introduction to the Christ, and Daddy did make it through with just some minor hearing damage, but shit, he never listened to anyone in the house anyway.

He thought about his mother; what she would say now with the reality of extraterrestrial life in her face? She would most likely say that God made them too.

In the end, it is all about faith, and Mac knew it was really going to be tested today.

He looked around the room and thought about the people in the room and their belief system; they didn't seem too concerned. It was like a bee's nest in there; everyone had a job to do. They were too busy to really think about what was actually going on and the implications of today.

It was a good day to be an atheist; for them, it was just another assignment.

Mac let his mind calm as the voice of the senior agent began to seep back in as he ran down the drill of how today was going to unfold.

"The subject will enter the establishment and will be under total monitoring from that moment on," the senior agent began.

"What about the people who are in the restaurant. Will they be at any risk?" Magen asked.

"The patrons are all ours. We have the whole day reserved," the agent was happy to provide that information.

"Agent, you had mentioned that the subject would be totally monitored during the encounter, Could you please elaborate on that statement, please?" William Dean was still concerned for his friend.

"We are utilizing state-of-the-art surveillance equipment. The subject will be on video, infrared, and also a biofeedback device that we believe will assist us in verifying the truthfulness of its answers." The agent seemed impressed with the concept.

"Is there a plan B ready to roll, just in case the spider doesn't wish the flies to catch it?" Mac only half joked as he took in the data.

"Officer MacDonald, is there something you wish to add or find fault in our methods?" The agent leaned back in his chair and grinned.

"Well, I spent only a few minutes with this thing, but one thing became crystal clear to me," Mac began, and then paused.

"What would that be?" The agent appeared to be slightly agitated.

"When we were on the roof, this Cain was all smiles and friendly right up to the second a thought flashed through my mind to pull my piece and blast him!" Mac paused again, reliving the encounter.

"I have no intel that the subject has demonstrated the ability to read thought. It is a highly emotional event to be pressed into a situation of this nature. Could you have possibly misinterpreted the reaction?" the agent asked with obvious concern.

"I suppose that there is a possibility that I gave something away with the look in my eyes or body language. I was heightened and afraid, but he stopped cold when I thought about my gun and looked at me like he knew just what I was thinking!" Mac stated with fear clutching on each word.

"If they could read minds, they would have had us at the hotel. Telepathy doesn't add up," the voice of Agent Phyllis Capaso answered from behind Mac.

"Agent Capaso, nice to see you made it out of the hotel," William Dean stated.

"Thank you, Mr. Dean, you are always the gentleman!" Phyllis smiled and turned to the man who was standing to her right.

"Will you be joining us for lunch with the cloaked alien from outer space?" Mac joked.

"Unfortunately, I am without an invitation. However, I would like to introduce you to the fourth member of the encounter team, Dr. Alfred Kowalski."

Mac looked closely at the odd-looking lab coat with stains and the seventies Hush Puppies on his feet. This was someone who didn't get out much, ever.

His hair had not seen a comb for a long time, and his eating habits were ridiculous. Mac was stunned that the United States was about to sit down with an extraterrestrial and their representatives from planet Earth were Hot Lips, Bashful, Old-Timer, and Dopey here.

This just kept getting better!

CHAPTER 84

He shook hands with Mr. Dean and then moved to Magen. He could see her make an instant disapproving face, but didn't know why until he turned to Mac and slammed a cold wet hand into his. Mac winced as the cold wet fish squirmed in his hand.

The geek quickly adjusted his glasses and turned to stand back next to Agent Capaso. She was smiling like a kid in a candy store, and that was disturbing, to say the least.

Magen glanced over at Mac and winked as she read the expression on his face. There was a brief moment of silence, and then Magen broke the moment with a pointed question at the new team member.

"Dr. Kowalski, can you tell us what exactly is your field of expertise?" she asked with genuine interest.

"I flew in from Switzerland this morning. For the last several years, I have been working on a side project at Lucerne, Switzerland. The prime focus of my research has been neutrino particle acceleration, or the real application of deep space travel. When I was contacted this morning, I immediately saw the potential to accelerate my current research!" The good doctor could hardly contain his enthusiasm.

"Doctor, can I ask you a question?" Mac asked and quickly saw the smile escape from Agent Capaso's face.

"Of course, Officer, if there is anything I can help with!" Dr. Kowalski replied.

"Have you ever had any connection with NASA or any of their affiliates?" Mac asked.

"Dr. Kowalski has a history with Apple Physics. I know this because I signed his checks for a few years when I took over there."

"This was several years back, and then he was transferred to Silicon Valley, as I recall," Mr. Dean chimed in.

"That is correct. You have an excellent memory! I actually attended one of your lectures during my time there. You were a true leader!" the doctor voiced his obvious admiration.

"Have you ever met this being Cain before?" Mac asked.

"I have. Twenty years ago, he came down to the lab and spoke with me for a few minutes about the direction of my research," the doctor admitted as he occasionally looked over at the face of Agent Capaso.

"Was there anything more?" Mac asked.

"I can say that I was highly impressed with his grasp of my field. He redirected me away from a path that would have stalled my work for at least a decade." The doctor adjusted his glasses again and then looked at Mac as if to say, *Anything else?*

"Please understand this is not an attack on you or your justification for being here. I really like to know what I'm dealing with," Mac explained his questioning.

"Well, I'm glad that all of that is out of the way. We have a lot of wiring to do before we sit down with our friend," Agent Capaso emphasized.

"Let's get it done!" Mac said with a big smile that seemed to irritate Agent Capaso.

CHAPTER 85

The team was hustled into a large room that closely resembled an operating theater. There were four separate privacy areas where each member was ushered in and asked to disrobe. The team of doctors and scientists then methodically took turns with their own expertise.

There were physicals and measurements taking place in all three areas.

Magen had a whole team of females attending to her, and she was busy asking questions. Mac was all right with the poking and prodding, but he became anxious when one of the physicians began to shave some of his chest hair to apply electro-monitors. The doctor was dealing well, considering that he was the focus of the most evasive medical enhancements.

There was a censor chip being installed in his scalp, directly behind his left ear. This was placed in the outside possibility that all the other transmitters were eliminated by Cain.

Mac thought about the unlikely prospect of that happening. Cain had no interest in limiting the dialogue; he wanted to be heard. Cain had an agenda; there was absolutely no doubt about that fact.

Regardless of what scenarios Mac ran through his head, he knew that he was going to be in for one interesting brunch.

After forty minutes of processing, the fearless four emerged to an adjoining room that served some high-test, fairly passable coffee.

"Did you enjoy that as much as I did?" Mac joked with Magen the instant she entered the room.

"Well, I have had worse! And at least their hands were warm," Magen shot back with an accusing smile.

"Funny! I think this is all too much. If this thing wanted to avoid communication, we wouldn't even know about him," Mac expressed to his new friend whom he had grown fond of all too fast.

"This is really just standard protocol, Mac. They push this stuff when they feel uncertain about outcomes," Magen claimed as she rubbed her shoulder.

"Are you feeling all right?" Mac asked.

"I'm fine, but my shoulder is screaming at me to stop moving," she admitted.

"I would listen to the screams. The body knows," Mac shot back with some genuine concern in his voice.

The older agent came into the room with two other men. Mac recognized one of the men from the hospital. Mac thought to himself that this agent must rank fairly high to have his own bodyguards. The old-timer must have seen some real action in his day. He often thought that the only way to move up in the CIA was to live longer than your enemies. They spent some time talking among themselves, and then all three turned to address the room.

The newest member of the group was the last to enter the room.

Due to the extra special attention that was paid to him, Dr. Kowalski looked like he was in more pain than Magen.

The agent walked to the middle of the room and began to round up the bunch. He was in his element when he was running the show; some people are just born for leadership, and he was one of them.

"People, my name is Smith. We are on a timeline, and this operation is now active. We are going to file out the gray door to your left. On the other side of that door, there are two black SUVs that are ready to transport the four of you to the prearranged destination. We will be arriving several minutes early.

"The restaurant is under the highest surveillance. We will enter the establishment prior to the subjects' arrival and wait. You are not alone. Every patron in there is ours. Your only concern should be what you will be ordering from the menu. Are there any additional questions that you feel we haven't covered?" The agent scanned the team.

"What about traffic? Midtown can really get a little heavy during the early morning hours," Mac asked.

"There will be no traffic today. We have secured a route directly to the destination," Smith stated with absolute confidence.

"Wow! I bet that took some doing," Mac said, not hiding the fact that he was truly impressed.

"If that is all, then it's time to make history! I want to say that it has been a pleasure working with all of you, and I envy your next few hours." The agent finished his speech and then stood back and laid out his hand toward the door.

The cool, fresh air was a wonderful feeling when they stepped out of the door. Mac was reminded that he had been in and out of vehicles since the shooting. He found himself pausing for a second and enjoying the sensation; Mr. Dean and Magen also felt it.

They piled in the two blacked-out GMC Denalis, and off they went at an alarming rate of speed.

At the end of the block, two blue-and-white NYPD police cars joined the convoy, one up front and the second in the rear.

He glanced over at Magen and smiled; she reached out and grabbed his hand. They had only gone half a dozen blocks when a loud buzzing noise came from the internal radio.

CHAPTER 86

> I find men far less interesting as a rule than the female of the species. Truly not sure why this is, nor do I feel a need to justify the statement!
>
> —That crazy Cain

Cain sat back in the limo watching his new young friend. Joshua loved all the buttons in the large vehicle, and the fridge with soda was far too much for him to handle.

Cain watched the youngster for a good while; he tried to recall a time when he was that innocent. Joshua smiled as he studied the look on Cain's face; he was fully aware of the positive energy that Cain was feeling, and Cain knew it.

What an amazing gift this child has, Cain thought as they pulled down the block of the restaurant.

He glanced over at Mr. Pierce, who was silent for the majority of the trip. He had been through quite a lot in the past few days; time to process was appropriate.

The instant they made the left onto Madison, Joshua's face changed. Cain caught the change immediately and leaned over to the youngster.

"Joshua, what are you feeling?" Cain whispered.

"Everything is ugly out there!" Joshua stated as only a child could.

"Marcus, we will not be stopping. Please just drive on through," Cain said to the driver as they came close to the restaurant.

"Yes, sir!" Marcus rang back from the back.

"Why are they so angry at you, Mr. Alex?" Joshua asked with sadness in his voice.

"Joshua, they aren't angry. They are just afraid!" Cain assured the scared child.

"Most of them are afraid, but some are really angry!" Joshua stated with absolute certainty.

"They just don't know me like you do!" Cain said as he rubbed the child's head. "Marcus, we are going to the Oak Room. Are you familiar with that location?" Cain asked.

"Ten minutes and we're there!" Marcus announced.

CHAPTER 87

There was some buzzing with the military, and then the cars began to slow. They pulled off the side of the West Side Highway and sat for a few minutes.

Magen looked back, trying to get a better view of the rear car to see what was going on.

As they sat, the lead agent walked up to the rear window.

"We have a game change. Our guest just called. He would like you all to join him at the Oak Room," the agent announced.

"Those burgers cost some big coin. Will this be on the government dime?" Mac smiled as he gave the agent that "told you so" look.

"We have made adjustments for this development, so we will proceed with the engagement. Let's roll out!" the agent announced and turned to return to the rear vehicle.

"I could have seen this coming, and I would say this isn't the last surprise of the day!" Mac offered.

"He is just keeping things interesting, and I imagine doing his best to even the playing field," Magen responded.

"Or he is playing us like the monkeys we are," Mac said with his sarcastic tone.

"I don't think so, Mac. If he had no concerns, we would be eating at the first location," Magen reasoned.

"I don't know, Oak Room burgers are mighty tasty!" Mac joked as Magen smiled.

The two GMC Denalis rolled up in front of the restaurant at a fast pace. The valet guys jumped out of the way, not fully understanding what was developing. The team jumped out and began to group at the entrance. There were some last-minute instructions, and then the team ascended into the restaurant.

Mac immediately assessed the situation and realized the lighting was not working in their favor. It was practically dark, and they would need some time for their eyes to adjust.

The hostess approached from the left with a big smile on her beautiful face. She addressed William Dean first.

"Are you the Cain party?" she asked.

"We are!" Dean said after a brief pause.

"Please, right this way," the hostess gestured with her hand and began to lead them down the aisle.

Mac moved slowly, picking up the rear; he studied the faces of the patrons. He thought for the first time that Cain might not be alone. He studied the faces of those people he passed, looking for that which didn't fit. He recognized two of the mayor's aides. If they only knew what was going on in their city, they would shit bricks. He guessed that the big table off to the right was a pack of Wall Street fat cats. Since the occupation movement started to camp out on their doorstep, these guys would rather be anywhere else. *Can't say that I blame them. You can only feed people lies for so long.*

As he scanned the crowd, nothing was standing out as unusual, until they arrived at the table.

CHAPTER 88

There they sat, Cain and a young black child and another black gentleman who he surmised as one Cornell Pierce.

Mac didn't remember Cain being so young, and sitting close to the child made him look even younger. It was then that he realized that both William Dean and the good doctor had never seen this being. Most likely they were expecting the bogeyman. Surprise!

Mac found that he was unable to take his eyes of the child. His eyes were pale yellow, and this black child gave Mac the willies. He wondered if the child was human or like Cain. The child was looking right at Mac when a large smile broke across his face, like a jack-o'-lantern. Mac never took well to children to begin with, but this child really put the hook in him. After what was felt like a lifetime, Magen broke the ice.

"Really nice to see you again, Cain. I want to thank you for the invitation." Magen opened the dialogue.

"Welcome, Agent, and may I say thank you for accepting my lunch invitation. Were you hurt?" Cain asked.

"Yeah, I ran into a little trouble this morning. Nothing that would keep me from lunch," Magen said with real sincerity.

"You, sir, must be Mr. William Dean, the catalyst to this meeting?" Cain said with a reassuring smile.

"I am Mr. Dean. Forgive me for staring. You are not what I expected!" William said, almost embarrassed by his reaction.

"It's good to see you, Mr. Dean," Cornell broke into the conversation.

"Cornell, I can't even begin to tell you how good it feels to see you!" Dean stated with pain evident in his voice.

"Thank you, sir!" Cornell responded.

"The return of Mr. Pierce is a simple token of my intention. Feel free to return among your people outside," Cain stated as a choice. However, it wasn't.

"I will speak with you soon. Thank you!" Cornell announced as he removed himself from the table.

"I would like to introduce you all to my young friend. This is Joshua," Cain stated as he placed his hand on the youngster's head.

"Hello, young man, how are you?" Magen said with her best loving look.

"I'm good. I really want a hamburger," he said with a little giggle.

"That's so funny. Detective MacDonald has been talking about the burgers at this place for a while," Magen stated.

"This place has the best burgers in this town. Detective, you know your stuff," Cain stated.

"Thank you. This is my town, and if there is one thing I know is where to get the eats," Mac returned.

"I agree. This is really some town. My heart may travel along spoon and fork, yet my only true love be New York!" Cain said with a deep smile.

"Who said that?" Magen asked.

"I just did, or I heard it through the years. It really is hard to track that kind of thing after centuries of human dialogue dancing through my skull!" Cain continued to jest with a wide beautiful smile.

"Sir, I would like to take this opportunity to introduce myself. My name is Dr. Kowalski, and I am so honored to finally meet you," the doctor chimed in, almost desperate to open a dialogue with the extraterrestrial.

"I am so glad they sent a scientist to converse with me. I was afraid that I was going to get drilled by some Nazi Central Intelligence agent," Cain stated with relief.

"Would you be willing to tell me what method you utilize to travel through the universe?" the doctor asked with a hopeful tone.

"I have to be honest. There are so many things I could tell you that would eventually lead to your destruction, so please don't think that I am being difficult. I will say that metals need to be removed from the body and replenished at the point of entry. I know that may sound vague, but how much do you really know about the vehicle that drove you here today?" Cain offered.

"That is outstanding! What is the time frame of the transport?" the doctor snapped, hanging on the words of the alien like an addict.

"The time lapse is immeasurable! But let's talk about why we are here," Cain stated.

"Forgive me, Mr. Cain, I can barely control my enthusiasm!" the doctor admitted.

"Nothing to forgive and this is not the first time we met! However, I need to claim my intention and have your superiors review my proposal," Cain stated.

"We have met before?" Dr. Kowalski was surprised that he was remembered from so long ago.

"What is the deal with cattle mutilation? I have always wondered about that?" Mac asked, breaking into the conversation.

"Cattle autopsies, yes, I have heard such things. There are other beings throughout the universe that might have curiosities about such things, but not us!" Cain stated.

"What kind of curiosity are we talking about?" Mac pressed.

"I would imagine that it could come down to one or two things. First, it's not aliens at all but random human crazies, and we both know there is no shortage of those here on Earth!" Cain smiled at his guests.

"What's option two?" Mac and the rest of the team seemed interested.

"Well, it could be an advanced life form just checking your expiration date!" Cain smiled and laughed.

"I'm sorry, but I am the nonscientist at this table. What do you mean?" Mac asked, slightly confused.

"I imagine a smart species could narrow down your life expectancy by examining your nutritional input, to the millennium."

"Why would they do that?" Mac shot back.

"They might want your planet after you're done with it!" Cain stated, becoming slightly bored with the conversation.

At that time, the waiter walked over to the table and asked if there was anything he could bring or do for the group. The child spoke up first and requested the cheeseburger with his off-center smile. Magen looked over at Mac and smiled as if to say, *Go ahead, get your burger*. Mac looked back over at the young black child; deep in the child's gaze was full knowledge of Mac's thoughts.

Mac could feel the child's mind blanket him, and a ferocious pain began to well up within his stomach.

There was something really wrong with the child.

Mac began to think about what purpose this child served Cain. At first, he thought that the kid was protection for Cain.

If he was holding the child on the way out, there would be no shooting.

The more he thought it over, the more the scenario didn't add up. Cain was up to something, and this child played a role.

Mac began to suspect that the youngster in front of him was not human at all. As the thought ran through his mind, the child's smile faded, and he turned his head. The timing scared Mac deeper, as he worked to free his mind of all thought.

There were a few moments after the waiter walked away that the silence was deafening. Finally, Magen leaned over the table and asked, "Are there females of your kind?"

Cain smiled and looked around the room; he seemed to be picking out the couples and watching them closely.

"The females of my race are different. The birthing process has been altered in my world. Females no longer give birth. That process has been fully eradicated from their DNA. All Zen birthing is done in a sterilized environment, under flawless monitoring. There are no miscarriages, stillbirths, or defects. Each of my kind enters this state of consciousness as equals. However, we all get to choose the path we take. Free will demands much of us. I will say this. If the woman of my species could see your females, I think they would be rattled. They have sacrificed so much to rise to the level that they have achieved.

"Nine hundred years ago, they attempted to take over my entire galaxy. They would have succeeded if they were not divided among themselves. Today, the relationship between the male and female of my species is most difficult. The wars lasted for more than three centuries by your time frame. A billion and a half were lost. I look around the room and see the way that humans interact, really quite beautiful. The planet that I am from, a large population of males view the female species with both caution and contempt. Much like Afro-Americans view white males here on Earth. I must confess that I am jealous of your race and those little things that you are yet to lose." Cain sat back in the booth and smiled. "I apologize for my rambling. I'm sure that I answered your question several times over," Cain stated through sad eyes.

"I understand, but can I ask, are there any women here with you now?" Magen asked.

"The privilege of space travel is reserved only for the male of our species. This is something you might not understand, but it became necessary at a political level. I am one who will not discriminate based on gender, but many council members do. The wars have molded us as a people. Please understand that this is truly a form of prejudicial treatment. These are rewritten laws of God that I have protested publicly. These protests have not truly endeared me to many of the senior council members. In a roundabout way, this brings us to the reason we are all here."

"You have no intention of returning to your world!" Mac said out loud, recalling his earlier conversation with the Israeli.

"You are correct, Officer MacDonald. I am impressed!" Cain stated.

"As much as I would like to take credit, it was a theory that someone else had suggested," Mac admitted.

"I imagine that one of you, if not all of you are transmitting to superiors outside of this restaurant. I would like to arrange a second meeting, after you have had time to consider my proposal. I have much to offer a society like the children of Earth. As of this moment, I will not consume, terrorize, or manipulate any of this planet's inhabitants!" Cain paused as the child next to him began to shake.

CHAPTER 89

"What is it?" Mac's eyes began to follow the child's field of vision.

Through the swinging kitchen door, a man appeared tall and focused; he was dressed as a waiter. However, he appeared too physically fit and tanned to be someone who worked indoors for a living.

Mac then noticed his boots, military-issue.

Instinctively, Mac reached for his weapon, only to remember that it was taken by the Feds before he left the building.

Mac could only watch as the man approached.

At twenty feet out, the man dropped a red cloth napkin from his hands, revealing a large-caliber handgun with a long silencing device. His pace began to quicken as he approached the table.

He raised the weapon in Cain's direction and fired. Mac sprung back from the table and turned to see the first bullet hit the booth's back cushion.

Cain had his hand pointed at the gunman, and then flipped his wrist. The gunman's momentum stopped immediately, and his body and face quickly contorted and was thrown against the back wall as if he was struck by a wrecking ball.

The crowd at the Oak Room didn't start running, even after the gunshot. Everything happened so fast that there was really no time for the situation to register. Many were attempting to look over to the table to assess the situation.

"Sorry, folks, waiter made a small error. All is well!" Cain announced as people quickly returned to their lives.

"Who was that?" Magen announced as she moved to the twisted body ten feet from the table.

"Well, you can't make an omelet without breaking some eggs!" Cain stated as he began to rise from the seat with the youngster in tow.

"Is that the end of the meeting?" Dean asked, still confused by the events that had just taken place.

"This was a good start! This will not be easy, but I am deeply hopeful that you and your people will see the sacrifice that I am making for this world. We will talk soon." Cain smiled and gently touched Dean's arm as they shifted past.

"I have so many more questions!" Dr. Kowalski stated.

"In time, my friends. Come, Joshua!" Cain called back to the child who was already sliding out of the booth.

Mac watched as the alien walked toward the exit with the small child holding his left hand. His mind was reeling by the speed of how wrong things had gone. The child looked back directly at Mac and stared for a second then smiled.

From the side of Mac's field of vision, he could see dark figures exiting the kitchen. Cain and the child were ten feet from the door. It was at that moment the front door erupted with a sea of federal agents.

Mac was frozen with anticipation of what he thought would be a significant conflict. However, to his amazement, the agents ran right past Cain and the child. Cain didn't even alter his pace or direction; the agents coming through the door simply moved around him. Mac was stunned and confused, and was really having a problem formulating a theory of what was unfolding in front of his eyes. He looked around the Oak Room and noticed that even with the flood of agents pouring into the building, the patrons were not running. They were aware of the men with machine guns running around them, but there was no hysteria.

His attention turned to the man who opened fire on Cain; he was being assisted by Magen. Mac could see blood coming from both the nose and eyes of the man.

"Where is he?" The senior agent was standing in front of Mac and his question was directed in his direction.

"Where is who?" Mac stated.

"Officer MacDonald, I am asking you where the subject is?" the senior agent was now looking at him, truly puzzled.

"You and your men ran right past them as they walked out the front door!" Mac stated.

Cain watched from the back of the limo as the troop of agents filed into the Oak Room. He turned back to the youngster and tilted his head and said, "What a nice bunch of people!"

"Yeah, but I'm starving. We left before I got my burger," Joshua said with some annoyance in his voice.

"Hey, we are going to roll over to Jackson Hole and grab a burger!" Cain called out to the driver.

"Yes, sir!" the driver responded, as they turned off the block and headed uptown.

CHAPTER 90

The debriefing room back at the makeshift command center was buzzing.

The intelligence people were consumed with the assassin who took a shot at Cain. The scientists were busy taking blood from the patrons and the staff and the Oak Room, and of course, the four of them were stuck first.

The senior agent was watching a video and playing over all the available tape. There was a pounding in Mac's head that was slowly fading; it started the instant they drove away from the restaurant.

The rest of the crew also reported suffering from either a minor headache or high sensitivity to light. Dr. Kowalski was briefing a team of white coats on his analysis. He was sure that there was brain chemistry manipulation taking place in the restaurant. He was waiting for the blood tests to be finalized, but he thought that the delivery of a chemistry agent would need to come directly from Cain himself.

The initial thought was that there was some device being utilized, but the good doctor was standing firm that the theory was not viable. His platform was that Cain must be releasing some type of chemical that can affect both right and left side of the brain. He felt that there were multiple scenarios taking place within the restaurant.

First, there were the patrons who hardly blinked after the shot at Cain. Second, how could Cain and the child walk past an army of armed men undetected? His argument closed as he held some paper he was scribbling on.

"These are the two areas of the brain that are being manipulated. Unless he is utilizing a new chemical, we will be looking at multiple chemicals being released. As I was trying to follow the logic and importance of what was being explained, there was a large commotion out in the warehouse. When I finally made it to the door, I was just in time to see the Israeli Barack being led away under guard." His eyes caught Mac at the door; he looked confused and slightly unnerved.

The senior agent walked up behind the group and stopped to talk with Dr. Kowalski.

"What's going on?" Mac asked.

"It turned out that the shooter from the restaurant has a connection with the Mossad, and that is a problem that we need to deal with," the agent stated with some noted regret in his voice.

"Do you think that Barack has anything to do with the shooting?" Mac stated in disbelief.

"I don't have the luxury of judgment. I have to act on the facts in front of me!" the agent claimed.

"This is just crazy. That guy has some of the best intel regarding Cain!" Mac couldn't help but come to the aid of the Israeli.

"The fact remains that Barack is the closest connection to the shooter. We need to do our investigation!" the agent continued.

"What is the shooter saying about his motive? I bet it is not even related to his politics," Mac asked.

"He died on the trip back, massive brain injury. Whatever Cain did to him really scrambled his melon," the agent stated.

"You seem like a really intelligent professional, and I am guessing that you are not new to the level of deception that operates in government agencies?" Mac stated.

"I am aware of how things work. I still have a process that needs to be followed. Do I believe that he is guilty of treason? No!" the agent admitted.

"I didn't think so. The whole thing is too easy. The man is smart enough to avoid any implication if he wanted to," Mac voiced his theory.

"Well, my thinking is slightly different, but we get to the same overall conclusion," the agent stated.

"How do you mean?" Mac looked puzzled.

"I have known Barack for some time. I don't think he would have used some wack with a gun. He would have blown him up!" the agent turned to walk away.

"Agent, we have had several conversations. Is there ever going to be a time that we learn your name?" Mac asked with a light smile.

"Smith!" he finished and turned and was gone.

"Why not Jones? Smith sounds almost made up?" Mac joked, and both men smiled just a little.

CHAPTER 91

The army cargo plane's wheels touched down at Andrews Air Force Base and came to a grinding halt. The giant bird was slowly taxied to a hangar that was currently unoccupied.

There was a cloak of secrecy surrounding the cargo plane, and that was not that uncommon at Andrews. So, the fact that a plane was landing there without documentation was not really cause for alarm.

What did stand out that day was a team of Special Forces that was standing by at the hangar. The day officer was driving past during his routine inspection and caught sight of some of the soldiers standing guard at the hangar entrance. He reviewed the daily manifest and saw nothing for Hangar 17. He motioned the driver to circle over and investigate.

The driver pulled the wheel and started heading over to the hangar. They weren't able to get within fifty yards when the soldiers trained their weapons up on the vehicle.

The day officer grabbed the arm of the driver, indicating that they should bring the vehicle to an abrupt stop. The young officer quickly jumped out of the jeep and began to approach the hangar, scolding the soldiers as he came closer.

When the officer reached twenty yards, a burst of gunfire from a silenced weapon snapped around his feet.

"Have you lost your mind?" the young officer barked.

From the hangar came a towering man of about 6 foot 4, who began to walk toward the officer. He was dressed in civilian clothing of all black linen complete with short sleeves. He was 240 pounds; he placed his age in the early fifties. His Marine haircut was glistening in the afternoon sun, although it was not that hot. Still, he utilized a white handkerchief that he continued to run across his beaded forehead.

As the big man got closer, the officer was quickly taken aback by the steel gray eyes that burned deeply into his young soul.

"How can I help you, young man?" the large man boomed with some agitation in his voice.

"Who the hell are you guys? And that man right there just fired on me!" the officer blasted out, trying to sound angry in the face of such a large man.

"I'm Jed. Who be you, young man?" the old soldier said with a notable Southern accent.

"I am the day officer of this base," he began and was quickly cut short.

"The day officer. Listen, you get your ass on the phone to your superiors, then take your skinny backside back in that carriage before I shoot you myself. Are we clear?" the large man boomed.

The big man's red face and neck and angry eyes were too much for the young officer. He quickly returned to the jeep and called in to the command office. He was able to reach a captain and explained the situation. There was a pause on the phone, and then the captain came back and said, "Avoid the hangar for the next twenty-four!" and then the phone went dead. The day officer drove away.

CHAPTER 92

Dr. Mazza began to come out of the haze; he had taken several tranquilizing darts to several parts of his body. Fortunately, they didn't all deploy the full amount of sedatives, or he could have had some cardiac problems.

There were two paramedics assigned to the doctor; they hung back a few feet behind the soldiers. They moved quickly down the hall with the Central Intelligence officer Jed leading the procession.

There were several SUVs waiting outside with the engines running. There were additional soldiers spread throughout the parking lot; they were redirecting traffic away from the vehicles.

The CIA agent directed the teams to divide and load the doctor in the rear SUV and put the two cages into the front car. They had accomplished all this in record time and were now on their way to Route 95.

Jed was holding a walkie-talkie to his ear, and was ordering the helicopter above them to continue down the highway and feed back traffic information.

The doctor was calling out from the back of the vehicle; the drugs were still on board, and it was almost impossible to understand the words coming out of his mouth. His brain was still not connecting with his body, and everything resembled drunken speech. There was absolutely no movement at all coming from the other two cages.

The beeper on the CIA officer's side began to vibrate; it was their destination.

Jed read off the address to the driver, and they were now en route to a safe house in Davidsonville, Maryland; his guess was twenty-five minutes at the speed they were maintaining. The old agent sat back and closed his eyes, unable to sleep with the steady rambling from the back seat.

CHAPTER 93

New York

"They're heading for the safe house in Davidson, Maryland. Get this finished!" Helen Worthington turned from the window overlooking New York City and spoke loudly so she could be heard over the speakerphone on the table.

She sat down at the desk and looked around the room at her partners. There were a mixed bunch of distinguished individuals, some military along with some of the mega rich. However, they seemed to be most focused on the small Italian gentleman who sat at the far side of the room. His name was Vincenzo Coppola, and he was a member of the Vatican's preferiti, next in line to possibly succeed the current Pope Benedict XVI.

He was a slight man without any pretense; his strength came from both his position and from the darkness in his eyes. He sat with his right leg easily draped over his left, sipping some tea and paying close attention to what was being said. His two aides flanked both sides of the cardinal and kept their eyes on the room; their only focus was the safety of the man at their side.

"What's our exposure?" Worthington asked the attorney Daniel Shift at the center of the room.

"We need to clear this up now. Our position will be practically undetectable and much easier to manage," he said with little to no emotion at all.

"What about the bodies that Mazza laid across a lawn out there in Long Island?" asked Mr. Fanning, an aide to a local senator right here in New York City.

"That has been dealt with and is no longer an issue. We have been able to fully clean the lab and erase all connection to any of our companies!" the young attorney assured.

"So now we are about to level a residential home in Maryland with a dozen American soldiers inside, just to clean house!" Fanning belted out in some passive aggressive rant.

"That is exactly what we are going to do, Fanning. There is no stopping this train, and you knew the stakes here!" Worthington snapped.

"Don't lecture me, bitch. We should have terminated this operation the minute we knew Cain had returned!" Fanning shot back.

"Please, I need to interject some thought at this point!" Cardinal Coppola raised his shaky hand from his chair, and all conversation stopped.

"I am sorry, Your Eminence!" Fanning stated humbly like a child.

"Compassion for your fellow man is something one should never apologize for. This is difficult for everyone in this room!" the small Italian stated with obvious sincerity.

"Yes, sir!" Fanning said as he returned to his chair.

"When we began this endeavor, it was for the love of man and to bring God back into the hearts of man. In hindsight, when the evil returned, I should have ordered the elimination of the project. This is my fault!" the cardinal stated in a low tone.

"Your Eminence, please, we are all in this together. There is no reason for you to bear this pain!" Worthington came to his defense like the daughter of a guilty man.

"We were so close to bringing the Nephilim back to the land of man. Greed overtook me, and it is I who should apologize!" the cardinal continued.

"Maybe we should attempt to salvage the two chosen children, and continue our attempts at Cain's termination," Fanning chimed in, seemingly reversing his position.

"If I thought that wouldn't put the world in grave danger, it could be open for discussion! However, if the fallen one became aware of our plan, the planet may not survive," the Italian let his imagination go to a dark place.

"All will not be lost today. We still have DNA in the Vatican archives that we can work with when the threat is gone," Mrs. Worthington offered, directing this at the cardinal, hoping to please him.

"The only saving grace to this tragedy. It was my deepest hope to see the rise of the angels in my time!" the old cardinal sighed and then stood and made the sign of the cross to all those in the room.

The cardinal was assisted from the room, up to the roof where the helicopter was waiting to take him to Kennedy Airport, then off to Rome.

The Italian walked through his team of conspirators with his hand out and palm down, allowing his people to kiss the holy ring.

He stopped at Fanning and paused after the businessman finished kissing the ring; he looked at the old man deep in his eyes. "I do feel your pain, my son. The founder of my society once said, 'To kill a heretic is not a sin!' Lately I have taken great solace in those words!" The old man turned and disappeared through the door.

Fanning returned to his chair and stared at the woman behind the desk as she began to dial the phone.

"Talk to me, Major. Where do we stand?" Worthington stated.

"Three minutes from the predetermined destination!" a voice came from the phone.

"I know this is not what you want to deal with, so if you want me to just put this to bed, that's fine," Worthington offered.

"I do appreciate that, but I need to take responsibility in my part of this failure!" Fanning shot back.

"Can I ask you what the cardinal said to you as he left the room?" Helen's curiosity was overwhelming.

"There is no sin in killing a heretic," Fanning stated, not feeling there was any secret that needed to be guarded.

"His Eminence always has a way of saying something supportive," Worthington said with respect.

"Or maybe he just knows the right thing to say at the right time!" Fanning stated with a big smile, showing his bold veneers.

"I will miss him when this is all put to bed!" Worthington voiced, showing real emotions.

"I have considered this lately. I guess that would be best, but I really would have loved to see the children rise and become!" Fanning said through some pain.

"I understand how you feel. Getting this close makes the loss even greater!" Worthington agreed.

"Well, no point dwelling on a loss. We know this is God's will!" Fanning closed his eyes and rubbed the stress out of his forehead.

"Team A and B in position. Are we a go?" a rough voice came from the phone speaker.

"You're a go, Major!" came after a slight pause. Fanning made the sign of the cross over his chest and sat deep into his chair.

Major Andreas Schmitt chucked the phone in the back seat of the Suburban, then motioned the six men to the back of the vehicle. He popped the trunk by the remote key in his left hand, exposing two large mounds in the back covered by a camouflage tarp. He whipped the tarp off the first pile displaying four M4 striker-style machine guns that were quickly seized. Under the second tarp were two multibarrel Gatling-style weapons; these were handed slowly to the two larger members of the team. The major retrieved an M25 grenade launcher, and then laid out a positioning map at their feet.

"Gentlemen, the two cannons will hold positions at the front of the house. The rest need to flank both sides of the house," the soldier began at several nods of understanding, "The B team will focus their firepower in a pyramid formation, so avoid the front center of the house. There are two snipers at location one and two, so avoid these areas!" He pointed out the areas. "We have two roads in and out, with agents posted six hundred yards down the road. This will buy us an additional three minutes. When we light up these woods, the local police will be notified of a drug bust, which will buy us an additional two minutes. Please set your watches. This vehicle rolls out in seven minutes!"

There were nods of understanding, and then they were on the move.

CHAPTER 94

Dr. Mazza was awake and trying to clear the fog that consumed him. He knew that he was in the back of a moving vehicle, and the last few miles they were off the highway.

The intermittent darkness told him that they were in a highly wooded area, and the smell was not Long Island. *South*, he thought. He initially tried to talk, but reason was the farthest thing that was exiting his mouth. He realized that he needed time to get past the paralysis and nausea.

Thoughts of children began to flow into his mind, along with a sense profound sadness. His angels were taken from him; that was his deepest fear.

Nine years of his life destroyed in one day.

How did they find him, and more importantly why didn't that bitch protect him?

Thoughts of Worthington ran through his head, and he began to consider that maybe those holding him were her people. She had too much invested in this and would never let them go if she could help it.

He began to smell Old Spice aftershave. *Soldiers*, he thought.

He wanted to identify the leader and attempt contact; his brain slowly began to come online.

Just in time, the vehicle began to slow and make a slow left onto a dirt road. The Suburban finally came to a full stop; there was the sound of running in all directions.

The doctor could hear dirt under their feet and leaves rustling, and this confirmed that he was definitely in a wooded area. As he lay in a fetal position at the back of the vehicle, he practiced moving his mouth and tongue.

It felt like an eternity as the soldiers secured their area; breathing was becoming difficult in his position. Finally, he heard the latch on the Suburban click, and then the back rose up, slowly letting the afternoon light snap his eyes shut. He felt a pair of hands pulling him out from the back. He had made an attempt to stand with limited success. His eyes began to become less sensitive, and he started to focus.

There, in front of him, was an old jarhead soldier, most likely CIA. He grabbed the doctor by the face and looked deep in his eyes.

"You in there, fuck stick?" the old-timer yelled in his face, really displaying his Southern accent.

"Do you work for Worthington?" Mazza was able to push out of his fuzzy mouth.

"I work for the good old Uncle Sam. I don't know who you're talking about!" the old soldier released the doctor's face and motioned the other soldiers to take him into the house.

"We are all going to die today!" he said, realizing his situation as they dragged him to the house.

"Not on my watch, son!" he said out loud, but scanned the woods with his eyes.

The doctor was placed in a dining area toward the back of the house. The house was basically empty, a few chairs, and a foldup card table. There was a strong wooden chair that was connected to the wall by a link chain which looped around a load-bearing column.

This was the chair that he was placed and secured in with straps. He wondered how far away Worthington's people were. He really didn't know how long he was out cold from the drugs, or what day it was. His wound had been addressed, and he was starting to clear; he wondered why he was alive.

The more the drugs wore off, the faster the pain was resurfacing throughout his body. He knew that he needed to convince the redneck that this was not a safe situation.

The big question was how could he do that and not sound like a total nut bag.

Mazza watched as several soldiers carried two large containers into the living room.

They were the children; he did everything in his power not to scream for them. The thought of his angels wounded and afraid, he could hear them both breathing fast and hard. Tears welled up in his eyes as he watched the jarhead who joined the soldiers and ordered them to put the cages in the back. He seemed upset that there was no basement in the house; he seemed edgy. Mazza saw this as an opportunity to plead with the big agent.

"Hey, you need to give me just one minute. It's really important!" The doctor did everything he could to stress the importance of some brief dialogue.

"First, I don't need to give your crazy ass the time of day. Second, I am really busy at this time, son. Why don't you relax?" Jed turned his back and began to walk away.

"Please, one brief statement, then I will shut my damn mouth!" the doctor pleaded with the man.

"Damn, let's have it son. Anything to shut that hole under your nose!" The big man pulled up a chair in front of the doctor.

"We have to get the fuck out of here, right now!" Mazza really stressed the situation.

"Why do I bother?" Jed began to rise.

"No, please, it's a setup. Do you think it's a mistake there is no basement in this fuckin' isolated dwelling?" Mazza was practically crying at this point.

"Boy, you are crazy. What makes you think that you're so damn important that someone is going to risk life and limb to kill your silly ass?" Jed stated, attempting a shot at reason, but deep down he was concerned about the absence of a basement.

"It's not me! I mean nothing to these people, but the children are everything." The doctor needed this man to understand.

"Those little monsters that you hatched in a lab are on nobody's Christmas list. You're not making sense!" Jed stated with aggression in his raspy voice.

"No! You're wrong. Those children are divine, and there are those who will burn heaven and earth just to possess them!" the doctor stated with tears in his eyes.

"Divine! What the hell are you talking about?" Jed asked, truly puzzled.

"I know you can't fathom what I'm talking about. Just know that if we stay in this house, we will all die!" His full belief of this fact was apparent.

"You keep saying that we are all going down today, and it's all because of the two freaks in the back." Jed turned to walk away.

"Listen, you fuckin' redneck, don't you get it? The same person paying you also pays me!" Mazza lowered his head and wept, and that truly began to worry the big agent.

Jed looked into the face of the soldier who was flanking the doctor. His eyes spoke volumes; it was clear that he was afraid that what he was hearing could be the truth.

The other soldier on the right was wringing his weapon in his hands. Clarity was starting to grip the big agent that possibly there was more going on, and that it was not going to end pleasantly.

Jed snapped his fingers and pointed to the two soldiers; taking both his middle and forefinger, he raised them to his eyes indicating toward the windows at the back of the house. The soldiers fanned out and began to focus on the woods to the back of the house.

Jed had seen combat in some of the darkest parts of the world and really knew what to look for. What was more important was that he knew what not to look for. Then he began to realize that there was no sound coming from those woods. Nothing, just silence.

He began to question his situation; was he under siege, or was this crazy doctor making him crazy?

He knew that sitting still was never the optimal plan; he needed to test the waters. He withdrew his Beretta and screwed on a silencer, which was a gift from his second wife. He thought about how he would plan a blitz on the house and estimated where the opposing forces would position themselves.

Jeb took a knee and leveled the weapon out of the window and squeezed off nine shots, spacing them a foot and a half apart. After he fired, Jeb quickly lay down on the floor, awaiting a response.

After several seconds, he began to chuckle and shake his head at his actions. He looked at the doctor who was bracing for return fire.

"You really had me going with that crazy shit. Don't I look, silly?" Jeb stated as he began to raise himself off the floor.

There was a thumping sound that came from the woods; he guessed not more than thirty yards. Jeb knew the sound of an M-50 grenade launcher and knew at that very second that his worst fears had been realized.

CHAPTER 95

He began to bark fire orders to the men in the room, but it was too late. The side of the house exploded, and the impact sent Jeb feet overhead, slamming against the far wall of the house.

The concussion of the explosion had blown both eardrums on the old soldier; all was silent. Jeb was able to gather enough faculties to see bullets dancing around the room like a mosquito swarm. He knew that if he attempted to stand, his life would be taken.

He watched as two lines materialized across the wall and both soldiers were caught in the line of the Gatling-style weapon. He turned his attention to the doctor who had been working feverishly to release himself from the wall chain. He had taken two bullets to the neck and was now choking on his own blood.

Jeb thought to himself that this was definitely not an extraction mission; this was termination protocol.

As he watched a second line of bullets rip through the baseboard, he realized that they were sweeping a lower trajectory, attempting to terminate anyone seeking shelter on the floor.

Jeb timed the sweep and jumped out of the line of fire. When he landed, a sharp pain from his belly made him wince. He reached down and felt blood and what he imagined to be rib bone. He was not sure if he had been shot or the impact from the explosion was responsible.

The other side of the house was still under fire, and some of his men were engaged with the imposing forces. Jeb realized that he was exposed and needed cover; he grabbed a weapon that was no longer needed by the dead soldier. He then used the body of the terminated soldier to shield himself as he worked his way to the opening.

He could now see several soldiers dressed in all black emerging from the woods, laying down a steady field of fire at the source of return fire.

Jeb checked the ammo in the weapon; it was empty.

He reached around the dead soldier and checked him for additional ammo. He found two clips for the M-16 and discharged the old cartridge. Jeb sat for a second and thought out a strategy; he knew that he needed to get to the woods. He wasn't sure if he could run and maneuver with his wound, but he needed to try.

He saw his 9-millimeter on the floor at his feet, and realized that he still had a few shots left in that clip and a second on his belt. Jeb knew that he was better with the handgun than with the rifle. He quickly retrieved the gun from the floor and made sure that the weapon wasn't damaged from the explosion. When he was sure that everything was working, he counted to three and began.

He quickly stepped through the explosion hole on the back wall, into the backyard. He raised his weapon at eye level and began to limp toward the woods.

One of the soldiers bearing down on the house noticed him immediately.

He turned to fire on the large man exiting the house, but was too late. Jeb was able to get off two shots that both entered the left lens of the soldier's Ray-Bans; he went down instantly.

The other soldier who was moving toward the house was not even aware of what had taken place forty feet away. The two mini cannons were generating so much noise; the two silenced shots went unnoticed.

In one fast motion, Jeb was able to get off an additional two shots, then took down the second soldier, discharged the clip, and then replaced it with a full one.

He began to bolt toward the woods, holding his sides and gritting down on the pain. He was starting to get some sound recognition back in his right ear, and he was really thankful for that.

He had made the woods and started zigzagging in random patterns as he ran. One of the large soldiers holding the mini caught sight of Jeb running and changed his fire direction. Jeb hit the ground just in time as the woods erupted in a haze of splinters. He crawled on his belly away from the soldier's field of fire. When the big man took his finger off the trigger of the weapon to survey the damage, Jeb stood up and put one shot in his chest.

The big man hardly flinched and seemed only to be aggravated that his target was still alive. Jeb slid down a sharp embankment as his previous site erupted from a hail of bullets. Jeb double backed ten feet and raised his weapon once more. He caught the big man in the kneecap and started to run again.

He could hear the monster of a man scream out in pain. Jeb didn't wait around for his friends; he was moving at steady pace and was able to deal well with the pain; adrenaline is the ultimate painkiller.

Major Schmitt turned the corner of the house just in time to see his soldier's knee explode and snap out from under him. He then caught the sight of two more of his men down, bleeding on the damp Maryland ground.

Instinctively, he lobbed three shots from the M-50 into the woods and shielded his eyes as the woods exploded. He was unable to see the man running, but he could surely hear him moving away.

He was determined that the three shots that he had laid out there didn't have much chance of success of hitting a moving target. He started barking at one of his men to move on the noise of the large man running through the woods. The soldier didn't hesitate and was moving through the woods before the major could finish his directive. The large soldier with the leg wound was holding in his pain, and attempted to get off the ground.

Schmitt pulled a syringe from his top pocket and jabbed it into the choking man's throat. The big man looked up, unsure of what he was just injected with, fearing the worst.

"Morphine. It will take the edge off until we can get you out of here!" the major reassured the wounded man.

"Sir!" came a voice from the front door of the house.

"What do we have?" the major asked as he quickly positioned to the front of the house.

"Not sure what we have, but you want to check this out!" the soldier said with noted confusion in his voice.

Schmitt walked into the house, stepping over dead soldiers. He would be lying if he said that it didn't hurt his heart to be stepping over American soldiers, but orders were given and accepted. This was the code he lived by, and it served him well through many battles.

The front of the house looked much like Swiss cheese, and smelled of gunpowder and death. He spotted a man chained to the wall, with most of his face gone and blood still spilling out of a neck wound.

He looked through some photos in his hand and determined that he was looking at Dr. Mazza.

It was at that moment that he heard a bloodcurdling noise come from one of the interior rooms. He had never heard anything quite like that sound, but it filled him with dread.

CHAPTER 96

"What the hell is that?" the major said out loud.

"That's what we called you in for. This, you're not going to believe!" the soldier stated, putting heavy emphasis on "believe."

"Show me!" Schmitt directed.

"Yes, sir!" the soldier stated, removing his glasses, holding an open palm toward the room.

The major entered the room slowly and cautiously; anything that made that noise was potentially dangerous. The light in the room was compromised from both the lack of electricity and the smoke from the assault. However, he was capable of making out the two cages in the middle of the floor and the occupants of those cages.

At first glance, he wondered why there were two young children in cages in front of him. Then he began to see that they were different. Their pale skin was evident and alarming, even in the poor light. The male of the two had wrapped its hands around the high-grade steel bars that kept them bound.

He could see the shape of their hands and the claws that resembled razors. Then a low-pitched growl came from their mouth as their dark eyes followed the major as he kneeled and came closer.

He stopped cold when the abomination began to open its mouth and displayed the line of needlelike teeth protruding from black gums.

The eyes of the little monster had locked the major in his tracks; he was frozen. He snapped out of it when one of the soldiers shifted on his feet. He looked over at the other cage and saw the female equivalent of the nightmare in front of him. She was bleeding from an upper arm wound; it didn't look like a fatal wound. However, he couldn't be sure about anything regarding the evil in front of his eyes.

The major reached his hand into a pouch on his side and pulled out a dark round item. He rolled the hand grenade in his sweaty hands for what seemed like minutes.

Several of the soldiers who had been behind him had exited the room, anticipating the blast. His orders were to terminate all within the house, but he needed to be sure.

He snapped to his feet and pulled out his cell phone. An unfamiliar voice came on the phone, asking for a code. After he provided the number sequence, the voice returned, asking how she could be of assistance.

"Helen Worthington!" he requested.

CHAPTER 97

The big wounded agent continued his run through the woods, as branches sliced his hands and whipped his face.

Jeb was no stranger to the bush, and as he ran, nothing escaped him. He read the moss and the wind and fully knew what direction he was going. He knew that the potential was there for one or more of the soldiers to be hot on his trail.

Jeb knew that he couldn't go to the road; that would be a fatal mistake.

He knew that teams like this one would be very aware of the noise that they were creating. If they were the professionals that he knew they were, there would be point crews on the roads.

His best guess was that local authorities had roadblocks throughout the area. His only chance was to stay in the tree line and get some distance from this area.

As he ran, Jeb noticed a fallen tree and decided that this was his best opportunity to make sure that he wasn't being tracked. He quickly jumped the log and pulled the pistol, taking a deep breath so as to not give away his position. His lungs were on fire, and he slowly released the air that was making him dizzy.

His hearing was improving, but far from adequate to hear deep in the woods for a trained soldier. He twisted off the silencer because at this point of the game noise didn't matter, and it only threw off his aim.

He raised the weapon over the log back toward the direction that he came from. He did his best to slow his breathing, but it was near impossible. Jeb was years away from his best shape and was really regretting the added weight he had put on over the past few years.

He sat there waiting for what felt like an eternity. The woods gave nothing, and he had fairly good vision of the area.

He began to psych himself up to get up and start running when he saw the soldier.

Jeb figured him to be about seventy feet away; the pistol shot would be wasted. The man wasn't moving that fast and seemed to be moving from tree to tree for cover. Jeb knew that the soldier was better suited to prevail in this situation.

His loss of hearing was a major deficit, and he really didn't want to tangle with this guy.

The soldier picked up some leaves on the ground, and started in Jeb's direction.

He had quickly closed the gap to Jeb's position and seemed to be tracking the blood trail. Jeb looked down at his hand and saw the blood leaking from his fingers. He shook his hands and realized that he was leading the soldier right to his location.

Jeb raised the weapon toward a break in the tree line where the soldier would appear if he continued his same course.

As Jeb waited for the man to materialize he began to see movement twenty yards in the opposite direction. The soldier had doubled back, investigating an area of knee-high vegetation.

The soldier pulled at a chord on his neck and began to speak. The man nodded his head and did one last scan of the woods and then began to jog back the way he had come.

Jeb realized that he had been called back to the house, but he didn't start his escape. He could feel the cold from the ground and smell the woods, and it helped soothe his mind. The ringing in his ear was still causing him great discomfort, but it was slowly improving. His chest had stopped heaving, and the only real pain that was concerning was the wound he had suffered at his ribs.

He took a moment to review the damage; he had seen worse, he thought.

He rolled out from behind the tree, and continued to run as fast as his old body could take him.

After what he guessed was three or four miles, he collapsed near a small water runoff from the bay. He knew that his position was too far south for the water to be fresh. He guessed salt water this close to the Annapolis area. However, the wound could be dealt with, and the salt would help with minimizing potential infection.

Jeb sat down and thought of his next move; he needed a plan, or he would not make it out of this area. He realized that his best shot was to find his way to the Annapolis marina and liberate a small boat. Then work his way south, and find some help that he could trust.

The voice of the psycho doctor continued to sound in his head, "We work for the same people!"

It had to be true; they were set up, nowhere was safe for him, and he knew that to be true.

Jeb looked down at the wound on his side and knew that if he didn't address this soon, he would be dealing with infection, and that could be fatal. He cut up two sections of the bottom of his shirt and redressed the wound, and off he went.

CHAPTER 98

The headache was gone, and Mac began to feel really sleepy. Kowalski said that this was the end result of being exposed to Cain. He couldn't be sure if Cain himself released the chemicals or if he was utilizing some type of device.

The blood work had come back, and it was confirmed that some neurotoxins had been detected, and they were further being analyzed.

Mac had listened to the scientist talk about their theories but walked away more confused than before.

Magen walked through the door, and he could see that she was also struggling with the effects of the meeting. He wanted to get her home and break out of all this crazy stuff.

She smiled at him as she continued to respond to questions from one of the science geeks.

She shot him a look that said, *Enough already.*

Mac got to his feet and came to the rescue, placing himself between Magen and the lady scientist.

"We have been at this for some time. We need to take a break!" Mac stated, not leaving any room to argue his point.

"I understand. Please see me after you get some rest," she said as she turned and walked out.

"Well, Ms. Cummings, can I offer you a warm bed and a tasty breakfast in the morning?" Mac laid out his plan.

"I thought you would never ask. How do we get the hell out of here?" Magen asked.

"I need to get my hands on the agent named Smith and see if I can borrow one of his vehicles," Mac stated as he headed for the door.

"He has been locked in the interrogation room for the past two hours!" Magen stated as she joined him out the door.

"This place has really calmed down over the past few hours. Let's see if we can get his attention." Mac pulled her into the room.

The room was dark and deserted, but through the one-way glass Mac could see the big agent and Barack having some dinner.

It appeared to be Italian takeout, and the smell of garlic permeated the room.

There was a bottle of red wine on the table, and it really didn't look like Barack was being treated too harshly.

Mac was about to reach for the door when he heard Barack start talking about the news of the newly deceased Dr. Mazza, and how their plan and focus needed to be changed.

Magen looked at Mac and put her hand over her mouth. Mac turned and placed a hand on her arm making an attempt to comfort her.

Barack finished the bite of food in his mouth and turned to Smith and asked, "Do you know who the mole is that gave up the safe house?"

Mac looked at the doorknob and thought that maybe they should announce their presence. Magen pulled him back on his sleeve and held up one finger, indicating for a little more time.

The agent took a second and sat back, lighting a smoke. He shook his head and said, "If I knew the why, then maybe I could figure out who!"

Magen released the grip on Mac's sleeve and motioned him toward the door. Mac turned from her and grabbed the knob and entered the room.

"Good evening, gentlemen, I take it that you have been cleared of any misgiving?" Mac smiled at Barack.

"Officer MacDonald, it is good to see you, and, Agent Cummings, may I say that it is always my honor!" Barack laid on the charm.

"Thank you, glad to see that things have been worked out," Magen added with true sincerity.

"I'm glad you're here. There is something that we need to discuss!" Agent Smith announced.

"Is there no way we could put that thought on hold for just a few hours? We need some sleep!" Mac pressed, testing the waters a little.

"Sorry, I know what you both have been through, but there is something that just came through. It can't wait." The agent rose to his feet and offered the chair to Magen.

"No thanks, I would fall out if I sat down." Magen smiled as the agent nodded.

"At three o'clock today, just minutes after the arrival at the safe house, Dr. Mazza and the team of men assigned to him were killed," Smith began.

"Wow!" was all Mac could muster, not wishing to linger long with the news.

"The two unidentified were not on the scene when the second team arrived. We are certain that we are compromised here at the facility!" Smith seemed more irritated by the breach than the loss of the doctor.

"This type of thing just doesn't happen. There must be clues from those responsible. Any theories yet?" Magen said with conviction.

"The house is still being processed as we speak. So far, all we have are two thousand rounds of untraceable rounds found around the perimeter." Smith seemed slightly defeated as he responded to Magen's question.

"Do you think Cain might have some responsibility in the attack and retrieval?" Magen asked.

"We are ruling out nothing at this point! However, we have moved to a lockdown scenario and will need to restrict team movement," the agent announced without skipping a beat.

"Are you saying that we are not leaving to get some sleep, and if so, what is your plan?" Mac asked with obvious agitation in his voice.

"I know you're tired. We have made arrangements at the Hilton to secure housing for all team members, and we are running transport every half hour." The agent seemed regretful to impose restrictions on the two agents.

"Agent Smith, I truly understand your situation, but I am going to need a change of clothing soon!" Magen seemed to emphasize "soon."

"We understand, and there will be clothing delivered to the hotel. There will be someone there to assist you before you sleep. Sorry." Smith ended and grabbed his cooling coffee and took a drink.

"Looks like you thought of everything. We will see you in a few hours!" Mac stated and turned for the door.

"Officer MacDonald, I know you really got dragged into all this by an unimaginable set of circumstance. I lost one of my oldest friends at that house tonight. Please keep all contact in the house."

"I am sorry about your friend, but I will need you to call my captain and explain our lockdown status, please," Mac, too tired to confront the agent's reference, turned for the door.

"That I can do, and thank you!" Smith said as he watched the two leave the room.

"I like them. Cain made a good decision dragging them into this!" Barack said with a hearty smile.

"How long do you think they were listening at the door?" Smith asked.

"A minute, two tops!" Barack smiled at his friend and pulled hard on his cigarette.

CHAPTER 99

Jeb walked to a clearing that funneled into a bridge.

He knew that this was going to happen sooner or later; the whole area was a series of bridges and swamplands. He needed to start taking some risks, and it looked like that time was now.

He thought about doubling back and sticking to the woods, but that could be just as dangerous.

Jeb took a few minutes getting his act together; his clothes were covered in leaves and dirt. The blood in the front of his shirt was still a hard stain to explain to anyone who saw him. He did the best he could to hide the damage under his large arm.

Jeb took a deep breath and got out on the road and headed for the bridge. The day had moved on, and he could feel the sun beating down on his bald head.

Initially, the feeling of the heat was really comforting, but as he moved closer to the bridge, the heat really began to work against him. He had been in the woods for hours, and wasn't sure just how much ground he had covered. His best guess was seven miles, but when you are running blind in the woods, it is hard to make a safe assumption.

As he approached the walkway to the bridge, he began to hear a car engine behind him, maybe a quarter mile off.

Jeb began to take longer strides as he began to ascend up the walk; if he timed this right, he might avoid being seen altogether.

As he passed the peak of the bridge, he cursed the years of smoking that was really working against him. The first few downhill steps felt strange on his legs, and he stumbled slightly. The car that was coming up behind him would be visible in a few seconds, and Jeb would need to make a quick turn to assess the potential danger.

He was getting close to the bottom of the bridge when he heard the vehicle clearly and knew that he was exposed. He did a quick twist of the neck between strides and then turned back in hopes of not to appearing to be too concerned.

It was a Buick, and it appeared to only have one driver. Jeb felt relieved that it wasn't a Crown Victoria or GMC, the preferred operative vehicle.

That thought made him sad; he had given his life for his country, and now he could possibly be hunted by his own people.

The vehicle began to slow as Jeb stepped off the bridge walkway and continued on the side of the road. As the vehicle came alongside him, he saw that it was an older female and he felt slightly better, then he saw the brake light.

The vehicle made a complete stop ten feet from his position, and the door began to open. A woman in her late forties got out of the car with a blanket in her hand and said in a sweet voice, "Are you hurt? Please let me help you!"

Jeb's mind was running like a two-stroke engine; he was trying desperately to read the situation. The woman was coming right toward him, and he was considering diving into the woods to his left. Then the possibility clouded his thoughts that he was just being paranoid and he was really dealing with a Good Samaritan.

Then an extremely clear thought ran through his head about the soldier back in the woods, finding his blood on the ground and running it between his fingers. Then Jeb asked himself how did this woman see his injury from her vantage point?

His decision was finalized when he caught the sight of her eyes behind the three-hundred-dollar sunglasses. They were cold and calculating and without any concern for her own safety.

Jeb couldn't put the whole picture together in his mind; it just didn't add up.

The woman and her clothes fit the Buick, but the sunglasses and that cold stare were way off-center.

Jeb stepped toward the woman, giving her the idea that he was fully accepting her assistance. He timed his steps perfectly; as he stepped toward the blanket, the woman smiled.

With the reserve of strength that he had left, he raised his right fist and caught the smiling woman directly on the nose. The woman's face exploded as her nose broke and her pricey glasses flew up in the air.

More important was the 9-millimeter that now danced across the street. Jeb smiled as he realized that he had guessed correctly. His joy was short-lived as he became aware that the woman was back on her feet and all her sweetness was gone.

"Let's dance, fat boy!" the woman announced as she began to move in on the older CIA man, blowing a blood clot out of her left nostril.

"You're on, lady!" Jeb shot back out of instinct, but his eyes betrayed his shock at her resilience.

The well-trained operative began to rain down blows on the agent. Jeb did all he could do to minimize the shots on his face and arms. The second blow to the temple almost sent Jeb down to Queer Street, but he was able to recover long enough to send a punch into the groin of the female. She fell backward and let out a wince of pain; the blow would have sent most men to the floor for hours. Unfortunately, this only seemed to agitate her deeper and sprang from the ground and came right for Jeb's eyes. Her fingernail dug into the side of Jeb's face right under his eye; he could feel the skin peel away, and horror filled his mind.

He was using way too much of his remaining strength to get her off. Finally, he just decided to use his own weight to his advantage and take this fight to the floor. He took two steps and stumbled over the embankment, landing hard on top of the strong woman. The impact was enough to break her iron grasp. Jeb took just a second to compose himself and gain footing.

He sent three consecutive shots into her face, but she shook them off and came right back at him, this time digging her index finger into the wound on Jeb's side, digging deeply at the exposed bone. Jeb let out a scream and could feel his legs buckle.

It was at that moment Jeb considered the possibility that he could die right there on the side of the road outside of Annapolis, Maryland.

Anger welled up in the big man, and he twisted his body so that his face was parallel with the assassin's neck. Jeb opened his mouth as wide as he could and wrapped his teeth around the woman's windpipe and bit down as hard as he could. He began to taste the blood in his mouth and feel the crunch of cartilage under his teeth.

Even with her death en route, the woman still would not release her grip. Slowly, her strength began to subside as her last few breaths escaped past Jeb's teeth.

He was breathing hard through his nose and crying from the trauma and the exhaustion. He sat there with his jaw locked around the woman's throat for what seemed an eternity. As he regained his senses, he quickly released his grip and prepared himself for another attack that didn't come.

Jeb fell back and stared at the sky as the blood dripped down his face and into his mouth. He was quickly shocked back to reality when an air bubble popped through the dead woman's broken throat.

Jeb came to his feet and was preparing himself for additional battle. He fell to one knee and reached to his wound that was now reopened and bleeding. He knew that he needed to get the hell out of there; his life depended on it.

Jeb gathered what he could; there was some cash and papers in her pockets. The keys to the car were still in the cylinder, and he also grabbed the blanket and the gun. He was about to throw the vehicle into drive when he quickly opened the door, stepped to the embankment, and sent two bullets from the 9-millimeter into the dead woman's listless body.

He screamed at her as if she had taken something from him.

He returned to the car, looking around for any approaching vehicles. He caught sight of himself in the mirror and almost jumped at the sight of his face. He thought about the evil bitch who almost sent him to the boneyard and wondered who would have such a nightmare on their payroll.

He needed to find some place to patch up his battered body and work a plan, but most of all, he needed help.

CHAPTER 100

Helen Worthington ran around her office for the next twenty minutes, barking orders at her team. Fanning and the attorney were still in the room starting to piece together what had happened during the phone call that flipped the switch in Worthington. She stopped to breathe for a second and quickly grabbed the phone and ordered whoever was on the other side of the phone to have the cardinal's helicopter turned around at Kennedy Airport.

Finally, she sat back down and reveled in her second chance. It was at that moment she had the epiphany that God was working through her and wanted her to succeed.

This was a second chance that she couldn't fail.

She closed her eyes and prayed, then vowed to God that she would stop at nothing to see his will finalized.

Helen looked up from her desk with new purpose. Fanning was looking at her with deep anticipation to learn the new events that seemed to have changed everything. She seemed to be looking through her two cohorts and lost in her own world.

Finally, she smiled. "Gentlemen, it seems that we have been dealt back in the game!" Helen stated with great elation.

"They escaped the military?" Fanning said with some surprise.

"Not escaped. They have been liberated and are being delivered back to us!" Her sheer joy did not even slightly waver.

"Was the good doctor also rescued from confinement?" Daniel asked.

"His life has been sacrificed in the assault on the safe house. However, the children are practically uninjured!" she informed them as if explaining some miracle.

"How will we control the spawn without Mazza? He was considered both mother and father to them," the attorney stressed.

"This was my first consideration when I first heard the news. I am having Wilson call in an expert in wildlife," Helen said with some confidence.

"Wildlife expert? We may need a little bit more than that!" Fanning added with a hint of his standard sarcasm.

"We will get what we need, that I can assure you. The important thing is that all is not lost!" Helen continued through her bliss.

"We still have Cain to deal with. If he finds out about the existence of the twins, we will not survive," Fanning continued to play devil's advocate.

"Cain has been a factor since the beginning. We are in this for a reason! The only thing that has changed is the fact that God has given us another chance." Worthington was rolling and heightened.

"Where are the children now?" the attorney chimed in, attempting to calm the moment. He could see that his employer was caught up.

"They are currently in Maryland, but we are working them toward a facility farm in upstate New York, small area near the Tappan Zee Bridge. We own a soybean farm up there." Helen seemed happy about the facility.

"A really large piece of property and really secluded, it's perfect!" Fanning chimed in, remembering his trip to the facility several years back.

"We can start some conversions to the existing structure using our own contractors, not to draw any local attention," the attorney stated.

"Let's get to work on that. The children are going to need room to grow. I am going to need all of Mazza's notes and computer data that hasn't been confiscated or destroyed. We need to move the local connections out there in Long Island." Helen shot off direction after direction, and the attorney worked feverishly to write it all down.

Fanning slowly reached over to scratch his hair, but really, he was catching the sweat that was slowly creeping down the side of his face. He didn't want Worthington to notice that he was in a full-out panic, and was starting to realize that she just might be insane.

CHAPTER 101

Mac held the door for Magen as they entered the aging hotel. The building was well maintained, considering its years.

Magen pointed out the lighting and a large fresco of Naples that dominated the far wall near the elevator. The woman at the front desk offered a sharp smile and quickly jumped into a rehearsed apology for not having any available rooms.

Magen held up her badge, indicating that she was from the government. This initiated a new volley of apologies from the woman, stating that she didn't think they looked like the federal team that had been coming and going. Mac made a joke about them looking too honest and human, but they were only contracting. There was some laughter from both the ladies as Magen took the key card for the room and her identification card and thanked the woman.

They entered the old elevator, and Mac pulled the iron door closed. There was a pause, and then Magen reached out and pushed the button for the fifth floor. As the small unit began to rise, Magen walked over to Mac and pushed him against the wall. She grabbed his shirt by both collars and slammed her hot mouth on his. He was caught off guard, but he quickly relaxed into her warm body. He ran his hands up the side of her body, gently touching her firm breasts. She pushed his hands away and gave him an evil smile as she clawed at his chest.

Mac had no problem with Magen's dominating actions. Mac had always been secure about who he was as a man, so he smiled and let her take control. Finding the role reversal extremely arousing, he placed the back of his hands against the wall and let her in. Magen reached down to Mac's crotch and grabbed a full handful of balls. His breathing began to intensify, only to be matched by hers.

She had unzipped his pants and made an attempt to free his penis from the stressed confines of his pants. She quickly became aware that his penis had become so hard that she was not going to be able to retrieve it through the small slot in his pants.

The elevator was coming to their floor; she turned her back to Mac, still holding a firm grip on his throbbing penis. The door opened, and the hall was empty. Magen slowly began to walk to the room that they had been given. Her grip on Mac was still secure; she turned to flash a sexy smile. He was obviously enjoying the game, his breathing was really heightened, and he was sweating a little.

Magen slid the key card, and the door popped open; she pushed through and was thankful for the bathroom light. Mac was thrown on the bed, and she reached down and pulled his belt through the hoops and dropped it to her feet. Mac reached to remove his pants and was stopped immediately by her hands. He was surprised by her strong grip and hungry mouth. Magen stood between his legs, running her hand over his eager cock, gently brushing against the swollen head.

Mac was trying to slow his pace; her gentle touch was nearing him to climax. Magen slowly removed her shirt and skirt, standing there in a black bra and panties. Mac was near the breaking point as she began to rub her inner thighs together in front of him.

With sure, confident hands Magen reached down and undid Mac's pants. Without hesitation, she bent between his legs, released him from his underpants, and took him into her mouth. He let out a deep moan as his body slightly convulsed with pleasure.

Magen enjoyed the control she had at that moment and was amazed at his hardness. She really didn't focus on his penis while having sex the prior night, having been caught up in the hunger of the moment.

Tonight was for her; she was feeling her woman come back, and she missed her deeply. Magen stood up and removed the remaining clothing that both Mac and she had on.

She was careful taking off her bra, due to the pain she still felt from her shoulder.

Her hands reached out and grabbed the base of his shaft, and then she straddled him, guiding him into her. Magen felt him enter her; there was just a brief moment where she winced slightly as his penis stretched her.

Slowly she began to feel the tension ease, and the joy came flowing in. Magen lowered her body fully on Mac now and then placed her mouth to his. They sat there, not moving; his arms pulled her to him with true desire. Magen began to ride him as she felt the pressure inside of her build.

Mac could feel his pleasure growing as well; he began to back off in hopes of staying with her. Their passion was for that brief few minutes all there was in the world.

The pace increased as the moment of climax was closing in for both of them.

Magen began to thrash up and down upon his hardness, soft noises escaping her throat.

Mac tried to slow his pace, but that was becoming too difficult as he reacted to Magen's body. He let out a deep moan and then began to climax. Feeling this, Magen released and began her own orgasm, grinding hard on Mac.

The moment of bliss hung out there for what felt like minutes, and then they both fell into the bed, shaking and spent.

For some time, they both just lay naked in each other's arms, letting their breathing even out.

Magen ran her hand through the hair on Mac's chest, enjoying the warmth that surged through her body. The breathing began to slow, and the night closed in as Magen embraced sleep.

Mac lay there, letting the day's ugliness drift away, no thoughts of governments, military, and no Cain!

CHAPTER 102

Smith reached the focus room sometime after 2:00 a.m. and found some of the remaining scientists mulling over data.

According to one of the military strategists who was trying to compile the information from several teams of specialists, they hadn't made any real headway from earlier in the evening.

Smith reviewed the data for a few minutes and then rubbed his eyes.

The strategist walked over and sat down next to the section chief and began to update him on the past few hours. He began to explain the connection of the past events and the increased dopamine levels. The young man stopped himself every few minutes and reminded the section chief that at this point everything was conjecture and nothing could be confirmed. He went on to clarify that the current consensus was that the neurotoxins were equally spread over an area that was confined to the restaurant. Blood samples of people outside the area confirmed this.

The majority of the teams feel that Cain himself has the ability to disperse the toxins, as opposed to the possibility of him having a device.

There are several accounts of both animals and plant life right here on Earth with the same ability.

The strategist started to go over the identified compounds found in the restaurant, but nothing seemed to be out of character with all things that should be found in this environment.

Smith reached down into his pocket as he felt his phone that was set to vibrate.

He reviewed the number and didn't recognize its origin, and his phone recognized every call it had received for the past decade. Then Smith took a deep inhale as he recognized that it was a Maryland number from the first three digits.

The section chief quickly moved away from the table, nodding at the younger man. He hit the "Accept" button as soon as the door closed behind him.

"This is Smith!" the agent announced into the handheld.

"Sir, this is Jeb. The house was compromised, and I am hit. Please advise!" the old soldier shot back as he peered over his shoulder from the gas station outside of Annapolis.

"Jeb, I'm not sure to what level the deception goes. Will call back in five minutes, this number!" Smith hung up the phone and began to move through the hall with regained energy.

Smith turned off his phone and grabbed the large doors leading out to the motorcade. He saw the soldier that he was looking for and moved toward him at a steady pace.

The soldier saw the incoming section chief and snapped to attention.

"Soldier, I want that phone in your side pocket!" Smith said with total confidence.

"Sir?" the young soldier said.

"Give it up!" he stated.

"Yes, sir!" the soldier said as he fished the phone out and handed it over.

Smith nodded to the young soldier who was looking forward and waited for some type of reprimand that never came.

He had opened the garage door and walked out before he punched the numbers in and reached out to his friend.

Smith looked over the area one last time to make sure he was alone.

"Jeb, the phone is clean. Talk to me!" Smith stated.

"The house was compromised. I didn't recognize the team, but their methods were all too familiar," Jeb said between deep breaths with a noticeable wheezing.

"What is your position at this point, and can you be safely extracted?" Smith asked his old friend.

"I am moving in five minutes. This area is not safe! Do you remember the day your oldest graduated from the citadel?" Jeb probed his friend's memory.

"I do. We went out to a restaurant. You fought me about paying the check!" Smith recalled the day.

"That's right. I'm going to walk into that place in three hours. I need a doctor." Jeb laid it out there and hoped his friend was able to follow his plan.

"I am on it. Jeb, were there two crates that came with the doctor?" he asked, just for confirmation.

"I shot my way out the back. Nothing survived the attack! They came from every angle. If anything survived, it would be a miracle," Jeb explained as he continued watching the area.

"Understood, my friend, I will not contact you for the next three hours. I just need to find the right people to bring you in!" Smith held the phone slightly off his ear.

"Thank you, my friend! See you soon." Jeb hung up the phone.

CHAPTER 103

Mac and Magen woke to the bedside lamp turning on. Magen instinctively went for her weapon; Mac didn't even budge.

"Forgive me!" Smith said as he slightly recoiled from Magen's fast movement.

"Is this some kind of joke?" Magen voiced as she pushed on Mac to wake.

"Please, I can explain!" Smith added as he turned to see Mac's eyes cringe from the light.

"What is going on that couldn't be handled in the morning?" Mac stated as he adjusted to the light.

"Let me first say I am deeply sorry for waking you like this!" Smith said quietly as he held up a paper that he read.

"So, what is it that we can do for you?" Mac asked, shrugging his shoulders.

"Dr. Kowalski has noted some side effects from today's meeting. Nothing serious, but an eye scan had detected a grouping of broken blood vessels, and we were hoping that you would be open to a quick scan, five minutes tops!" Smith had laid out an almost believable scenario that would give them a head start on whoever was watching.

"I suppose that we could be ready in just a few minutes!" Magen added as she held the sheets tightly around her ample body.

"Of course, I will wait downstairs. Again, I apologize for the inconvenience!" Smith turned and moved toward the door, leaving the envelope at the small table by the door.

Mac snapped out of the bed and quickly moved to the door and removed the envelope and began to open it.

He held up a set of keys and a letter.

Magen had already retrieved her clothes and was heading for the bathroom to change.

Mac began to read the letter and then passed it into the bathroom. Magen exited the bathroom a few minutes later, having read the note, nodded, and motioned to the door.

Mac slid on his shoes, and out they went.

Neither one of them talked until they saw Smith near the elevator.

"It seems that this party just will not end!" Mac stated as he watched Smith push the button for the first floor.

"I can't thank you enough for your help!" Smith stated as he blocked the camera on the panel and placed his index finger to his lips.

"Don't listen to him. He's just cranky. We are happy to help!" Magen added.

"I know you two have been burning it at both ends. I wouldn't push if it wasn't really critical," Smith finished as the doors opened and they moved into the lobby.

"You are so right about burning at both ends, but we play for the team, so lead on!" Mac stated as he motioned Smith to the front door where the Denali was waiting.

"What the hell is going on?" Magen snapped as soon as they were in the vehicle.

"I received a call from my old friend who was the point agent at the house that was compromised. He was able to get away, but he is hurt and in some real trouble. I have no choice but to send in an outside party. I feel that I have absolutely nobody within the organization that I can send. The agent's name is Jeb. I have worked with this man for thirty-plus years. He is not only extremely valuable as a survivor, but he is a really close friend, and I feel a level of responsibility to bring him in safe.

"When we pull up to the building, I need to go into the building, but you two can jump into the car I have in the lot. Everything else you need is in the folder on the front seat, restaurant address, photos, and directions."

"I have listened to stories about this man since I was a young cadet. I am honored to be part of his extraction," Magen voiced, her hero worship evident as she realized who was involved.

"I can't trust my phone or any other form of communication, so to some degree you are acting alone," Smith stated as he threw the vehicle into park.

"Understood. To be honest, I like it this way!" Mac stated and jumped from the car and fished the keys from his pocket, pressing the alarm button to locate the vehicle.

A loud beep pinged back at the two as they walked through the lot, dedicated to the staff that was working at the control center.

Mac smiled as he saw the lights on the BMW X5 flicker. Magen looked at his boyish smile and shook her head.

As they entered the car, they immediately saw the large envelope taped to the steering wheel. Mac pulled it off and handed it over to Magen who opened it and began to read.

Mac threw the vehicle into gear and slowly rolled out of the parking lot. He moved slowly as he drifted out into traffic. Magen noticed that he was not familiar with the vehicle and seemed to be milking the gas pedal.

"At this rate, we should get to Maryland for Christmas. Do you need me to drive?" Magen said as her smile lit up her face.

"Oh, I'm sorry, was it your turn to be really funny? There is the train station a few miles down the road!" Mac said, acting like he was affected by her remarks.

"Train station, that might work, then we can both sleep, not just you," Magen joked as she pressed down on his right leg to manipulate the gas.

"Stop it! Do you want us to crash?" Mac belted out as he picked up the BMW's speed, the needle passing seventy-five.

"There you go, big boy. Glad to see you still got a pair!" Magen smiled.

"You enjoy that illusion of control, sweetness!" Mac stated as he passed the traffic camera at seventy-nine miles an hour, too fast to notice the flash from the camera.

CHAPTER 104

Cain sat in a leather chair overlooking the lower half of Central Park. He thought deeply about the meeting that had taken place earlier.

Joshua and his mother had gone back home to deal with all those things that they had placed on hold over the last few days. Cain missed them and hoped to reconnect soon.

He didn't mind the silence of the room, or being alone. His brain continued to process every aspect of the meeting. The shooter was not part of the agencies that were monitoring the lunch, this he was pretty sure of. He would only be guessing if he tried to verify the failed attempt motivation.

He knew long before he made the decision to stay on Earth that there was going to be resistance. He is an unknown commodity among an endless sea of greed and corruption. There was only one way that this was going to work for him, he thought. He needed the buy-in from the American agencies that most likely feared him most.

The woman, he thought, was a possible ally; he felt she was holding something back from him.

Cain could read her easier than the others. Her thoughts and questions were fluid and pointed, but there was something that she was holding on to.

She had been recently wounded; he smelled the blood and antibiotics. It wasn't from the hotel; it was days later.

Maybe she knew about the assassination attempt, he thought for just a brief second, and then dismissed the idea.

Both she and the police officer who was more concerned with her safety than cheeseburgers were both in shock when the gun came out from under the napkin.

Kowalski never looked away from the table; he just withdrew as the table reacted.

Dean was in the path of incoming fire. If he had anything to do with the attack, he would have sat elsewhere, simply because he was trained to do so.

Cain stood and paced in front of the large glass window and began to realize that it wasn't those at the table, and that could mean that the CIA was still ready to work with him.

How could he confirm his theory without giving too much away?

His best course was to open a side dialogue with the woman, Magen; she would need to come clean about what she was hiding.

Cain pulled up a chair and sat watching out of the thick glass. He retrieved a long, thin pipe and a pouch. Moments later he was breathing in the sweet smoke and exhaling evenly. He sat thinking about his situation, and the best course of action. The smoke was helping him relax and focus.

Cain pondered that he still had resources that could assist him in utilizing information from the military. Thomas was gone, but there were still connections that were working the evacuation. He knew he needed to get into this and try and see in just what direction the wheels of fate were spinning.

Cain moved his chair to the middle of the room and retrieved several round ball bearings from his pocket and sprayed them out at his feet. There was a faint buzzing noise that began to escalate as the round balls rose from the ground. They hovered about a foot above the ground. Cain thought about the pending feeling of being totally broken down and reassembled elsewhere.

He has utilized fast travel since he was a child; still, the feeling of pulling it all together was nauseating. He felt the wave coming; he used to start holding his breath at this point. Now he couldn't be bothered.

Light erupted in the room, and he was gone.

The pipe sat on the table near the window as the last few wisps of smoke tangled toward the ceiling.

CHAPTER 105

The office of Helen Worthington was buzzing; people were running with a sense of purpose. Helen herself was finally calming down and now sitting at her desk, then came the sharp knock on the door.

Her video analyst Adam something came in with laptop in hand, slightly out of breath.

Helen thought this was odd, knowing full well that this man's office was only fifty yards away. She motioned for him to take the seat in front her. The young assistant placed the laptop in front of his superior and began to state his findings.

"It appears we have a bit of an anomaly that I felt needed to be brought to your attention."

"You're right, Adam. You have been monitoring the command center in Brooklyn?" Helen stated.

"Yes, Mrs. Worthington. Adam Mensal, I am the communications specialist who has been monitoring the Brooklyn grid," the young man said sheepishly.

"Well, Adam, please feel free to dazzle me with your findings," Helen said, not really too concerned.

"Yes, well, we have been keeping a close eye on the traffic coming and going from that section of Brooklyn. Nothing of real concern has come through our net over the last two days. However, a few minutes ago, Anderson in voice was talking about a conversation that was picked up in the garage at the command center. He made reference to the primary Agent Smith confiscating a soldier's private phone at 4:14 a.m.!" The young analyst took in a deep breath.

"Help me put this together, please!" Helen stated, slightly agitated.

"Well, voice also has the same Agent Smith barking orders at a team of Special Forces inside to command center at 4:56 a.m. However, the NJT ran a plate number at 4:48 a.m. on the agent's private vehicle heading southbound at a high rate of speed!" Adam cocked his head, trying to assess if his data was getting through to his superior.

"Who is driving the car would be my first question," Helen's brain began to piece the puzzle together.

"That, and where are they going in such a hurry?" Adam added.

"Right, I need the make and model on the vehicle. Have we determined if it is LoJacked? I need a full team meeting in fifteen minutes!" Helen was up on her feet, snapping out questions and commands.

"I'm on it. I will have your answers before we sit down for that meeting!" Adam stated as he reached the door.

"Good work, young man!" Helen stated as she waited for the door to close, and then picked up the phone.

"Major, we may have a slight issue heading your way. It seems a vehicle was commandeered early this morning and is southbound on the New Jersey Turnpike moving at a high rate of speed. Is there any possible reason you can think of that would motivate the lead agent in Brooklyn to secretly send someone your way?" Worthington probed.

"We did a head count at the house, and we are down one!" Schmitt stated without emotion.

"That is unfortunate. This situation needs to be contained as soon as possible. I will get you more information when I have it!" Helen stated with slight agitation being conveyed.

"There was blood found on the ground in the woods, so he is injured. I am missing one of the contracted personnel. She hasn't made contact in the past hour. We will clean this up sooner than later. No worries," the major stated with confidence.

"That is good to know. Is the other package still in Maryland, or have arrangements for transfer been made?"

"Those things are off my plate, on schedule to the location you specified," Schmitt stated with obvious distaste.

"How severe is the injury on the female?"

"I wish that I could tell you. It has been cradling the injury, and nobody has attempted to get close enough for a proper evaluation!" the major said with limited concern in his voice.

"I am going to send you coordinates of a safe location to meet with a doctor who can address her wounds, then proceed with that individual to the original destination. Clear?" There was firmness in her voice.

"I will be awaiting your transition. The team is en route already. Should I slow them down?" Schmitt asked.

"That will not be necessary, sending coordinates now. You will be looking for Dr. Jason Daly," Helen finished.

"Receiving information. Instructions are clear and a go!" Schmitt clicked off.

CHAPTER 106

The Turtle Back Zoo was located in Essex County, not far from the exit off the New Jersey Turnpike. This was really good news to the soldiers in the back of the Denali, who were becoming uncomfortable with the evil gaze from the two caged passengers.

Dr. Jason had already been at the zoo for several hours when he received a call from the chief of board of directors Grayson Stone informing him to expect a call from a military commander that was of the highest importance and that he was to assist in any manner possible. It would be of great benefit to the zoo. He attempted to ask some questions to Grayson; however, the phone went dead.

He was always ready to do his part for the zoo; these people had been really good to him and his research. He was not too happy about having any involvement with the military. He couldn't, for the life of him, fathom what benefit he could be to the military. It all seemed unimportant when he locked the gate to the wolf cage and turned to see a middle-aged man in a black suit flanked by two soldiers in full combat gear.

"Dr. Jason Daly?" the man wearing the suit spoke first.

"Yes, that's right. Good morning!" Jason said slightly alarmed at the sight of the armed officers.

"Good morning, sir. I am Dean Skelous, Federal Bureau of Investigation. We are going to need you to accompany us this morning!" Agent Skelous stated and gestured his hand in the direction of the parking lot, not waiting for a response.

"I received a call from the board of directors early this morning that you were coming. I am not really sure how I can be of any assistance to the military," Jason talked as they walked, becoming uneasy as they neared the parking lot. He had hoped for some additional information; however, the agent was indifferent to his statement.

"I am going to need you to enter the back passenger door of the second vehicle, please!" The agent motioned to the large black SUV with several additional soldiers flanking the vehicle.

"Do you mean that you wish me to go with you? I was unclear with that, and I thought someone just wanted information," Dr. Daly began to protest.

"Sir, I am on the tightest time frame known to man. I need you in this vehicle now!" The agent pulled his jacket open, exposing a weapon that Jason recognized as a tranquilizer gun mostly used on carnivores, primarily the Felidae family of big cats.

"Am I being kidnapped?" Jason snapped as fear began to overwhelm him.

"The United States government does not kidnap its citizens! However, if you don't get into the back seat of the second vehicle now, I am going to shoot you in the face with one of these big ugly darts!" The agent motioned again to the door.

"This is unconscionable. I will discuss this with the board!" Dr. Daly stated as he slid into the back seat.

"Roll out!" the agent shouted as the soldiers quickly mounted the vehicle, and they were moving before the doors had a chance to close.

CHAPTER 107

"What in God's name is that smell?" Jason stated as the Denali leaped back on the road.

"That would be our little guests, Doctor, or maybe I should say your guests!" a young soldier said from the seat in front of him.

"What guests are we talking about?" Jason stated as he held his nose.

"Doctor, I would like to introduce you to Eris and Keris, our young guests that we are delivering!" The young soldier turned in his seat and offered some Vicks VapoRub, a trick that medical examiners have used to deal with the smell of rotting flesh.

"Thank you!" Dr. Daly said to the young soldier as he dabbed the rub under his nose.

The soldier was pointing to the back. "I remember the names Eris and Keris from my Greek in college!" Jason stated as he shifted in his seat to look into the back of the vehicle.

He recognized the containers as high-end animal transporters. He lifted the checkered picnic blanket that was covering the containers and adjusted his eyes.

The face of a sickly boy looked up at him, and then his eyes shot over to the young girl who seemed wounded. Horror began to spread through him as he wondered what type of people would imprison these young children.

The caged boy child moved closer to the steel door, and wrapped its hands around the reinforced bars. The child seemed to be sniffing at the air, smelling him. Jason saw the dark fingernails on the boy begin to grow. Then the eyes began to take on a new form.

The eyes on the child began to emulate that of Canis lupus!

"They smell the wolves, and they are adapting!" Daly said out loud.

"Did you say something, Doctor?" the young soldier said, amazed that the man wasn't freaking out by what he just saw.

"What? No, I mean, yes, we need to turn around and get back to the zoo. I have my things there, and this child needs medical attention," Jason said, trying to emphasize the importance.

"Sorry, Doc, this train doesn't make stops and we never go backwards. Your lab has been recreated at our destination," the soldier in the passenger seat stated.

"That is not an option! Do you know what you have back there?" Jason voiced.

"No! We don't. Can you please enlighten us?" the soldier stated from the front seat as the rest turned to hear the answer.

"The behavior that I have witnessed from that male specimen is not standard normalcy of human behavior!" The Doctor struggled for answers as his indecision blasted through his brain.

"You're as clueless as the rest of us!" the soldier who handed him the VapoRub said with a smile.

"My best guess is that they are both some form of genetic alteration. However, something like this just doesn't fall from the sky. They would have been raised in a lab with unlimited recourses!" he stopped talking long enough to notice that the soldiers had gone silent.

"There was a doctor!" the soldier began.

"Shut the fuck up, Manski!" screamed the higher-ranking man in the passenger seat.

"Bullshit, he's part of the team now. He's going to know everything when we hit base!" The young soldier pleaded his case, and the other man turned and looked out the window.

"We are not authorized to provide data on the package!" the higher-ranking soldier stated, but with limited conviction.

"The doctor who cared for these things, he's dead, took a bullet to the throat! He said they were angels!"

The full car of soldiers turned to look at the new doctor; he could feel the fear.

"What do you mean? Like angels that float down from heaven?" Jason laughed a little at first, thinking that the men were trying to put something over on him, but no one was laughing.

"He was crying like a baby when he said it. I saw the honesty in his eyes!" the young soldier stated, still making the slightly older man uptight.

"I helped raise two wolf pups after the mother was killed by a hunter. I think I might have called them my angels once or twice," Jason tried to keep his thinking based in reality.

"It wasn't like that. He was crying. He said they are angels!" The soldier was holding firm and seemed angry about being challenged.

"I am not sure what they are. What they are not is human, not like we understand the classification!" Jason stated as he looked back and peered into the eyes of the young male who now seemed sad and in need of someone to trust.

He smiled just a little, and the ghoulish creature caged in the back of the vehicle smiled back slightly.

Jason could feel his heart leap in his chest.

This was big, really big, he told himself as he dabbed a little more rub under his nose.

CHAPTER 108

After nearly three hours on the road, Mac turned into the seaside village of Annapolis, Maryland. He felt like he had just taken a pleasant step back in time.

There were people on the streets making their way to work. He recognized hospital staff and young cadets from the naval academy.

This wasn't the first time he had made the drive down here. He enjoyed this town; unfortunately, he drank way too much the last time he was here, and his memory was vague.

They knew how to live down here and play as well. Mac rolled down the window in hopes of getting a breath of that sea air. Not disappointed, he took a deep pull through his nose and smiled.

Rolling the window down woke Magen from much-needed sleep.

"Are we here already?" Magen asked, not too happy about being awake.

"That is too funny. You slept the whole ride down! One minute you were complaining about my driving, and the next, you were out like a light," Mac joked as she yawned and gained her bearings.

"I love the smell of the Chesapeake!" Magen said as she rested back in the seat.

"I do, too, reminds me of my early childhood!" Mac stated as he tapped the brakes at an approaching stop sign.

"How do you mean that?" Magen asked, realizing that she didn't know all that much about the man she had been sleeping with.

"When I was a child, my parents had a home out on the north fork of Long Island. It was a place called Mattituck, and from what I have heard that was an Indian word for 'Great Creek'. They had a small summer home near a place called James Creek that lead out to the Long Island. It was an amazing place. Everywhere you looked there were boats. You could walk around the beach half the day and not see anyone. There were clam bakes that my father put together. He would just dig holes right in the sand and pull out handfuls of fresh steamers." Mac could imagine the taste as his father would hand him one off the grill. The brine would enter his mouth first, followed by the clam; his dad always squeezed some lemon on them before he handed them over. The lemon worked perfectly with the taste of the sea and the slightly chewy clam.

As Mac sat there explaining to Magen about those beautiful summer days of his past, he was totally unaware of the large red Hummer H2 speeding at them over his left shoulder.

CHAPTER 109

Jeb let the paper fall to the table when he heard the crash outside.

People in the café were scrambling to the window to see what was going on outside. Jeb held back a second thinking that it might be a trick, a sniper trying to draw him to the window.

He needed to know, so he held the paper to his face and found a vantage point where he could see the action, and if someone opened fire, none of the patrons would be in the cross fire.

He watched as a middle-aged soldier stumble out of the passenger seat of the downed Hummer and opened fire at the BMW; a short burst across the windshield bounced off neatly from the bulletproof glass.

The Beamer still had some movement potential as it slammed ahead and crunched the dazed soldier between both cars. His scream was painful to hear, as both legs were shattered in multiple places. His weapon let out a final burst as he began to lose consciousness.

Two running bystanders were hit by the random fire, and a bank window exploded. People were screaming and fleeing the area. The BMW limped down to the corner and hung a right.

Jeb guessed that must have been the cavalry that his friend sent to bring him in.

Jeb slowly withdrew toward the back, pushed through the double doors, and walked slowly past all the kitchen staff who were twisting their necks to see the terrible tragedy that had unfolded on this beautiful morning.

Jeb stepped outside into the fresh morning air and realized from the faint breeze that he was sweating. He was surrounded by old, stained brick and smelly dumpsters that filled the area. He only had one option, and that was to cross into the building directly behind the café and emerge out in the front of the next street over.

His guess was that the vehicle wouldn't make it that far.

Holding his side, he scrambled over a small brick wall then made his way through the gate. He saw the sign for Poplar Trail and he tried to hurry his pace toward Taylor Avenue.

He felt sharp pain every time he took a step. Jeb rounded the corner and saw the vehicle; it was smoking and finished; he could smell the oil burning.

There was a knockout blonde standing outside holding her shoulder and trying to conceal the weapon in her hand under her folded arm. Jeb could also see that the driver was slamming his left shoulder sharply against the driver's door, trying to force it open.

He wondered if the driver might be in shock, that door had no chance of coming free. Jeb had reached twenty-five yards from the car when the woman spun around and leveled a 9-millimeter at him.

Jeb stopped dead in his track and thought for just one second that just maybe he had calculated wrong.

The woman then dropped her weapon and breathed a sigh of deep relief; Jeb did as well.

She turned her attention back to the car and reached in and grabbed the man by the collar and yanked him to the passenger side of the car.

As Jeb approached, he could see that this action caused the woman incredible pain as she sunk to her knees. Jeb helped her up and then caught sight of the driver whose face was covered in blood.

He was able to get him out of the car and stand him up against the back door. The man was dazed and confused but not totally out of it and seemed to be clearing. The blood seemed to be coming from a two-inch gash right above the hairline.

Jeb dug in the hole just to see if the man's skull was compromised. Mac quickly snatched his hand and removed it, his focus returning instantly.

"There will be no need for all that!" Mac said with noted agitation as he cleared the blood from his eyes.

"Glad to see you're still with us. That was some extremely good driving!" Jeb smiled.

"I'm glad I could entertain you. Who are those sick fucks? I thought I saw a Special Forces tattoo on the one I hit," Mac stated as he continued to blink and wipe blood from his face.

"Later. We really need to get the hell out of this place and fast," Jeb said, still holding his own injury.

"Stop!" Magen screamed as she stepped into the middle of Taylor Avenue and lowered her weapon at a passing Buick. The vehicle locked its brakes and came within an inch of hitting her.

The man at the wheel looked angrier than upset. Magen placed her hand on the hood of the car as if this was going to hold the car in place. She turned to the two men and barked orders to move.

"Is she always like this?" Jeb asked as he and Mac worked their way over to the car.

"No, she is being extra gentle this morning!" Mac spat out from the blood in his mouth.

"Well, I guess we should get in the car," Jeb stated as he helped Mac into the back seat.

"I will need you to get out of the vehicle right this second!" Magen screamed as she opened the car door and leveled the weapon at the driver's shocked face.

"Okay, just don't shoot!" the young man, who was visibly shaken and confused, said as he ran from the vehicle.

"Is that wound addressed?" Magen asked, looking as she punched the gas.

"It will need attention in the next few hours, but I can travel," Jeb said with a slight smile breaking from his face.

"I have no idea how to get out of this town. I'm just driving!" Magen announced.

"You're doing just great. You want to make a left on Route 50, and you will be able to follow signs north from there," Jeb said as he turned to look at Mac, who was still dazed in the back seat.

"So, you must be Jeb. We were sent to come get you. Somehow, I thought that was going to be slightly easier," Mac joked and continued to hold pressure against his scalp wound.

"I could tell you what a horror show it has been to get this far, but it looks like you folks have had your own challenges," Jeb stated as both Mac and Magen acknowledged his statement with a weary smile.

"So, what agency is trying to kill you, and do they work for aliens or against them?" Mac asked, only to feel how crazy he would sound just saying it.

"I think it is our agency or some faction of the American government. I'm not sure what aliens have to do with anything," Jeb stated, but an automatic feel of guardedness began to creep into his mind.

"So, you are unaware that we are truly not alone in this universe?" Mac said as he stared at the back of the agent's shaved head.

"I am aware of discussions of that possibility!" Jeb stated as he looked at the window.

"Possibility. Would you boys at the CIA care to enlighten us on just how long those possibilities have been circling that big jarhead?" Mac's words shot out mixed with blood and spit; the agent in the front seat didn't flinch.

"The doctor and the two containers that your team were guarding at the house, where are they?" Magen asked and could see her words were hurting the agent deeply.

"I have been hearing of the alien talk for twenty-plus years. However, I understand that they may have been here much longer," Jeb stated slowly and with limited emotion.

"Standard CIA policy. Don't ask, don't tell, right?" Mac added as he found a T-shirt in the back seat and began to remove the blood from his face.

"So, who are you people?" Jeb asked as the car merged onto Route 40.

CHAPTER 110

Cain stepped out between two mammoth stones and took in a deep breath from the higher altitude and paused for a second just to allow his body to adjust.

He stood in the ancient ruins of Peru, South America. The old stone city was once known as Ollantaytambo; it had been reduced to mostly rubble over time.

Cain stepped out into the light and searched the area, taking in every stone, trying to remember where everything was back then. He recalled being on the same spot centuries earlier and taking his first human breath.

This was one of the four windows on Earth; they were all destroyed during the final war. He recalled the night the decision was reached by the council to evacuate and obliterate this site, the sadness that they all felt.

The thought of the window falling into the hands of the enemy would have been catastrophic. He took in his surroundings and remembered just how magnificent all this was back then; what greatness the council demonstrated back then. They were a glorious race in those brief moments in time; he lamented the loss.

He turned a corner to find two elderly women holding baskets. They were dressed in traditional work garments of the region, polleras and morteras; he knew that some of the locals came here on occasion to leave gifts of worship. They were most likely descendants of the original tribes of the region. He wondered if they were alone or part of a bigger party; he didn't need company.

"Good Morning," Cain said in flawless Quechua, an ancient dialect that he spoke in that same village a thousand years earlier. He was surprised that he was able to recall the language so freely.

The two women were shocked and quickly covered their eyes and began to pray in hopes that the ghost would go away.

Cain stepped past the two women and continued up the path to what was once known as the Field of Faces. He glanced back at the two locals who were helping each other down the hill. He thought of the wondrous stories they would be telling their friends and families that night. It was not uncommon to see Europeans investigating the ruins, but they never came alone and always came through the village. He realized that his presence and the dialogue he used at the greeting could only mean one thing for them.

He thought for just a second that it might be best to stop them, but the village was an hour from the temple, and he would be long gone in twenty minutes. He walked out to the base of the field and took in the wall of faces that were carved in stone. They looked at him with their cold expressions, and in his mind, he thought that they were happy for his return.

Cain could still hear sporadic grunts and yelps from the running women; their noise echoed through the ruins. He recalled the days when this place was alive and the ship that often hovered over the window. That's what was missing from his memory, the hum of the ship.

At first when he stepped from the portal, he thought it was the emptiness of the ruins that gave it that dull feel. Now he recalled the ship that would hover seventy feet above the window and let out a mild harmony that changed both the tone and the color of the entire city.

As he slowly made his way along the wall, he glanced at the faces and thought of the fine people who helped build this city. He knew they had scattered after the time of leaving, but he would always wonder if they had made the right decision.

Cain stopped at the bend in the wall and saw the face he was looking for; it was his, or at least the Cain who came first in the time of greatness.

He held his hand to the face, and it began to glow; light from his energy was interacting with the stone.

An opening appeared above the face.

Cain reached in and removed three round orbs and held them in his palm. It looked as if age had taken its toll on these marble-like relics. Then they began to glow from the energy within Cain; life seemed to flow from him and then back.

They began to rise from his hands and then spin counterclockwise. He looked satisfied at the development and let them fall back in his hand. He knew that if he was to stay here on Earth, he would need to be cautious of these power sources. Humans were developing fast, and it would only be a century or so before they were able to isolate the signature of such great power right on their own planet.

He knew just the three orbs that he held in his hand were enough to eradicate all organic life on the planet within moments. Before he made his peace with these people, the seeds would need to be dealt with.

Minutes later, he was standing back at the arch. He took one more deep breath and stepped backward. He was gone!

CHAPTER 111

A single tear rolled down the face of Heather Worthington; she had reached her breaking point.

She sat at her desk holding the phone to her ear as the major explained his absolute failure in Annapolis.

As he spoke, she contemplated his death; she needed serious reserve at this moment. Her job was far from completion, and she knew that it was going to take every resource that she had at her disposal. However, she was able to ease the pain of his incredible blunder by imagining cutting his throat herself.

She looked down at her hands; they were shaking from her anger. She knew how to deal with these moments of pure rage. She reached into her desk and pulled a pair of needle-nose pliers and latched onto the fingernail of her index finger.

She held the phone away from her face as the major rambled on about his inability to control his war dogs.

Helen slowly twisted her fingernail upward as blood began to trickle out and skin parted from the nail; she let out a faint whimper. The major stopped midsentence and asked, "Is everything all right, Mrs. Worthington?"

"No, Major, there is nothing all right. We have a significant cleanup that needs to be activated. You and your men should be a million miles from Annapolis by the time we hang up, understood?" Helen stated through clenched teeth, working diligently to remove the anger from her voice.

"Yes, understood. Do you wish for us to pursue and eliminate the CIA agent?" the major asked, half knowing the answer that would follow.

"No, you and your men and everybody else down there need to head north to await further instruction!" she said and clicked off the phone.

"Right!"

He heard the phone go dead and stared at it for several seconds.

The major walked to the van; they were at a rest stop off Interstate 95.

He opened the door and climbed into the passenger seat. The driver who had been watching his facial expressions since he started the phone call watched him now and recognized deep concern. He had seen that look on his commander's face only twice. First time was in Iraq minutes before an ambush almost killed the whole squad. The second time was when he accepted the money from the Worthington lawyer.

This whole thing felt wrong from the moment that envelope entered Schmitt's hand. They were now guilty of killing American soldiers, and the pain he felt in the pit of his stomach was not even close to the debt they owed those men.

"Are we going after them?" the soldier at the wheel asked.

"No, we are ordered to stand down and await orders!" Schmitt stated.

"That is total bullshit. We're fucked, aren't we?" the big soldier from the back seat said through clenched teeth as his shattered knee was being addressed.

"We don't know that. They must have a plan B that will tag the car heading up to New York, isn't that right, major?" the driver barked as he turned in his chair to stress his hopeful position.

"Well, I don't think so. I tend to think we are pretty much fucked!" Schmitt stated, almost smiling or at least coming to grips with the fundamental truth.

"I knew this was all wrong. How the hell did I think I could kill American soldiers and it would be okay?" the big man in the back seat yelled.

"To be honest, that isn't sitting well with me, not to mention those two little freaks of nature that we passed off!" the major said with anxiety in his voice.

"We need to get the hell out of the country. That crazy bitch is going to wax us first chance she gets!" the driver said.

"That is a harsh reality and something that we need to consider. I can get us to Mexico if we head south to Florida now!" Schmitt said softly, almost whispering.

"Shit, I hate that bitch!" the big man said from the back as the driver threw the van in gear.

"Yeah, I have a pretty high level of hate for her, and I'm not so keen on running away!" Schmitt stated with newfound resolution.

"Fuck Mexico. Let's end that Jason bitch!" the big man cried from the back.

"Sounds like a plan. Get them before they get us!" Schmitt stated as he pulled the seat belt across his chest.

CHAPTER 112

Cornell Pierce woke with a scream, grabbed at his hand to try to stop the bleeding.

He started to relax, then realized that his hand was just fine.

He was sweating and finding it really hard to breathe. He had spent about ten minutes of interview time with two of the scientists when he began to feel light-headed.

He was told that he was going to be fine, but some of his blood work was off.

He didn't know just how long he was sleeping, but he felt like his ability was returning.

Cornell really wanted to talk with Dean about what he learned about the aliens. He wasn't sure if they were all aware of just how dangerous these things were.

He rose to his feet and slipped into flip-flops that were on the floor and motioned for the door. The second he touched the door, the lights went on, and a high-pitched alarm began to sound on the other side of the door.

Cornell stepped back, trying to get a grip of what was going on.

"Mr. Pierce, we are going to need you to sit on the bed. You haven't been cleared by ID yet."

"I need to talk with Mr. Dean. It is really important," Cornell spoke out to the camera in the corner with dripping fear.

"We will arrange for a face-to-face in the next twenty minutes. Please continue present isolation protocol."

"No problem. I am not looking to make waves. I just want some straight talk!" Cornell stressed.

"Thank you, Mr. Pierce!" said the voice, sounding pleasant.

Cornell started to concern himself about being restricted to the room.

He sat rubbing his new hand, wondering if he had been infected somehow. His fear level was mounting, and he began to feel tight pressure in his chest. The voice in his head was fighting back, telling him to relax. However, the negative voice was simply stating that *you just don't get your hand back for free*!

The room was slowly closing in on him, and he could feel himself getting sick.

He thought how crazy this whole thing had been, his teeth being ripped from his skull, alien tigers, his hand being bitten off.

He had worked for the government for over thirty years, and he knew that he just wasn't going home to Helen, his good wife, and everything was just going to go back to normal.

Cornell began to weep.

"Cornell, what's going on?" the voice of Mr. Dean came over the speaker.

"I know too much, don't I, Mr. Dean? I have seen it all, and they can't let me go now, can they?" Cornell was somewhere between crying and angry as his voiced cracked.

"I'll be right down!" Dean clicked off, and in seconds, he had the door open and grabbed his friend.

"I'm sorry, Mr. Dean, I don't want to be acting this way, can't help it!" Cornell continued to grip his friend's arms.

"I know what you are thinking. We are not playing that game!" Dean yelled as his voiced cracked.

"I'm sorry, I don't want to cause no problem for you."

Cornell was emotional and fearful.

"Let's go! You just need to get the hell out of this room," Dean stated as he helped his friend to the door.

"It's all right. I'm just really having some bad thoughts, that's all. Don't get yourself all jammed up on my account."

"Open the door!" Dean yelled up at the camera and waited through a long, uncomfortable pause.

Bzzzzzzzzzzzzz.

"Let's get the hell out of here, Cornell," he said as they walked through the door into the face of Commander Smith.

"I know that it is difficult to be isolated after what you have been through. There are elements in your blood that are concerning," the commander stated.

"What kind of elements?" Cornell said with obvious concern.

"That seems to be the bigger question. The science behind what has happened to you and your hand is beyond our scope," Smith stated and placed his hand on Cornell.

"I don't really think isolation is necessary. This man is no danger to anyone!" Mr. Dean was firm and forceful.

"Oh, we are not afraid of him. We are afraid for him!"

Smith grabbed a small Geiger counter off the table and ran it by Cornell's hand.

The machine reacted.

"What does this mean?" Cornell looked at his friend.

"The radiation in your blood emanating from your hand is doing something to your white blood cells. We are not sure what that is. However, if your white cells are being vanquished from your body, even a common cold could kill you. The germs on Mr. Dean's arm could be fatal."

Smith looked at Cornell, who registered full understanding and backed away from his friend.

"I have been kidding myself when that monster bit my hand off. I knew that was going to be the end of me," Cornell said, softly accepting his situation.

"Listen, you need to have some faith. They are not saying anything, but they don't know. They just need a little time," Dean pressed his friend.

"Well, I guess that I will wait for the news. Don't make sense to walk out of here now." Mr. Pierce turned and reentered the room.

"We need to fix this!" Dean said to Commander Smith who nodded and reached for the vibrating phone in his pocket.

"Hello, Smith!" The commander recognized the Langley number.

"Smith, I am not looking for an answer. Early this morning we received word of a firefight outside of Annapolis, Maryland. Five minutes ago, we learned that there was a second event in downtown Annapolis, with two dead, weapons in the streets, and multiple car fires. I don't want to know what it is. It seems your personal vehicle was listed as one of the fires. I just hung up with CNN. Those idiots think the citadel is under terrorist attack. Like I said, I don't want to know, but someone humped the bunk on this one. It needs to go away!"

Then there was silence, not even a click from the phone hanging up. Just silence.

"Please excuse me, something has come up!"

He turned and walked away.

CHAPTER 113

"Let us please offer a sign of peace!" Father Frank Nica said with a great big smile and familiarity to the members of his congregation.

The good father had been the senior priest here at St. Michael's in Somerset, New Jersey, for the past seven years. He had completed his final tour in Afghanistan, hung up his helmet, and opened his Bible.

He remembered the day he left that ugly country for good, how tears wouldn't stop coming. People who looked at him and made attempts to console him thought he was just happy that it was all over. The truth was that he wept only because he would need to stop killing that day.

He knew God had given him a great gift to have the strength to look into the face of a man and take his life without judgment.

On that day, he felt fear and a loss of purpose. It was the first time he had felt those feelings since the rifle was placed in his hands.

Then the people came to him and gave him hope and direction, showed him the path.

Today he talked with his flock about the need for community and the importance of forgiveness. He loved this part of the mass when everyone stopped thinking about themselves and looked into the faces of their neighbors.

He could see their faces change gears from being alone to that sense of belonging.

Frank walked over to the altar boys, James and Timmy. They loved it when Father Frank would shake their hands; the other priests just stood by the big table watching the crowd.

There were others on the altar today, and Father Frank didn't miss anyone; validating his people was a great strength.

As he walked back to the podium, he turned and scanned the congregation. Three rows back in the middle of the pew was a small Arab child. Father Frank could see that the child's left eye was missing. As the child turned his head to shake hands, Frank could see that the back of the child's head was also missing.

Frank remembered the day he shot the child.

He blew off the youngster's ankle off with a .50-caliber from about seven hundred yards. The child hit the floor and screamed for his mother and father.

Frank would kill both the mother and father that day.

The child's father was an American-trained bomb maker named Hafi Nodal who thought it would go unnoticed that he was utilizing his skill to kill Americans.

Frank didn't care much about politics; to him, Hafi was simply the six of clubs.

The child's eyes locked with Frank's; they smiled at each other. The ghosts that visited St. Michael's were never really angry.

"Go in peace, to love one another!" Father Frank smiled brightly as he raised his arms and prayed for his parishioners.

As the people filed out, Frank contemplated how he would still do random works for his government from time to time. There were many things that people didn't need to understand about him.

Frank placed his Bible on the podium and saw that his phone was vibrating. The name that was illuminated on the screen was H. Worthington.

Frank thought to himself, *Think of the devil and the devil will think of you!*

He picked up the phone and held it to his ear.

"Hello, Frank, you are being called by your father!" Helen said with stainless conviction.

"Will I find the envelope in the confessional as is our agreed protocol?" Frank said, not wanting to discuss anything on the phone.

"I am sorry to change the process. We have reached critical mass here, and there is a soldier on the front stoop of your church."

"Helen, are you telling me that Hannibal is at porters?" Frank partially joked, recalling the whispered old tales. He then pulled a 9-millimeter from a compartment in the podium.

"I don't understand. He has a case that will provide you with everything you require," Helen added, confused by his statement.

"I understand!" he stated and hung up the phone.

However, he didn't understand. Frank instantly felt that his number had come up, occupational hazard of his line of work.

He leapt from the pulpit, folding his weapon under his robe. The church had emptied, and there was a great peacefulness that Frank felt as he moved briskly through the building. He pressed his back to the large wooden door and then snapped his eyes out the small stained glass window.

He then moved his face from the window with equal quickness.

His mind was trained to see so much in the cluster of seconds. There was an army officer standing on the second stoop of the church, the soldier was a major; there were two buttons on his lapel that indicated that the man had spent some time at West Point. The soldier also had seen combat and had suffered an injury; he stood as if he might be utilizing a prosthetic.

The roof across the street was empty; so was the top floor of the neighboring apartments. If they had sent another sniper to end him, that's where he would be.

Frank clicked the safety off his weapon and slowly pushed open the heavy door.

"Good morning, my son, is there no interest in coming into the house of God on this fine morning?" Frank stated, noticing for the first time that the man was Afro-American, extremely light skinned, but a black man all the same.

"I don't do steps!" the soldier said as he held up a black case.

"I noticed. Thank you for your service and for what you have contributed!" the father stated as he took the case and looked down at the left leg of the man.

"Okay then!" the soldier said and turned on his good leg and began to step off the curb.

"Go with God, my son!" the priest said as he backed to the heavy wooden door and went back into the church.

The priest placed the case slowly on the table and ran his fingers around the exterior to check for wires.

Nervously he clicked the first latch and then the second, almost bracing himself for a potential explosion. He lifted the lid only about a half inch, then, utilizing the overhead light, made another pass for wiring. Feeling that it was safe, he lifted the lid, fully exposing the contents.

There was an eighty-by-ten photo sitting right on top. Frank held up the photo.

"Officer MacDonald, what on earth have you done to anger the evil queen?" the priest said out loud as he picked up the second photo.

"Pretty lady, I can understand why the evil queen wants your head! Hey, you're a federal agent!"

Frank placed the photo down; he began to feel uncomfortable. The thought of killing an agent for the government was something that he had never been asked to do.

He glanced down at the third picture and froze.

The picture was an old shot of a soldier in full dress blues, all the pretty metals hanging off his barrel chest.

He knew that face; Frank's mind drifted back to Iraq when he was just a kid. There was a training operation that went wrong; IUD took out their truck. He was injured, and his eardrum had popped. He woke up in the evac chopper looking straight into those blue eyes that reassured him he was in good hands and he would live.

"No! This is wrong! I can't kill this man, you know that," Frank was talking to the life-size Christ that hung on the cross.

"Is this how it ends between us? If I don't do my job they come and end me, and I can't let harm come to this man!"

Frank sat back on a big chair to the left of the podium, letting the photos fall from his hand. He wrenched his hands together and prayed for several minutes.

Father Frank rose to his feet, keeping his eyes fixed on the statue of Christ, his eyes wet with tears. Then a great wave of relaxation spread through his face, and his jolly smile returned.

He realized that he had only one direction to take. There would be killing. God would guide where the dead would fall.

"Behold, your instrument!" he said aloud with hands raised.

CHAPTER 114

"We need to pull off one of these exits. Get our focus together," Jeb stated to Magen who was still breathing hard.

"What? I don't think so. We need to put some real distance between us and that assault team back there!" Magen said, confused by the statement.

"No, we need to pull off, change everything we are doing!" Jeb had real conviction in his voice.

"What are you talking about? We have orders to take you back to Brooklyn!" Magen still kept her high rate of speed.

"MacDonald, what's the fastest way to go to New York?" Jeb cocked his head and pressed the question.

"You take 95 to the Jersey Turnpike!" Mac answered, not yet following the logic of the CIA agent.

"How else would you go, if you wanted to avoid the turnpike?" Jeb pressed.

"I don't know. I never took an alternate route!" Mac sat up, wanting to follow the logic.

"Of course not, there really is only one way to go, unless you take a huge detour through Pennsylvania. They know this too!" Jeb finalized his point.

"There could be another team up ahead just waiting for us!" Mac said with acknowledgment.

Jeb could feel the car begin to slow down, at least to a reasonable speed. Magen breathed out a deep sigh and looked over at Jeb.

"They could mobilize a sniper in less than an hour. We need to get off this highway!" Magen had gained back her composure and realized their situation.

"We need to be somewhat spontaneous because predictable could kill us, and fast!" Jeb stated and rifled through the glove box in hopes of finding a map. However, it didn't seem to matter. Magen floated the car off the blacktop and turned the wheel and applied the brake.

The car slid on the grass for about thirty feet, then turned, facing the way they came. She gunned the gas; within seconds, they were heading back the way they came.

"I guess that was the spontaneous part!" Jeb stated as he released his white knuckles from the dashboard; the smell of burned rubber was overwhelming.

"She's good at that!" Mac stated from the back.

CHAPTER 115

Dr. Jason Daly stepped out of the car and took in several quick, deep breaths that didn't have the smell of the two passengers in the back boot.

He saw the sign for South Nyack right before the vehicle turned off the interstate.

He knew the large bridge that loomed over the treetops about a mile away; he just couldn't remember the name.

They seemed to be at some type of large farming building. It was too dark to make out everything, but he could see several buildings from the vehicle headlights. He could smell the woods and pine, but no sound.

A dense stretch of woods like this without any sound didn't make sense.

Jason was not sure why they drove all day just to make a five-hour trip; he assumed that they needed to make sure they were not being followed.

The cages were taken quickly from the vehicle, and then he was led by the man not in uniform to another section of the building.

The young man swiped his badge, and the latch on the barn door popped with a buzz. He opened the door, and the light was severely bright, causing Jason to shade his eyes.

It took a few seconds for both men to adjust their vision and begin to walk through the large structure.

Jason still couldn't decipher what kind of building it was. He saw large generators and even larger tanks against one wall. There were vaulted storage areas throughout the structure. He was led to a small office that looked like some type of control room. At the back of the room was a door, which the man pointed to. Jason stepped through the opening, and the light instantly clicked on.

It was an elevator; Jason smiled at the man, who didn't return his enthusiasm. The man opened a keypad and placed his eye over a glass cylinder. Green light ran the length of the eye, then there was a slight pause.

All at once, it felt like the floor fell from under him.

It was just two to three seconds, but he estimated that he had descended at least a hundred feet.

"I don't mind if you're not a talker, but a little warning would have been reasonable!" Jason stated with some conviction; still no response from the man as he reached for the handle and swung the door open.

"Holy shit, are you kidding me? Who the hell built this?"

Jason stood in awe as his eyes spread through the immense structure. He wasn't much of an engineer, but he estimated that the multilevel structure was the length of four to five football fields.

It was arranged almost like a beehive with chambers branching out from the center. He could make out storage rooms that were open; other rooms were vaulted. There were weapons and vehicles, and that was just what was visible. Jason thought that this must be some type of first-response facility in an event of nuclear detonation in Manhattan.

He continued to marvel at the sheer size of the facility until the soldier called at him.

"Doctor, please stay with me, not much further from here," the soldier stated as he turned to find Jason twenty feet behind.

"Yes, sir! Coming." Jason broke free from his shock and hustled over to the man with the unhappy disposition. "I know you are under orders, but can you guys give me some type of clue why I am here?" Jason appealed to the man who didn't seem overly interested.

"Just stay with me. The scientists that are waiting for you can explain everything!" he said with some distaste, not looking at him at all.

"Scientists? What do I have to offer?" Jason stated, now more confused.

The young soldier shrugged his shoulder and pointed to a series of large doors. As they approached, the large vault door opened, most likely on a type of computerized release.

As the two entered the area, they could instantly hear the voices of several people and the churning of computers. A group of white-coated physicians stood looking at him. They were gloved and masked, appearing ominous and cruel. When they noticed his arrival, there was a lengthy pause. Two of the men removed both mask and gloves and approached him. The others went back to scrambling with several boxes of equipment.

CHAPTER 116

Lighting went on in the adjoining room, and the wall to the left illuminated, indicating some type of viewing station.

As Jason stepped to the window, a deep chilling pain rose from deep in his belly. Before him was an exact replica of Tiger Mountain at the Bronx Zoo. He had spent three years at that zoo completing his dissertation. Jason stood there in total shock at the sight before him. He thought to himself that the original took almost fifteen months to build. This is not something that has just come to light, as the agent said when they picked him up in New Jersey this morning.

This habitat didn't take form overnight, even with a city of military people working on it.

Jason then laid eyes on two familiar cages that he traveled with. They sat side by side in the open viewing area. Jason started to breathe deeply, finally realizing why he was here.

He was the new caretaker to the strange subhumans that stared out their cage doors, with fear in their dark eyes.

He turned to look at the men in all white that were flanking him. He nodded his head and held up his arms for them to hold their ground. The scientists were approaching with spray sanitizers; he thought that would not work in his favor.

"I think the spray would confuse these two. They seem to be activating on a primitive level," Jason stated, and the white coats held up.

"What about cross contamination from you to them?" the man closest to him stated.

"I think I'm more concerned with their feeding cycle. When did they eat last?" Jason asked as he continued to gear up, waiting for a response that didn't come.

"Our data is incomplete on their eating habits," the older gentleman stated with some noted anxiety.

"Well, I think before I go in there we should at least see if they are hungry. What do you think?" Jason said with a hint of sarcasm in his voice.

"Again, we really don't have a point of reference on what these beings are capable of eating," the older man stated and then realized that silence had grown within the room.

"That is the first time that I heard anyone refer to those creatures in the cages as beings. I think I am not being provided with adequate data!" Jason stated with both confusion and growing anger.

"Dr. Daly, my name is Perry Bolton. I am employed by a gentleman named Fanning who has a considerable investment in our young friends in the cages. I would like to bring you up to speed, if you will allow me?" Bolton stressed with a long smile that seemed to stretch around his head.

"I am open to any and all light that can drag me from the darkness," Jason continued in a sarcastic tone, but the man just laughed and led him to a section of chairs.

"We recently came into possession of our two friends. Their primary caregiver was killed in an unfortunate accident, not related to our two children!" Bolton began.

"Well, that is some good news, I guess. What are they?" Jason asked.

"That is a very difficult question. We are not sure, and we also think that they may have been tampered with!"

Bolton was searching the room as he spoke, as if that part of the conversation was uncomfortable.

"How do you mean tampered with, like genetics?" Jason shot back, confused.

"Possibly. We think that behavior modification was not utilized effectively. It appears the prior trainer was feeding their aggressive nature!" Bolton rose from his chair and walked to the viewing room as he spoke.

"Have they demonstrated aggression toward humans?" Jason asked, half knowing the answer to his question.

"Yes, there have been people injured. I don't have all the facts," Perry turned back to Jason, lying with his best straight face.

"So how was I recommended for this assignment?" Jason was curious.

"I am not really sure, but you do come highly recommended among your peers, and all of this is really at your disposal." Bolton was selling, and he really didn't want to come off like that.

One of the white coats approached at that moment. He was older and carried himself like he was familiar with having authority; he began to explain that they had reached a decision on how to feed the two caged beings.

They had placed small explosives on the locking pins that could be remotely detonated. They had arranged for a goat to be tied twenty feet from the front of the cage. They would blow the pins and allow the beings to feed. After that, they felt they might be approachable and much easier to deal with.

"I think if you utilize explosives anywhere near the cages, they will never return to them," Jason stated, fully aware of the fact that he was volunteering to join this insanity.

"How else would we open the cages?" the older man asked.

"Well, I'm not here to stand on the sidelines. I will need to remove the charges, and I don't want to blow my hands off!" Jason said in a take-charge way.

"This is highly unadvisable. The two guests are in a heightened state! It is too soon!" the older man was passionate about what he was saying.

"You are most likely right, but I am still going in. I feel that it's time!" Jason stated as he began to walk to the window.

"What makes this the right time?" Bolton asked as he stepped next to Jason at the window.

"If I don't do this soon, I'm going to chicken out and be of no use to anyone!" Jason said through a smile, but he knew he was being somewhat honest.

"I do like your style, Dr. Daly!" Bolton laughed.

They both started to the door then Bolton turned to stifle the small protests of the scientists.

Jason stood at the viewing window with his palms sweating.

He was attempting to formulate some type of strategy in his head on how to survive contact.

From where he was standing, he could see the face of the male of the species. Jason could see that its dark eyes were fixed on the viewing area. However, from that angle, it would be impossible to see its own reflection, so what could it be focused on?

Jason moved around to both sides of the viewing area, looking at multiple angles and becoming more puzzled.

Bolton walked up next to Jason with a quizzical look stretched across his face.

"What are you looking at?" Perry asked, trying to line up his vision where Jason was looking.

"I'm trying to understand what our little friend is so intently focused on!" Jason said.

"He seems to be looking in this direction. Don't you think he is looking at us?" Perry asked, still puzzled.

"This is a viewing port. There is a reflective surface on the other side, and my first thought was that it might be looking at its own reflection, but the angle is not lining up," Jason stated as he continued looking around.

"That is strange. Maybe that thing has X-ray vision!" Bolton joked, but Jason and the older scientist looked at each other with acknowledgment that maybe this being's vision operated at a different level.

"Is there any way we can test if this being is capable of infrared sight?" Jason asked the scientist who was already formulating that very test.

"I think there is a way we could determine that!" he stated as he picked up the phone.

"There is a very good chance that our friends in there don't see life the same way we do," Jason said to Bolton, but he could see that he had only confused him more.

"The equipment we need is on the way!" the older scientist stated as he called over to his team to stop what they were doing and join him near the viewing port.

"So, my comment about X-ray vision was just a joke, you know that, right?" Bolton stated as he watched the room start to churn with energy.

"You would be amazed at just how many animals on this planet have optical variations and see life on a different level!" Jason said as he watched the being that continued watching from the cage.

"Nothing amazes me anymore, Doctor. Are you thinking that this being can sense where we are?" Perry asked.

"There is a possibility that it can track a heat signature, possible infrared. I am not sure," Jason stated as the scientist came back into the room.

"Okay, I have six pairs of night vision optical enhancement glasses and these three lead heat shields. I think we should line up and place these glasses on and turn out the light. Three of us put these heat shields on and the others walk into the next room. Now, if the being follows the others walking into the room, then you might be right about that infrared ability!" the older scientist stated as he handed the long heat shields to both Jason and Perry.

"This should work. Is there any way we could hit the lights in the big room?" Jason said out loud.

"Tell me when you're ready!" the older man said as he fitted the night vision glasses.

"Let's do it!" Jason said, and the lights in the area went dark.

"Please, gentlemen, if you would just walk into the adjoining room so we can test this theory!" the scientist in charge motioned to the three white coats without heat shields.

"I am having difficulty seeing the subject even with these glasses!" Jason stated with frustration in his voice.

"There is an adjustment slide on the right-hand side. Move it slightly upward!" the scientist said as the three other white coats walked to the other room.

"Not a flinch! Subject's eyes have not even shifted," Jason stated with obvious disappointment in his voice.

"The strange thing is that this being seems to be focused right here at the viewing port!" Bolton stated as he looked deep into the eyes of their guest.

"Dr. Daly, I would like to attempt to investigate one other theory if you are willing," the older scientist requested.

"What do you have in mind?" Jason was surprised by the request.

"Would you be open to joining the team in the other room?" he asked, almost embarrassed by his request.

"What? Why do you think that would change anything?" Jason cocked his head with confusion.

"Just a theory. You sat near the cages for five hours. Your scent might play a role in what is going on."

"All right, let's check that possibility out!" Jason said as he removed the heat shield and started walking.

"Wow! I think you have a stalker. You are being tracked from your first step!" Bolton called out with amazement.

"You're kidding. It's me that has it focused."

"Well, maybe going into the cage isn't the worst idea I originally thought it was. You seem to have made a connection!" the older scientist stated as he removed the glasses and flipped on the lights.

"Unless it associates me with its imprisonment, then I am toast!" Jason spoke more to his own fear than the men in the room.

"That is a distinct possibility. You're right about that!" the man said.

"I once went into a snow leopard's cage and removed a shaft of bone that was logged in its jawbone!" Jason stated openly, in hopes that his courage would be jump-started.

"Well, that does give you some bragging rights in this room!" Bolton said with an apprehensive grin.

"We need to do this now. If I wait any longer, my brain is going to stop me from entering that room!" Jason said as he walked to the door.

"We can provide you with a bomb suit if you think that might help?" one of the white coats near the door asked.

"No, but can we turn the lights down? It might calm them!"

Jason stepped through the door and stopped as the large door shut behind him.

CHAPTER 117

He had not ventured more than three steps when the smell of the two beings found his nose.

Instantly, fear dragged its bony fingers along the cut of his spine. Jason fought the initial feeling to run for the door.

The goat that had been staked out there for a food source had shifted and made what was most likely a plea for help. Jason had forgotten about the goat in all the excitement and was frightened beyond all reason when the noise came.

He sat there shaking and gripping his chest, hoping that his heart wouldn't leap from his body. In his mind voices battled with him to accept reason and flee from the room before it was too late. He knew that animals could smell fear and sense when prey was weak.

At this point controlling his fear was not working out too well.

The lactic acid was building up in his body, and everything hurt. His stomach was a boiling volcano that was creeping its way up his throat.

He had reached the back of the cage and then stopped. His hands were trembling, his breathing was erratic and he found that sweat was now streaming down both sides of his face.

He saw where the charges were connected to the cage locking pins. He moved to the cage where the damaged female of the species was curled in a fetal position. He was unable to see her face.

He pulled in a deep breath and held it.

Now positioned on the side of the cage, he reached out and removed the charge. Jason placed it slowly on the ground and then moved to the cage of the male. He didn't approach from the front; if he looked in that creature's eyes at that very moment, he would run away screaming.

After removing the charges and securing them, he removed the first locking pin from the cage of the female, then the second.

The cage showed no movement; he wondered if she had possibly died of her wounds.

Jason moved over to the second cage; he bent slowly and slid out the first locking pin. He exhaled, then took another deep breath and reached for the final pin.

As his fingers neared the mechanism, the cage door exploded as a dark shadow raced from the container. Jason reeled back and fell on the side of the cage. He picked up his head just in time to see the creature use both mouth and claws to rip the goat in half. The goat had put up only mild protest as his life was taken long before it saw the attacker.

The being turned the animal over and with his extended claws removed the skin and fur almost instantly. Then with the speed that it displayed on exiting the cage, it returned to the female cage.

Jason sat there shaking, his skin cold from fear. Then he began to hear the banging on the viewing window and there were voices yelling over the overhead system.

"*Run, run!*"

The words were starting to drill through his fear.

He managed to get to his feet and stumble to the door. There was a horrifying feeling that kept racing through his head that he was not going to make it. He looked back several times, half expecting to see the being on his heels.

There was no sign of the creature that butchered a goat in the time it took him to raise his head.

Jason reached out his hand for the door, wondering why it hadn't been opened already. Jason stopped cold only to find that his hand was holding the small hand of the creature who somehow managed to beat him to the door.

The banging had stopped as well as the screaming over the intercom. Jason turned his head and found himself looking directly into the eyes of the male being.

The dark red eyes fixed him like a stone, and for just a second, Jason felt as if his heart had stopped.

Blood leaked through small openings in the razor-like teeth that sprang from black gums. He was close enough to smell the foul, rank breath that he could only connect with death, maybe a crypt or a graveyard. Then it happened in that split second. Jason released himself from the chains of fear and accepted his death.

The creature moved his mouth slowly toward the side of Jason's head, and he felt the being's mouth begin to open. As he waited for the bite to come, he tensed up his body, most likely a natural reaction.

He waited and gritted his teeth.

However, the bite didn't come, only three words, "Please help us!"

Then it was gone, and the cage of the female rocked on its side.

Jason began to breathe again. His mind was struggling with what he had heard; maybe it was just his imagination.

"Dolittle has made contact and still has his head!" Bolton, who had moved to the corner, spoke quietly into the phone.

"Excellent! Well done, Mr. Bolton!" Helen Worthington turned off the speakerphone and raised her eyes and smiled at the aging Italian man from the Vatican.

CHAPTER 118

"We need to get rid of this vehicle as soon as humanly possible!" Jeb said to Magen who was still hard at work doing her Dale Unser impression.

"There are some fast-food joints and a few hotels off the next exit," Magen wasn't asking if she should get off there, she was just informing him where she was going.

"That will work for us! If I didn't know better, I would have to say that you are not new to this!" Jeb said, looking at Magen with some admiration.

"You have no idea, Colonel!" Magen stated as she exhaled, thinking of the past few days.

"I want to thank you both for coming here and risking your lives to bring me in!" Jeb said, his tone sincere and heartfelt.

"We really didn't have plans for anything else!" Mac said from the back that forced laughter through the car.

"You don't need to tell me anything if you don't want to, but who were those people trying to kill you?" Magen asked, with respect and some hesitation.

"They are a military task force out of Fort Dix. I recognized one of them when the wall exploded at a safe house not far from where you picked me up!" Jeb stated and reached down to feel his wound.

"Why are they so hell-bent on your elimination?" Magen asked.

"My whole team was annihilated. This Dr. Mazza took a bullet in the throat and was dying badly as I took to the woods!" Jeb was getting angry as he spoke.

"You two know this guy? I am not sure about the things in the cages. I know bullets were ripping through everything in that house. If they survived, it was an absolute miracle!" Jeb was confused about their connection to this doctor.

"We know this doctor only too well. They dug a bullet out of Magen yesterday that he put there!" Mac stated with nothing but contempt.

"So, it is by no mistake that Smith sent the both of you to pull me out! I was ordered to safeguard what was deemed a high priority but a low-level risk. Then all hell broke loose, and my team is dead." Jeb paused for a second then added, "It was those altered children they came for, wasn't it?" Jeb started to put a few pieces of the puzzle together.

"I am not sure! They didn't seem to care who lived or died. I'm not even sure that they were altered children!" Magen said with conviction.

"You're Magen Cummings, aren't you?" Jeb asked, fully knowing the answer to his question.

"I am. What pet name did you know me by?" Magen asked. Her anger was evident.

"The alien chubby chaser, I believe it was!" Jeb said without skipping a beat.

"I guess that's just as funny as all the rest!" Magen stated with some indifference.

"Not anymore!" Jeb stated with a realization that there was more going on than he realized.

"Well, the game has changed. Your friend Smith had us sit face-to-face with a one Mr. Cain. Do you know that name?" Magen asked.

"No, who is he?" Jeb seemed puzzled.

"Not who, but what is he?" Mac shot from the back seat.

"What?" Jeb turned to look at the still bleeding Mac, who caught his eye and started to nod.

"Not a joke. We sat down with an extraterrestrial yesterday, right in the middle of Manhattan!" Mac said, still trying to grasp that concept for himself.

"The real article, we didn't have long to talk, due to some religious zealot opening fire in the restaurant, but I think he wants to stay here on Earth!" Magen stated as Jeb's face tried to process the new data.

"How do Mazza and the two pale creatures connect to all of this? What does it want here on Earth?"

Jeb knew from the moment that he saw the American soldier in the woods that this situation was bigger than he could imagine. Now sitting in the car listening to the latest developments, he became afraid for the first time that he might not survive this.

"I am not sure about the connection with Mazza and his experiments. I had the feeling that Cain was only really concerned about his own status," Magen stated, but in her head, she knew there needed to be some form of connection.

"There has been thousands of high-ranking military and political personnel reported missing over the past forty-eight hours!" Mac stated from the back.

"You mean like they were kidnapped or killed?" Jeb turned his head quickly at Mac, not believing what he was hearing.

"There is an Israeli back at the command center in New York. He feels that the moment these aliens were identified, an immediate exodus began!" Mac reflected on the words Barack had said.

"So, they had been embedded in our infrastructure all along?" Jeb was astonished at the concept, but to a military man, it made perfect sense!

"Like I said, it is just a theory from this Israeli guy. I started down this road two days ago when I was investigating a death at a train station in downtown Manhattan!" Mac said, thinking just how crazy the trip down the rabbit hole has been.

"The subway homicide turned out to be a scientist who was working on some type of amino acid that broke down fat in the system, so they sent in the chubby casher!" Magen said with an air of arrogance.

"I am guessing you are feeling some validation in all this?" Jeb smiled as he looked at the bruised woman next to him.

"I handed my data in to my superior four years ago. I have been the blunt of a bad joke since. Now they are dissecting my old data like it was the Dead Sea Scrolls. Yeah, 'validation' is a good word!" Magen stated with some anger recalled.

"I have a question for the both of you," Mac announced from the back seat.

"Yes, sir!" Jeb stated as he turned to look in the back seat.

"For an American Special Forces team to attack an established safe house full of American soldiers, those orders must have come from high up, right?" Mac asked, knowing the answer, but felt the reality from the look on Jeb's face.

"Yes! I know where you're going with that question. It gets worse. I was almost killed by an assassin four hours ago. I'm pretty sure that she was CIA!" Jeb stated, quickly reliving that trauma in his head.

"She! You were attacked by a woman?" Magen was surprised to think about the woman who would attempt to harm the big old soldier.

"She was a total professional and deadly beyond belief. I got lucky." Jeb's hands shook as he talked about it.

"What I think am hearing is that there is a faction within the United States government that is working to secure their agenda at all costs," Mac stated openly.

"It would need extremely high clearance to activate teams from both military and intelligence!" Jeb stated, thinking about the level of deception that must be underway for something like this to happen.

"Who has the power to bring down the wrath of the full community?" Magen asked.

"Your boss Gregory had mentioned that he felt Langley itself was compromised!" Mac stated.

"Are you talking about Timothy Gregory?" Jeb stated with surprise that Magen was on his team.

"He is my acting superior. I report directly to him!" Magen stated.

"That's too bad. That guy is a first-rate shithead!" Jeb smiled at Magen.

"I have been trying to tell her that since I met that tool. She does nothing but stick up for him," Mac howled from the back.

"I really appreciate the loyalty to a superior, Agent Cummings, but Gregory is shady beyond description," Jeb pressed.

"He has been working his ass off on this case for seven years. I know he is hard to like, but I can say for certain he is not the bad guy!" Magen was firm about her statement.

"Well, maybe so, but I still can't stand him!" Mac barked from the back as he and Jeb laughed.

"I will say this, Jeb, the odds that you know the person who has betrayed us is pretty good!" Magen said this not out of anger, but to get everyone back on track.

"That is safe to say, I give you that. I have been around a long time. I am sure whoever is responsible for this betrayal, I will know them," Jeb said with an element of sadness.

"How do we get back to New York? I'm hungry," Mac said from the back.

"Funny, I was thinking that there could be an answer to that dilemma. I know this is going to sound crazy, but it might work," Jeb stated and pondered the solution.

"I think that I just pooped myself a little!" Mac joked.

"Where should I go? I think we need to try something crazy before crazy catches up to us."

"I saw an H for hospital for the upcoming exit. I am going to guess that there's a high probability for this area that they have a heliport!" Jeb said with a smile.

"Mother of God, please be joking. That idea is sounding slightly over-the-top there even for an old war dog!" Mac winced at the thought of dying on the roof of a hospital.

"Prince George County has a fleet of helicopters. We need to secure one of our own!" Jeb remembered his early years with this area.

"It's a sound plan. Where is our access point?" Magen added.

"I am not sure if we can secure one at the hospital, but at the very least, we can find out where to liberate one," Jeb stated as Magen pulled off the highway.

CHAPTER 119

Cain focused his vision as he shifted back into the Manhattan apartment.

He took several deep breaths and balanced himself. The kitchen granite tabletop was cold under his hands and it felt fantastic.

He walked to the window overlooking the Brooklyn side of New York and smiled. The thought of Indian food filled his taste buds, and he refocused on an eatery on the corner of Second and Seventy-Fifth; the order had already been placed, and he waited for a knock on the door.

The smell of finely cooked curry filled his nose; it was blissful. He always recognized home when it came calling.

As he waited for the food, the thought of the black woman crept into his mind. The thought of her naked body connected to his deep animal feelings that he worked hard to suppress.

That would have to wait; Cain was starting to feel that something was off. The fact that there was no real push to locate him was extremely odd.

He sensed nothing, and if they had even made some attempt with the local authorities, he would have been notified.

Not all of his kind have left the planet; there were still a handful in the military and other security factions.

It was time to pay a visit back to Fort Meade and see if he can get a better look into what is going on.

He was hungry and feeling impatient; he was aware that these feelings came when something was out of joint. What could me more important than finding the alien visitor that you know is in town?

No, he thought to himself, *the actions are not matching the priorities.* Something else was distracting their focus; it was the only explanation that made any sense.

Cain sat in the dark; the noise from outside was more of a slight hum, much less activity from earlier that day. He needed these moments to ease his thinking process. At the rate his brain functioned, it needed to be eased down slowly at the end of the day, much like human sleep.

As he wound down, he started to prioritize what he needed to do, but thoughts of Cleo's skin came back, and his lust turned to hunger.

He stood and walked to the window, watching the lights flash around town. He needed to make an additional three stops throughout the planet and disable all possible transport windows. Timing was important; by now, the council on Zen would be aware that their decision to send him back was a mistake. He knew there wouldn't be any assassins authorized to come for him, at least for the next two lunar cycles.

The council never really moved all that fast, the price of wisdom.

He looked up at the stars and guessed it was slightly after two in the morning. He knew if he shifted to Tell Mozan, Syria, it would be midday and there would be no way to retrieve his three orbs without cloaking himself.

The cloaking process used considerable energy; he thought it would be better to hold on until later.

He reached into his pocket and fished out a parking ticket. The meter maid had handed it to him with a smirk as he exited Jackson Hole's takeout.

Cain opened the door of the master bedroom and flicked on the light. There, on the bed, was the young meter maid tied and gagged; her wide red eyes told a tale of pure horror.

Cain sat next to her and tried to soothe her, much like someone would deal with a small child. She was sweating and shaking. The sheets of the bed were soaked in urine; she was broken and in shock.

Every time Cain touched her with one of his razor-like fingernails, she stopped breathing.

Her ability to scream was long gone, most likely lost in the trunk of the limo.

She worked her head off the table and turned into the face of something she just couldn't grasp. Cain looked down and opened his mouth with a chilling stretch of his jaw muscles with the sound reminiscent of steel cables being pulled to their maximum.

His teeth latched onto multiple areas of her flesh. Her flailing body went tight, grasping at the final strands of life, and then everything went limp.

There was nothing but silence in the room, all hope lost, and Cain fed.

CHAPTER 120

Jason Daly paced back and forth in the observation area with three words racing through his head.

Please help us!

He knew that it wasn't imagination; part of him wished it was.

Jason didn't say anything to the men in the room about the words that the young being said to him. There was something in the tone of the young one that forced him to reassess his reason for being here. He knew at some level that these beings needed to be cared for and protected. The reason he needed to hold back on the staff was simply a matter of trust.

His head was spinning with the voice of the being.

He walked to the door of the enclosure and looked at the cages. He saw nothing, but he could feel them somehow, as if some connection was forged between them. He needed to get back in there and try to make sense of this.

His fear was fully gone; it had been replaced with a feeling of warmth and purpose.

Bolton had come back in the room and joined him at the viewing window.

"I know that I am not receiving all the information regarding these two. Is there anything you can help me surrounding their origin?" Jason asked.

"I am really not sure where they come from," he lied.

"Is there anyone that I could talk to that could answer some questions that I need?" Jason pleaded.

"I will try and assist you, Dr. Daly! My name is Mrs. Worthington. I am in charge of this facility." Helen had jumped into the limo as soon as the word came through.

"Thank you, I have heard mention of you from several of the soldiers that accompanied me here." Jason reached out his hand and was met with a cold hand that squeezed and disappeared.

"How can I be of assistance?" Helen asked and then guided Jason by the arm to the large staging area, mostly for privacy.

"I was hoping that you could give me some background on the origin of the two beings?" Jason asked.

"Let's walk a bit, please," Helen said, pulling him out of earshot of Bolton and the team.

"Sure!" Jason said as they walked. He couldn't help but find the isolation from the rest of staff deliberate and almost mean.

"I pulled your file, and I am fully aware that you are an intelligent individual, so I am not going to waste your time with protocols or deception!" she stood before him and spoke directly at him, burning her hollow blue eyes into his.

"I really do appreciate that, saves so much time!" He was cautious about the tone he was using. He could see that this woman wielded extensive power.

"Yes! Time is something that I no longer have on my side. You need to know what you're dealing with," Helen said as she peeled her eyes around the area one last time.

"Please, I need to try and understand what they are?" Jason seemed to plead.

"You asked about origin. That is a difficult question. We need to start with the fact that their origin is not Earth bound!" Helen began.

"What?" Jason said out loud, but at some level, he was open to the possibility.

"I need to tell you a story. This is not an easy story to tell, and you will initially have doubt. I will assure you that eventually you will come to believe what I am saying! In 1985, a small faction of the American government became aware of an alien presence on this planet. They were living among us, working, and thriving right next us. Their motives were unclear at the time, but now we have learned that they have manipulated historical outcomes for centuries. The more layers we pulled off, the deeper the penetration was evident within our very structure. Military, political, they had penetrated all areas of power and authority. We slowly began to see what they were and how this situation didn't happen overnight. One of the scientists who worked with us began to put together that these beings had been on Earth for long periods and they were not immortal, that maybe there were remains.

"You see, we can't see what they really look like unless they wish to reveal themselves to us. However, in death, they are instantly revealed. In any event, this scientist researched this theory for six years, and would you believe that he found what he was looking for? We sanctioned several archeological digs at the location he recommended on the west slope of a mountain in Israel. In six months, we found what we were looking for, bones of a being not seen on this planet for ten thousand years!"

"Bones? Are you saying that the bones of extraterrestrials were found here on Earth?" Jason asked, fully gripped into the story that was unfolding before him.

"That is exactly what I am saying, two complete skeletal remains of one male and one female, amazing bone structure, fiber compounds off the chart. So, this doctor who realized all of this began to formulate that there must be multiple alien species evolved from this structure of the alien force here on Earth. The bones that he found appeared to be the ruling class that found Earth and cultivated it. However, the bulk of the visitors were not of this class. They were more or less servants or a watered-down version to these advanced beings. Then the good doctor explained that he was able to find these beings utilizing just one literary resource, the Koran, Bible, and Hindu text.

"You see, early humans knew of these beings, and they called them angels, amongst other things. That is what you are dealing with in that room, DNA extracted from the bone marrow and cloned in hopes of breathing life back into our dying world. Do you understand the significance of what I am saying?" Helen asked as she took in a deep breath.

"I'm not sure we are dealing with angels or anything of a religious matter. There might be a connection with extraterrestrials!" Jason began to dispose of the religious content then stopped himself as he noted the woman he was talking with began to become visibly angry.

"You will take the information I gave you and draw your own conclusion. I am not attempting to convert you. I need them to learn and grow. It is with our deepest hope that you can assist with that end," Helen stated with a coldness that wasn't there just seconds ago.

"Please let me apologize. I was by no means trying to upset you!" Jason spoke up, immediately sensing the complete shutdown from the woman.

"We are extremely hopeful of your success. Please let me know if there is anything you need," Helen finished and began to walk away.

"Is there any research that I can follow? Also, the scientist or doctor who initiated this, is he available?" Jason pressed.

"He is dead, and we are in process of retrieving his research. As soon as we secure his notes, we will have them here. I think at this point just developing trust with the two beings will suffice!" Helen's anger began to wane, and she even forced a smile.

He watched her walk away and tried to process the information that he was just given. He was also really surprised by her reaction related to his comment.

Did she really think that these two were fallen angels?

The fact that they were extracted from ancient bone marrow was strange enough and amazing.

He tried to calm himself and think clearly without the rain of possibilities that were running through his head. He needed to get back in the enclosure and continue to work with the two. As he walked back into the viewing room, he looked at the staff personnel who were all staring at him.

He walked back over to Bolton who was standing at the window.

"What is their problem? They seem to be eyeballing me," Jason asked, not looking at the science team.

"The evil queen never comes down from her tower. They are staring because they are starting to see that this is not just another project!" Bolton kept his eyes frozen on the crates.

"Do any of them know what these two are, or where they were generated?" Jason asked, basically to monitor Bolton's response.

"That is an interesting word, 'generated.' I am really not sure what they know. This whole thing just unfolded. My understanding is that up until forty-eight hours ago, these two were an unknown!" Bolton stated, obviously telling the truth or at least believing what he was saying.

"I put their age anywhere between four and seven years! How does someone keep something like this a secret without some strong help?" Jason asked.

"I see your point. Let me rephrase that. I had no knowledge of their existence," Bolton stated.

"I need to get back in there and work with these two. Can I make that happen?" Jason asked, not knowing the protocols that were put in place.

"This is your show! You seem to have the blessing from the high command!" Bolton said with a smile.

"Then it is time for me to get back to work. Thank you for everything!" Jason pushed out his hand out toward Bolton who accepted without hesitation.

Jason stepped out into the pod and waited for the door to close. When it latched shut, he proceeded into the enclosure.

CHAPTER 121

The fear he had during his initial trip was absent this time in. Not that he felt all that safe, it was just that he knew that if these beings wanted him dead, that would be enough. They were just too fast and dangerous.

During his first trip into the enclosure, he had considered the danger and what it would take to escape. This time around, he knew escape would be pointless.

He made his way toward the cages; his sense of smell slowed his pace as he came closer. He removed a pad from his pocket and sat down a few feet from the cages. The skeletal remains of the animal were now sitting at the area where it was first retrieved. The bones were ripped and splintered, as if a large cat or possibly a hyena had spent some considerable time with them.

Jason heard a faint noise behind him and turned to see both beings not more than four feet from where he was sitting. Then he realized that the harsh features were gone; the dark razor-like teeth were also gone.

Before him were two children who you would find running for a bus or playing in a field.

He attempted to stand but was unable to get his legs to obey the commands of the mind. He sat back down and stared at the beings for what seemed an eternity, unable to turn away. His heart began to slow down from the pounding drum that was sitting mid chest, looking to leap from his body.

Then through all the fog and disbelief, the one word he needed came to his mind: communicate!

CHAPTER 122

Jason slowly got to his feet, his eyes still glued to the beings; he brushed his hands down his pants. This was a habit that most zookeepers found themselves doing.

Working with the multitude of animals, it was almost impossible to avoid dirt, hair, and tons of hay that rolled through the place every week.

In this case for Jason, it was helpful to dry his palms that were wringing wet from anxiety.

He started his approach with a smile and then stopped, thinking that on a primal level they might consider a show of teeth an act of aggression. So, he wrapped his lips around his teeth quickly and began his approach slowly.

He thought the best approach would best be a version of primate submission. Jason realized his vantage point was several feet above the small beings. He dropped to his knees and began to crawl, easing his way toward the feet of the beings who had not changed their position.

As he closed in to where they stood, Jason held out his palm. He raised his eyes up and saw the look of confusion on the beings' faces and decided to back away.

The female began to approach slowly at first, and then walked straight to a front position just inches away from him.

Jason looked for the male, realized he was gone.

At that very second, he heard movement directly behind him.

There was a brief stiffening moment of fear, and then Jason grounded himself and knew that he was alive for a reason.

As these thoughts ran in his mind, the male being walked up from behind him and joined the female. She looked deep into Jason's eyes and motioned toward her clothes. He looked at the rags that covered the both of them and realized that she wanted new clothes; this was the connection.

He became excited and motioned to his own clothing, and the being smiled at the recognition.

Instinctively he opened a large grin of his own, happy that the initial communication was made.

He walked over to a viewing window that was crowded with faces.

"Can you guys hear me?" Jason asked loudly.

"Yes! Is everything all right out there?" a voice came from overhead.

"Is there a woman on the team that I can talk with, one who has clearance?" Jason requested.

"Yes, we have someone in data analysis that we are calling up, just a few minutes," the voice rang from overhead.

Jason turned his head to the transformed children who seemed confused about his dialogue.

Not upset by any means but still testing the waters on just how much they can trust him, he needed to make some type of gesture that would secure it.

Jason walked over to them slowly and sat five feet from their feet. Their body language relaxed, and they mimicked his actions. Jason motioned slowly to his clothing, and the female did the same, forcing a smile. Jason thought the behavior that they were demonstrating was much more wolflike than feline.

As she shifted, Jason was able to assess the area where the young being was injured. There was absolutely nothing visible to the naked eye, not even a scar.

Jason was frozen at the reality in front of him; it appeared that they had extensive healing properties that were manifested after they ate the animal. He thought to himself that the two children he was looking at right now didn't look like this at all. They were able to generate some type of cloaking device that made them appear less frightening. He knew that there were several species throughout the planet that were able to demonstrate similar behavior; the chameleon came to mind.

His mind raced as he heard his name being called.

"Dr. Daly, I was asked to come down and talk with you. How I may be of assistance?" the young woman spoke nervously into the microphone.

"What is your name?" Jason asked, slowly turning toward the window.

"Excuse me?" she shot back, confused by the whole scene.

"It was a simple question. What is your name?" Jason stated with a bit of arrogance.

"Ann Marie, my name is Ann Marie Colleran!" she answered, not sure if she was being tested.

"Ann Marie, do you have children?" Jason asked.

"Excuse me! I'm not sure what we are doing." Ann Marie couldn't understand the level of questioning.

"Ann Marie, I am going to ask you questions, and you're not going to say excuse me. Please just answer!" Jason was becoming agitated, and he noticed the two beings could sense this agitation.

"I have no children. I am sorry, it is just the line of questions I find strange. I'm a programmer," she attempted to justify her answers.

"Do you have a niece or nephew in your life?" Jason asked.

"Well, yes, I have three nephews!" she answered quickly.

"Excellent! Now we are getting somewhere. I need to find clothing that will fit these two, nothing too wild but not cheap. Can you help?" Jason asked, half expecting to hear another excuse me.

"I will need credit cards and transportation. All documentation is taken when we commit to this assignment!" she stated.

"Is Bolton still up there?" Jason asked.

"I have cash and a vehicle coming around to the front. We will have everything back in your hands in two hours."

"Dr. Daly, if you would please hold up your hand to the young girl's foot," Ann Marie asked.

"What? Why would I do that?" Jason started.

"Please hold your hand next to the young girl's foot!" Ann Marie said in a similar tone to the one he used just seconds earlier.

"You're looking to gauge size for footwear. Well played, Ann Marie." Jason smiled as he eased slightly closer; averting his eyes from the male being, he held out his hand just inches away from her right foot.

"Thank you!" Ann Marie stated, and off she went.

CHAPTER 123

It was extremely windy on the roof of the hospital. Mac could taste brackish water in his mouth, and the taste was unmistakable and unpleasant.

The wind must be pulling it right out of the Chesapeake Bay. The noise from the helicopter was winding down, and Mac couldn't help but think about the movie *Apocalypse Now*.

The three of them stood against the far wall of the building, waiting in the dark recess away from the light that blazed above the sliding door.

Mac was able to count three EMS workers and the lone man on the gurney that was being raced toward the sliding doors and into the hospital. The door closed, and the three began to move on the copter.

Jeb was the first one to roll back the door of the whirlybird and confront the pilot who was more than slightly shocked by the ambush.

"We are trailing down. Watch your heads, the blades dip when this bitch turns off!" the young pilot yelled as he twisted his neck to see the man enter from behind.

"Son, I am going to need you to start this bitch up again right now!" Jeb shouted over the sound of the engine.

"That's not going to happen. I am on schedule to run a patient up to Hopkins," the pilot stated.

"That trip has been canceled. Start it up, or get out and I'll fly this thing myself." Jeb held up his CIA identification where the pilot could see it with the same hand as his weapon.

"My wife is going to kill me!" the pilot yelled and started up the helicopter.

"Thank you, son. I most likely would have dropped this thing in the bay!" Jeb laughed.

"I need a heading, Captain. Where are we going?" he asked.

"Brooklyn Navy Yard. We just need to get close to Pier C, off the East River!" Magen said as she strapped herself into her seat.

"We are going to be really close on gas, but I felt a good south to north headwind. Hopefully it's still flowing that way," the pilot stated as he pulled back the stick and pulled off the roof.

CHAPTER 124

Cain stepped out of the limo at Fort Dix and was instantly greeted by a party of the few remaining seeds that he held in place, just in case.

The first of the group to reach his position was Colonel Randall Smokehouse III. Cain has had dealings with him for over four decades, and had assisted with his growth over that time. Cain could tell immediately that the good colonel was put off by the young appearance that Cain possessed, and there was a brief moment of strong uncomfortable feelings.

As fast as that thought came, the colonel quickly realized just who he was dealing with and responded accordingly.

The others that flanked him were lower-level ranks, but still key to the information that he would require.

It was drizzling a bit, so there was no delay in introductions, and the colonel ushered them into a conference room just off the main entrance.

As they settled down in the room, they were joined by a younger man who seemed to be confused by the sight of the young man who seemed to have excessive power.

"Mr. Cain, this is Sydney Bloom. He is our guru on domestic terrorism," the colonel stated as the informal introductions were made.

"Extremely good to meet you. I hope that you can help me with my quest!" Cain stated with a large smiling grin.

"That's why I'm here. Can you give me parameters of the scope of what you're looking for?" the analyst asked.

"I am looking for the *unusual* that came across your screen in the last forty-eight hours!" Cain stated.

"Well, the first thing that comes to mind is the event in Annapolis yesterday. Are you up to speed on that fiasco?" Sydney asked.

"Please bring me up to speed. Think of me as a blank slate!" Cain stated with more than a little arrogance.

"Yes, sir. There was a shoot-out involving military personnel with one confirmed fatality," the analyst began.

"I have been monitoring the news stations up in New York. Why have I not seen anything on this?" Cain asked as he removed himself from the table and began to walk around.

"Annapolis is a military town, and we were able to suppress the event as a motor vehicle accident without much resistance," Sydney stated.

"Can you pull up any video at the scene so I can take a look?" Cain asked.

"That is no problem. I have two camera angles from the bank across the street!" Sydney stated.

"I like your style. Can you pull it up on the big board, please?" Cain requested.

"This is the primary view. As you can see, a nice easy day in downtown Annapolis, then watch as the BMW rolls up the street!" the analyst was doing the blow-by-blow.

"Can you focus in on the people driving the vehicle?" Cain asked.

"No need. Watch as the second vehicle comes into the picture. Here it comes. Wow, big hit! Now watch as they back away and speed off!" The youngster was pointing at the image for effect.

"Is that weapon fired?" Caine asked.

"It is! Now watch as the BMW makes its limping getaway. See the woman in the passenger seat. We have been running the image through the system. Nothing is coming back."

"Magen. How extremely interesting. What are you up to, my little fearless child?" Cain said with a mischievous smile.

"You know this person?" the colonel asked.

"She is a federal agent, I believe. Strange that she is not turning up in your system!" Cain sounded surprised.

"Do you know the driver?" the young analyst asked.

"I am going to take a bit of a stab and call the driver Mac something, NYC police officer!" Cain stated but deep down wondering what was going on with this scenario.

"Why are they here, running wild down in Maryland?" Sydney asked.

"That is the most important question of the day, my young friend!" Cain looked out the window, trying to piece the events together.

"There must be a sound reason why they are down in Maryland and not here trying to gain a step on me," Cain said out loud, but was more or less talking to himself.

"There was something that happened yesterday, but I'm not sure if it had anything to do with your friends!" Sydney stated.

"What was it?" Cain listened closely.

"There were over twenty-five 911 calls yesterday, all coming through in a six-minute time frame, then nothing," Bloom stated.

"What do you mean by nothing?" Cain pressed.

"I mean, not another word. Police went to investigate, and there was no radio chatter on the result or outcome!" Sydney shook his head.

"Did you assess the possibility of other government agencies that may have been involved?" Cain stood directly in front of the young man, interested.

"I put out feelers to every possible clandestine agency and even got Homeland involved. Nobody came forward." Sydney watched the young guy who seemed to have endless power, and waited for a response.

"So, we have some type of firefight that nobody knows about, or even worse nobody is taking credit for?" Cain paced the front of the table.

"Yes, sir, then less than fifteen hours later, we have the crash with weapon discharge, all within a ten-mile radius!" Bloom went on.

"Now what on earth could bring these two down here? What was so important?" Cain looked around the room.

"The BMW was registered to a black ops colonel who is on assignment in New York. It's his private car!" Sydney seemed even more confused by the incoming data.

"That would indicate that the trip was one of secrecy, and trust was extremely important, but why?"

"It was an extraction, sir! The BMW is abandoned two minutes later. A third party is seen leaving in a carjacked vehicle with these two!" the analyst stated.

"Can you bring up his face? Now we are getting somewhere," Cain said with some enthusiasm.

"I regret to give you additional bad news. He seems to make a practice of keeping his head low and avoids contact with the buildings. I wasn't able to lock on to anything with him," Sydney seemed upset with his perceived failure.

"We can at least assume that he is most likely a professional, trained to behave this way in the middle of chaos?" Cain threw this out much like a question and the room agreed.

"We are still waiting on interviews and the rest of the camera analysis, but we have relieved some intel on the third person if you care to hear it?" Sydney seemed back on his game.

"I want it all, Mr. Bloom. No detail is too small!" Cain motioned his hand as if to signal *Now would be good.*

"He is a white male, age range 40 to 60. The weight range appears to be plus 250 pounds. Two people said he wore glasses. Four people said he didn't. He seemed to know where he was going to connect with the vehicle!" the analyst began.

"Who said he had glasses, people inside or outside?" Cain was visualizing the scene.

"People outside said yes. Those inside said no or didn't remember," Sydney stated and waited for a second.

Cain nodded.

"He pushed past a busboy as he cut through the building. The busboy from Mexico reported that when the man jumped the fence he saw blood on his shirt!" Bloom emphasized this point.

"Of course, he has blood on him. Six hours earlier, the man was in the fight of his life nine miles outside of town!" Cain said as the clarity of events were now coming into focus.

"The last time the vehicle was seen it appeared to be heading north. However, we have not been able to locate it!" Sydney said with some reservation.

"The only reason you can't find the vehicle is that it doubled back and most likely is currently underwater. I'm sure they are working out an alternative means to their destination!" Cain stood and bowed slightly and motioned for the door.

"Sir, I just received a transmission of a northbound helicopter that is off course and not responding. Should we shoot it down?" the young analyst asked.

"Oh, no, we are back in the hunt. I need a satellite on the bird right now, and I want coordinates shot to my phone as soon as it lands, clear?" Cain said with authority that wasn't questioned. He was happy with the visit, his sense of understanding was validated, and now it was time to act.

"I can have a jet to take you to New York if you wish?" the colonel asked.

"That will not be necessary. I have made travel plans in advance!" Cain leaned into the ear of the colonel. "At this time, I also need to let you know if you are still on Earth at the start of the second lunar cycle, you will be a permanent resident!" Cain looked him in the eye to assess recognition of his words.

"Thank you. It has been a privilege!" the colonel stated with real sincerity in his voice.

Cain nodded and was gone.

CHAPTER 125

Heather Worthington arrived back in New York City shortly before six in the evening and went right to her office.

As she walked through the door, her eyes fell on Cardinal Coppola and his aide who were enjoying some tea. There were smiles from all three faces.

Helen was so thankful that the cardinal was able to postpone his flight. He was happy to see her, but he really wanted an update on the little ones. She could read him so well.

She thought of her father and how they were able to communicate by just a system of looks. She missed him dearly. However, having the cardinal around made things almost manageable.

"We have contracted a doctor from a New Jersey zoo who was able to make contact with our guests!" Helen stated as she sat down and smiled from ear to ear.

"Outstanding! This is fantastic news. I feel that we are being guided by the hand of the almighty himself!" Cardinal Coppola said with elation in his aging voice.

"Yes! I feel that to be true!" Helen said with tears welling up in her eyes.

She poured tea for the cardinal and herself.

"I am quite proud of you and how you have handled this crisis!" the cardinal said to Helen as they sat.

"Thank you! My cardinal, I must confess a certain amount of personal pleasure surrounding the events of the last few days," Helen said with a hint of guilt in her eyes.

"Nonsense, you have every right in the world to feel a sense of pride. There should be no guilt!" Vincenzo said and reached out and patted her hand.

"You are too kind, my cardinal!"

Helen didn't feel it was relevant to tell her friend that she only felt good that Mazza was dead and she now controlled the children.

CHAPTER 126

Major Schmitt opened the vehicle and stood, trying to focus his binoculars on the building where he would find Helen Worthington.

The driver also exited the vehicle and came next to the major and slipped on night vision glasses.

Sergeant Morris Campbell had worked under Major Schmitt for the past nine years. The air was cool, and it was good to stand after the four-hour drive.

He ran the full length of the building but was unable to locate her. However, he was sure that the evil queen was there. He counted almost twenty men, all armed and some with submachine weapons. He realized that this was all he could see; there could be bigger issues the deeper he got into the building. He estimated that on the initial wave he would eliminate a dozen men just based on their poor positioning.

"Wake up our friend. There is some work that needs to be tightened up!" the major stated as he lowered the binoculars.

"That is not going to happen. The big man is dead. Bullet must have nicked an artery, bled out!" Sergeant Campbell shot back.

"We need to move him to that bench over there so he can be found and we can utilize the vehicle."

"He would have really helped with this building today!" Campbell said as he pulled the big man from the seat.

"That is unfortunate. Damn good man!" Schmitt stated as he looked back at the vehicle and thought of just how bad the mission had gone.

He lowered his friend to the bench.

"Well, I have a feeling that we will be joining him sooner than later!" the thick sergeant grunted with a forced chuckle.

"That is starting to look like a strong possibility. We really don't know what is waiting for us in there. Our flank is fully exposed and we have no support!" Schmitt said with a grin as he armed his weapon.

"Sir, it has been my absolute pleasure serving with you!" Morris snapped a salute.

"No, Sergeant, it has been my pleasure and absolute honor!" Schmitt returned the salute.

"Taking out this bitch is the right thing, and it is truly a good day to die!" Morris pulled back the arming mechanism on the weapon and stood and readied his charge.

"It is a good day!" Schmitt stood next to the sergeant and gritted his teeth; then a sound came, *beep, beep, beep*.

Schmitt looked at his friend who simply rolled his eyes and then bent back behind the vehicle to keep their weapons concealed.

"I don't recognize this number. Who is calling?" Schmitt asked, a little more than slightly agitated.

"So, Major, your plan is to run into that building and get yourself dead?" the voice of Father Frank Nica came through the phone, and the major's heart skipped a beat.

"Frank! Is that you? Where the hell are you?" Schmitt asked with pure astonishment in his voice.

"Yeah, long time, Major. You seem a little busy at this moment. Would you like for me to give you a call back?" Father Frank joked as he watched through his scope.

"Where are you, Frank, and what are you doing?" Schmitt asked, hoping that he wasn't working for the Worthington woman.

"I'm on your six and about three hundred feet in the air, but please don't start looking around!" Frank asked in the same jesting manner.

"Are you working for Worthington or not?" Schmitt asked, this time with more authority.

"If I was working with the evil queen, we wouldn't be having this conversation!" Frank stated with a cheerful tone.

"I can't tell you just how happy I am to hear that. We are going in. Your help would be appreciated!" Schmitt added, almost short of an order.

"Your target is on the seventh floor. I will attempt to be your eyes in the sky. Do you have a wireless piece?" Father Frank was working out his system for best-placed shots.

"I am going to wireless right now. Nice to have you on board!" Schmitt said with newfound hope in his voice.

"It will be my pleasure, Major. May I suggest the garage-level entrance where you will find the least resistance!" Frank assisted the major in the plan he had worked out in his head just hours earlier.

"I thought of that. However this puts a significant force behind us that would eventually bottle us up in a building we can't escape!" Schmitt had worked several options out, and the frontal assault was the best-case scenario.

"Well, I was thinking if you knocked out the elevator on the eighth floor, it would force the soldiers to take the stairs and they are wide open. Fish in a barrel?" Frank stated, hoping the major would follow the logic.

"Don't take this the wrong way, Frank, but I'm not totally confident that you are on our side!" the major stated, still having difficulty in accepting outside intervention.

"I understand, Major. it is not easy to trust anyone in our business, but I need you to consider two things. First, I do have a unique perspective from up here, and second, if I had any evil intentions, you wouldn't even hear the shot!" Frank laid it out as clear as an unmudded lake, knowing his idea had the greatest margin for success.

"All right, Frank, let's do this your way. We still have a fair amount of explosives. We will take care of the elevators," Schmitt stated as they began their insertion into the lower garage.

CHAPTER 127

There were four men in the base of the stairwell; two of them were sitting and half enjoying some local calzones from around the corner. The other two had their back to the door and seemed to be listening to a joke only killers could revel in.

Schmitt placed a single-barrel field glass to his right eye. He was able to read the lips of the man who was narrating the joke. A smile broke across his face as the punch line was revealed. Laughter broke out from the men in the stairwell, and Schmitt knew it was time to move.

He motioned to his sergeant who nodded his head and removed a flash grenade from his front pocket.

Sergeant Campbell stood and, utilizing some earlier softball skills, lobbed the device toward the men with a great deal of precision.

Schmitt twisted the silence barrel on the Beretta and stormed into the stairwell.

The first two shots caught the stunned faces of the two men that were sitting as the flash grenade went of almost at the same time. The other two were shot assassination style as they attempted to lift their suffering bodies from the floor.

Schmitt and his second charged the stairs, taking them two at a time when the sound of weapon fire erupted at the front of the building.

Father Frank was flawless with his well-placed shots, and before the guards realized that there was a sniper, six men littered the entrance to the building.

At the moment the alarm system initiated, Frank could see those remaining men head toward the elevator and then the stairs. He was able to take out the lead man and then wound the next two men with high leg shots.

The screaming could be heard from his high position even with the city traffic. The full metal jacket rounds didn't slow down when they hit bone, just splintered them! This stopped all progress on the stairs as the two wounded men were dragged to safety.

The major would have the time he needed, but just to be safe, Frank swept his weapon through the second floor and blew out several windows and spread panic and a stampede of office workers.

He raised his eyepiece up to the eighth floor and watched as the evil queen and an elderly gentleman who looked somewhat familiar were motioned out of the room through the back!

"Major, what's your current position?" Frank spoke into his headpiece.

"We just turned the corner heading past the fifth floor, over!" Schmitt yelled into his phone, pushing his large frame up the stairs.

"The queen is on the move out the back, possible freight elevator out of my line of sight!" Frank voiced.

"Understood. Try and keep her on the grid. We are close!" Schmitt chimed out.

Schmitt and Campbell came through the door at the eighth floor with guns drawn. Weapon fire erupted instantaneously, and Schmitt saw his friend's shoulder explode in a burst of red off to his left.

Schmitt turned his weapon and released three short bursts. Two men fell, and Schmitt could see the evil queen standing in an elevator against the back wall. Her eyes were glued to his, and darkness poured from her as she realized just who was moving against her. She said nothing as Schmitt raised his weapon and pulled the trigger, releasing the final bullet in his clip.

The bullet landed against the back of the elevator just two inches from her head. Worthington didn't even blink as the doors from the elevator closed; she just shot those evil blue daggers deep into his soul!

Schmitt grabbed his friend and pulled him back into the stairway, taking the weapon off his injured friend and sending the barrel out the door.

Several bursts from the weapon stopped the other two minions of the queen from advancing on his position.

"We need to move, Sergeant, that elevator is heading for the roof!" Schmitt ordered.

"I am leaking gravy, Major, I would be finished within three flights. I will cover your escape!" Campbell said with a smile, grasping his fate.

"That is an unacceptable outcome, soldier!" Schmitt snapped at his friend.

"Take to the roof, put a bullet in that bitch, and come back for me. I can hold off the night watchmen all night long!" Campbell stated and motioned his commanding officer off.

"I will put the bitch down and be back before those clowns grow enough ball hair to come through that door!" Schmitt stated as he leaped up the stairs.

Frank began to hear the sound of the helicopter engine start to power up. He raised his eyepiece up, but he was unable to display the position. He could see the top of the roof, but there was no shot; he was about twenty-five feet below it. He swept his weapon down to the eighth floor in time to see a priest standing in Worthington's office. He could see that the young dark-haired priest was afraid and praying silently to himself. Frank scanned the other windows and saw a young man come into view; this well-mannered man didn't seem to pose any threat.

Confusion began to increase in Frank as he watched the nicely dressed young man walk forward and then pounce on the man like an animal. Frank watched as the facial structure of the young man began to change; he backed away from his eyepiece, rubbing his eye.

He was not sure that what he saw through the lens was reality.

Frank refocused his left eye to the scope just in time to see two long talons rip into skin just above the hairline of the now screaming priest. There was a sharp jerking motion from the distorted thing that was holding the man, and instantly the majority of the priest's face was gone.

Frank turned his head and dropped his weapon on his lap. He could feel his early dinner working its way up the back of his throat.

He began to hyperventilate; his mind was moving in too many directions, and then he realized that the major was still in the building.

"Major, come in! You need to get out of there right now!" Frank yelled into the headset.

"On the roof, Frank. The chopper is out of my range. Do you have a shot?" Schmitt shot back.

"No, Major, you need to get out of that building now!" Frank shouted.

"I can't do that. Campbell is down, and I need to extract him. What's coming my way, Frank?" the major asked without much anxiety, realizing that he was between a rock and a hard place.

"Just get out!" Frank yelled between his long deep breathing and pulled off the headset.

Frank began to pack his gear and get as far away from the building, then the scream came, and he stopped dead in his track.

He had been a sniper for better than twenty years, and he knew that the scream traveled about eight hundred yards through thick painted glass from a priest without a face.

Fear was something Frank didn't let consume him; he had been in hundreds of life-threatening situations. Yet here he was trembling, afraid to even look at that window. Then a thought came to his mind that the reason he was so was afraid was because the thing in that room that was once a nice-looking young man was, in fact, evil. He knew at some level that it was not human, but he also knew that he couldn't run away like a coward while a man of faith was being tortured.

Frank took three deep breaths and brought the scope to his eye and aimed it at the eighth-floor window.

The priest was still in the grip of the beast who was talking in his ear.

There was no fight left in the man who just swung in the clutches of the monster. Frank took one last deep breath and fired the weapon!

CHAPTER 128

The window was a quarter-inch thick but no match for the full metal jacket that passed through and caught the failing priest in the back of the skull. There wasn't too much blood splatter as most of this man's blood was already pooled at his feet. Frank swung the weapon quickly to the beast which was looking right into the lens as if he knew exactly were the shot had come from.

Frank stared into the blackest eyes he had ever seen; the being seemed not so much angry as annoyed.

Frank regained some composure and began to squeeze the trigger, when in the blink of an eye, the being was gone.

Frank stood from his kneeling position and swept the room; nothing, it was gone.

Frank went into automatic pilot, breaking down his weapon in seconds as he had done so many times. He pocketed the shells off to his right, counting them in his head as each one made it to his pocket. As he gripped his hand around the field bag, Frank heard the sound of light breathing directly behind him.

He released his grip on the weapon and the bag. He turned slowly to find the young man standing there; the beast he saw through his scope was gone. The look on the young man's face was not one of anger, but maybe slightly perplexed or even amused.

"I can imagine that this is all slightly confusing to you. I must admit that you have surprised me a little as well!" Cain said with a slight smile.

"What in God's name are you?" Frank found his mouth working.

"That answer will need to hold. What is more important is who are you, and who do you work for?" Cain asked, his eyes narrowing.

"There are three of us here, two others inside, one hurt. We came to terminate one Helen Worthington!" Frank felt honesty was the best path and might just save his life.

"Interesting. By any chance do you know what that crafty woman is up to?" Cain asked as he took a slight step closer.

"I received a package yesterday to kill an old Marine. I couldn't do that. The other two in the building were involved with some operation that she sanctioned, and somehow we met on the path to the same place!" Frank thought about the words he was saying and how bizarre it sounded.

"Almost like *The Wizard of Oz*, but darker?" Cain smiled and laughed.

"I guess that's not too far off!" Frank shot back, startled by the laugh coming from the young being.

"Where is the rendezvous point with the two others?" Cain asked as he picked up the rifle and bag.

"We didn't arrange one, but their transportation is down on the street!" Frank was confused by the question but knew he was in deep and there was a reason this being was picking up his gear.

"Hold on tight!" Cain said as they stepped off the roof into the cool midevening air.

CHAPTER 129

Frank felt the wind pick up as his descent increased.

Fear grew automatically, but he fought the feeling because somehow he knew that this was not the end of his life.

As he spiraled down, he thought of his God and wondered if he was really ready to talk to him; was he truly worthy of his grace?

It was at that point he knew that there were things that he left undone and unsaid, and then fear returned.

Frank reached out and held on to the only hope on the table!

The thing that he held tight to was not even remotely concerned with the acceleration toward the pavement. Then as if time itself slowed, so did they, and they slowly came to a stop on the ground without so much as a jerk from a sudden stop.

Frank still held the being with blazing white knuckles until he realized that he had closed his eyes. As he opened them, he saw the young face gazing at him with a look that would appear to communicate that everything is fine, he can relax now.

Frank released his grip and stumbled toward the major's car. He took two deep breaths and steadied himself with the aid of the vehicle. The nonhuman popped the trunk of the jeep and placed the gear in the back in what Frank could only consider being an effortless action.

Frank watched him as he went about these actions and realized that something wasn't right. He smiled at his own thought. *You bet your boots*, he thought, *something was far from being right*.

Then he knew what it was. It was the breathing; no matter what this being did, his breathing didn't change. This thing just jumped seventeen floors, and its breathing pattern didn't even waver.

As Frank watched the strange being, he began to consider running or taking an aggressive action; it was how his mind worked. Then his reasoning came back on line in Frank's skull.

He was alive only because this being wanted him around.

Frank turned his head to see the major coming out the front doors pulling Campbell. He froze for a second and then pulled out his sidearm and scanned the area, providing cover if it was necessary; it wasn't.

The front entrance was littered with bodies; the other men who were on the eighth floor never continued their pursuit of the two men shooting at them.

Frank wondered if they came across a faceless priest and lost the will to fight.

Cain opened the vehicle doors and motioned to aid the major.

"We need to get our asses out of here. The police are close. Do you work with Frank?" Schmitt asked, confused by the presence of the young man.

"Alexander Cain. Frank and I are working on our relationship. Let me help with your man!" Cain helped the man in the back of the jeep and climbed in next to him.

"Are you a soldier? There is something familiar about you. We have served together, haven't we?" Schmitt asked Cain but never took his eyes off Frank who avoided the major's eyes as they climbed in the jeep and turned the key.

"I knew a Lieutenant Andrew Schmitt, rifle company, 1969, Mekong Delta!" Cain said as he inspected the other man's wound and realized that if he didn't assist, this soldier would be dead in minutes.

"Yeah, that would be my father!" Schmitt stated as he pivoted in the chair and leveled his Beretta at the youngster in the back seat.

Cain smiled and pulled the shirt away from the bloody chest of Sergeant Campbell. It must have been a large-caliber bullet; the damage was significant and most likely fatal.

Schmitt's eyes danced from Frank to the wound on his friend's chest, and back to the smiling young man in the back seat who seemed to not even slightly be fazed about the weapon pointed at his heart.

Cain raised his hand to the wound and then opened it to reveal three round balls that slowly rose from his hand and seemed to turn in midair; gray light filled the back seat.

The two end balls traveled counterclockwise, the middle ball traveled in the opposite direction.

Campbell, who was close to passing out, began to feel his chest being ripped to shreds. Cain raised his finger that seemed to be growing and placed it into the central energy of the floating balls; in one swift motion, he dragged that energy into the wound.

There was a sharp flash of light as the round spheres fell back into Cain's hand. It took a few seconds for his eyes to adjust, but when they did, he saw his sergeant running his fingers over his chest that was now minus one fatal wound!

There was a pause of silence as Schmitt lowered his weapon, not sure what else to do.

Frank finally broke the silence in the vehicle as they made the right on Second Avenue and headed uptown.

"I am almost certain that he is not human. I'm not sure what his intention is, but he could have killed me ten minutes ago!" Frank spoke low as if he was in shock.

Two police cars passed them going the other way.

"You are a very intelligent man, for a priest slash hit man. I think it would be safe to say that the three of you have never been as safe as you are right now!" Cain said as an ear-to-ear smile broke across his face.

"What the hell are you?" Schmitt said as he holstered his weapon and grabbed his right hand with his left to stop it from shaking.

"I am Cain, and we seem to have a common enemy. Worthington, who has worked for me for years now, appears to have betrayed me!" Cain stated as the smile fled his face.

"You look like you're a teenager, but the words coming out of your mouth seem to be from an older man!" Campbell said, feeling uncomfortable about him *proximate* to something that he couldn't understand.

"I know this is strange, but I need you gentlemen to assist me, and that works out for all of us. She seems to be up to something, and I need deep understanding this!"

Cain held his hands up as if to ask for help.

"This has something to do with the two little freak shows that we acquired in Maryland yesterday, doesn't it?" Schmitt said as he recalled the faces of the two abominations.

"Freak shows? Please elaborate." Cain's interest was now fully piqued.

"The dark queen sanctioned my team and I to storm a high-risk target outside of Annapolis. We eliminated nine soldiers, most likely a CIA operation. There were two beings found after the operation. They were not human, as I understand the term."

"Where are these abominations now, Major?" Cain asked, his anger growing.

"We were instructed to hand off the two transport containers to a secondary team, and then we were to find and eliminate a soldier who escaped the house."

"Let me guess, that didn't go well, and the man was liberated by a man and a female!" Cain stated as he began to process the series of events.

"Who were they?" Schmitt turned in his seat, anger welling up in his face.

"Not even slightly important. They were simply acting as errand boys under orders, but trust me, Major, those responsible will pay dearly!" Cain stated with a great deal of confidence.

"You're not from this planet, are you?" Frank broke conversation with the one question that he needed answered.

"You already know the answer to that question. Why don't you ask that what you truly want answered, priest!" Cain said softly.

"Does your race believe in a God?" Frank blurted out as if it was a question; he was not sure that he wanted it answered.

"Of course, there is a God, this you know. Your deeper question concerns the Nazarene!" Cain pushed as Frank slammed on the break and pulled next to a fire hydrant near Seventy-Fourth Street.

"Yes, you seem to read me well. I do need to know. I'm not sure what you are, but I do see both evil and honesty in you. Maybe it is just a weakness in me that continues to question."

"I followed King David long ago into battle for Canaan against the Philistines. After a three-day fight, I sat bruised and bleeding with my back against a well in some smelly farming village. The holy one walked up and drew some water to drink. He then knelt beside me and washed blood from my face. In his eyes I saw real, true love, something that I was not familiar with. I sat and wept like a small child for what seemed an hour. Is he the son of man? I truly would like to think that he is. I know that in my many centuries in countless galaxies, I have yet to feel that much warmth and goodness in one being's hand!" Cain stated slowly as if he was watching those events unfold just yesterday.

"Thank you. I will help you any way I can!" Frank gargled through his constricted throat.

"I need to leave you men now. Track down the errand boys. I need to find those abominations and you three to stay together, are we clear on that?" He grabbed the door handle and twisted his head back toward the major who acknowledged agreement.

"Find them!" Cain said, and then he was gone.

CHAPTER 130

Mac was freezing his ass off in the back seat of that damn helicopter.

He couldn't stop thinking about food and how hungry he was. All he wanted was a Greek gyro with onions and that smoking cucumber sauce. Mac knew a place in Astoria, Queens, that carved it thick off that nasty meat wheel. There used to be a place on Forty-Second Street that was superior, but that was before Giuliani cleaned up the Square. He could almost feel the grease dripping down his arm.

Magen was a few feet away looking at the NYC skyline, trying to process the events of the last few days. He knew she was thinking of the research she had done over the years and how it was all coming to life.

Mac knew she was beating herself up on what she considered a missed opportunity.

The fact she didn't press Cain about the countless doctors and scientists that his people killed over the years. In his mind, it was simple. Cain and his buddies were stocking the pantry; keep us fat and slow, and we are easy to catch.

She smiled when he said this to her, but Magen felt there had to be more to the story. He looked at the side of her face and marveled at her natural beauty, and then knots began to well up in his belly.

She was so far out of his league; some part of his brain was warning him not to get that close. Unfortunately, that was just impossible now having tasted her mouth, and the warm tight feel of her pussy when he was in deep was making his hands shake.

Mac realized at some level that he could live the rest of his life and not find another woman that made him feel this way. The way she dug her nails into his rear end flesh when she came! Holy smokes!

He smiled as he watched her shoot off question after question to the older CIA agent that was doing his best to keep up with her barrage. The pilot barked something that was inelegible, but Magen responded, and the helicopter banked hard right toward Brooklyn.

They had made really good time, and somehow, they were not blown from the sky by Homeland Security; he thought Smith might have helped with that.

Mac looked out the window and marveled at his vantage point; his city was glowing and blinking.

He wished more people could see it how he did, feel it like he did.

He wondered if his whole philosophy would change when he got back to his job. He tried to imagine himself doing the job, and he just couldn't see it.

As the helicopter banked hard along the Hudson, Mac saw several bridges come into view. The Brooklyn Bridge gleaming in the night was by far the brightest. Mac couldn't help but smile as his city flew past him; the stunned looks on the faces of the rest of the passengers left him with a feeling of deep pride. The feeling of coming out of the darkness in the dead of night and finding this magnificent display of light was inspiring. Even the pilot raised the face shield on his helmet and let his mouth hang open for a few seconds.

Just then, the older CIA agent pulled off his headset and turned in his seat, facing Mac. He took his two fingers and forked them at his eyes then pointed to the side window. He heard him yell, "Ten o'clock!"

Mac moved his face closer to the window; initially not seeing anything, he turned back toward the CIA agent with a look of confusion on his face.

Again, the older wounded agent yelled, "Ten o'clock!"

Mac looked again, and his eyes went wide as the silver-skinned drone materialized through some clouds. His first thought was that it must have been sent to intercept the stolen helicopter. However, the fact that nobody at the controls was panicking and screaming led Mac to believe that it was simply an escort from Smith most likely.

He marveled at the gray drone's ability to blend into the night sky. The two Hellfire missiles that were strapped to the underbelly didn't blend as well.

Mac turned to see everyone smiling at him; he guessed that the military folks like to see civilians in awe of their cool toys.

Mac raised his middle finger, and the compartment erupted in laughter. Mac noticed that even the pilot who was kidnapped less than two hours ago was grinning from ear to ear. Mac shook his head and thought that things couldn't possibly get weirder; he was wrong.

The helicopter banked right toward the Brooklyn side; the drone lifted away and was gone in a flash. The factory where Smith and what looked like half a division of soldiers was lit up like Times Square. Mac was slightly taken aback by the firepower, but considering the last twelve hours, he understood.

A team of Green Berets flanked the dock as the copter touched down.

There were two teams of medical service people standing by, and they rushed to the compartment as soon as the skids touched down.

Mac watched as they began to triage Jeb's wounds when some young nurse jumped into the seat in front of Mac and began probing his right eye with a powerful light.

"All right, all right, no need to blind me. I made it this far!" Mac protested and pushed the light away from his face.

"Please, Officer MacDonald, you have been involved with a head-on collision. This is standard protocol!" she fought back.

"I know you have a job to do. I am sorry! I need to wash up and eat, so please, no gurney, no blinding light," Mac said, attempting to make peace as he moved past the tech.

"Yes, sir!" the young tech stated as she moved slightly to the right, allowing Mac room to pass.

"Well, there is no shame in my game. I would love a gurney and some morphine, stat!" Jeb called out as he allowed two of the techs to assist him on the stretcher.

"You should have someone look at that scalp wound, Mac! I want my honey to be all right," Magen stated as she grabbed his behind.

"I'm going to wash up, and then if I need to deal with this, I will roll down to the infirmary. Besides, I feel just fine, sweetness," Mac said as he walked over to where Jeb was being strapped into the gurney.

"Hey, flatfoot, I just want to thank you and that pretty lady for saving my old ass!" Jeb said with deep appreciation in his voice.

"I'm not sure who saved who, but you take care of yourself, Jeb, and thank you!" Mac said as he reached out and took the big hand of his new friend.

"I'm not sure where they will be taking you, but I will find you, so you make sure you're good to the nurses!" Magen said as she bent down to kiss him hard on the lips.

"I don't usually take to Yankees, but you two are making me reconsider my stand on things!" Jeb stated with a big smile as the medical service team raced off with him.

"I understand that my car looks like a pretzel and was towed to some police impound yard in Bumfuck, Maryland!" Agent Smith stated as he stepped from behind the helicopter.

"Yeah, we are fine! Thanks for asking!" Magen said without skipping a beat.

"Annapolis was in a tailspin. They thought they were under attack from Muslim fundamentalists!" Smith said as he shook his head.

"I understand the team that attacked us was a group of American soldiers. Now that is slightly disturbing, to say the least," Mac said, trying to read any automatic responses that his question sparked in the colonel.

"We have not received all the data back from Langley on the identification. However, there seems to be reasonable intel that these men have been employed and trained by our government," the agent said with some deep regret written across his face.

"I can see that this does not sit well with you also, Colonel. So what are we dealing with?" Mac asked, hoping for some better understanding.

"There have been some new developments here in New York during your trip back. I think we need to take some time and debrief and let me bring you up to speed!" Smith stated as he held his hand toward the dark Hummer parked just outside of the line of soldiers.

CHAPTER 131

As Cain stood in front of the large panel of tempered glass overlooking the city, he closed his eyes and reached out his hands to feel the glass.

They were cool and vibrating from the wind gusts.

His thoughts were on the policeman who had called him on his desire to stay here on Earth.

He was there on the roof of the hotel; now he is running operations down in Annapolis.

Cain wondered if was he missing something.

He knew the officer wanted to shoot him on the hotel roof, but his fear changed his mind. The skinny federal agent was never too far away from this policeman, and that might be something he could use to his advantage.

He took a deep breath and decided in that second that he needed to turn up the pace. Worthington needed to be found and dealt with. He still needed to close two additional portals here on Earth before they were used to extract him.

It was time to draw the line between friend and foe.

He had a highly positive feeling about the woman agent. There was absolutely no evil intent behind her eyes. This was something he would need to count on. He could not say the same for the police officer; that human would have no issue pulling the trigger of his Beretta. Not that a bullet could end his life force, but he was enjoying the current body that he inhabited.

His phone buzzed on the table; he had placed it on vibrate because the noise was starting to bother him.

He picked it off the table and held it in front of him. It was from Smokehouse. It read, "Helicopter down pier 22 Brooklyn Naval."

Cain pushed the off button and smiled.

They were set up less than a quarter mile from the warehouse where Thomas had processed the New York hive. They hadn't been on the ground long, and Cain assumed there would be some discussion before they disbanded.

He thought to himself that the timing couldn't be better.

He placed a smoke at his lips and lit it; pulling in the smoke felt good, and he enjoyed the smell.

He opened the closet door and pulled out a nice black leather jacket and rolled his arms through the sleeves. He smiled in the mirror at his resemblance to the Fonz with smoke dangling from his mouth and the cool jacket.

Cain held up both of his thumbs and said, "Hey!"

Then he turned to the door and out he went.

CHAPTER 132

Jason Daly sat at a child's picnic table drawing the young beings in the recently built menagerie.

The young male was becoming much more comfortable with his daily presence. They even seemed to be comfortable with the fact that they were imprisoned. He guessed that these beings have been held somewhat captive since their birth.

Now they had food and much more room than they ever had in the past.

Jason tried to imagine these two confined in some basement laboratory in the suburbs. Where were the police or the countless government agencies that should have been tipped off at some point? The scent alone that emanated from these two was enough to send every single dog and cat in a five-mile radius into frenzy.

He had met with the science team that had evaluated them since their arrival. There was some discrepancy over their age; it was difficult to gauge without a reference point. His feeling was that the beings ran between four and six years of age. One of the leading members of the team said that they could be as young as twenty-six months, depending on their rate of growth.

Their diet seemed to be more in line with the carnivorous animal species than human.

The scientist requested that Jason assist them with a blood draw that he quickly denied. He asked them to utilize the blood that was on the cage, but they had said it was compromised with the female's saliva.

He thought about that for a while; the fact that hunger drove her to lick her own blood sent a chill up his back.

There had been no additional dialogue from the beings since the male asked for his help. This point consumed half the meeting time, and the team really wanted to push for additional verbal confirmation. Jason felt that there must be a reason why they weren't attempting further engagement. At this point, the theory was that they were able to communicate between each other on a telekinetic basis. This fact was not currently provable; however, there were times where they seemed to be locked in deep discussion without either one whispering a single syllable.

The infrared camera was unable to capture any heat signature, so they were determined to be cold-blooded.

Jason thought to himself just how amazing this whole experience was.

Yesterday, he was so sure about the way the world worked. Today he felt like a child in a candy shop.

There was a slight shift at the back of his ear, and he realized that as he was daydreaming, the male had circled behind him and was looking at his drawing. Jason could now feel breathing like gentle wind; initially, he grew rigid, but fought with himself to remain calm. Instinctively, he wanted to turn his head right, but that would expose his wide-open face to a set of teeth that could rip his skin clean off.

Jason fought off the initial anxiety and went back to drawing, even though he felt the being edging closer.

He took a steady deep breath and exhaled low and slow, and then it came.

"We can't stay here. He will find us soon, and everyone will die!" the being said in the voice of an older man.

"Who will find us?" Jason stated as he swung his head in the direction of the voice, but the being was gone.

CHAPTER 133

Bigger than New Year's Eve, more important than the Fourth of July!

—Additional day in May noise

The two guards at the gate were very much aware and heightened as the black limo pulled up twenty feet from the base of the pier.

When the young man exited the back, they looked at each other with some confusion on their faces.

Cain adjusted his tie and straightened out his dinner jacket in the reflection of the back window. He liked the way this suit framed his shoulders; it wasn't easy to find a gifted tailor these days, very sad.

Cain had managed maybe ten steps toward the back gate when the older of the two guards stepped up and said, "That will be far enough, young man. This is a restricted area. Back in the limo and go!"

His eyes became fixed, and his finger flipped the safety off the M-16.

"Yes, you men are doing an outstanding job, and it is not going unnoticed!" Cain said with a heartfelt smile.

The guard began to feel the pressure in his skull and started to squint. He flipped the safety back on and then stood up straight and motioned to the other guard to do the same.

"Thank you, sir!" the guard said out loud.

"Punch me through the gate, please, Sergeant. I'm running late for the meeting," Cain said as he slapped the soldier on the back like they were old friends.

"Yes, sir, will you need anything else today?" the guard asked, looking only to be helpful as he pushed the six-digit code, snapping the gate open.

"Thank you, Sergeant. You two are doing a fantastic job. Carry on!" Cain said with enthusiasm and walked to the back hangar door.

"Who was that?" the younger guard asked when Cain was out of earshot.

"Some tight-ass captain, real ballbuster!" the guard stated.

Cain walked right into the motor pool and took in the full area just in case he needed to make a hasty retreat. He was fairly certain that the people involved here were reasonable and smart. However, humans had a tendency to be somewhat unpredictable when they are caught off guard.

Cain walked slowly to the back of the large garage and entered an area that was obviously a power station with several generators.

The amount of computers that were operational in this building required a significant amount of juice. He knew the next area was most likely the command center as most of the power lines led into that area.

He thought of just waltzing in, but then thought better of that approach.

He grabbed a soldier and asked him if there was a conference room in the area, and who exactly was in charge.

"Well, Commander Smith is running the show, and the conference room is right down that hall," the soldier stated and pointed to the left, away from the command center.

"That is perfect. I just need you to do me one more favor, and then you can finish what you're doing," Cain said slowly as he placed his hand on the soldier's shoulder.

"How can I help, sir?" the soldier stated, only hoping to please.

"Could you alert Colonel Smith that Mr. Cain has arrived and is waiting in the conference room?" Cain asked with a smile.

"It would be my pleasure, Mr. Cain. Please have a seat, and I will locate the colonel."

"Thank you, Marine, you're a good man!" Cain said as the soldier walked away to carry out his mission.

CHAPTER 134

Mac was sitting next to Magen as Smith reported on the soldiers and hit squad that they were able to identify from the scene down in Annapolis.

Face after face was added to the large screen overhead along with their military history. Smith seemed almost ashamed when he listed off the names and their ranks.

The Israeli who seemed to be back in good standing was also in the room. Mac made a point to acknowledge his return the moment he saw him. The Israeli smiled when he saw his new friend and seemed genuinely concerned about his smashed-up face, but the bag of ice that he was holding to his eye made everything just fine.

Smith then emptied the big screen and placed the face of an officer the full size of the screen.

"I believe that this man, Major Schmitt, is the leader of this band of traitors. He is one of our Special Forces rejects. He became tired of taking orders and rolled off after his last tour in Afghanistan, taking half his crew with him. Three of those men are being transferred back to Fort Meade from the Annapolis morgue. Schmitt's last known whereabouts were unknown for the past six months. Although there were rumors that he and his team were involved with the theft of Egyptian relics, this cannot be confirmed. It is currently unclear whom he is working for at this time. One strange piece of the puzzle comes from the CIA. They report that he entered back into the country with a diplomatic service team from the Vatican."

"I would say that strange is an understatement!" Mac said, dealing with his own puzzlement.

"There must be some type of connection, angels, monsters, and now Vatican involvement!" Magen pointed out.

"I didn't say that there was Vatican involvement. For all I know, he passed himself off as a member of their team without their knowledge!" Smith said firmly.

"He really doesn't look like someone who can move around without being noticed. Look at his eyes," Magen shot back.

"I agree, he is memorable, but I still only have a small piece of a larger puzzle. To draw any conclusions at this point would be ridiculous!" Smith seemed firm on this.

"Sir, I am getting a report of some type of firefight in an office building in midtown!" a slightly balding man said from a computer post.

"Who is sending the report?" Mac shot back.

"I am intercepting some cross talk from the local Leos. I could put it on the overhead if you want?" the man at the computer asked.

"Let's hear it, Corporal!" Smith snapped.

"We haven't found any survivors yet, Captain. Lots of bodies, blood everywhere, and shell casings everywhere you step. My men are going through each and every floor. So far, just dead suits and they're all packing! I have four men down at the entrance with headshots, looks like sniper rounds!" the voice finally paused.

"Sergeant, listen, I need updates every fifteen minutes. Find me at least one living body! I don't care if he is a good guy or a bad guy! I'm calling the Feds. This is soon to be out of our hands, but I need to know what happened and if the bad guys are in the wind."

"Yes, sir. Captain, I was told that a body on the eighth floor appeared to be tortured. You will have a full report on all findings in two hours."

The voice on the radio was interrupted by the captain who asked, "Just how did you determine torture, Sergeant?" he said in a slightly mocking tone.

"The man was holding his face in his own hands. It looked to be surgically removed!" the sergeant stated as if his words were not his own.

"What?" The captain's voice trailed off.

"His wallet identified him as a priest from Rome, of all places. I can't wait to hand this one over to the Feds. I'm not ashamed to tell you that me and a few of the men really have the willies over this one," the sergeant stated.

"Understood. We need to secure that crime scene. That is priority one right now!" the captain finished.

"Yes, sir!"

The transmission ended.

"I need to know the name of every single body in that building. I want information on every business connected to that building, and I want it now!" Smith's voiced boomed, and the room snapped into overdrive.

"Do we think this is the work of Cain?" Mac asked.

"Don't you remember the hotel? Cain and his buddies don't need guns. They just eat their way through the crowd," Smith shot back.

"What about the removed face? That seems a little off the beaten path," Mac stated as he raised his eyebrows at the section chief.

"To be honest, it reeks of drug cartel. They love all that shock value bullshit!" Smith said.

"I'll give you that much. Maybe it's just the timing that has me wondering," Mac stated.

"Sir, there is a visitor waiting for you in the conference room!" the young soldier stated as he approached and came to attention just a few feet from the command desk.

"Who is waiting for me in the conference room?" Smith looked surprised.

"There is a Mr. Cain waiting, sir. He requested that I come personally to escort you," the soldier stated as silence fell over the room.

"Is this some type of joke, soldier?" Smith stated as a puzzling look stretched across his face.

"Hold on, Colonel, his eyes are dilated. He's possibly being manipulated!" Magen stated as she walked closer to the soldier.

"Do we have a camera in the conference room?" Smith boomed again.

"Sir, we don't even have audio in the room. We really didn't think interrogation was part of the current scenario!" the lead engineer stated.

"Well, let's not keep our guest waiting!" Smith stood and began to exit the command room.

"Are you planning to go alone? Would you like some company?" Magen stated, confused by the section chief's actions.

"I think it time for Cain and I to get better acquainted. If I need anyone, I will call, but I feel some alone time is in order," Smith stated and turned toward the hallway.

CHAPTER 135

"Mr. Cain, my name is Smith. Some people call me Colonel Smith or just Smith!" Smith stated as he sat slowly at the other side of the table.

"I am Cain. As you can imagine, they call me many things!" Cain said and allowed a large smile to spread across his face.

"I see. Just how we can help you today?" Smith asked.

"I am not aware of any pending crisis. Is there something you are not sharing with me, Mr. Smith?" Cain faked a look of mild confusion.

"Well, I'm sure your council didn't send you here to Earth to end the greatest secret of all time!" Smith said firmly.

"No, they certainly didn't. However, here we sit, and you seem to have the inside track on information!" Cain stated calmly.

"Will they come for you?" Smith asked with some mild concern apparent.

"They will try. However, I am currently working on closing the gate from my system to here," Cain said.

"That is a good thing. Would hate to think that a superior alien force was en route to make things right, so to speak!" Smith said. His obvious sarcasm was blinding.

"I have the feeling that I am not the first alien that you have conversed with, am I correct?" Cain asked.

"You are correct. We have been aware of the presence of your race for some time!" Smith stated without even the blink of an eye.

"I take it that you are Central Intelligence, and the rest of the party outside of this room is only slightly informed?" Cain stated as if he had lived that moment before.

"There are several of my government's agencies involved, and you're correct. They don't have all the facts!" Smith crossed his arms.

"Right, I have no desire to rain on your parade. I will need a few things for my stay here on Earth!" Cain said as if all formalities were finished.

"What can I do for you, Mr. Cain?" Smith said, happy to get down to business.

"I will require an island, small but with adequate soil and vegetation, somewhere tropical, Caribbean possibly, but not too far south!" Cain made a thumbs-up gesture as Smith wrote on his pad.

"That's very nice. Anything else?" Smith asked with a mocking tone.

"Yes, there is a woman named Imogen. She is a photo model from London. I will need her as a mate!" Cain stated as he slid a picture of a young green-eyed woman across the table.

"She is a beauty. I am guessing that this is cut from some random magazine?" Smith almost joked.

"What am I missing, Smith? You would think that every agent in your world would love to be sitting where you are?" Cain asked, beginning to get annoyed.

"Cain, we have become an extremely technology-driven world. Secrets are becoming harder and harder to keep. At fifteen hundred hours today, we tracked in 112 agents from foreign governments, and more are coming. They know about you, Cain, and they want you, but if they can't have you, then your death is just fine just as long as the United States doesn't have you!" Smith paused and drew a deep breath.

"I see your point. Much like the restaurant today, it's just going to keep happening," Cain said sadly.

"That's right. To be honest, I'm surprised the Chinese haven't already attempted some type of kidnapping or assassination! Cain, thinking about assassination, were you at a building in midtown earlier this morning?" Smith asked.

"Helen Worthington, she has betrayed me and has cloned a male and a female of my species. They must be destroyed at all cost and Worthington also, by my hands!" Cain made that point clear by letting his canine teeth creep down the outside of his mouth.

"Worthington! I am familiar with that name, many friends on the hill!" Smith stated, slightly shaken by the sight of the teeth. It was all too easy to forget that one was dealing with a monster under such a youthful appearance as its camouflage.

"Were you aware that a faction of your own government was involved with this treachery?" Cain asked as he leaned in closer to get a better scent of the man in front of him.

"I have no prior knowledge of her dealings with these two experiments! What I do know is that I have American soldiers killing other American soldiers to possess them. This I can't allow to continue!" Smith said with deep conviction.

"Excellent, you are telling the truth. Worthington is rouge and unsanctioned. I will need to know her location so I can end this tyranny!" Cain said as an evil smile erupted on his face, and his eyes grew dark and rage filled.

"I don't understand. I am aware of some of your capabilities. You should have no issue finding her or at the least two of your own." Smith looked across the table confused, but sensing that something might be off.

"I can almost smell your mind working, sensing a possible weakness, is that right? Be careful, Smith, I have been around. I know where all the bodies are buried!" Cain stated as his dark eyes dug deep.

"What is it? Why can't you locate her?" Smith shot back, dismissing the threat.

"I have sent back over 90 percent of the organic structure that formulated and maintained the global net around this planet. I have closed two of the four ports. This is what I needed to do, but it has come at a price!" Cain said without any regret.

"So, your ability has been limited by the changes that you placed in motion?" Smith stated, fishing for information.

"Smith, I know that Central Intelligence has trained you to always manipulate any possible weakness. I can smell your wheels spinning! However, I need you to understand that I could raise my hand and send this whole building spiraling into the Hudson River! More important, I would be standing at the event horizon urinating on your smug face as you scream for your life. Finding another CIA shithead to deal with would take me slightly less than twenty-three minutes. Are we clear?" Cain leaned back in his chair and began to relax and waited, unblinking through an extremely long pause.

"We will assist in the finding and terminating the experiments. The island, I can make happen. Kidnapping a citizen from the UK could be problematic, but we will make arrangements!" Smith said slowly in methodical sentences as if he was reading from a script, the air of confidence gone.

"Thank God, I was starting to worry about you!" Cain said as he pulled his chair closer to the table.

"Not out of the woods yet, Mr. Cain. We need to talk about some developments that have recently come to light," Smith stated with some unease.

"Damn, you were doing so well!" Cain said with an evil smile.

"The motherboard back at M-Tac has been lighting up like Christmas. Your presence has initiated a tidal wave of intelligence teams to emerge on New York!" Smith stated, shaking his head.

"Did someone let the cat out of the bag regarding my arrival?" Cain asked, dropping his eyebrow for effect.

"No, I think it was the Internet video of you and your buddies slicing your way through a midtown hotel!" Smith said with obvious agitation.

"Well, how did someone get the video out of the hotel?" Cain asked, seeming slightly confused.

"Everyone and their mother has a phone with a video application. Your team went viral in ten minutes. They're calling you and your pals the Broadway Wolf Pack. Please feel free to have a look!" Smith stated as he handed Cain his iPod.

Cain turned the viewing screen toward him and watched the seven-minute clip of absolute chaos as he and his team went wild in the grand entrance of the hotel. There were times he winced and others where he smiled and fought back the laughter.

The screaming echoed through the room.

When it was over, he turned to Smith and asked, "May I keep this device?"

"No, I will make sure you receive a copy prior to your departure!" Smith said.

"Departure? Am I going somewhere that I am unaware of?" Cain asked, almost bewildered.

"I'm not sure what we should do with you at this point. The folks outside this door must be losing their minds!" Smith said as he shook his head.

"I suppose that my fan club will need some time with me, questions upon questions. You run along and secure my requests, and I will play the fun-loving alien!" Cain smiled and held up a double thumbs-up.

"Does your list have a priority order?" Smith asked as he stood from the table.

"Smith, I want that girl. Don't play with me!" Cain's smile disappeared.

"All you have is a photo. You don't know where she is, and this might not be her real name!" Smith attempted to reason.

"I don't give a shit what her name is. Start looking around Kent. How fuckin' hard could it be to find a green-eyed angel with good teeth in England?" Cain shot back.

"Is there anything else we can help you with, Mr. Cain?" Smith offered, half hoping that their business was finished.

"Yes, I seriously need you to pull your whole team together and help me through this," Cain stated.

"Yeah, that's not going to happen." Smith sighed, wishing he never asked the question.

"Well, how many men can be spared? I need access to a jet at least. Gates need to be closed, and I can't be in two places at once," Cain pushed.

"Sorry, we will not be able to sanction that!" Smith stated.

"What the hell has happened to your agency? I remember a time when the CIA would have moved heaven and earth and not give it second thought!" Cain seemed slightly puzzled.

"Well, we are a much more transparent organization these days," Smith stated as he motioned for the door. "Cain, none of this discussion is shared outside of this room, or your requests will not even be considered," Smith stated as he turned the knob on the door, placing the list in his jacket pocket.

"Not one syllable will breach my lips, but you need to unfuck yourself and get with the program!"

CHAPTER 136

Cain eased back in the chair and gathered his thoughts as Kowalski came through the door with wide, eager eyes.

"Mr. Cain, it is good to see you again. I was wondering if I might be able to convince you to part with just one small vial of blood?" Kowalski asked in a highly sheepish manner.

"Not a fuckin' chance. Why, do you think I am tracking the two abominations for my health?" Cain's patience was wearing thin.

"I was not aware of the connection between the two offspring. Please forgive me" Kowalski stated.

"I find it hard to believe you being a scientist never formulated the probability that some form of connection existed between me and two alien children," Cain said, puzzled and wondering if the man in front of him was a dimwit.

"I was informed that a Dr. Mazza was performing some genetic research off the grid," Kowalski stated as if backpedaling.

"Off the grid is one of those statements that people like you coin to clarify." Cain smiled and tilted his head slowly.

"Mr. Cain, I am truly sorry if I offended you!" the doctor stated, still in his defensive posture.

"I don't feel at all that offended, more overly aware of the facts that you are just a small pawn in this mystery." Cain smiled.

"You know what it's like for a scientist in this company. I am given the information I need, nothing else," Kowalski stated, clearly upset about the dialogue.

"My good doctor, I know you are working on limited information, but I am working on the assumption that all those connected with this are just full of shit!" Cain said and leaned back in his chair.

"You will not receive an argument from me on that truth, but I am simply trying to learn from you," the doctor pleaded.

"I know you are, but you must see that everything I tell you has the potential to destroy every living being on this planet!"

Cain leaned in and peeled his eyes at the scientist, looking for some acknowledgment.

"Could you answer any questions regarding the origin of the human race that wouldn't have dire consequence?" Kowalski requested.

"I respect your persistence, but to be fully honest, I'm not absolutely sure how you made it. You're an absolute anomaly!" Cain smiled.

"The research that has been compiled on you shows that you have been moving in and out of our history for centuries. Have you been manipulating history?" Kowalski stated.

"This question should seem obvious, but again, the answers to your investigation could not serve you to any positive end," Cain stated.

"Is Earth just one of many inhabited planets in the universe?" Kowalski asked.

"I think you know the answer to that question, and would you believe that DNA matches throughout?" Cain volunteered.

"Well, that can only mean one thing. We are not some amazing mistake!" Kowalski stated with some enthusiasm.

"Does that make your life more manageable?" Cain smiled.

"I never know when you're being elusive or deceptive. Is that by design?" the scientist pressed.

"I so enjoy our talks, but it is now time I take my leave from you!" Cain stated.

"There are several different agencies awaiting the chance to conference with you tonight." Kowalski barely had the words out from his mouth when he realized Cain was gone.

CHAPTER 137

Jason Daly stood in the habitat monitoring the behavior of the two beings that he was now affectionately calling Trouble 1 and Trouble 2.

Fortunately, their demeanor had calmed significantly since they devoured the goat. Now they presented like young children exploring and playing without any sign or symptom of metamorphosis to their altered state.

The initial fear that Jason felt concerning his safety was gone. However, he was quite aware that a deep bond was manifesting itself between him and the children.

There were no further attempts by the scientific team to enter the habitat; he initially welcomed the control he felt over the assignment but now was slightly concerned. He began to wonder just how long those in charge would allow this to continue. He was aware that there were several tests being performed by the team from a distance, but at some point, this would change.

He was no stranger to research, and for solid empirical data, eventually they would require blood tests, tissue samples, and possibly even more evasive tests. The little ones didn't seem overly concerned with the faces behind the glass. He imagined that their lives were riddled with erratic events and endless inconsistencies. Jason had never met this Mazza individual, but from his outcomes, he had regrettably become insane. There was no doubt that the man must have been brilliant; he would kill to have just an hour with his notes and data sheets.

This guy was eons ahead of the curve in genetics. Unfortunately, he saw the look in the eyes of the Worthington woman and knew he was only going to receive limited facts.

Thoughts of his own safety also circled in his head; could they actually just let him leave now that he had seen these two creations?

"We need to leave here soon!" the voice of Trouble 1, the male being, was whispering from inches away.

Jason was so preoccupied with his own thoughts that he was unaware that the being had advanced just inches away.

"Why? No one here wishes to harm you or the little one," Jason stated, only half believing the words that were leaving his mouth.

"We can feel him out there. He stopped being concerned about us just hours ago. There is only one reason that would happen!" Trouble 1 spoke softly with his hand over his mouth to avoid detection from the science team.

"Who is it that you feel out there?" Jason pressed, trying to understand their fear but at some level realizing he was being told the truth.

"I don't know his name, but we can feel his power. He is not what he appears to be," the being stated, still holding his hands over his mouth.

"I am not sure what I can do. This place was hard enough to get into, let alone get out with the two of you in tow," Jason muttered more to himself than the being to his right.

"We will help. We are really good at hide-and-seek!" the young female said, now cross-legged in front of him with her back to the partition.

"There must be three battalions of extremely armed soldiers within this structure along with a state-of-the-art camera system," Jason said softly through stressed lips.

"We will help. We trust you, and you're good!" The little being smiled and reached out and touched his hand.

"Dr. Daly, you are needed in the focus room, please!" a melodic voice sounded from the PA system.

"I will be back!" Jason stated as he motioned toward the door, confused and shaken.

Jason entered the briefing room to find Ike, the youngest member of the science team squinting at the computer screen. The CIA liaison was slumped in a chair reading the sports page. He seemed extremely uninterested with his new assignment.

"Dr. Daly, is everything all right with you? We have detected a spike in your blood pressure over the past four minutes?" the young man asked.

"No, I am feeling fine. Why are you monitoring my blood pressure?" Jason asked, slightly concerned.

"It's impossible not to add you to the program. There is too much movement going on within the habitat," young Ike stated.

"I saw those little critters getting up close and personal. Maybe you were feeling a little tense!" the liaison chimed in.

"Maybe, but I don't think so. They seem much less aggressive since they ate!" Jason added.

"I think that I would crap my pants if they got that close to me," the liaison chuckled.

"Makes me wonder how this Dr. Mazza was able to sustain their existence not just once, but to create a second being was pure madness," Jason stated.

"Really not sure what they have been feeding you, Doc, but there was only one experiment. Those two have the same birthday," the CIA agent volunteered.

"That's impossible. There's easily a year-and-a half difference between those two!" Jason said, astonished.

"Hey, you're the doc. I'm just telling how it is. One birthday, two critters!" the liaison stated then turned his head back to the paper.

"Dr. Daly, I am picking some muffled dialogue. Are you receiving any communication from either one of the beings?" the young scientist asked.

"Nothing, no recognition of vocal stimulus is evident!" Jason said as he headed back toward the habitat.

When Jason passed back through the door, he leaned against the door and expressed a large breath of air.

They had been lying to him from the very beginning. The agent said "birthday," and he said it twice. Mazza was working for them from the start. The Worthington woman was crazy; he saw it in her eyes when he met her.

He realized that he wouldn't survive if he didn't get the hell out of this insanity.

Jason stumbled along the path almost in a fog. When he came into view, Trouble 1 saw the look on his face and tilted his head slightly.

"We go, yes!" Trouble 1 whispered quietly at the back of his head.

"They have been lying to me since the beginning, but you knew that, didn't you?" Jason said through tearful eyes.

"You are good, and we feel that as we feel her and the old one!" Trouble 2 was back at his feet.

"Who is her and who is the old one?" Jason probed.

"You know who she is, and you know she is bad. The old one is a being that is here from far away!" the little one stated.

"Being from far away, do you mean an alien?" Jason asked the question he considered since the first time he saw them transform.

"He is angry that we live!" Trouble 1 said with a hint of sadness in his voice.

"It seems this old one is not alone. I have worked out every possible scenario, and we don't survive any of them," Jason said, his fear apparent.

"We need to leave!" the little one said with a smile.

CHAPTER 138

"What do you mean he's gone?" Magen stated in disbelief.

"I turned my back to it, couldn't have been more than a fraction of a second, and when I turned back, he was gone!" Kowalski stated, his own confusion evident.

"How is that even possible?" Magen stated.

"Well, we are talking about a being that jumped eighty feet into the air last night. Not too much will shock me after that," Mac chimed in.

"I need the forensics team to process the room. I have a theory!" Kowalski announced.

"I love a good theory in the morning!" Mac stated, knowing his joke was poorly timed, yet out it came.

"What if Cain was never there in the room in the first place?" Kowalski said.

"Is that even possible?" Smith asked, seeming to have his interest piqued, his head cocked to the left.

"It would make so much more sense if Cain wasn't there and was simply projecting an advanced version of his consciousness," Kowalski was formulating.

"Well, I saw what these guys can do with film from the kid they killed off the subway last week!" Mac stated, trying to wrap his mind around things.

"How is he able to make contact with other objects if it is a simple hologram?" Smith asked.

"Well, my guess is that there is nothing simple about this, but I need more data!" Kowalski stated as he hustled down the hall.

"Just like a kid on Christmas morning!" Mac said with a long smile stretching across his face.

"However, if he is right, we could finally get the chance to one-up Mr. Cain!" Smith stated as he excused himself.

"Smith spent an awful long while in that room with Cain. Should we be concerned?" Mac whispered to Magen.

"I'm not as paranoid as you are, and I'm concerned. It is highly irregular to see a section chief isolate himself with the target of an investigation," Magen said with disbelief in her tone.

"I find you extra sexy when you agree with me, but I guess you already know this?" Mac joked.

"You're a sweet man, Officer MacDonald, but I'm going to do some nasty things to you when I get you alone!" Magen told Mac as she grabbed his slight Scottish ass.

"Don't threaten me with a good time, Agent Cummings," Mac said as he moved into her personal space.

"I don't make threats!" Magen began and lowered her voice as Smith returned.

"Agent Cummings, we are slightly understaffed here. Would you and Officer MacDonald mind interviewing Mr. Pierce?" Smith asked.

"Interview him? I'm not sure I understand," Magen glanced over at Mac.

"We need an edge. Cornell might have some small piece of information that can help us pin down Cain!" Smith seemed motivated.

"Cornell has been through way too much over the past thirty-six hours, and I am to blame, so I would like to be involved with this interview!" Mr. Dean stepped up.

"You are very close to this one. I'm not sure it is a good idea, but if you think you can assist, I am not opposed to your involvement!" Smith said as he turned to leave.

CHAPTER 139

As the group entered the holding area, they quickly realized that things had changed. There was a full medical team processing data on Cornell.

There was a sense of heightened activity, almost excitement among the science geeks.

Cornell was sitting at a steel table that was a new addition to the room. He seemed calm, considering the wires that were connected to both his head and chest.

Another addition to the room was a young black soldier that was posted just outside the door. He was standing tall, and the M-16 across his chest was menacing. The two techs that flanked him were working on his new arm.

An older man with gray hair and an air of authority came over quickly and approached Mr. Dean with an open hand.

"Can I be of assistance? I am Dr. Irving Stillman, team leader of the science probe," he stated, his English accent evident.

"Good afternoon, my name is William Dean, and we are hoping to get a few minutes with my friend Cornell," Dean said as the two men shook hands.

"Yes, Mr. Dean. I recognize you from the string theory symposium last year at Colombia College. Quite brilliant I thought!" the doctor said with sincere openness.

"Wow, I was not sure that anyone actually was awake through my portion of that presentation," Dean joked.

"Nonsense, it was quite well received, as I recall!" the doctor stated.

"I am really glad to see that Cornell has calmed down, and he looks to be in relatively good spirits," Dean remarked.

"It's a bit of an anomaly really. His hand strength has doubled in strength in the past three hours!" the doctor said with puzzlement in his tone.

"This might sound somewhat strange, but Cornell seems to look younger!" Dean stated as he squinted his eyes.

"Are you sure?" the scientist seemed highly interested.

"Well, I can't be absolutely sure, but we did have one long adventure together," Dean stated.

"I am going to have some additional tests run on some blood we took less than an hour ago," he stated as he shuffled off.

"Is it all right if we go in and talk with Cornell?" Dean asked.

"Of course, it will be good for him. I'm sure he is growing tired of being poked and prodded!" Dr. Stillman said.

"Cornell, you are looking so much better. Are they keeping you busy?" Dean said, puzzled by his friend's recovery.

"Really feel much better. I know it's something that son of a bitch did, but damn if I don't feel amazing," Cornell said with a wide smile.

"Have they made mention of any physical problems that they might be looking for?" Magen asked, seeming concerned.

"No, in fact, they are more interested on all the positive side effects that seem to be going on!" Cornell said.

"What positive side effects are you experiencing other than the hand?" Dean asked.

"Craziest thing, my left knee needed surgery for the past two years, and now I am kicking like a mule," Cornell said, lifting his leg up and down.

"I am just not seeing a downside to this!" Mac said, looking for feedback.

"I hear you. I hate to say it, but Cain hooked me up. Not sure that was his plan, but it works for me," Cornell stated.

"Do you remember everything about your time with Cain?" Magen asked, recalling why they were there in the first place.

"I was thinking about it just a few minutes ago. He was here in this building, wasn't he?" Cornell asked in a probing manner.

"He was here. How did you know that?" Magen asked.

"I think I can sense him. Not really sure how or why, hard to explain!" Cornell stated.

"Was there anything about the place you were being held that you can remember, now that you've had chance to rest?" Magen asked.

"It comes in small pieces. I can tell you one thing for sure, it was here in Brooklyn!" Cornell said.

"You seem really sure about that, why?" Mac asked.

"The smell of the Navy yard has its own bones, unmistakable!" Cornell said softly, almost to himself.

"Are you saying Cain has been here all along in Brooklyn? Where?" Dean asked.

"I'm not sure, but it was close, and it was somewhere that was significant to tourists," Cornell said, a bit shaken.

"Why do you think that?" Mac asked.

"Trust me, you really don't want to know, but trust me on that one!" Cornell stated, trying hard to block the images of those screaming people out of his mind.

"Was there anything else about the place that you think might be important?" Magen asked.

"It was a warehouse, a lot of machinery, but there was also the bank," Cornell stated as if he was recalling pictures through a dense fog.

"What bank?" Mac asked.

"It was downtown, older bank. I'm sorry, just small glimpses coming through," Cornell said.

"Anything you can remember about the outside would be extremely helpful!" Mac probed.

"I know I'm not really helping. My memory is all broken, like small flashes!" Cornell said with stress in his voice.

"Don't be upset. This is not anything you can help!" Magen said in a slow, compassionate manner.

"There was the smell of food. I can still smell the chicken and the fish. It was baked, not grilled!" Cornell stated, looking across the room, recalling the smell.

"In the bank, you could smell all that going on?" Magen asked, seeming puzzled.

"I know that sounds crazy, but that's really what I have been pulling out of my broken head," Cornell said, almost angry with himself.

"Maybe there was a restaurant next to some bank in the city that is sending their exhaust air into the bank?" Mac stated.

"The smell wasn't outside, and it only got stronger the deeper we went into the building," Cornell added.

"Cornell, what makes you sense that this was a bank at all?" William Dean asked.

"I remember the vault, round with brass gears. The vision of it is so vivid in my mind!" Cornell stated as if pleading a case.

"Okay, we need to put the puzzle together, that's all!" Dean said as he got up to leave.

"One last thing, Cornell, do you remember going into the vault?" Mac asked.

"I'm not really sure. I have been trying to see past the vault, and there is nothing," Cornell responded.

"Thanks, Cornell, you take it easy. I will be back later to check on you!" Dean said as he embraced his new friend.

CHAPTER 140

Evan Masters moved through the halls of the midtown building with swift determination. His flight from London was brutal, and he was in need of a shave and a shower.

The woman on his right was attempting to bring him up to speed on the past twelve hours. Evan was taking in the data to the best of his ability; however, his concentration was drawn to the lack of information that had developed over the past hours.

The Americans never did such a great job with keeping secrets; something was not adding up.

There should be more data and at the very least some photos of the alleged alien. The fact that there were only small pieces of unconfirmed data was alarming to him.

Too much was happening here to progress any further without sound intelligence.

The whole concept of an alien from outer space was hard enough to process. Now the thought that the CIA had flipped this anomaly was too much for MI-6 to deal with.

The question that resonated throughout his mind was is this for real, or is it some big CIA hoax?

Big joke just to see how far the English lads would go.

He needed more information before he mobilized his team and put them all in harm's way. The information was out there, and he needed it now. He stopped mid stride and turned to the handler and said, "Where is the intel? We must have some of our own people still in the mix!" Evan pleaded.

"There has been an exodus of personnel in the past thirty-six hours. We have only what is in the file," the young woman said.

"I am not sure I understand the concept of this exodus. Where did our people go?" Evan looked puzzled.

"My understanding is that over two thousand high-profile individuals have simply vanished!" she said almost under her breath.

"Two thousand people just don't vanish. This is a trap!" Evan stated.

"The Chinese and the Russians are here in New York. There is something that is drawing all this together. The PM is all over this. He feels that the Yanks are not creative enough to dummy up a story like this," the woman stated and continued down the hall.

"This has to be some kind of joke or an elaborate hoax. I am not buying into this nonsense," Evan stated, fully unable to process the information.

"You need to look at this!" the woman said as she handed him her cellphone.

"Where did we get this from?" Evan asked, studying the footage.

"This has been trending online for the last twenty-four hours. My nephew sent this to me first thing this morning, asking me if it was real!" the woman said.

"Holy mother, they look like humanoid cats. How are the Yanks even communicating with them?" Evan asked, astounded by what he was seeing.

"The leader known only as Cain possess the ability to transform into human form, and from what I understand, he presents extremely young and quite handsome!" The woman smiled.

"Transform into human form? Do you hear the words coming out of your mouth, love?" Evan eyed the woman with a strange look.

"I know that this all sounds beyond crazy, but you need to come to grips with one significant point!" The woman became slightly defensive.

"That significant point would be what?" Evan returned.

"You have been charged by MI-6 with the leadership of this team, *and they need to believe this hoax!*" the woman stated as she handed him the file.

"I see your point. Time for the game face," Evan stated as he reached for the doorknob that led into the conference room.

CHAPTER 141

There were six people seated around a long dark wood table; they had been talking prior to his arrival.

His guess was there was a fact-finding conversation of why they were pulled out of their deep-cover operations to sit around a table in New York.

Evan recognized only two of the six agents at the table; the others were young, He began to wonder about the extent of their experience. Then he remembered the files that he reviewed on the plane.

Collectively this room was responsible for seventy-one assassinations.

The youngest of the group, the woman to his immediate right, had compiled a third of that number.

The team was a good one; there really was no doubt about that, but they are about to get their whole world rocked.

He glanced over at the handler and placed the folder on the large table. The woman who was briefing him walked over to the tech that was setting up the video feed and handed him a small zip drive. She nodded at Evan and then to the rest of the room, then walked out of the room.

"Right, lads, I know you all must be quite confused about why you are there in those seats," Evan began.

"Seeing the talent in this room, I can only imagine that someone is in need of a killing!" one of the older men who was sitting stated.

"You are quite right about the talent in this room, but this goes much deeper than a killing," Evan stated.

"Would you be acting team leader, Mr. Masters?" a young woman asked.

"Yes, I am. However, this assignment is not like anything you have dealt with in the past!" Evan stated.

"Are you trying to scare us?" the older man said.

"I suppose I am attempting to prepare you, and maybe that's a poor judgment on my part," Evan said as he gripped the back of the chair in front of him.

"Please, the suspense is killing me," the young female stated.

"Right, ladies and gentlemen, it appears that we are no longer alone in the universe!" Evan stated to a moment of deafening silence, then collective laughter.

"This is some form of test, a hoax, yes?" the woman said, more of a question than a statement.

"No test or hoax. It would appear that an extraterrestrial presence has made contact with governing bodies of the States!" Evan continued.

"Bollocks! We would have heard about this. Everyone knows the Yanks can't keep a bloody secret," one of the younger men said as he swiveled in his chair.

"I wish that were true. The video feed you're about to watch was taken three nights ago at an upscale hotel only blocks from this location!" Evan nodded at the tech.

After one minute and seventeen seconds of absolute carnage, the team sat in total disbelief.

Evan did nothing to break the silence; he wanted the data to sink in. He paced the front of the room, glancing at the team. Their faces showed a mix of emotions ranging from horror to denial.

After watching the film for a second time, he found himself slightly more shaken than his first viewing. Watching this on a bigger screen, he felt he was able to see the true nature of the beast.

Their eyes were extremely dark, almost lifeless. Deep down, Evan hoped that he would never come face-to-face with such an empty being.

His concentration was broken by the young man who wasn't buying the data. "This is pure madness. The Yanks are putting one over on us, and this footage reeks of bloody Hollywood!" the man stated.

"We don't know where they came from, or what they want. The motive for this attack is unknown. The news reports stated there was a propane explosion in the kitchen resulting in three injuries. We counted thirteen humans who were attacked in this video who couldn't possibly have survived. There is a leader who is known as Cain, who possesses the ability to transform into human form. There seems to be an ongoing dialogue between this alien Cain and certain factions of the Central Intelligence Agency. However, we are not sure of who or what faction. I am going to come clean with you all. This is the reaction that I initially had, but the Russians and Chinese are fully committed," Evan stated.

"Wow! This is unbelievable. Is there a kill order on those things?" the young woman on the right asked.

"No, the total opposite. This is a protection team!" Evan stated to the full disbelief of the table.

"Why in God's name would we want to protect this extraterrestrial and those things on the screen?" the older man stated, pointing to the video still on the wall.

"We can't have another nation taking technology off this being. Even a blood sample could tip the tides on this planet," Evan voiced.

"How do we locate this being and avoid detection from the CIA?" the older man stated in a tone that projected understanding and acceptance of the mission.

"The Chinese consulate ordered two fully loaded SUVs for immediate delivery. We feel they will be passed off to their team that has been forming downtown since this morning!" Evan began to lay out the plan.

"Where are the Russians?" the woman up front asked.

"They seem to be spread out with several arrivals at both LaGuardia and Newark International. We feel Brooklyn will be their final destination." Evan was obviously guessing. "We have been able to plant transmitters on both vehicles, and will monitor them from the moment they are delivered," Evan said with a pause as he studied the faces in the room.

"Remember you are professionals, and you will act as a team. I realize that most of you have never worked together. However, that is not going to matter today, because today the crown needs you to work as one. You leave this room knowing much more than you did when you entered. One thing hasn't changed, and that is England is counting on you. We didn't bring the best together to cock it up!" Evan's words broke like iron on calm seas.

He paused for a few seconds, glancing once more at the nightmare frozen on the screens, twisting the Oxford ring on his left finger, and then turned to the table.

"For queen and country, lads!" he stated as he lowered his eyes and let the room empty. He realized that he was holding back tears; he quickly searched his feelings. Evan never was what he would define as emotional, and he had sent countless people to face death. So why now was he on the verge of cracking?

He glanced back at the screen, and his eyes locked with the face of the alien. It was then he realized that he was angry, maybe even hateful. He had awoken this morning with a solid grasp on his world, only to realize that life on planet Earth would never be the same.

Every scenario that he ran through his head ended with a negative outcome. These beings will change everything, even if the Yanks didn't think otherwise.

In that moment, Evan knew what he needed to do.

Cain and the rest of these animals need to die with all the proof of their existence suppressed.

He had never disobeyed an order from the crown, but he knew that he was about to, and that filled him with guilt and pain.

He sat himself down slowly in the chair facing the screen. He put his face into his shaking hands and just for a second allowed himself a moment to weep for what he knew he needed to do.

CHAPTER 142

Jason sat in the habitat wrenching his hands and working really hard to remain calm.

The two beings seemed to be content, exploring the habitat.

He stood and took in a deep breath, then slowly made his way to the compound door next to the viewing window. Jason waved at the tech whom he had spoken to earlier. He heard the door click, and he walked in; the tech nodded, but after sixteen hours in that chair, he was physically shot.

The CIA agent was still busy with a newspaper, his eyes at half-mast.

The tech started to scramble around the board. Jason started to make a head count of the scientists in the next room. Three wasn't bad; he had seen as many as nine at one time. The tech started to increase his computer board scramble, and then he stood.

"Something's wrong! I am not picking up any heat signatures. Where are they?" the tech called out.

"What the hell are you talking about?" The CIA agent was out of his chair with his hands pressed against the viewing glass.

"I need you both to listen to me right now. Slowly start walking to the habitat," Jason stated with a calm demeanor, but still forceful enough that they knew it wasn't a joke.

"What are you talking about?" the tech asked, and then he started to see Trouble 1 emerge behind Dr. Daly.

"What the hell did you do?" he asked in total disbelief.

"What the fuck!" the CIA voiced in full outrage, then quickly motioned for his weapon.

"Please don't move!" Jason stated, but was too late. Trouble 1 had leaped onto the chest of the CIA agent and was now digging his talons through his skin.

"Take your hand from the weapon. Don't take it out. Just remove your hand from it now!" Jason said in a very clear, easy tone.

"What's going on, Doc? Why did you allow the subjects to breach the perimeter?" the young tech said, his voice cracking from progressing fear.

"No harm will come to anyone if you will all just slowly walk to the habitat. I don't have time to explain," Jason stated as Trouble 2 slipped past him and went into the other room.

The screaming sounded the minute the primary saw Trouble 2.

Instinctively, the scientist raced for the door, intending to exit. However, that was a drastic mistake as Trouble 2 leapt like a panther and sliced the scientist's hand to the bone.

The scientist scrambled to the other side of the room, clenching his hand like a child who grabbed a hot pot.

The CIA agent watched the exchange then turned back to Trouble 1 who was inches from his face, razor-like teeth on display.

Any thought of rebellion ended that second.

Jason motioned to the other scientist to move out of the room and walk slowly to the habitat. Trouble 1 moved off the agent, allowing him to get to his feet. Jason walked over and removed the weapon from his holster and motioned him to follow the others.

"Daly, they're going to kill you and everything you care about for this. Do you know that?" the agent stated as he was being ushered into the habitat.

"I never really had a chance to leave this zoo. You made that clear, and I can't let you hurt these beings," Jason stated as he closed the door and clamped the lock.

"Stay behind us. It's time to go!" Trouble 1 said as they opened the door and started down the hall.

Trouble 1 stayed close to the wall, working the shadows, as Trouble 2 took to the ceiling and moved a few feet ahead.

Jason was surprised that there were no guards posted outside the door, but he knew that there would be plenty of issues before they were free. When he turned the corner, he saw the first body was lying on his back. The second soldier was propped up against the wall, eyes wide open and blood squirting from his right ear.

He was astonished that there were no sounds of struggle, no yelling; they were perfect predators.

As he moved along the halls that seemed to be endless, he found himself stepping over no one alive.

They had reached the loading dock that led to the outside and the cover of the woods. Jason ran as fast as his feet would carry him. He came within ten feet of the door when the alarm sounded.

CHAPTER 143

Cain sat back in the cockpit-style chair within the vault, several displays and communication devices shooting out information.

His brain was processing countless frequencies of all levels of government, both foreign and domestic. He was surprised at just how little was coming through. On the surface, everything looked like business as usual. There was some limited data coming out of the command post in Brooklyn. The science team had been requesting some advanced diagnostic testing equipment. He guessed that had to do with the changes they were seeing with Mr. Pierce. Then he heard some orders for silicone residual testing and knew that Dr. Kowalski was starting to figure out a few realities.

Cain was slightly surprised at his ability; he wondered what it was that tipped him off. He wasn't that concerned at this development; his primary focus was still the two abominations and the Worthington woman. He would circle back and deal with the good doctor.

He was able to keep tabs on Schmitt and the priest; their phone was sending out a solid ping from some shitty hotel off Queens Boulevard; he guessed they were resting or licking their wounds.

He would need them soon enough; he just needed to find the lynchpin in all the data.

The woman agent was still in Brooklyn along with her new friend. Smith was right about the intelligence community; they were pouring into New York like it was Black Friday.

As his mind continued to process the data, he began to see the reality of his situation. The world had changed greatly over the past twenty years; for each step humanity took forward, there were two steps that made them fall back. His presence here in this time was not going to be received well. He knew that he could only oppose his will upon them for so long; eventually they would find a way to destroy him.

He regretted sending so many back through the gate; he didn't realize just how complicated things had become here on Earth. There was still one gate open outside of Japan; he knew that he needed to close that soon, or all hell would break loose.

There was something that was keeping him from ending all ties with his world. Cain searched his mind and he couldn't understand what divided his feelings. He thought maybe it was the loneliness of being the only one of his kind imprisoned in this world. His conflict was alarming him, and it was something he was not familiar with. Cain knew he wanted to live out the remainder of his life force here; he knew this at his core, then why the conflict?

He wondered if his irrational thinking was part of his exploration into the human experience.

He stopped processing data for just a second and opened his mind to the concept that his conflict was a side effect of human interaction.

The beautiful black woman that he had enjoyed at such a passionate level had called him last night angry for reasons he couldn't understand.

The CIA agent Smith wanted him dead, and he apparently wasn't alone.

Cain couldn't find rationality in any of them, except maybe the woman. The female agent seemed to only have one agenda, the truth. Maybe he could utilize her in this equation somehow. He knew if he was to survive, he needed to change the players. The Worthington woman had betrayed him, and that he understood, but her motives were confusing.

He understood human greed, and at some level, he even respected it; he felt it made them a bit more predictable. However, her motivation was almost of a delusional nature, and that needed to be dealt with, but this would have to wait.

Something was really off with the incoming intelligence or the lack of information. His mind entertained the thought that maybe Smith was closing in on his Houdini act and was limiting just how much was getting out.

Then it happened; an alarm when off at an army facility just outside of Tarrytown, New York.

Then the puzzle all came together. Cain smiled and thought to himself, *There you are!*

Cain let all those negative thoughts slide away and pulled up Schmitt's cell number.

"Schmitt!" a single voice said.

"There is a facility on the far side of the Tappan Zee Bridge. You will find what you and I are looking for there."

"We are on it!" Schmitt stated with eagerness.

"I am sending you GPS coordinates now. You are not going to be alone out there," Cain warned.

"Understood. We still need to come to an understanding of what to do if we find your two assets," Schmitt probed.

"They need to be terminated. The Worthington woman is not to be harmed. That will be my job!" Cain said with a solid tone.

"Will you be there to handle that?" Schmitt asked.

"I am already there!" Cain stated.

"Copy that!" Schmitt ended their dialogue.

After he discontinued the call, Cain began to disconnect the rest of the devices. It was time to operate at a much higher level considering the testing that Kowalski was engaged in.

It was only a matter of days before the vault was penetrated; he needed to prepare for his new life.

He had to admit that he was impressed by just how fast the food was learning. He had underestimated their ability and that wouldn't happen again.

Cain closed his eyes and began transcending into the air above the chair; there was a snap of light, and he was gone.

CHAPTER 144

Smith saw the alarm light go off, and at first, it was only a blip on a large board. He almost let that single wisp of light go past, and then it hit him. It all made sense; the facility had been decommissioned and was sold to some Maryland holding company.

The only reason that hellhole would be sounding off an alarm was if there was an attack or a breach.

It was a quick ride by copter from the city, it was perfect, and Worthington had manipulated this whole chain of events. She had the connections to pull this off, no doubt in his mind.

It was time to mobilize the forces and put an end to this saga.

He took a deep breath and being a longtime chess player, he worked through a handful of scenarios then leaned over and pushed the brown button on the intelligence board.

The plethora of screens in the room all turned to the facility in Tarrytown. Smith ordered the lockdown of the command center, no information in or out. Then he began to bark orders in fast repetition.

"I want all data on the Tarrytown allied facility, phone records, shipment manifest, crew rosters, and any camera feeds in or around the facility!" Smith barked with severe intensity, causing a freeze of all activity in the room.

"We might have a small problem with that request, sir!" one of the computer techs stated with fear in his voice.

"Please enlighten me, soldier, what that would be?" Smith said, obviously becoming annoyed.

"That facility is no longer in the hands of the United States government. The firewall seems to be marked classified at level thirty-seven!" the tech added, sounding confused.

"Son, level thirty-seven is CIA. That's us. Why can't we work through our own damn firewalls?" Smith stated, equally confused.

"Sir, these are marked with diplomatic immunity. We would need a presidential clearance code to proceed," the tech stated.

"What the fuck are you talking about, son? What country is listed as the owner of record?" Smith asked. The steel in his voice was deafening.

"It appears to be the Vatican, sir!" the tech stated.

Smith slowly rose up out of his chair; his mind scrambled with the infinite puzzle pieces. The mutilated body in the midtown office building had Vatican ties. Smith saw some photos and immediately thought Cain had something to do with it. Then the federal agent and the city cop had mentioned a Vatican lawyer at the hotel; it was starting to come together.

There were shell casings all over the building and in the street; why would Cain need weapons?

As hard as he twisted his noodle, it wasn't adding up. However, it didn't need to.

All his answers were a short trip north, on the far side of the Tappan Zee Bridge.

Smith slowed his mind down long enough to get control of the room and the frozen faces that were awaiting orders.

"First, I want the two F-16s at Fort Hamilton scrambled to the air in three minutes." Smith pointed at different players as he continued, "Second, I want everything at our command in the air two minutes ago with a target destination of Tarrytown, New York." He cocked his head at the soldier who hadn't moved on his command; the soldier began to run.

"Major, I want that president dragged out of bed. I need those codes. If he has even a slight issue, remind him just how cold it gets in Chicago this time of year!" Smith was moving toward the exit, snapping off commands as he placed live fire clips in the several weapons he had on his person.

CHAPTER 145

Jason stumbled but didn't fall; he could feel the damp pine needles in his hands.

The woods were dense and dark; it felt really good to be out of the hotbox down in the bunker.

Both the Troubles had taken to the woods like wolves. He could hear them sometimes right and sometimes left as he ran.

Every now and then, he would hear the sound of a body hitting the floor of the forest. He assumed that it was a soldier that entered their perimeter.

Jason took in short breaths as he ran, cursing his weakness for cigarettes as he heaved. After about a mile and a half, he needed to stop just long enough to vomit the contents of his stomach. He continued along a path that he thought was most likely from deer. He hit an open clearing after another quarter mile.

Trouble 2 was standing there; he could see her outline from the moonlight. As he came closer, he could see the blood on her clothing and face; he knew it wasn't hers. Trouble 1 came in fast from behind him; he was also covered with blood mostly around his face, but both hands seemed to glow black in the moonlight.

Jason knew this was going to be an issue as they traveled further away.

If he was to keep these two safe, distance was needed to put between them and this evil place.

Bloody children will be difficult to hide and near impossible to pass through any type of law-enforced checkpoints.

Trouble 1 saw Jason's face and looked down at his bloody hands and the face of his sister. There was a brief moment where Jason thought he saw some slight embarrassment in the face of Trouble 1. That initially shocked Jason; he had worked with predators half his life and never saw any form of regret. He began to see them in a slightly different light. Their feeding behavior was primal and instinctual, but the Troubles also wanted to be part of the environment they shared with their food.

The conflict must be difficult, especially for these young two. Jason watched as Trouble 1 led his sister down by the water's edge to clean up. They returned quickly and without any evidence of their activity.

CHAPTER 146

"What's going on up there?" Mac asked his new friend from the Mossad.

"Smith seems to be in high gear. He has mobilized the whole unit, and they're rolling out," Barack stated, rolling his eyes.

"I wonder why we haven't been given an invitation to the party!" Mac joked, looking back and forth between Magen and Dean.

"It appears that this part of the team has outlived its usefulness. We have become obsolete!" Barack stated, not really too concerned.

"I have been chasing Cain for too many years just to sit back and play second fiddle," Magen stated, her anger evident.

"There is a full communication ban up there. I don't even know where they are going," the Israeli stated.

"Do you think we can get out of here?" Mac asked, his mind racing.

"That will not be an issue. There is hardly anyone left at this compound," Barack said with a smile.

"Why am I getting a nervous feeling in the pit of my stomach?" William Dean stated as he looked at Mac.

"I know this is going to sound crazy, but something Cornell said about where he was being held has me spinning," Mac stated.

"Mac, Cornell is my friend, but his data is not reliable. He is just hanging on in there," Dean said with sadness in his voice.

"I agree, but something he said about the vault and the smell of food jogged a memory," Mac continued.

"What is it, Mac?" Magen asked.

"What if it wasn't a bank at all? What if it was a restaurant that was once a bank?" Mac asked, aware of the confusion he was instilling in the others.

"Do you know such a place?" William Dean asked.

"There is a place just a few blocks from the initial meeting place that Cain arranged to meet," Mac stated.

"Really? That's interesting, almost too much of a coincidence! What's the name of this place?" Dean asked.

"It's called the Holy Trinity. Huge vault right in the middle of the place, decent food," Mac stated.

"It would need to be shut down, the whole place closed down!" Kowalski stated as he stepped into the room.

"Why is that, Doc?" Mac asked.

"Cain would need time and room just for the power source alone for what he's doing," Kowalski began.

"I take it that you're on something, and we need a break," Mac stated.

"Cain said something to me when we first met about how he arrived here on Earth." Kowalski paused then continued, "He said that in order to travel through space, all minerals needed to be removed from the body. That made me think, he would need to get those minerals back into his form upon his arrival." Kowalski was rolling. "Well, if he could do that between planetary systems, then movement on one single planet would be easy," Kowalski paused to let his words sink in.

"Now try and follow this. Just maybe with this machine, he can appear anywhere as a solid mass, and not even be there!" Kowalski took a step back and watched his colleagues.

"I'm lost, so the times we have come face-to-face with this thing, he wasn't there?" Mac asked, trying to grasp the doctor's theory.

"Let's say this machine can project a type of solid hologram and his consciousness controls it. I think that would answer so many questions on how he keeps coming and going. I took some really strange chemical readings out of that holding room where he disappeared from! However, he would need a point position and a significant power source, not the middle of a restaurant," Kowalski stated.

"Do you get Internet on that phone of yours, Magen?" Mac asked.

"Yes, what are you thinking?" she asked, somewhat confused.

"Try and make a reservation at Holy Trinity!" Mac said then winked at her.

"He would need solitude and room. More important, he would have security. My guess is that it would be some type of warehouse, extremely isolated!" Kowalski stated as he envisioned the environment that would be ideal.

"Unable to book reservations, closed for repairs!" Magen snapped as if she was screaming bingo.

"Well, what was it you said about coincidence?" Kowalski stated in Mac's direction.

"That there was no such thing!" Mac said as his mind kicked into overdrive.

"We need to contact Smith. I am not sure where they are heading, but I don't think they are there heading in the right direction," Magen added, looking for agreement from the others.

"Not possible. There is a total communication blackout. Smith can be slightly paranoid at times!" Barack stated, his tone indicating that he was still agitated about being left out of the loop.

"I'm down for a little drive into the city. Some recon couldn't hurt!" Mac announced.

"Why not? Besides, sitting here waiting for Smith's return sounds unproductive," Magen said with a smile.

"I will take some liberties with the command center and try and assist you from within!" Barack stated as he reached out his hand toward Mac's.

"I need to stay behind as well!" Kowalski added.

"I thought you would be interested if your theories were correct. Why the sudden direction change?" Magen asked.

"I don't think Cain likes me too much, and I feel that if he finds me in the proximity of his hive, he would pull my head off my body!" Kowalski grimaced, considering the mental picture.

"He would know immediately that you smoked him out. I agree you need to stay behind," William Dean stated as he placed his hand on the doctor's shoulder.

"Seems that the three amigos ride again!" Mac stated with a wide smile.

"I want to take Cornell. It might help his memory if he sees the place," Dean added, but he wasn't asking permission. He was telling the team how it was going to be.

"Right, I can have him transferred upstairs for something, not a problem. Just give me two minutes," Kowalski stated, and then he was gone through the swinging doors.

"We are going to need transportation, something less discreet than the assault vehicles outside!" Mac stated.

"What about weapons?" Magen asked, not really sure why they would help.

"Better to be ready. However, I sure don't want an M-16 jammed up my ass tonight!" Mac added with a painful grin.

"I'll stick with some low-caliber handguns, much easier to be removed from your rectum," Magen added with her own smile.

"Thanks, honey!" Mac stated as he headed to the parking garage.

"That will be all, soldier!" Kowalski said as the guards ushered Cornell into the room.

"We have orders to stay with the subject at all times!" the young soldier stated in his best military tone.

"Son, this is not a subject. He is a hero, and he is on our side. Now that will be all!" Kowalski stated as he tried to push his heart back down his throat, but remained firm.

"Yes, sir!" the soldier snapped and backpedaled from the room.

"Why am I here?" Cornell asked as soon as he heard boot steps moving away down the hall.

"We are taking a trip to find a monster, thought you might like to help," William Dean stated as he walked in from the adjoining room.

Cornell just smiled at his friend; no words were necessary.

CHAPTER 147

"I have the goods. Let's roll. Glad you could make it, Mr. Pierce!" Magen came in holding up a duffel bag full of small arms.

"This was the best I could do!" Mac yelled out over the noise of the military Hummer that he pulled up in.

"Were there no tanks available?" Magen joked as they all piled into the vehicle.

"I can't drive a tank. Not part of NYPD training!" Mac stated as he was sad about the admission.

"Thank God!" Magen said as her head was thrown back from Mac's fast departure.

"GPS has us three miles out. In a minute, I'm going to look for a viable landing area!" the pilot yelled into the cabin.

"Roger that, Private. We need to get lower. This facility is highly armed. I'm not looking to get blown from the sky tonight," Smith stated as he turned in his chair to one of the soldiers at the radar station.

"When we get about a mile out, I want infrared through the woods. Concentrate mostly on the south side," Smith stated, passing a map to the soldier.

"Yes, sir!" the soldier said, his eye never leaving the screen.

"I want the tactical units on the ground to approach from north and south. We are going to come in from the west, bottleneck them toward the river," Smith continued shooting orders out.

"Is there any support in the river, just in case?" the pilot asked.

"Nothing that we could have called into action in the time frame necessary."

"Sir, my infrared is picking up significant action throughout the woods!" the soldier stated.

"Talk to me. What are we dealing with?" Smith asked with pure focus.

"We have about thirty troops moving away from the facility, and there are three nine-man teams moving towards the facility about a half mile out," the soldier stated.

"Three teams! I knew the Chinese and the Russians would be joining the party, but I can't wait to find out who else has joined the parade," Smith smiled but was slightly annoyed.

"There is a clearing coming up. Do you want me to land this bird?" the pilot asked.

"Yeah, I want on the ground now. I'm sure they see us on radar, so don't put us in the middle of these teams and get my ass blown off," Smith cracked as he pulled on the seat belt harness, anticipating a fast descent.

"I have no signs of the targets. I scanned two miles out, not seeing any grouping of three anywhere," the soldier at the radar stated.

"You are looking for just one target moving away from the guys with guns. Two of the subjects will not be showing up on infrared," Smith said, thinking things through.

"I don't understand, sir. How is that possible?" the radar man looked up.

"Two of the subjects are cold-blooded!" Smith stated as if it was common knowledge.

"Right, I will rescan the area and look for a lone runner," the soldier stated as he went back to the screen, trying hard not to appear too shocked.

"When we hit the ground, I want the men to fan out fifty yards and hold the perimeter. No order to engage," Smith barked at the pilot.

"Sir, wouldn't we be handing one of these retrieval teams a little bit of an advantage if we don't engage?" the pilot asked, somewhat confused.

"I anticipate that there will be no shortage of death in the next half hour. No reason for us add to the chaos!" Smith said calmly.

"Sir, I just finished the infrared scan of the area and have found no single runners," the radar specialist stated.

"We need to take the scan out further, get a satellite online. If they got out, they're moving fast away from the facility!" Smith stated.

"We will have SEC 1 online in six minutes. Is there a direction that we should use as a priority?" the radar tech added.

"What direction are the soldiers from the facility moving?" Smith asked.

"North to south!" the soldier added.

"There you have it! I want a three-mile parameter on that facility, and it's time to get some coverage on the water," Smith stated as he stepped off the helicopter.

"I only have one pair of night vision glasses, so I am going to need both of you to stay on my six!" Sergeant Campbell stated to Schmitt and the priest as they hit the heavy brush.

"Right on your heels, Sergeant. Head for that ridge over by the river!" Schmitt announced his order broken by the sound of suppressed gunfire and bullets raking the tree line in front of them.

"Holy shit, we walked into the meat grinder!" the priest yelled at Schmitt.

"Who the fuck are these assholes?" the sergeant snapped.

"I can't place the weapons, might be Swiss or maybe Chinese!" Schmitt whispered, trying not to give away his position.

"I really don't care who they are, Let's get the hell out of here," Frank Nica yelled then heard a noise at his feet. It was a grenade; instinctively, he picked it up and threw it from the direction it came.

CHAPTER 148

Jason heard the blast from the grenade and then the rapid fire of several weapons. His guess was that it was a little less than a mile away, but out there in the field, there was total silence, so sound traveled.

Both of the Troubles stood wide-eyed, looking in the direction of the firefight. Trouble 1 seemed puzzled, while his sister only appeared fearful.

She gripped his hand tight, the nail on her index finger drawing a little blood. He winced a little and pulled her finger out a little and smiled at her. She grinned back, seeming to be a bit embarrassed.

His focus had been on the noise from the woods and the pain in his hand that he didn't realize that he had stepped out onto a concrete road.

A vehicle came around the bend about two hundred feet behind him. By the time he realized that he and Trouble 2 were fully exposed, it was too late to do anything about it.

Trouble 1 crouched low in the weeds, waiting to pounce on the vehicle as it slowed right next to them, and the side window slowly rolled down.

"Folks, this is not a good road to walk on at night. Can I offer you a lift?" an elderly man asked.

"That would be fantastic. My son is going to the bathroom. One second, please," Jason motioned Trouble 1 to come up from the bush.

"No problem, when you have to go, right?" the old man stated with a bit of a laugh that was more a snort.

"Can't thank you enough. We had some car trouble. You kids put your seat belts on," Jason said, trying to sound relaxed.

"That's fine. I don't recall seeing a car on my way in. You folks roll in a ditch?" the man asked, not yet driving away.

"No, just pulled it off far enough so it wouldn't get hit," Jason shot back, getting slightly concerned that the old man was not moving.

"What are your names?" he called back to the children, only to receive silence.

"That's Jake and Rachel!" Jason shot back after a short pause, not sure where he pulled the names from.

"Hi, Jake and Rachel, can you two please buckle up?" the old man asked with a big smile.

"Oh, right," Jason stated as he turned to help both of them buckle up, realizing that they had no idea what a seat belt was.

"There you go, kids!" Jason stated as the both of them just sat there smiling.

"I'm Jake!" Trouble 1 announced almost with pride.

"And I'm Rachel!" his sister shot back as if she was testing out her new name.

"I am Walter, and I am so happy to meet you," the gray-haired man said as he threw the vehicle into drive.

"Thanks so much!" Jason said in a happy manner, but there was great sadness ripping his insides to pieces. They never had names before; they were experiments. He just wanted to hold them.

"Well, I just couldn't leave you out there for the horseman!" the old-timer laughed.

"Who is the horseman?" Jason asked.

"You know, the Headless Horseman. You are in Sleepy Hollow you know!" he said, repeating the same laugh.

"I thought this was Tarrytown, New York?" Jason stated, then looked behind to see fear on both faces.

"No, you left Tarrytown about a mile from where I picked you up. This is Sleepy Hollow," Walter said with a hint of pride.

"Sleepy Hollow, you mean from the Irving novel?" Jason asked, surprised at what he was hearing.

"One and the same, and that's why you shouldn't be out there in the dark!" Walter laughed as he spoke.

"It's just a story, nothing to worry about. Everything is fine," Jason said as he saw the fear on Trouble 2's face.

"So where are you heading in the middle of the night?" the old man asked.

"We are going to meet my brother at a Marina nearby," Jason lied as he anticipated the question.

"You mean the old Bill Gardiner place?" Walter asked.

"Oh, right, isn't there a dockyard on the other side of the Hollow?" Jason asked.

"I guess so. Haven't been there for years, but there might be a dock on the far side!" Walter said with puzzlement in his voice.

"It's my wife's brother. He's meeting us there with a boat," Jason lied.

"At night with the rain coming in? You must like living on the edge," Walter stated, not really buying the story.

"Yeah, he's just crazy, but you can't pick family, right?" Jason said, attempting to recover.

"Young man, I have been lied to by much better than yourself in my many years!" Walter stated without even a blink.

"Not sure I know what you mean, Walter," Jason mumbled.

"Really, should I just drive over to the sheriff's office?" Walter asked.

"The military want to capture and kill these children!" Jason said after a long thoughtful pause.

"Why in God's name would the military want to harm these kids?" Walter stated as he turned his neck to look at the faces of the two children.

"They have been subjected to some experimentation, and now they wish to cover up their actions," Jason added.

"When I was at Columbia University, we realized that the government was capable of just about anything!" Walter said through gritted teeth.

"Will you help us? I can't get them away alone!" Jason asked.

"You need to meet someone who can help you, but yes, I believe you. I have been watching these military people spending money hand over foot over the past several months. Enlighten me!" Walter stated with anger in his voice noted.

"Thank you. Walter!" Jason said as he turned and smiled at the Troubles.

"I knew they were up to no good in that place, telling everyone that they were closing the place, all those food trucks rolling in and out, buying supplies like they have a blank check!" Walter snapped.

"They are coming for them. We really shouldn't stop!" Jason pressed.

"Oh, we need to stop. My friend Keith is skilled at this type of thing. Two tours in Vietnam. You will we see!" Walter managed a sly smile as they pulled up to a small pharmacy.

"Keith is a pharmacist?" Jason asked, somewhat confused.

"Not a good one, poor eyesight. You always need to make sure you're getting the right meds. Come on and bring the kids!" Walter said as he opened the car door.

"Walter, time is critical. I am appreciative of your help, but we need to go. These are evil people!" Jason continued to press.

"Son, didn't your dad ever tell you not to bring a knife to a gunfight?" Walter stated as he opened the door.

"What are you talking about?" Jason said as he followed Walter in, holding the hands of both Troubles.

"Keith, how are you my friend? We need your help!" Walter stated as he locked the front door and flipped the "Closed" sign.

"Walter, you flipped my sign. Why did you flip my sign?" Keith seemed confused.

"Keith, the government is after these people. They wish to do harm on these children!" Walter stated simply.

"Would that be our government? What is special about these children?" Keith asked, eyeing the Troubles up and down.

"Show him, Jake!" Jason asked as Trouble 1 held up his right hand and allowed his talons to extend and detract.

"Mother of God, Walter, did you just see that?" Keith snapped, his shock evident.

"Keith, they have been experimenting on these children, and now they are coming to kill them!" Walter said, attempting to break the trance Keith seemed to be in.

"Not going to happen. Let's go!" Keith said as he led them out the back to a freestanding garage that looked like it could fit an airplane.

"Hiding is not going to be effective. They are going to rain down on this town like a plague!" Jason tried to emphasize as he allowed himself to be led through the door.

"Welcome to the jungle!" Keith said as he waved his hand over the room full of weapons.

"Holy smokes, what country are you waging war on?" Jason joked as he watched Trouble 1 smell one of the large-caliber weapons on the wall.

"I don't wage war, but I love a good fight. Now let's get you and these kids out of here!" Keith stated as he pulled the tarp off a 1970 black Plymouth Barracuda.

"Wow!" Trouble 1 stated as he looked at and smelled the car.

"Hop in, kiddies, and, son, would you please grab two of those LAW rockets off the wall!" Keith pointed over to the wall with the anti-tank weapons.

"Do you really think this will be necessary?" Jason asked.

"I certainly hope so!" Keith said with a sly smile.

"That would be my cue. I have put you in the hands of a man born for this, and alas, I must take my leave of you!" Walter said with mocked sadness.

"Walter, I don't know what to say. You saved us!" Jason stated with sincere admiration.

"You take care of those children. Be well, Jason!" Walter said and was gone from the garage.

CHAPTER 149

Cain took a deep breath as he stepped from behind a large pine. He could sense movement in several different directions. Things were going to heat up in these woods before long. Cain heard a small twig snap just a few feet away, and a sinister smile spread across his face.

The Chinese agent was not doing an extremely good job on a stealth approach. It was no wonder it was only six hours earlier that he was setting type at the *New York Times*.

As he stumbled through the cold woods, giving away the position of his team, fear ran out of his pores. He had just made reservations at a new restaurant on the Upper East Side, and then the phone rang.

Cain could smell the slightly overweight agent now. His cholesterol was high, and he was cooking some early prostate cancer, but he was still going to taste great.

"Good evening!" Cain said in flawless Mandarin.

"Who is that? Chow, is that you?" the agent called out, shock and surprise in his voice.

"No, your luck isn't running that good tonight, my friend!" Cain stated as he raised the talon on his left index finger.

"Chow, stop goofing around, You know I'm dying out here!" the agent whispered into the darkness.

"You certainly are!" Cain stated as he pierced through the man's chest plate and severed his right ventricle.

There was a minor gasp, then came the feed.

CHAPTER 150

There is a beautiful calmness in the woods at night; it can really intensify one's senses.

As the teams moved in from multiple points, the sound of a human body being ripped to shreds was unmistakable.

When the chunky young man's hip bone was snapped out of the socket, it sent a loud pop that could have been heard from a quarter mile away.

There was no screaming or pleading, just ripping and the sound of tendons snapping under stress. Then there was the smell slowly creeping through the woods. The violated body was releasing gasses and chemicals that just had no place in those calm damp woods.

The Chinese team was the first to pick up on the stench; they froze and tried to make sense of what was going on. One of the younger agents began to gag as vomit began to crawl up his throat.

That was all it took.

The woods erupted in a hail of bullets! Then there was screaming as the rain of hot full metal jackets couldn't help but find random targets.

"This is ridiculous. They don't even know who they are shooting at!" Smith stated as he heard the firefight begin.

"We could utilize this event to penetrate the building if you wish," his second-in-command suggested.

"Let's do it. I want Worthington alive!" Smith barked as they entered a trail that would lead them away from the firefight.

CHAPTER 151

The streets were loud and cold as Mac rolled the Hummer close to the restaurant's location. There were people moving in all directions.

Mac smiled at the thought of Cain operating out of such a busy area right here in his city.

The cop that he was instinctively began to dissect the block.

He soaked in the faces, vehicles, and even the shadows that the buildings offered; there was nothing that he would consider out of place. He couldn't identify any lookouts or even a vehicle that just didn't fit in.

The thought that he had made a mistake briefly ran through his head. He looked at Magen who was also studying the area. Her face spoke volumes, and there was nothing out of place.

Mac glanced into the back of the Hummer to see Cornell's face pale and ashen. There was a vacant look that wasn't there minutes ago; he looked almost dead.

"Mr. Pierce, is everything all right?" Mac said as everyone turned to see the stress grow in Cornell's eyes.

"He is here, and he knows that I'm outside!" Cornell stated as his breathing intensified.

"What? How do you know that, Cornell?" Mac asked as he cut off a yellow cab to get to the curb.

"I can feel him inside my head!" Cornell yelled as he dug the tips of his fingers into the loose flesh at his temples.

"It's okay, Cornell. Take it easy, my friend!" William Dean said as he placed his hand on Cornell's then snapped it back fast.

"What is it, Mr. Dean?" Magen asked, watching his reaction.

"His hand is on fire, and there is a live current running through it. Incredible!" Dean stated as he cradled his hand like a child.

"What the fuck is he doing in my head?" Cornell yelled as he reached out and grabbed his good friend's coat.

"I'm pulling over. Take it easy!" Mac said as he swerved and cut off a yellow cab to get to the curb.

"It's all right, Cornell!" Magen managed as she noticed an older woman on the sidewalk stop in her tracks and turn her head and peer right into her eyes.

"I can feel him smiling at me!" Cornell continued, his stress growing.

"Mac, we might have a problem!" Magen stated as she saw the woman start to run at the vehicle.

"What!" Mac said as the woman ran face-first into the window behind him, causing him to jump.

"What the fuck!" Mac snapped as he watched the bleeding woman back up a few feet and charge the vehicle again.

"We need to get the hell out of here!" Cornell yelled, watching the woman take her second charge.

"Is she crazy?" William stated out loud as he tried to make sense. Then the roof of the Hummer buckled as a body fell from above.

"Mac, please, we need to go!" Magen screamed as blood began to roll down the back windows.

"We are gone!" Mac stated as he pulled off the curb with both sides of the streets clearing and chasing after the car.

"What the hell is going on out there?" Dean yelled as they sped away, chased by perfect strangers.

"Cornell, how does Cain control these people?" Mac barked as he darted in and out of traffic.

"I don't know!" Cornell whispered as his body seemed to deflate.

"Oh my God!" Magen shouted as the body rolled off the roof as Mac sped up.

"We need to call Smith, let him know to get his ass out of the woods!" Mac stated as he turned off the avenue.

CHAPTER 152

Schmitt threw his back against a thick pine tree as bullets began to breeze past.

He called back to his sergeant who was scrambling on the ground, holding his left shoulder.

Frank Nica was lying flat on his belly, waiting for the shooting to stop, but he was in no real hurry to move.

Schmitt pointed his weapon around the corner and squeezed off a burst in the direction where the tracers were coming from. Another blast of bullets lit up the tree to his left, starting a small fire at the base.

After the return fire, he reached out and grabbed his friend and pulled to the tree. Two grenades exploded about twenty feet from his position; a few small fragments hit his ankle but not hard enough to penetrate the skin.

Schmitt worked on his breathing, something he learned to do in countless firefights in every corner of the world. He wondered how he could have walked into such an obvious trap. How could he listen to that alien or whatever the hell it was?

"Are you guys having fun yet?" Cain said. He seemed to appear out of nowhere.

"Where the hell did you come from?" Schmitt screamed.

"We don't have time for all that. You have much work to do!" Cain stated.

"What the hell are you talking about? We're getting our ass kicked out here!" Schmitt shouted, sending another burst around the corner of the tree.

"Would you please stop shooting at the Chinese? They will just keep firing back," Cain stated as if the whole situation was exhausting.

"Why are the Chinese out in these woods shooting at us?" Schmitt asked, confused about what he was hearing from Cain.

"They're here following the Russians, and the English are out there somewhere also, but the prize has slipped out the back door!" Cain said as he looked in the direction where the children were.

"What? How do you know that?" Schmitt asked.

"Excuse me, be right back," Cain said and then was gone.

CHAPTER 153

Evan kneeled on a bluff three hundred yards off the developing firefight, attempting to focus his infrared scope; when the two grenades went off, he totally lost focus as the field of vision flashed, slightly blinding his left eye.

He turned away from the scope and blinked several times then refocused. He could make out a slightly heavy male lying prone on the ground; another male was being dragged to the base of a tree to avoid fire. Then the infrared picked up something else; it was a figure but unlike the others, and it had no distinct form.

Evan knew that this was the alien.

He took several deep breaths and gently squeezed the trigger. The weapon kicked a bit but not enough for Evan to lose focus, but the figure was gone.

Then Evan realized that he was not alone; someone was kneeling next to him.

"Did you get him?" Cain asked.

"Apparently not, my target appears to be a bit on the wily side!" Evan stated as he scrambled to his feet, surprised at the alien's youthful appearance.

"If I was a paranoid being, I might think you possessed an agenda that wasn't too Cain friendly?" Cain stated as he arched his eyebrow.

"That's right, Cain; is it? My orders are to extract you, but I certainly am not in agreement with those orders. You are in need of a killing!" Evan stated as he pulled a smoke from his top pocket and lit it with a Zippo lighter, offering Cain one as well.

"I must say I am intrigued. You seem like a decent man. Why would you need to snuff little ol' me?" Cain asked as he allowed the British soldier to light his cigarette.

"Your existence is going to destroy this world. The sheep are far from ready for a new breed of wolf!" Evan stated as he pulled deep on his smoke, fully aware that it might be his last.

"I remember a time when you English were the wolves, ravaging the planet, and now look at you, the shepherd!" Cain stated as he looked out over the field of dying men.

"Well, I suppose that is true, but you will add nothing to this world, only pain and suffering!" Evan stated and then held his hands behind his back.

"I have been adding to this world longer than your line has walked the land!" Cain stated then turned to the soldier and placed his finger in Evan's eye.

There was a flash, a pop, some smoke, and Evan was dead.

Cain was gone.

CHAPTER 154

"So where was I?" Cain said to Schmitt as he phased back.

"Where the hell do you keep going? We have a bit of a situation here!" Schmitt yelled as he held a field dressing on his friend.

"At ease, soldier, you need to collect the priest who apparently is in no hurry to meet his boss, and back out the way you came!" Cain stated with a hint of sarcasm.

"What about my man? He needs a medic. He still has a bullet in his shoulder," the major pressed.

"You can leave him here with me. I will take good care of him!" Cain offered as a smile spread across his childlike features.

"No, I have him!" Schmitt stated as he began to pull his friend up and then whistled to Frank.

"There is a small town about a mile south. Look for a marina. It is the only option that makes sense!" Cain stated as he began to walk off.

"Is there a reason that you're not going after these two kids? You seem to be able to come and go as you please," Smith asked, obviously angered and confused by his situation.

"I have some issues to deal with back in the city, after I correct our mutual friend!" Cain stated with a chilling focus, then turned and was gone.

CHAPTER 155

"I want them found. Nothing is more important, Captain!" Helen Worthington screeched through gritted teeth.

"We are on it. I need some air support just in case they clear the woods!" Captain Elman stated as he pointed to the grid map on the wall.

"You will have it. Do we know who is attacking my facility?" Worthington asked, more than slightly annoyed.

"We are making out three groups. The primary team was engaged from the left flank. Not sure who the others are shooting at!" the captain stated.

"It is harder and harder to keep secrets. I'm guessing that there is a laundry list of factions out there that wish to secure the offspring!" Helen said with noted defiance.

"There is much more going on out there than we understand," the captain stated with obvious confusion.

"I'm not sure I follow, Captain," Helen stated, giving him full focus.

"There are two highly trained teams of elite soldiers blowing themselves to pieces in our backyard. That's not adding up for me!" the tall soldier stated, still watching the monitors.

"You think Cain is out there creating his own brand of chaos, and eventually he will be heading my way?" Worthington stated with a hint of anxiety.

"That is looking like a strong possibility. We may consider the need to move you to a secondary location," the captain pressed.

"The children need to be found and secured. Everything else is secondary!" Helen slapped her hand on the desk in defiance.

"I applaud your valor, Mrs. Worthington, but I have to consider your safety and the success of the project!" the older soldier stated with firmness in his voice.

"There is absolutely no project without the return of the children, but I do understand your position," Helen yielded in her own way.

"I am getting your helicopter ready on pad three. Cleared for departure in six minutes!" the captain stated as he turned back to the video monitors.

CHAPTER 156

The Barracuda roared from the garage, its large engine breaking the silence of the small town.

The scream of the tires and the rapid acceleration filled Trouble 1 with fear. It also caught the attention of a small drone that was released from the facility upon the escape of the children. The drone's primary design was to monitor traffic patterns. However, after several alterations by the government's R&D department, these devices have become much more.

The drone locked into the fast-moving Plymouth and began to send data back to the facility. Keith was well versed on the ability his government had at their disposal. He was well aware that his actions were being flagged, but there was no other choice.

The way Keith saw the developing scenario was really quite simple. He was either going to outrun the storm or die trying, but there was no hiding from this one.

Keith threw the shift stick down into fourth, and the vehicle leapt, whipping his head back.

Jason glanced over at the speedometer that was quickly rolling past ninety; he looked away just as fast.

Even with the escalating speed, the drone had no issue tracking the vehicle. It wasn't long before the drone had coordinated the vehicle's location with the two Apache helicopters just offshore.

Keith was the first to spot the two sets of blinking lights in formation heading his way.

"Change of plans. We can't outrun this on land!" Keith stated. A sense of commitment in his words confused Jason.

"What's going on?" Jason pressed.

"We have company at my eight o'clock, and they're coming in fast!" Keith said without any fear, but his realization shined through.

"Shit, that didn't take long!" Jason snapped as his tension doubled.

"I wouldn't be surprised if they didn't have a drone or two circling the area," Keith stated as he pushed the gas pedal to the floor.

"What is your plan? I can't let these bastards get their hands on them!" Jason yelled over the roar of the high revving engine.

"I have a boat. We are going to get you and the kids on it and roll you out of here!" Keith stated.

"A boat? We are going to outrun a military helicopter, that's your plan?" Jason shouted, trying to wrap his mind around what he was hearing.

"I will take care of the helicopters, and you will slip out with the children. It is the best chance for survival," Keith shouted loudly over the screaming engine.

"Have you lost your mind?" Jason shouted back.

"Long ago, son, but that doesn't change the fact that you're only going to get these kids to safety by being a little unpredictable," Keith yelled over the screaming engine, then flashed a smile that you could tell was foreign to his face.

"Holy shit, this is your plan?" Jason stated as he sunk back into the chair.

Keith slowly reached down and gripped the rubber handle of the emergency brake. His heart was beating like a drum, as he performed a silent count in his head.

With a fast jerking motion, Keith ripped the brake upward, bracing his body for the inevitable reaction. The wail from the screeching tires was deafening as the vehicle locked up and spun across two lanes.

The Cuda came to rest in front of a nine-foot chain-link fence.

Keith cocked his head over at Jason and smiled slightly through his close-cropped beard. He then spun around to make sure the children were all right.

Both Trouble 1 and his sister were in the process of full transformation as a result of the stress and increase of endorphins.

The black eyes of Trouble 1 were locked on Keith's face. Keith remained expression free, not so much as a flinch or a blink from his eyes. Then he broke his gaze as he followed the right arm of Trouble 1.

His focus rested on the long talon that had punctured through the front seat of the vehicle, just inches from Keith's neck.

"What the hell have you sick bastards been doing up there on nightmare hill?" Keith asked softly. His disgust was evident as he popped the car door and exited the car, not waiting for a response.

"I am not part of their insanity. All I want is to save these children from pure evil!" Jason stated as he pulled the front seat forward to allow the children out, calming them with easy motions and a warm smile.

"The thought that my tax dollars have gone to altering these children makes me sick. My government has lost its way!" Keith muffled as if small balls of shit were rolling around inside of his mouth.

"These people aren't government. They're much worse and they are powerful!" Jason stated as he continued to ease the troubles. Their human form almost completely returned.

"I am guessing that as soon as the helicopters make their turn, we will have two teams dropped right on top of us. Rangers most likely!" Keith spoke as he clipped a link in the fence and pulled it open, allowing just enough room for them to get through.

"What are you doing?" Jason snapped, confused by Keith's instruction.

"You need to take these keys, get in the boat right behind the brown shed, and get these kids out of here!" Keith stated as he tossed Jason the keys and began to pull weapons from the trunk of the car.

"This is crazy. I can't drive a boat. You need to have a plan B," Jason pressed, not happy with the new developments.

"Well, you better figure it out, and damn fast, because here they come. Get going, young man!" Keith snapped as he flicked on the laser sighting on the AR-15 and leveled it on the jeep rolling up the block.

CHAPTER 157

Schmitt was turned in the front seat of the jeep holding a field dressing on his friend's chest, attempting to limit blood loss.

Campbell was sprawled across the back seat, his eyes open, but his skin pallor was pasty and gray.

Schmitt lifted the dressing quickly to assess the damage, then immediately replaced it as a thin line of blood squirted across his sleeve.

Frank Nica glanced back at Campbell as he continued to accelerate; he was angry, and his face showed it. He wondered just how he had arrived at this point. He watched the alien murder the English officer and saw the absolute absence of feeling that was shown.

Why was his God testing him? What was it that he needed to understand that his Lord was trying to reveal to him?

He looked back at the dying man and caught his eyes as they passed by a streetlight. Then a moment of clarity descended upon him; his vanity drove him from his sanctity. He knew at that moment that he needed to stop doing the bidding of this off-world being. It was human life that was important, and it was time to find a hospital!

"I'm done with this. We are finding a hospital!" the priest announced, leaving little room for debate.

"We have orders, Frank. Campbell will hold on until we execute those orders," Schmitt snapped, but the strength of his conviction was weak.

"He is going to die if we don't change our course. I have seen enough death to know when the reaper is close," the priest stated as he brought the vehicle to a complete stop in the middle of the road.

"Okay, Frank, let's deal with Campbell now, and we will track down Worthington later if she survives Cain!" Schmitt stated, the defeat in his voice replaced by hope.

It was then that all hell broke loose.

The front windshield of the jeep turned to Swiss cheese from machine gunfire. If the two of them weren't leaning into the back seat at the time, they would have been finished.

Schmitt immediately dove on top of his friend to shield him from splintering glass and additional fire. This selfish act goes against every natural law of human self-preservation, yet a trait often found in old soldiers.

The priest went fetal and prayed to his God for forgiveness until the shooting stopped and the glass and lead stopped dancing around the interior of the vehicle.

The second the shooting ended. Schmitt jumped into action, grabbing his friend and pulling him away from the direction of the gunman.

Campbell protested as every movement brought additional pain.

Frank slid across the front seat and helped Schmitt move the wounded soldier. The three of them sat there with their backs against the bullet-ridden vehicle, waiting for additional fire that never came.

Schmitt was confused for a brief second, then he saw the helicopter swing out past the tree line, maybe five hundred yards away.

Slack lines fell, and a team of heavily armed men began a rapid descent. The thought of making a break for cover crossed Schmitt's mind but then realized that he could get caught by either side.

Schmitt worked at keeping his friend quiet as the team of nine men approached from the east. Frank turned to him and shot him a "holy shit" look, but Schmitt smiled as he looked at the helicopter and thought only of the opportunity.

"I am going to need a hand with Campbell on three!" Schmitt motioned in a direction of cover.

"Where are we going?" Frank asked, somewhat confused but happy to be leaving the middle of the road.

"Seems that our ride is about to touch down. Let's go!" Schmitt said as he motioned at the helicopter.

"Holy mother, but it's still better than here!" Frank stated as he grabbed the arm of the wounded soldier and off they went.

"We can circle around the team's flank and ask the pilot to take us the hell out of here," Schmitt stated as they picked up a good rhythm in their pace.

"I'm not sure the pilot is going to see our side of the story," Frank joked.

"Well, I can be somewhat persuasive at times!" Schmitt stated as they closed in on the helicopter.

"Hold it! I don't know who you are, but you are in the wrong place!"

A lone soldier left behind to cover the team's exit was about six feet off the path, training his weapon on the temple of Schmitt's skull.

"Hold your fire, soldier. This is Major Schmitt, and we have a wounded man here!" Frank stated a tone that presented as more of an order than a request.

"Take another step and I will drop all three!" was all the soldier was able to get out before Schmitt's bullet caught him in the face. The bullet followed the nasal passage and went right through the top of his head.

He dropped like a plank of wood.

CHAPTER 158

"I need this bird in the air right now," Schmitt stated as he pressed the hot barrel of his weapon to the base of the pilot's neck.

"Hey, who the hell are you people?" the pilot winced, pulling off his headphones and slowly lowering his left arm to the weapon at his hip.

"Son, put one finger on that weapon, and I will end you right here. My chubby friend is a fairly good pilot!" Schmitt stated and quickly reached around.

The assault team stopped in their tracks at the edge of the road after the shot rang out of the cold woods.

The team leader took a second to process the new development when he saw the helicopter begin to lift off.

He lifted his weapon and considered opening fire on the bushwhacked vehicle; however, his attention was drawn to the sound of something metallic that bounced in the street and came to rest near his feet. Then there was a second noise, also metallic, just a few feet away.

It was then that the first response team standing on the cold road without a ride were about to have their day ruined by two grenades that were older than all of them.

The explosion was practically simultaneous as both pins were pulled at the same time.

Bodies flew in different directions; the team leader was among them.

The whole crew suffered immediately from the blast, disorientation, hearing loss, and the burning shrapnel.

The few that were able to scramble to their feet were met by machine gunfire from behind the dark-colored Barracuda parked across the street.

As his focus returned, Keith could make out a large body on the street. Next to him was the leg of another man. Just a few feet away was what looked like a Swiss assault rifle with a right hand still attached at the trigger.

Keith winced as he surveyed the area and wondered what would his neighbors think about the way he converted their peaceful town into a horror show of smoke and screams.

He knew that when they learned that wacky pharmacist was involved, they would somehow get that. His train of thought was broken by the sound of the twin Yamaha outboard engines.

The second team was swooping in from the north and had watched the carnage on the ground. Before they even propelled down the lines, they opened fire on his position. The Barracuda erupted from the onslaught of bullets; glass and steel flew in every direction.

Keith took a hit in the face, and it dropped him to the floor. Initially disorientated, he quickly regained his composure and spit out the mouthful of teeth and blood that the bullet had destroyed.

Keith pulled his handheld LAW rocket from his duffel bag and took aim.

The second team was on the ground and moving fast on his position. The secondary team leader saw the assailant go down from a direct hit to the face and was more than a little surprised to see a missile heading in his direction.

He quickly dove behind a four-door Buick and held his ears. The rest of the team didn't have the reaction time.

The missile struck a vehicle twenty feet away from the approaching team. The blast took out two additional vehicles that were grouped together. One soldier was killed instantly, while another two were disabled.

The secondary team leader rolled out from under the vehicle and viewed the damage with shock and disbelief. Out of the corner of his field of vision, the leader saw a bright orange boat pulling away from the boathouse. He was fully aware that his mission was to secure the children and terminate the doctor that had abducted them. However, he wasn't about to walk away from this; he lifted his weapon and began to fire.

Keith smiled as he saw the twenty-one foot Scarab roll out of the boathouse. He knew that if he could hold on for another two minutes, there would be no catching that machine.

Keith ripped a piece of cloth from his shirt and stuck it in his mouth. The pain from the exposed nerves in his mouth was being kept at bay by the overload of adrenalin pulsing through his body.

Keith heard boots on the pavement and reached for the AK-47 and pulled the slide back. He had purchased the weapon online from a seventy-five-year-old woman from New Mexico, which seemed funny at the time. Her name was Agnes, and they had developed quite a relationship; she never trusted the government either. She had sent some fresh baked cookies just yesterday, and he wanted to wait until the weekend to eat them.

He would trade all the remaining teeth in his mouth for just one damn cookie.

He jumped to his feet and unloaded a full clip at the direction of the pounding boots. He capped the first soldier in the shoulder and spun him like a top. The second soldier was caught dead center of his flak jacket, and even though the bullet didn't pass through, the force was enough to stop his heart.

Keith dropped back down and reached for a second clip, found it, and snapped it in.

Then the shadow, he could see it in the wheel well, someone had snuck up on his six. His shoulders sunk, he was finished and he knew it.

He threw the weapon a few feet to the left as a distraction and then grabbed for the German luger, attempting one last effort.

Keith never heard the shot as two entered the back of his head.

CHAPTER 159

"Who the hell is this asshole?" one of the soldiers who emerged at the destroyed Barracuda shouted.

"We need to get after those kids!" the team leader stated.

"Fuck those freaks. Let's bury our friends!" another soldier stated, his anger evident.

"It would have been nice if we had some solid intel out of this fuckin' place. Chasing two kids and we get Rambo!" the soldier who had shot Keith stated as he kicked him over to look at his face.

"Shit!" was all that one of the soldiers could muster as a green grenade without a pin rolled from the smiling dead man's hand.

Smith stood in the middle of the woods, his right hand holding the headset to his ear.

He stood looking up at the sky as if he was waiting for something to drop on his head. His face looked pained as if the information he was receiving was physically hurting him. He wondered if this scenario could get any worse; he could still hear gunfire in the distance.

The chaos was ridiculous, bodies spread out all over the grounds of the federal facility. The powers that were back in Washington would be looking to rip his balls from his body and have them nailed to the White House front door.

Even with the best technology known to man, two children and a fuckin' horse doctor had managed to slip from under his net.

There was a whole town on fire three miles away, and on top of all this, there seems to be a helicopter missing.

He pulled the headset from his sweating forehead and began a brisk walk back to the waiting helicopter.

"I want this bird off the ground now. Head back toward the city!" Smith barked at the pilot and his second, as he jumped into the back of the helicopter.

"What's going on, sir?" the communication agent asked, his Southern accent more prominent with the added stress.

"Who the fuck knows? Russians killing Chinese, Americans killing Americans, and now I hear there is a British team out there dying in style!" Smith continued to dish out the realities to the stunned agent.

"Should I bring in a containment team, start the cleanup process?" the agent asked.

"Too late, this assignment was a full failure. I'm guessing twenty dead in the woods, another fifteen in a town three miles away, and to make matters worse, we seem to be missing one of our Apaches!" Smith stated as he threw the headset on the floor.

"Holy shit, we are so damn fucked. We are going to make the papers, aren't we?" the agent said as he placed his face in his own palms.

"Well, I suppose we could hit the *New York Times* building with a drone strike that would change the tide of this debacle!" Smith smiled as he considered the act.

"Wow, yeah, that would change everything!" The agent laughed at first then realized that his senior agent wasn't entirely kidding.

"The way things are going, we would screw that up just as well. Let's get back to the city!" Smith said as he connected the harness across the chest.

"Sir, there is an emergency call coming in from a William Dean. You can pick it up on the blue headphones!" the pilot yelled over the sound of the whirling blades.

"Put him through!" the second agent yelled back to the pilot.

"Mr. Dean, I am in transit. Can we talk when I return?" Smith pushed, not really interested in talking.

"We believe that Cain is not where you are looking. There is strong evidence that his physical being is in here in the city!" Dean was yelling into the phone.

"Are you positive about the intel? Where have you located him?" Smith responded, instantly seeing the opportunity to get out of his current issue.

"I know this will sound strange, but we believe that he is operating out of a bank vault in the old Trinity building on Broadway," Dean explained, not sure of the response he would get.

"You know, Mr. Dean, it really doesn't sound that strange to me at all!" Smith stated as his wheels continued to turn.

"It seems that Cain has the ability to control other humans at will, even to act against their basic natures," Dean had stopped yelling and was attempting to articulate his theory but was unsure on the mechanism of how.

"I am sorry, Mr. Dean, but I'm having difficulty following your story!" Smith stated.

"Well, it appears that there were people connected to him. They were chasing us, jumping from windows with no apparent regard for their own safety!" Dean felt as if he was falling short in his explanation.

"What does connected mean?" Smith probed.

"To be fully honest, I'm not sure, but it was obvious that they were protecting his location and they were being controlled!" Dean said firmly.

"Did you take Mr. Pierce along on your little recon adventure?" Smith asked.

"We did take Cornell, and he did manifest some strange behavior as we approached the building!" Dean confirmed.

"I have a question and please think this through. If you had gone without Mr. Pierce, do you think you may have avoided detection?" Smith knew the answer to the question he had asked but still wanted to hear it out loud.

"That is difficult to decipher based on what we know. However, I will say there is a high possibility," Dean offered.

"Mr. Dean, please bring Cornell back to Brooklyn. I'm en route back there now, and, Mr. Dean, thank you!" Smith clicked off and removed the headset.

"The look on your face is telling me that we are back in business!" the agent stated, reading the ear-to-ear smile on Smith's face.

"We might have a shot, but it could get really nasty!" Smith said with an evil glint in his eye.

"Tell me what you need. I think we reached the point of no return, so whatever it is, let's just fuckin' do it!" the agent stated, his attitude shifting as a direct result of self-preservation.

"We are going to need a jet, something fast, F-15 maybe, and a bunker buster!" Smith stated as he gazed out over the tree-lined river heading toward Manhattan.

"That's not going to be an issue. I can have one of those in the air in ten minutes. What's the target?" the agent asked with some caution.

"I think our alien is working out of a bank vault in the city. When I confirm this, I may need to strike fast!" Smith announced, slowly putting his plan together in his head.

"You will never get sanctioned to open missile fire within a city grid!" the agent stated, not wanting any part of the plan.

"We don't need anything sanctioned. We have a runaway Apache helicopter, remember?" Smith raised his finger to highlight the point.

"Where is this bank that you're looking to target?" the agent asked, almost fearful of an answer.

"The Trinity building on Broadway. The vault is on the first floor!" Smith smiled, seeming to enjoy the discomfort of his second.

"You know if we miss the mark, they will hang us!" the agent stated as he slouched back into his seat.

"We can paste a laser tag on the location, but make no mistake, there will be casualties!" Smith stated, scanning the agent to test his loyalty.

"It would seem that the plan is changing as we go!" the agent said, displaying his disappointment.

"We are forced to change direction. The children are out of my reach for now. Cain has always been priority one!" Smith stated, seeming firm on the point.

"My jacket on Cain states that he is not to be terminated. The powers that be are interested in developing a relationship with him!" the agent pushed back.

"I know what's on paper. I wrote the fuckin' dialogue, but I have new data that Cain can't be extracted. Those powers don't have a clue of what's really going on!" Smith stated. His anger was growing.

"Boss, help me out. What is going on?" the agent probed, trying to understand this new perspective.

"I am not sure that I fully understand how he is able to do what he does, but it appears that Mr. Dean and the others have found where Cain hides his true self," Smith stated, trying to unroll his theory.

"So, he isn't in the places that we have had contact with him? The restaurant, the hotel, all some type of projected hologram?" the agent seemed confused.

"No, much more than a hologram. The scientist Kowalski tells me that he has the ability to pull energy from just about anywhere!" Smith struggled to explain what he didn't really understand himself.

"This is how he is able to change form and murder at will?" the agent probed.

"Don't misunderstand, Cain is very real, and I am not sure how his whole process works, but I believe he needs a central location to operate from!" Smith emphasized that he didn't have all the answers.

"So, your plan is to take out his operation platform which I get, but still we have the initial problem!" the agent stated.

"What problem is that?" Smith winced at the response.

"Our orders are not to terminate. Should we brief the farm and try and get a blessing to proceed?" the agent asked.

"They see Cain as a prize only because they don't understand the alien!" Smith's demeanor seemed to change, frustration or impatience.

"From what you are telling me, it sounds like the technology alone is reason to work with Cain, wouldn't you think?" the agent stated as he unhooked his harness to return the phone to the front of the cockpit.

"Hey, I'll take that!" Smith motioned for the phone, then grabbed the wrist of the agent and pulled him across his chest and out the open helicopter door into the cold night.

"What happened?" the pilot screamed, realizing that he had lost a passenger.

"Poor decision-making!" Smith stated and then initiated the code into the phone that would set his plan into motion.

CHAPTER 160

Dean hung up the phone and explained the instructions that he received from Smith.

Mac was fine with returning to Brooklyn as he recalled the blank expression of the woman who slammed into the car. The dull look in her eyes and the aggression in her face was something he would rather not deal with.

Magen wanted to take a closer look at the building; however, she was also shaken by the events back on Broadway.

Mac wondered how Cain was able to manipulate so many people at the same time.

One thing that he was absolutely clear about was that Cain needs that building protected at all costs.

His mind was racing with the events of the past few minutes that he almost shot through a red light. He applied the brakes quickly, causing his passengers to jolt. His preoccupation was broken by the sound of the back car door opening; he turned his head long enough to see Cornell bolting from the vehicle. Mr. Dean slid across the seat with the intention of pursuit.

"Cornell, where are you going?" Dean yelled after his friend.

"William, stop!" Magen had grabbed his arm, pulling him toward her.

"We need to get him back. Why are you holding me back?" Dean snapped at the agent holding his arm tightly.

"He needs to go. I'm not sure why, but for some reason, I understand his decision."

Magen and Dean watched as Cornell turned the corner and was gone from sight.

"Smith seemed to be interested in Cornell's connection to Cain when I told him what happened back on Broadway," Dean stated as he slunk back into the seat, a feeling of defeat stretched across his face.

"I think whatever Cain did to Cornell created some type of psychic connection that plugs him into his reach," Magen said, finding it difficult to explain her theory.

"Well, unfortunately there is only one way to test this hypothesis. We need to go back to Trinity!" Mac said, looking deep into Magen's eyes, wishing for the first time that she wasn't there.

"We have come this far. Don't look at me like that. We can do this!" Magen stated, reaching over and squeezing his hand.

CHAPTER 161

Schmitt sat in the back of the helicopter holding his friend as the priest held his weapon on the pilot. He knew they were still fifteen minutes from the hospital, and the bleeding was not letting up.

He wasn't sure if it was the cold from the night air seeping into the cockpit, or was his friend's body temperature dropping fast.

Campbell had been with him a long time; if he had to label their relationship, he would have to say they were brothers. They had killed men on every continent of the planet, and he was the one person on Earth that always had his back.

Schmitt wondered just how the hell he wound up in this position. He couldn't count the times that he was saved by the man that was dying in his arms.

As he stared at the blood leaking out of his friend, the rage began to build. In a moment of clarity, Schmitt stood up, resting his friend's head on a gunnysack.

He slid into the seat next to Frank and leaned in to talk over the roar of the engine.

"We need to turn this bird around and finish that bitch off!" Schmitt stated, his face icy and chilling.

"What about Campbell? We are ten minutes from the hospital" the priest stated, confused by the new development.

"He isn't going to make the hospital. Campbell is going to die right here in this helicopter!" Schmitt stated, looking over at his friend.

"Major, I know this isn't easy, but you don't know that!" Frank pressed the soldier who was now fully focused on vengeance.

"My friend has lost too much blood to survive. He will not make the hospital!" Schmitt stated, fully accepting this as the truth.

"Sir, I have seen that look before. You don't want to go down that road!" the priest began but realized his words were falling on deaf ears.

"Let's turn this around, Frank. The bitch dies tonight!" Schmitt stated with an icy tone that left no room for compromise.

"We are going to need to turn around back to the Tarrytown facility!" Frank yelled at the pilot who was already unhappy with his situation.

"What? Are you people out of your mind?" the pilot began to scream over the roar of the engine, his anger near the breaking point.

"No time for that bullshit. Let's go!" Schmitt stated as he leveled his Glock, spitting out a round that just nicked the pilot's headset and continued out the window.

"Turning around, hold on!" the pilot stated, his anger gone, replaced by fear of the old soldier covered in his friend's blood.

CHAPTER 162

Cornell turned the corner off Cedar Street. There was a large red structure standing in the middle of a park.

The Trinity restaurant was just past the structure, and the area was flooded with hundreds of people.

He had gone to school in New York and was familiar with the area, but he didn't remember that big thing in the middle of the park. Masses of people stood looking at the structure with vacant expressions.

Cornell could feel the pull of his energy as he came closer.

He needed to back away from the area because the pull was overwhelming. He could feel a connection with the people in the square and knew they felt his presence as well.

He wondered what the hell Cain did to him that made this possible.

However, these people in the square were being totally controlled, and Cornell was able to maintain control over his decision-making.

The dark thoughts ran through his mind about the day in that warehouse. Cain had taken and given his hand back, but something else came along with the return of his limb.

He realized that he wasn't totally safe here in the park close to the red structure.

There was no way that he would be able walk through these people and get to the entrance to the building. Cornell looked at the surrounding buildings then scanned the rooftops.

As he sat there making up his mind, he began to hear the low hum of an engine. The military helicopter turned onto Broadway and hovered over the park.

The hundreds of people that were gathered in the park broke their trance instantly and ran toward the building entrance and began to form a human wall.

"We are coming up on the facility landing pad just over that tree line," the pilot yelled into the headset.

"I'm down to maybe a half clip on my .45, about the same on the M-16. How are you?" Frank asked the major who hadn't spoken a word since the helicopter turned around.

"I have one full clip that pilot has in his Glock. I sent my last round through that windshield over there!" Schmitt stated, lifting his eyebrow as the pilot turned and scowled.

"I'm guessing the heliport is going to be covered with men, at least a detail. What's your plan?"

"Frank, I'm going to kill that bitch if I have to hit the deck with my knife. Stay in the bird if you need to," the major shouted over the loud engine.

"I fully believe that woman is in need of some killing, just not sure I'm ready for a suicide mission!" the priest shouted back.

"Not ready to meet the skipper just yet, Father Frank?" Schmitt smiled at his own joke.

"My skipper can forgive rage and vengeance, but suicide is something he really frowns upon!" the priest shot back.

"Rage and vengeance is truly in the mail, so it's good to know I can slice off a bit of forgiveness after I dispatch Worthington!" Schmitt stated as he pressed his weapon to the head of the pilot.

"Hold on, I have done everything you asked!" the pilot shouted over the loud engine.

"How many soldiers are on that pad?" Schmitt stated with chilling ice in his voice.

"Half dozen tops!" the pilot snapped without hesitation.

"What is the firepower capacity on this death machine?" Schmitt asked.

"Rockets were pulled, but the side gun is fully loaded!" the pilot stated.

"I'm going to need you to roll in fast and bank right on final the approach. Fuck with me, and I'll kill you with your own gun!"

"Yes, sir!" the pilot stated and cleared the tree line, the lights of the heliport clearly visible.

CHAPTER 163

The facility chief, along with a handful of soldiers, was accompanying Helen to the heliport.

The plan was to move her out and clear up the firefight in the woods. Then the facility would need to be tanked, all data destroyed.

Government forces were on their way by now, and there would just be enough time to get her out and burn the servers.

As they approached the door leading outside, they could hear the distinct sound of helicopter blades cutting through the air.

The chief's first thought was that that the departure chopper was getting ready. Then he realized that the helicopter was incoming.

He had just stepped out in to the night air when the full extent of that information registered in his mind. The chief stopped in his tracks and placed his right hand on the shoulder of Worthington. The helicopter came in fast and banked right then seemed to brake in midair.

The side mounted gun erupted, and the heliport was raining bullets. The soldier in front of the chief disappeared into a mist of red, like a wine-filled balloon popping!

The chief barked instructions to get Helen back into the building, and then there was a great stinging pain on the right side of the chief's body.

He reached for his arm, only to find an empty space.

The hijacked copter continued to fill the yard with destruction as bodies flew in all directions. The soldier at the rear was able to secure Worthington until a stray round caught him flush on the back of his heel.

The rapid fire from the helicopter's mounted weapon continued, but the screams of the fallen soldier filled the hall. Worthington was ushered through a series of doors and emerged in a courtyard where a black Lincoln town car was idling.

She was practically thrown into the vehicle as the last remaining team member scrambled to the other side of the car.

The storm of bullets could still be heard at the other end of the building; the team member reached for the door handle, only to find it locked. He bent down to motion to the driver to let him in, squinting to identify any shapes through the dark tint. Then the Lincoln leaped forward, and within a blink, it was beyond the soldier's reach.

He raised his weapon instinctively; he then lowered it, realizing that he might hit his primary. He watched as the Lincoln drove off and smiled, realizing that nobody was left to call him on his fuckup.

CHAPTER 164

Helen watched the soldier from the back window, her brain trying to search for understanding.

She turned to look at the driver who hadn't turned around and appeared to be humming. In that brief instant, fear gripped her like someone reached down her throat and squeezed her stomach.

Helen dug deep for her breath and some balance, fighting the fear as it welled up from deep, dark places. There was a part of her that knew the probability of this moment was absolutely unavoidable. She grasped for composure and silently prayed to her God for protection.

Helen often found instant relief when she gave her will to her maker, but today the fear was fighting back and winning.

"Cain, I was wondering when we would have some time together!" Worthington stated as she fought for composure.

"Nice try, Helen, but the smell of fear is almost making me dizzy." Cain laughed as he shot a look in the rearview mirror.

"I'm sure you are enjoying that, but I suppose at some level that's why we are here," Helen shot back, attempting to secure the moral high ground.

"Oh, really, I thought we had arrived at this junction due to your blatant betrayal!" Cain's voice displayed an increase in intensity and anger.

"That's almost laughable. Betrayal has been your primary goal here on Earth," Helen snapped.

"I'm sure you have all the justifications you need rolling around that twisted skull, don't you?" Cain shot back, shaking his head back and forth.

"Killing and eating your way through history is what I consider twisted," Helen stated, her passion in her cause evident.

"I'm really not interested in the delusions that hold you together. I want the two abominations that you created," Cain said, seeming uninterested in her words.

"That is going to be somewhat of a problem. They were liberated from my charge two hours ago," Worthington stated, attempting to hide a twinge of shame she felt from that statement.

"Liberated by whom? Where did they go?" Cain said as he stamped on the brakes.

"My last intel has them in a speedboat heading for open water. Unfortunately, we were unable to pursue," Helen stated with a sense of blame at Cain.

"This is really a bad day for you. Lose your children and soon to lose your life," Cain stated as he eyed the woman in the back seat.

"I'm sure you will do what you do best, but it will change nothing," Worthington stated as she held her ground.

"There is really nothing to change. Your skinny pig from Rome is dead. The children will be found, and you have stabbed your last back!" Cain said as if reading a laundry list.

"So many know of your existence now and the children as well. They will come for you soon enough. You're finished!" Helen stated with some aggression.

"You don't have a single clue in your delusional skull. Did you wake up in the same America as me this morning?" Cain threw his head back with a mocking laugh.

"Laugh if it makes you feel better, but your vision of defecting to this planet is a pipe dream," Helen continued to press.

"Well, I think my little plan is going quite well. The only concern I have is your little abominations. Really not happy about this, Helen!" Cain opened his door as he spoke.

"You can kill me, and it will change nothing. You are soon to meet your own fate!" Worthington struggled to remain strong as Cain let himself into the back of the vehicle.

"Your betrayal has pained me deeply, Helen. We have done so much for your world, saved you from your own self-destruction!" Cain eased closer in the seat.

"So your kind has taken such great pleasure in reminding us, but you have taken such liberties with our world," Helen stated as she shifted in her seat.

"Liberties, you must be talking about our feeding habits, as if your behavior is any different," Cain smirked.

"You will not find us snacking on those we serve!" Worthington shot back.

"I admit we may snatch up a few of the fatted sheep along the fringe, but your kind devours full flocks with a push of a button," Cain stated with no hesitation.

"So who is doing the justifying now?" Helen said as she began to weep, thinking about her death.

"Tears of fear. Tell me what is it about your life that you feel the need to leak from your eyes, you soulless bitch?" Cain stated as he leaned into her face, allowing his fangs to extend.

Cain's eyes locked, and he froze, as if he was looking into himself; his teeth retracted.

His house was under attack. The seeds were gathering around the bank; trouble was unfolding.

Worthington's death would need to wait; it was time for war.

They were moving in close; he knew it was only a matter of time.

It was time to turn his attention to the city; he would have to tend to this evil betrayer and her two atrocities later.

Cain vanished like mist, leaving Helen in the back of the vehicle sitting in a puddle of her own urine, weeping.

CHAPTER 165

Mac slammed on the brakes, instinctively reaching out his right arm to protect Magen from lurching forward.

The square was filled with thousands of wide-eyed people surrounding the bank. They weren't charging the car, but they were aware of the new arrivals.

The crowd seemed to be much more focused on the helicopter that was hovering above the avenue.

Getting anywhere near the bank would be impossible with all these people packed in so close.

The helicopter seemed to hover over the crowd, not fully ready to commit to full slaughter.

The crowds continued to grow as new people arrived and joined the human chain. Magen looked over at Mac, and then noticed the face of Cornell Pierce in the crowd.

"Mac, look, it's Cornell!" Magen pointed out his window at the man doubled over on the sidewalk.

"We need to get him in here!" Dean stated as he reached for the door and pushed it open.

"Hold on, don't move too fast. I'm not sure how these people will react," Mac stated, but it was too late. Dean was on the move.

William Dean leaped out the back seat and ran to his friend's side.

Cornell flinched as if he was ready to fight off an attacker. He quickly realized it was William, and his whole body relaxed. Dean slipped his right arm around Cornell's shoulder to provide support and guide him back to the car. They had only taken two steps when they realized that there was a second pair of hands helping Cornell to the back of the vehicle.

William and Cornell lifted their heads and came face-to-face with Cain and instantly froze.

Cain gave them a reassuring look that allowed them to continue to the car. Cain helped Cornell get into the back seat; he then walked over to the driver's side window.

"Officer MacDonald, you look well!" Cain said as he hunched slightly at the window.

"Thank you!" Mac managed, not knowing how to respond.

"Magen, I know why you are here, and that's okay, but is time to leave," Cain stated.

"What is going on? Why are all these people here?" Magen pressed, trying to get clarification.

"None of this matters. If you are not far away from this location in the next three minutes, you will be terminated!" Cain voiced and lifted his hand to motion the large mob of seeds to create a path.

"Why are you helping us?" Magen asked.

"I'm just not ready to lose you. I feel we can do great things together," Cain smiled and stepped away from the vehicle.

"We are out of here!" Mac sped off, not needing any additional instruction.

"Honey, I think that alien is sweet on you. Not sure how I feel about that," Mac stated, his voice stressed.

He pressed harder on the gas.

"I know that is true. Cain doesn't care about any of us but Magen. I feel it!" Cornell stated. His statement was flat.

"Why would he have any interest in me?" Magen asked, confused by Cornell's statement.

"He needs you for something. That's how he thinks!" Cornell answered flatly as he stared out the window.

"Do you know what that reason is?" Magen asked as she turned around and stared at Cornell.

"I never see the reasoning of things when it comes to Cain. I can only see the truth of things," Cornell stated as if he was reading a script. His head snapped back slightly as Mac hit the gas.

CHAPTER 166

Smith stared at the vehicle speeding away through the crowd.

The agent who was sitting next to Smith looked over for some direction regarding the departing vehicle. It was clear that Smith refused to move his attention from what he saw as the prize.

He was consumed with only one task, and that was to dispatch Cain.

He didn't know until that moment just how much he hated the alien. Cain had consumed his every waking moment, his career, and his marriage, all decimated by this creature. He was never the same after learning of the existence of the extraterrestrial and felt the assignment was a punishment.

It filled him with great joy to think he was just minutes away from ending this lifelong nightmare. The pilot glanced over at Smith, who seemed to be smiling. He held up his left hand in hopes of getting his attention.

Smith held up his finger and pointed to the left side of the bank where he thought the vault would be.

The pilot flicked a few switches right above his head, and the green laser painted a clear target on the side of the bank. The F-16 released the weapon about a mile from Manhattan then banked left out to see.

In order to avoid the tall buildings surrounding the bank, the weapon was released at ten thousand feet. It would be passing over the Statue of Liberty in just a few seconds, then on to the Battery.

Smith could sense that a conclusion to his long nightmare was coming, and he smiled. The plans that were put into motion could not be reversed, and now the only thing to do was to back away from the area, after the laser locked the target.

Then the helicopter began to stutter, the lights began to flicker, and the vessel began to descend.

The smile on Smith's face disappeared as he began to realize that the chopper was going down. He saw the area begin to clear of people with only one person standing alone, not moving.

Smith knew it was Cain, and just before the helicopter hit the ground, Smith saw him smile.

CHAPTER 167

At 10:26 a.m., the American-designed missile struck the Trinity building at its base.

The weapon passed through the basement, missing the vault entirely. It then came to a complete stop in an abandoned subway tube that also housed several lower Manhattan gas mains.

The explosion was massive, affecting over nine city blocks. The Trinity building was claimed instantly, and seven other buildings were also extremely damaged. The vault had evaporated in seconds; whatever Cain and the aliens were holding in there added to the blast.

Since the explosion took place underground, everything in the vicinity was expelled upward. The report of raining debris along with body parts was documented as far away as Port Washington, Long Island.

Initially, the island of Manhattan believed they were under terrorist attack again. In one swift strike the financial district of the United States was destroyed. All power to the area was severed; even the streetlights were down all the way into the forties.

New York accepted this event as the most feared second terrorist attack. This was partially supported by footage of the charred remains of the military helicopter, as it was quickly becoming known as Ground Double Zero.

Within minutes of the explosion, New York took to the streets, making it twice as difficult for emergency services to mobilize. Of the 9.3 million people who were busy starting their day that morning,

4,015 would never see its end. Unlike the events of 9/11 where finding and identifying bodies was near impossible, this event filled the streets with blood, bone, and wounded people.

The subways came to an instant halt as the computer system couldn't handle the loss of so many programs. Twenty minutes after the explosion, any street movement was reduced to foot traffic in the downtown area. All vehicles were moved to one side of the street, allowing passage of fleeing pedestrians and incoming emergency service vehicles. The military were slow to respond on this morning; later documentation would support their investigative management was busy in Tarrytown, New York, trying to work through the previous night's confusion. "Plausible denial" was the term used most often on that morning by a number of governments.

President Obama took to the airways, emphasizing the need for calm as the professionals worked on the retrieval of evidence of the event. He had ruled out terrorism from outside forces at fifty-seven minutes after the explosion. The chief investigators at Homeland Security were working diligently with the Federal Bureau of Investigation; however, the Central Intelligence Agency was vague and guarded. Reports from them were limited to the fact that there was no indication of foreign terrorist involvement. There were side reports of several missing personnel that were stationed in the New York area, investigations pending.

The Air Force reported that one of their helicopters was seen in the debris; however, they felt this had nothing to do with the event. The last transmission from the pilot indicated that they were requesting access to Manhattan airspace in hopes of finding a second chopper that had gone missing. Of course, the Air Force reported no loss of a second helicopter, and this compounded the confusion of just what was the military doing at the epicenter of the explosion.

There were several eyewitnesses that reported seeing a missile pass over Castle Clinton down by the Battery, but their credibility was questionable. Several military experts broadcasting on CNN were providing a theory that it couldn't possibly be a missile that was involved. They presented diagrams and computer-enhanced scenarios that pointed out the flaws of the missile theory.

The media was on fire with possible connections to Ukrainian militants and Isis thugs. However, by midweek, the separation of a well-known pop star and her wide receiver husband took center stage.

Slowly people began to accept the accident scenario, that there really were no bad guys.

The gas mains were old and faulty; it was totally possible that the lack of appropriate maintenance was fully contributory to the event. People were more than happy to accept the safest possibility; this way the world could just roll back into their lives on Monday morning. No harm, no foul.

CHAPTER 168

The sun was baking the road to an extent that the tires on the vehicle were practically melting into the chipped, coarse cement.

Megan was drifting in and out of sleep; the only saving grace was the air conditioner that continued to feed the steady stream of cool air.

The journey to this island was just outside of eight hours from Virginia by an extremely fast jet.

She was slightly upset about her new appointed role as the chief of special projects. It seemed that after Smith died in the horrible helicopter crash, the company could only come up with one person who would fit the profile as keeper of the harsh truth. Initially she protested the assignment, but her dialogue fell on deaf ears.

There were considerable changes in her outlook over the past year. So, the offer was tainted with a large pill to swallow. The island was known as Palmyra Atoll; it was located about a thousand miles off the coast of Hawaii. The government came into the possession of the island long ago and really didn't do too much with it. They used it for a brief period during World War II as a staging point to attack Japan. The problem was the little rock was just too damn far away, and there were way too many options closer to the States.

The island also had a history of problems from ships sinking, people missing, to a highly publicized murder of a couple back in the seventies. This only helped keep the place free of the outside world; nothing like a little curse to clear the neighborhood.

Magen didn't care about any of that sailor fantasy talk; all she knew was that it was way too hot here. Her monthly visits to this desolate strip of beach were working her last nerve.

As the vehicle pulled up to the lagoon, Magen couldn't help but marvel at the postcardlike beauty of the place, magnificent white sand and the bluest water imaginable.

Just beautiful, she thought.

Just off to the right, near a large grouping of palm trees, was a large white tent, something you would find in the Arabian Desert.

Magen reached for the door handle and pulled; hot air filled the car fast. She opened the door and sat for a minute, half in and half out of the vehicle. She decided to remove her shoes; they were Italian and really not beach friendly.

Outside the tent, sunning her beautiful brown body, was Joshua's mother, Cleo. Magen knew her well from her previous visits.

"Hey, gorgeous, you think you chilling in the Rockaways?" Magen joked as she got close to the tent.

"Damn, girl, where have you been?" Cleo yelled as she got up from her chair to embrace her friend.

"Honey, you look so damn good living out here in paradise!" Magen squeezed hard on her friend.

"Magen, I have fish coming out of my ears. Don't play with me!" Cleo laughed at her new friend.

"Is that Magen makin' all that noise out there?" Imogen asked as she emerged from the tent with her big pregnant belly.

"Oh my God, wow, did you swallow a boatful of coconuts?" Magen ran to hug her friend.

"I know I'm going to pop any damn minute. Can't bloody stand it, all this cursed heat." Imogen laughed and hugged her friend, "Honey, you're looking so amazing. You're glowing!" Magen stated, holding her friend's hand.

"Thank you, baby. Did you know Bronx is pregnant now also?" Imogen stated, pointing to Cleo's belly.

"Are you kidding me? Is this tramp island I just landed on?" Magen screamed.

"I know you're not judging me, not much else to do on this little island. Tell me you brought some damn alcohol." Cleo laughed.

"Plenty of wine and rum, six bags of Victoria's Secrets, and two ounces of Purple Kush," Magen announced to the women.

"Oh, baby! The VS is all mine. That fat white girl can keep her secret," Cleo stated loud enough for Imogen to hear.

"Well, your fat ass can't hold a damn secret, you wanker!" Imogen shot back.

"Ladies, we can't fight with each other when there are so many men that need their asses kicked!" Magen snapped.

"No worries, love, I really do love my sister, and we are so glad that you're here!" Imogen announced as she reached to hug Magen.

"Really do love your visits, Magen, and thanks for the weed," Cleo stated.

"Thanks, girls. Where is he by the way? He wanted to talk to me as soon as I arrived," Magen asked.

"He is down by the lagoon with Joshua. They dive for oysters and other stuff every morning," Cleo stated.

"Isn't the lagoon filled with sharks?" Magen asked, surprise evident in her voice.

"Sharks fly out of there as soon as he steps into the water, something about magnetic fields or energy something. He tried to explain it to me once, but I wasn't really listening," Cleo informed, smiling at Magen.

"Well, I guess that makes some sense. Let me go see what he wants!" Magen announced and started off to the lagoon.

As she walked a few feet from the girls, she quickly looked back and saw the girls laughing among themselves. Magen began to tear up a little, remembering the early days when they agreed to Cain's terms. Cleo was not as upset as Imogen because she had already established a relationship with Cain. Imogen was practically kidnapped by the Central Intelligence Agency.

They were dark days in the beginning; Magen remembered crying herself to sleep every night. It was so hard to be part of something that she felt was monstrous. Her superior told her to hold the course, and Cain himself knew what she was feeling and continued to tell her that it was going to get better.

Her relationship with Cain has changed deeply since that day in New York. He had picked up Mac and her in a long black limo while the smoke was still in the air and laid out his plan that he wanted her to present to the powers that be.

She later found out that Helen Worthington was dead in the trunk of the vehicle that day. Those that were involved in her network were tracked down and incarcerated, and most were killed in the woods that night in New York.

She rounded a large dune and saw Joshua at the edge of the water, but there was no sign of Cain.

She thought that he must be diving for the clams or whatever was down there.

As she got closer, she realized that it wasn't Joshua at all; it was, in fact, Cain.

He turned and saw Magen and smiled, then instantly began to transform back into the Cain she knew.

Cain has always had the deep need to connect with children. Magen couldn't understand this part of Cain's condition, but she knew every chance he had he wanted to be with Joshua or other children. She thought it strange and knew there was some significance to it but just didn't understand.

Let others worry about that. Cain was fully transformed when Joshua emerged from the lagoon.

Cain smiled at his young friend and then turned to Magen. "Well, pretty lady, how are you?" Cain said with big smiles.

"I am well, Cain. I see the girls are doing well, especially Imogen. She is glowing."

"Yes, my family is well. Can you believe how great things have worked out?" Cain said as if he was announcing unbridled happiness.

"I have to admit, you were right about the outcome!" Magen stated, recalling his promise to her the day he talked her into being his liaison.

"So, tell me about the progress your people have made this month on finding Dr. Jason and the two children," Cain said, somewhat knowing the answer.

"They are moving a lot. I am told that they were almost intercepted in Brazil but managed to slip away!" Magen stated, just happy to be able to say something. Most months she just looks at the sand and says nothing.

"Oh well, you know an old Chinese warrior once told me if you stand on the riverbank long enough, you will see the bodies of your enemies float by!" Cain said as he helped Joshua out of the lagoon.

"We will get them!" Magen stated.

"I know, I have total faith in the process. Tell me, how is Mac?" Cain asked with honest interest.

"He is well. He sent a pastrami sandwich from the Katz's Deli. You wouldn't believe what we had to go through to keep it fresh," Magen announced.

"I so have a man crush on your fella. You are both so lucky to find each other. No need to thank me!" Cain joked, taking full credit.

"I think that gate swings both ways. He is always asking about you," Magen joked with Cain.

"Is he all right? I know he had reservations about us working together," Cain pressed.

"He might be a bit jealous of our monthly island getaways, but I still set the pace!" Magen couldn't help adding the little dig.

"Well, now that I have the human pleasantries out of the way, I need to talk about our future!" Cain stated, his tone changing just slightly.

"I knew this was coming. What is it that was so important that you felt we couldn't discuss over the phone or Skype?" Magen asked with a slight bit of nervousness.

In 207 days, Joshua will have a second baby brother. At that time, we will be leaving this island!" Cain announced in a calm manner.

"Wait, you said that this was the long-term plan, and as long as we secured this island, you would stay put!" Magen snapped back as her throat constricted.

"Magen, I love you, but I need to remind you that I promised nothing. I will not have my offspring be denied human contact," Cain stated, indicating there was room for compromise.

"Cain, I don't make policy on this. I only follow the orders of the section chief!" Magen began only to be cut off by Cain.

"I know where you're going with this. Magen, I am counting on you to convince your people that this must happen." Cain walked up and took her hand.

"You're making me old before my time, you realize this, don't you?" Magen joked, changing her demeanor, knowing this was not a battle she could win but her superiors were going to panic.

"We're going to need a town house or maybe a brownstone in the sixties. Cleo will help with the arrangements and interior design."

"What about Imogen? The official story is that she was killed in a car accident in London. We can't have her recognized on a New York street!" Magen stated.

"I think after the child is born, she will lose some of that childlike presentation, and if not, we can talk about some minor reconstruction!" Cain stated. He obviously considered the scenario.

"It sounds like you have made up your mind on this, and I know it would be pointless of me to take a negative stance." Magen smiled.

"I have considered thousands of possible problems we could encounter. Not one will deter our plan!" Cain stated, holding Magen's arm as they slowly strolled along the water's edge.

"What will you do back in New York, Cain? I know you have some type of agenda," Magen said in a tone that indicated she knew Cain all too well.

"I would like to audition for one of those singing shows like *The Voice* or *American Idol*, something like that," Cain stated with a big, broad smile.

"Oh, Jesus, Cain, you really think I can convince the CIA that it's okay for you to go public?" Magen stated, not believing what she was hearing.

"I think you are an extremely intelligent woman. As you recall, you knew about me long before your superiors even conceived of me!" Cain stated.

"Well, you know I will do all I can. They might want to meet with you to discuss details," Magen said, knowing fully well that there would be several meetings.

"I don't want to be too far from my family. If they want to come my way, maybe a yacht meeting or they are welcome here," Cain said in jest.

"They are going to flip out, and you know it!" Magen stated, fully aware Cain was aware.

"Yes, they will, but with your help, we can flip them right back in!" Cain pressed.

"Cain, can you even sing?" Magen realized she had never made the connection.

"Like an angel, my love, like an angel!" Cain smiled wide.

ABOUT THE AUTHOR

David Wendt was born in New York City in 1963. He has moved around several times in his life. His primary address is in Malverne, New York. Mr. Wendt is a master's graduate from Fordham University. He is the father of three children, Jake, Rachel, and Jessica. He's a master of several short stories, including "The Dog on a Day in May." For the past four decades, Mr. Wendt has dedicated his life to the pursuit of sheer joy and happiness. Things to consider: We are but scuttling claws upon the sands of silent seas! Party like a rock star, or get out of the way!